Christine has had a varied career working in education industry and the law. She is a member of the National Trust and Historic Royal Palaces and also does voluntary work. When not writing she likes eating out, going to the theatre and concerts. She is widely travelled and has recently sailed around South America from Brazil to Columbia, rounding Cape Horn and sailing through the Panama Canal. Christine lives in the West Midlands with her husband.

To Ian who has always encouraged and supported me.

To all who teach by example and by expertise

Christine Cameron

KINGSCOURT

AUSTIN MACAULEY PUBLISHERS™
LONDON * CAMBRIDGE * NEW YORK * SHARJAH

Copyright © Christine Cameron 2023

The right of Christine Cameron to be identified as author of this work has been asserted by the author in accordance with sections 77 and 78 of the Copyright, Designs and Patents Act 1988.

All rights reserved. No part of this publication may be reproduced, stored in a retrieval system, or transmitted in any form or by any means, electronic, mechanical, photocopying, recording, or otherwise, without the prior permission of the publishers.

Any person who commits any unauthorised act in relation to this publication may be liable to criminal prosecution and civil claims for damages.

This is a work of fiction. Names, characters, businesses, places, events, locales, and incidents are either the products of the author's imagination or used in a fictitious manner. Any resemblance to actual persons, living or dead, or actual events is purely coincidental.

A CIP catalogue record for this title is available from the British Library.

ISBN 9781788486651 (Paperback)
ISBN 9781788486668 (ePub e-book)

www.austinmacauley.com

First Published 2023
Austin Macauley Publishers Ltd®
1 Canada Square
Canary Wharf
London
E14 5AA

Table of Contents

Chapter 1	42
Chapter 2	64
Chapter 3	90
Chapter 4	113
Chapter 5	139
Chapter 6	160
Chapter 7	181
Chapter 8	205
Chapter 9	227
Chapter 10	253
Chapter 11	275
Chapter 12	299

Saturday to Monday

Kingscourt stood in a rolling valley sheltered by the wooded hills of the Tamar Valley. It was a mellow comfortable home, so hospitable that to stay there was to fall under its spell. In the late afternoon of a golden autumn day, it was peaceful and calm, an oasis of tranquillity.

To Simon Amory, jogging slowly up the drive in the King wagonette that had been waiting at the station for him, it seemed to offer refreshment to his jaded spirits. The sun, not so bright now as when he had boarded the train, glowed with a gentle radiance, giving the old house a welcoming air.

As he neared the house, the front doors opened and a butler and footman appeared. The driver steadied his horse and Simon stepped carefully down. Though he was now able to walk without a stick, alighting from a still slightly moving wagonette needed care.

'Good afternoon, Major Amory. I am Merridew, sir, Mr King's butler.' Simon was above average height but the butler had an impressive presence.

'Afternoon, Merridew.'

'James will show you to your room, sir, and tea will be served presently.' He made a small movement of his hand and the footman moved to pick up his bag.

'This way, sir. Your room is in the bachelor's wing.'

The entrance hall was an imposing galleried square, lined with pictures, Simon presumed, of long dead ancestors. James moved to a staircase just to his left which was adorned with trophy animal heads. I hope the rest of the place isn't this gloomy, was Simon's first thought.

'I'll unpack while you have tea, sir. Is there anything else you require?'

'No, thank you…James.'

The door closed soundlessly behind the footman and Simon gazed pensively out of the window. He could see the beautiful gardens surrounding the house, manicured lawns and well-tended flowerbeds. Through the partly open window, all he could see were rolling Devon hills beyond the formal gardens.

He leant against the window frame and closed his eyes, drawing a deep breath. His last few months in South Africa had been very unpleasant and although he had been in England some time, his mind still saw with horrible clarity the more gruesome images he had witnessed. Here, all was calm and tranquil, this house breathed old money, established customs, harmony. How on earth had Billy come to join the army?

He might have carried on daydreaming if a discreet tap on the door had not roused him.

'Tea is being served now, Major Amory.'

'Thank you.'

Sighing, he slowly took off his jacket and began to wash. By the time he had combed his hair and put on a fresh collar and his jacket, he was ready to face the King family. He went back down the narrow staircase and into the hall. From behind one of the closed doors, he heard muted laughter and James appeared.

'The white drawing, sir, this way.'

The double doors opened and with a mental squaring of his shoulders, Simon walked into the room, had a quick impression of a comfortable room full of sofas and chairs and people—quite a lot of people. On a small table in the centre of the room stood an impressive silver teapot, presided over by a plump matron. A figure detached itself and came over, hand out in welcome.

'Amory, is it? I'm Julian King. My brother is playing tennis but they'll be in soon.'

His handshake was firm and Simon looked into laughing blue eyes.

'I hope you didn't mind Billy inviting me?'

'Lord no, we're quite a party. Let me introduce you.'

Julian swung straight round and approached the lady behind the teapot.

'Mother, this is Major Simon Amory.'

A face that bore a strong resemblance to Billy scrutinised him carefully and a hand was held out.

'Major Amory, it is a pleasure to meet you at last.'

'Kind of you to invite me.'

'Not at all. Mr King likes to have young people around. Here is the tennis party so you can meet my other children.'

Four young people, all dressed in white and with tennis racquets in hand, came bursting into the room. Not much ceremony in this family then, Simon thought. It was a relief after some of the houses he had been invited to.

'Mother, we had a brilliant game and I thrashed Billy. Oh good, tea. I'm starved.'

'Grace dear,' her mother reproved gently, 'we have another guest.'

'I'm sorry, please forgive me.' The hand was small and soft, the eyes a brilliant shade of blue.

'Major Amory, my dear. My younger daughter, Grace.'

'You are forgiven, Miss King.' Simon surprised himself, he was not usually so glib with young ladies.

Julian, who had been talking to his brother, now turned back to Simon.

'I say, Amory, here's Billy.'

Simon looked into the young innocent face, well-scrubbed and with an engaging charm.

'Billy, how are you? Good game?'

'No, Grace and Hugo thrashed us.'

'Bad luck. Any chance of a return match against you and me?'

Billy laughed. 'Oh yes. Watch out, Gracie, when Simon and I play, we are unbeatable.'

Julian King intervened.

'Let me introduce you to my sister and brother-in-law, Amory. Celia, Hugo, this is Simon Amory, Billy's friend.'

Simon shook hands with a slim energetic young lady with a mass of chestnut curls and those same blue eyes, and a tall man whose limbs seemed totally uncoordinated.

'So you are the person we have to thank for saving Billy's life, Major Amory.' Celia Philips smiled.

'It is a pleasure to meet Billy's family.'

Julian King steered him towards a voluptuous beauty, stunningly dressed in a magnificent tea gown, who was reclining on the sofa.

'Lady Goldburg. May I present Major Simon Amory of the Light Horse.'

A perfumed hand was languidly extended and Simon bowed.

'Charmed, your ladyship.'

The beauty turned to Julian King and surprised Simon.

'The hero of Joubertskop. What an asset to the party, Mr King.'

Leaning against the fireplace was a portly gentleman of slightly foreign appearance. Across his ample front, an expensive watch chain shone.

'Sir Mark, may I introduce Major Simon Amory. Sir Mark Goldburg.'

Simon shook hands, concealing his surprise that this was the beauty's husband.

Julian King led him back to the tea table and took a cup from his mother.

'Tea, Major Amory?'

'Thank you, Mrs King.'

She nodded to a side table groaning with food.

'Help yourself. We stand on no ceremony here.'

Simon glanced at the table; the array of sandwiches and cakes was staggering and finally, he took a very small slice of moist-looking fruitcake, more for the sake of appearances than because he felt hungry.

Grace King came over and picked up a plate.

'So, Major Amory, you have been in South Africa and are now invalided home. I hope you are quite recovered?'

A shutter came down in his mind; he would not, absolutely not, think of that now. What was she saying?

'Have you met everyone?'

'Not your father.'

'Oh, he doesn't always come in for tea. I expect you'll meet him at dinner and he will want to talk to you, as we've heard so much about you from Billy.'

'Your home is beautiful.' He turned the conversation with a practiced air, determined not to think of anything else but this moment. It was pleasant to be in a comfortable room chatting with people who had the right number of arms and legs and were not hideously maimed.

In a moment she was off, telling him her great-grandfather had rebuilt the house and describing the countryside and its beauty. Simon watched her expressive face, the quick movements of her hands and how her eyes sparkled. Yes. She was lovely. Billy had not done her justice in his description of his "little sister".

All too soon, so it seemed, the ladies began drifting away to prepare for dinner and he was about to follow when Billy came up and sat beside him. The talk was all regimental chat but just as they were deep in conversation, the door opened and a footman came in followed by a tall bearded man.

'Crickey, here's the guvnor. Father, may I present Major Simon Amory.'

A pair of piercing grey eyes assessed him as they shook hands.

'I am always happy to meet friends of my children, major. You of course are doubly welcome, having allowed me to keep my son. I have heard a great deal about you.'

Simon had read one or two overblown newspaper reports of his actions and dismissed it lightly.

'You mustn't believe everything you read, Mr King. Some of the reports are exaggerated.'

Billy leapt to his defence.

'Come on, Simon, everyone knows you are a hero. You did save my life.'

'My son is right. The newspaper reports might have been exaggerated but this certainly is not.'

Silas King held out the book he was carrying and Billy read the title aloud, 'The Great Boer War by Sir Arthur Conan Doyle.'

'You were interviewed in South Africa, Major Amory?'

'Yes, several times.'

'Well, Dr Doyle's book is a compilation of many interviews he had with all ranks and in several of them, you are described as a brave and resourceful officer.'

Simon, rendered uncomfortable and speechless, gazed at his host. Billy laughed.

'Can't deny it, old chap, you really are a hero.'

Silas King had moved away to talk to his wife and Billy took his friend's arm.

'Come on, let's have a stroll around and a cigarette.'

Later, alone in his room, Simon sat in the small fireside chair, trying to remember his interview with Dr Doyle, but he had spoken to so many journalists! The stable clock chimed the hour and James came in quietly.

'Shall I draw your bath, sir?

'Thank you, yes.'

Simon stood up swiftly and crossed to the wardrobe. Suddenly, tonight, he wished to look his best. Grace King's sparkling blue eyes had made a deep impression on him, maybe he would be placed by her at dinner.

***

He spoke to her briefly before dinner; she looked very pretty in a modest cream dress, but he was disappointed that she was further down on his side of the table. He could not even glance at her occasionally. Lady Goldburg, seated on his right, was another matter and he found he had to be careful where he looked when she spoke, there seemed so much of her exposed.

Helene Goldburg seated herself at the table in the same languid manner she used in almost every action of her life. She noted that Silas King was seated at the head of the table and she was on his left, as befitted her status. This might only be a small Saturday to Monday house-party but she was very careful of her consequence.

She glanced down the table to where her husband was seated on Mary King's left. In evening dress, he looked swarthier than ever, his foreign origins very evident. Inwardly, she sighed, as she always did when looking at her husband in company and comparing him to…say, Julian King. Or Simon Amory. Well, she had known what she was taking on when she had accepted him—the lifestyle, the dress allowance, the jewels he showered on her.

One hand stole up to the ruby necklace, a present only last week and worn for the first time tonight. It became her well and the dress she had chosen specially to compliment it fitted her shapely figure to perfection. ; She had seen Julian's eyes on her when she entered the room, that swift blaze in his eyes that meant he wanted her. She smiled slightly to herself, remembering the summer evenings they had enjoyed when Mark was in Paris on business. Tonight would be impossible, of course, with Mark in the next room enjoying all a husband's rights of walking in whenever he chose.

She half closed her eyes, lost in a delicious memory, only to be sharply interrupted by her host.

'Are you feeling quite well, Lady Goldburg?'

Helene dragged herself back to the present and forced a smile.

'A little warm, Mr King, that is all. Perhaps some water?'

She indicated the glass and immediately, a servant was at her side. Helene took a small sip, put the glass down and gently moved her fan. Simon Amory, chatting amiably with Alice Trevelyan, had not paid her much attention and an imp of mischief put an idea into her head. She would see just how far Julian King could be pushed. How delightful it would be to make him jealous! It would be quite fun to watch as she flirted with Simon Amory. Helene did not doubt her power over men, she had always been able to seduce any man she chose, and when she tired of the game…why, there was always her husband and the solid wall of his money to retreat behind. Until the next time.

She was a practiced flirt but far too clever to be anything but utterly discreet. Her campaign began subtly enough and by the time dinner was over, she congratulated herself. She was so pleased that she spent the interval before the gentlemen joined them in talking to her hostess. By the time the two parties joined, she did not speak to Simon at all but caught her husband's eye and patted the seat next to her invitingly.

'A very enjoyable dinner, Helene, did you not think so?'

Her husband sat beside her in his usual pose, not quite close enough to annoy her but close enough to make his rights clear.

'Enjoyable indeed. You seemed well entertained.'

'Indeed yes. Mrs King is an excellent hostess.'

Helene discreetly smothered a yawn. She disliked hearing other women praised, even if they were as dull as Mary King. She half turned and smiled.

'Do you play bridge this evening?'

'I believe I shall be asked, yes. What will you do?'

The yawn became slightly more pronounced.

'I shall retire early. The country air is so enervating.'

'Then you may be asleep when I come up.'

'I shall see you in the morning then.'

She was undressed by her maid but her musings were interrupted by a sharp tug. Helene had thick auburn hair she was so proud of that she insisted on having it brushed night and morning until it shone. The silver hairbrush in her maid's hand had found a tangle of hair and dragged her head. Annoyed at being roused from her reverie, Helene picked up the other hairbrush and met her maid's eye in the mirror.

'I'm…I'm sorry, my lady. I hope I didn't hurt you.'

'Yes, you did.' The brown eyes, normally warm, turned cold as she half turned and deliberately rapped the girl's knuckles hard with the heavy diamond-encrusted brush. Two small beads of blood appeared and she smiled.

'Now you won't do it again, will you?'

Later, nestling in soft pillows and with the glorious hair all around her shoulders, Helene studied her small perfect profile in the little hand mirror that was never far from her. Such a pity Julian could not see her now, or even Simon

Amory. She pulled the lace nightgown a little lower down; she was proud of her ample cleavage and missed no opportunity to display it, even if she was alone.

She heard the stable clock chime 11:30 and doors opening and closing. Her husband's bridge must be almost finished by now and she snuggled down in the deep bed, imagining making love with Simon Amory. The soft sound of the door opening and closing escaped her and it was not until a pair of warm lips pressed themselves into her neck that she woke with a start.

Julian raised his head and looked into her eyes, a half-smile on his mouth.

'Julian, are you crazy? Mark may come in at any moment.'

She struggled to sit up but he had both hands on her shoulders, looking into her face quizzically.

'Isn't that what you want, my lady? A little danger. A little spice.'

Fear of discovery made her voice panicky.

'Julian, you must go. Suppose he comes in.'

'He won't. The bridge party hasn't broken up yet. I came in to while away your lonely hour.'

He moved as he spoke, discarding the dressing gown to stand naked in the firelight. Stretching like a cat and running his hands over his body, Julian turned and smiled.

'Any idea how I could amuse your ladyship?'

She was too frightened to feel aroused but she tried to smile.

'Julian, we can't do this. Not in your mother's house.'

One swift movement brought him to her bed and he pressed her shoulders into the pillows before kissing her passionately. His breathing was ragged and she struggled to move.

'Julian, please stop. Not here. Your mother…Mark…'

He lifted a flushed face.

'I'm not one of your flirtations to be picked up and casually dropped when you're tired.'

For a second she was afraid but then he laughed lightly, shrugged on the discarded dressing gown and went to the door. His face, though, as he looked at her, was grim.

'Remember Helene, one word from me to your husband is all it takes to change your life.'

He opened the door quietly and disappeared without a backward glance.

***

Silas King, sitting at the head of his dining table, surveyed everyone closely, mentally assessing each in turn. He was a sociable man and liked to entertain, to fill his large house with people and see his table well provided with food. His wife, placidly presiding at the other end of the shining mahogany, was as ever modestly dressed and quietly spoken but she was the hub of this house, the oil of its wheels. Silas knew he could never have achieved his chosen lifestyle without her always on hand to organise. The pearls he had given her at Julian's birth and to which he had added a row for each of his children were still her most treasured jewellery, worn constantly. She had several impressive sets of gems but it pleased him enormously that she clung to this sentimental reminder of the happiest of days, the births of each of his children.

John Trevelyan was his oldest friend, politeness itself but giving more attention to his dinner than such old friends as Mary King and her eldest daughter. That had always been his way; from their earliest days together, food had played a central role in his life. It was natural that when he married, his wife would keep an excellent table and many was the convivial dinner the four of them had enjoyed, lately joined by their children. Silas knew that John, like himself, would be overjoyed if a match came about between the two families. With no son, he dreaded the estate going to a stranger, depending on who Elizabeth married. Nether Bassett was not as grand as Kingscourt to be sure, but it was a much-loved house. It would fit neatly into the King holdings.

Celia, his eldest daughter, so much like her mother in character, was making a point to her elder brother, soup cooling as she moved condiments around. When Celia had announced her wish to marry Hugo Phillips, they had been slightly surprised; he seemed such a quiet young man and Silas could not see him being able to control the strong character of his daughter. He had been wrong about that and finally had come to the conclusion that Celia had picked wisely. The result of this marriage, Maryjane Victoria Philips, was asleep in the Kingscourt nursery under nanny's watchful eye.

Silas looked at his eldest son with pride. Julian had been blessed with remarkable good looks and the year he had spent abroad had given him an indefinable polish. He would inherit a great estate and as much money as Silas could make; what he needed now was a suitable wife.

Elizabeth Trevelyan's roman nose looked decidedly incongruous next to Julian but Silas thought again how very tidy it would be if John's eldest daughter married his eldest son. Nether Bassett adjoined Kingscourt and it would be a tidy arrangement. She was polite enough, rather colourless and insipid but viewed in the light of a potential daughter-in-law she was very suitable.

That brought him to Hugo Phillips, calmly eating his roast beef. Though it was a pity he wasn't the eldest son, he had an excellent relationship with his in-laws. The Risings, the house on the edge of the estate Hugo had bought when he married, was large and comfortable but they spent a good deal of time at Kingscourt and when Maryjane was born, it was natural that she lived in the nurseries with nanny.

His eye moved to Louisa Trevelyan, wife of his old friend and mother to Elizabeth. If her daughter turned out as well, Julian would be a lucky man and Kingscourt would be in good hands for the next generation. It was easy to tell mother and daughter and he saw that Elizabeth would come to resemble her mother as the years passed. He looked down the years and saw Julian in his place and Elizabeth in Mary's, and was happy.

That brought him neatly to his other companion. Helene Goldburg, wearing a dress which was somehow all wrong for dinner at a country house-party and showing far too much bosom (as he termed it to himself), was doing her best to charm Simon Amory. This was a woman who could cause trouble, too aware of her own charms and with a predatory eye on men younger than her husband. He had seen her eye Simon Amory up and down once or twice. There had been some nasty whispers last year that young Graeme had killed himself because of her. It had all been hushed up, of course—a shooting accident, his family said. Nevertheless, the Goldburgs had spent months in Vienna just after. Silas guessed she was in her early thirties and he knew how old her husband was, so it was evident she preferred younger men. Much younger.

His next guest, Simon Amory, was something of an enigma. Silas had been at a dinner in London and heard Arthur Doyle describing in great detail some of the sights he had witnessed in South Africa. And of course, he had saved Billy's life, which was a point in his favour. He had been pleasantly surprised on meeting him; there was no swagger or conceit about this modest young man, chatting amiably to Alice Trevelyan. Silas did not miss the look that passed between the tall young man looking splendid in his regimentals and his younger daughter. He would mention it to Mary after the party broke up.

Alice Trevelyan, a pretty little doll with engaging ways, was a favourite with Silas because she always came and talked to him merrily whenever they were in company together, unlike her more reserved sister. He wondered for a moment if Alice would be better for Julian, stop him being quite so self-centred.

His younger son was laughing at something Grace had said and Silas found himself smiling as well. The Kings had never been a military family and so when, from an early age, Billy had displayed an interest in all things military, Silas had been sceptical, a boy's whim. It would soon pass. Well, he had been wrong about that as well; the years passed but the whim did not and at last, his parents consented to his joining the army.

The dessert was served and his younger daughter turned to talk to Mark Goldburg. Silas was always pleased to see that she had what he thought of as proper table etiquette. That would be her mother's teaching. If she liked Simon Amory…well, he must talk to Mary.

Mark Goldburg was talking slowly and Grace, waving away dessert, listened politely. He had invited the Goldburgs in return for their hospitality earlier in the year to his wife and son and also because he was following Mark Goldburg's advice on investments. Though not overfond of the man, Silas admitted to himself that there was very little he didn't know when it came to money, and making it. If he was totally honest, it was more to do with his Jewish origins than the man himself but then, if the Prince of Wales could overlook that, so could he. There was no denying that so far, his advice had been profitable.

A movement caught his eye and Merridew was at his elbow.

'Shall I open more wine, sir?'

'Two will be enough.'

A bow and he was gone. Silas disapproved of lavish use of wines; his dinners were excellent thanks to his wife but there would be no over-indulgence at his table. He wished his guests to enjoy themselves and in his views, that could be done without a great many bottles.

Helene Goldburg was saying something to him and he kept his eyes away from her well-displayed charms and the magnificent ruby necklace she wore (far too ostentatious but nothing compared to the King rubies) and the mouth that certainly owed more to artifice than nature, and looked into her large limpid eyes.

'Your ladyship?'

'I was congratulating you on a splendid meal, Mr King.'

'Thanks to my wife more so, but I am pleased you are enjoying your stay here.'

The lips curved. 'Oh yes, more than I would have believed.'

There was something about her, Silas decided, that could drive men wild. He decided to pay closer attention to her behaviour.

His wife was rising discreetly, collecting ladies' eyes, and the footmen moved to open the doors. Time for Silas to play host and rotate the port. It was his custom to let his guests talk whilst he listened, putting in a word here and there. Simon and Billy were discussing the campaign with Mark Goldburg, Julian and Hugo were talking about the next week's hunt and John Trevelyan came to sit beside his old friend and smoke a cigarette before they re-joined the ladies.

He circulated the drawing room as he always did, untasted cup of coffee in hand, speaking to all the ladies before finally sitting down beside Louisa. When his wife began assembling the bridge party, he slipped away to his study for a quiet smoke.

It was approaching midnight but lights burning showed that the bridge party was in full swing so he ascended the stairs quietly and was about to turn into the east wing when he decided, as he sometimes did late at night, to put his head into the nursery and check on his granddaughter.

The sound of a door softly closing halted him. He stood against the wall and waited. Fond though he was of entertaining, Silas would never countenance misbehaviour under his roof, whatever happened in other country houses. His eldest son walked past without noticing him, dressing gown half open to reveal his naked body and face flushed. In an instant, Silas knew where he had been, who with and what had probably happened. Rage filled him for a few moments, and a loathing disgust of his son's behaviour, before his practical side took over. Of course, the boy had been seduced—and under his mother's roof at that—by that…she devil. Silas could think of many names bad enough for Helene Goldburg and mentally used each one.

In the safety of his dressing room he considered what to do next. His first impulse was to go to Mary and tell her. Calmer reflection convinced him that his wife must not know. Men sowed their wild oats, he himself had, but a prudent marriage was desirable now. Silas had always hoped his children would meet suitable partners but he firmly believed enduring love came along in its own time, as his own had. The very thought of someone like Helene Goldburg as a daughter made him blanch.

After a sleepless night, he rose the next morning with his mind made up. Julian would marry Elizabeth or Alice, that was all.

***

Sunday morning's breakfast was followed by the usual walk to church and during the long slow sermon, Julian savoured again the danger and spice of last night's visit,—what fun it had been. He was no novice but an experienced lover; he knew that in Helene, he had found the one woman who could keep him satisfied all his life. Quite how they would be rid of the inconvenience that was her husband Julian had no idea, nor did he trouble his head very much about it.

All his life, anything he wanted had a habit of coming to him in the end and the idea of failure never entered his head. That most of these things had been procured by his father's money also never crossed his mind. Naturally, there would be a divorce, which would be difficult, and they would be ostracised but after all—who cared about society?—and afterwards they would live at Kingscourt and raise an entire family of grandchildren for his parents to dote on. The getting of those grandchildren filled him with a joyous sense of well-being and he sighed deeply at just the appropriate point in the sermon. His father gave him a sharp glance.

Afterwards, striding along in the pleasant lunchtime sun, he mused again on how his future would look.

His younger brother caught up with him as the house came into sight and interrupted his thoughts.

'Our vicar gets more long-winded by the week, doesn't he?'

'Yes.' He entered the hall casually and Merridew came straight to him.

'Mr Julian, your father would like to see you. In the study.'

Julian stopped in his tracks and stared into the impassive face. Merridew had always had the power to make him feel like a naughty schoolboy.

'Anything up, Merridew?'

'I believe he wished to see you the moment you returned from church.'

Julian went to the door of the study and paused a moment, his mind going over anything he might have done which his parent would not approved of. Nothing came to mind and he tapped gently on the door and went in.

It was a small room by Kingscourt standards and seemed to catch the aura of his father's personality—close and secretive. It was a room he had instinctively hated coming to as a small boy when some misdemeanour had been detected. Then he would have to lie or blame his younger brother to get out of trouble.

His father was looking out of the window and did not turn to look at his son.

'I have been talking to your mother, Julian, and we think it is time you settled down.'

'Settled down, sir?'

'Why yes, married. Beginning to help with running Kingscourt. I shan't live forever, you know.'

His son laughed self-consciously. 'Nonsense sir, many years left in you yet.'

'That's as may be. Still, it's time you were thinking of marriage, children. Elizabeth Trevelyan is a most suitable young lady. A good match.'

'But sir…I mean, dash it all…I don't love her.'

'Love comes with time and intimacy.'

A vision of his wedding night with an insipid ignorant bride hovered in front of his eyes. He swallowed and opened his mouth.

'Father, there is…that is… There is a lady I care for…'

His father turned to look hard at him and the voice was steely.

'If you think I would ever countenance that particular lady in this family, you are mistaken.'

An awful pause ensued until Julian, aghast that his father knew and trying to collect his thoughts, cleared his throat.

'How did you know?'

'That is immaterial. This…liaison will terminate and you will marry Elizabeth. Failing that, you will go to India.'

'India! No sir, I couldn't. Not India.'

'Then marry Elizabeth. Or little Alice. It's your choice.'

Somehow, he stumbled from the study up to his room. He sat looking at the wall until the sound of the gong called him to lunch. No, he couldn't face it. He could not face his father or Helene.

Without even bothering to change he crept down the back stairs furtively and went out into the gardens. He walked fast, head down, his mind full of the awful thought of marriage to Elizabeth. He had known her all his life but the idea of her as a possible wife had never crossed his mind. Until he had met Helene, the thought of marriage and children had seemed remote but now he knew he could not marry anyone else.

He must think what to do. His first instinct was to go and pour out his troubles to Helene, they could plan their future together. In the time it took him to cross the gardens he decided against that. It was time for him to play the man, to tell her what they were going to do and for that he must have a plan with every last detail thought out.

He plunged deep into the woods; as a child they had been his refuge and delight. Now he walked without seeing, his mind whirling over plans. They would have to go abroad, of course, to Europe, and wait for her divorce. Later, after they had been discreetly married, he would bring her back to Devon and they could settle down and raise children. Once his parents saw how happy they were he knew they would like Helene.

To be sure quite possibly some of the county families would react badly but to him, that would be a small price to pay. To live here quietly with her, to go to bed with her every night and wake up beside her every morning! His mind was dizzy with happiness.

He emerged from the woods somewhat later, his mind made up, his one thought now to get Helene alone and dazzle her with the vision of their future happiness. The stable clock was chiming four as he crossed the front of the house; he had no idea he'd been so long and now he must make haste and change for tea.

When he went into the white drawing room later, she was draped on a sofa wearing a soft green tea gown with ruffles and laces partly concealing the charms he knew so well. He attempted to sit beside her but was foiled by his mother and was obliged to sit opposite and be as patient as he could. Patience did not come easily to him and when his mother announced that two of the county families were joining them for dinner, his mood grew darker. The thought of getting her on her own began to obsess him.

Somehow, he got through the rest of the evening and then had to watch her climb the stairs, candle in hand, closely followed by her husband. A restless night followed, for he dare not take the chance of visiting her room again, and he was down to breakfast before the table was even laid. He walked about in the gardens feeling very ill-used and when he finally went into the dining room he toyed with his food for a long hour and even tried to talk pleasantly to Mark Goldburg, though it was an effort. Going out afterwards for a quiet cigarette, he wondered why he had wasted his time when he knew very well that married ladies always had breakfast in their rooms.

Knowing she was under the same roof with her husband was unnerving. What was worse was knowing her husband had probably spent last night with her—it should be me, he muttered to himself. I can keep her happy and satisfied more than that…that old man.

In the end, it was simple. Smoking always calmed him and he went to the library, wrote a long letter to her and was just wondering if he could possibly bribe her maid when Mark Goldburg came quietly in.

'Sir Mark, what brings you here?' Julian was not aware he had spoken sharply but the older man did not miss the tone.

'I left my book…ah yes, here it is.' He picked up a small gold volume and eyed it as if seeing it for the first time.

Julian cleared his throat nervously. 'Are you leaving now, sir?'

'Later. My wife is dressing and I seek a little quiet repose.' Saying this, he sat down in one of the wing chairs near the fire and opened the book.

Julian slid the envelope into his pocket and stood up.

'I will leave you in peace then. It has been a pleasure…having you both here.'

Mark Goldburg, already beginning to read, waved a hand calmly. Julian could hardly wait to leave the room and go upstairs. There was so much movement of servants to and fro and just as he rounded the stairs her maid came out.

'Is her ladyship ready?'

'Not quite, sir.' The girl scuttled past like a frightened rabbit and ran down the stairs; he wondered briefly why she was so white. That was the thought of a moment, superseding it came the knowledge that he would have her alone at last. A quick glance up and down the corridor showed him there was no-one about and it was the work of a second to slip into her room and silently close the door.

She stood before the mirror, magnificently attired in black with a white fox fur stole draped over her shoulder.

'Helene…'

Their eyes met in the mirror and she spun around.

'What are you doing here? Go away!'

'You look stunning. Helene, I have missed you so.'

He went straight to her and slipped an arm round her waist. The heady perfume was wafting into his nostrils and the red lips were inches away.

'Are you mad? Mark may come in at any moment.'

'No, he's reading in the library. Helene, oh God, darling, I need you…I want you so badly.'

She stepped back coolly and turned once more to the mirror.

'It is a little early in the day for lovemaking, Julian. Now you have ruffled my hair.'

She smoothed the immaculate hair and picked up her gloves.

He gazed at her adoringly. 'You know the effect you have on me.'

'Certainly, but I will be late and Mark will be cross. I must go.'

'Helene, darling, you can't go. Please.'

She turned and smiled at him.

'Julian, I must go, you know that. We shall meet again soon.' Privately, she thought perhaps it was more than time to end this little dalliance.

She walked slowly across the room., his eyes taking in every curve of the voluptuous figure. He thrust his hands in his pockets and felt the crisp envelope.

'Helene…take this. Read it on the train. Please.'

She looked at the envelope with a frown.

'I cannot read it with Mark sitting beside me.'

'When you are alone then. It's our future, my darling, so please reply as soon as you can.'

'Our future, Julian?'

'I know you'll be as happy as I will when we are together.'

A small hand reached out and took the letter, tucking it into her muff. Decidedly, she must end it. Such a pity.

He put his hand on the doorknob but something in him could not let her go like this. His free hand took her chin and forced her to look into his eyes.

'I love you, Helene. Remember that. You are mine and always will be.'

'Let me go, Julian. My husband is waiting.'

He opened the door and she went through on a wave of perfume and was gone. He shut the door behind her and stared at it for a moment. Then he went and buried his head in the pillows, running his hands over the sheets where her body had rested and breathing deeply her perfume.

***

Mary

Mary King sat in the large room that had been called the linen closet for as long as anyone could remember. To outward appearances, she was placidly counting the huge number of sheets such a large household needed. It was Monday afternoon, the guests had left and she was absorbing herself in domestic duties and trying to distract her mind.

Inwardly, she was thinking of her eldest son and her thoughts were not pleasant. This Saturday to Monday, which for her had been a normal house-party, the same as many they habitually gave, had turned into something rather different.

Quite when she knew that Julian was Lady Goldburg's lover, Mary never afterwards knew, but it was a fact. She had intercepted several looks between them—no, she corrected herself, from her son only—which were too pointed to be ignored.

That part of her mind that detached itself from whatever she was doing thought sorrowfully of Julian's nature; he took after his single-minded father. In Silas, of course, that was a virtue, for his moral character was principled to a high standard, but in a matter of this kind, Mary feared it could be a disaster for Julian.

He had always been indulged, that was only to be expected as the eldest son but she had long suspected that this indulgence had been a mistake. Her son was too apt to believe he could have whatever he wanted, and all too often that had been the case. It had made him too inclined to indulge his every whim with no thought for anyone else.

Fleetingly, her thoughts turned to her other children.

Celia, her favourite child.

During her growing years, it became obvious that her eldest daughter would resemble her most in character. Celia had always been the one to tend injured animals and console anyone who was upset. As a grown-up, she became the strong calm person everyone turned to and relied on.

She had never shown any interest in the young men her brothers brought home and her mother despaired of her meeting anyone. Then, on a chance visit to Exeter to visit an old governess, she had met Hugo Phillips. To be sure he was a younger son but his family were solidly respectable and when Celia had told her mother she wanted to marry him, his income was all that Silas could wish for in a potential suitor.

Grace, her youngest and most energetic child.

Where she got all that energy from Mary could not tell, certainly not her parents or grandparents. Sometimes thoughtless, sometimes selfish, her redeeming qualities were a soft heart and an unwillingness to hurt anyone. With the right partner, she would turn out well.

Billy—what could she say about him? His wish to join the army she had at first dismissed as a schoolboy fad, soon over. Silas, she knew, felt the same. Time had proved them both wrong and the army had shaped him into a good man. Her only fear was for his safety when he went to the Cape.

No, her other children were, give or take a few faults, nothing to disturb a mother. But Julian was. Her mind refused to be distracted even by logic. Her common sense told her that all young men would sow wild oats, and at least it was with a lady (though Mary was not sure she would call Helene Goldburg a lady) and not (inward shudder) someone from the streets.

The very fact that she was a lady was the danger. Given his nature, it was only a short step from making love to someone to being in love with that someone, wanting to share her life. Mary tried to imagine "that woman", as mentally she was already calling her, sitting at the table in Silas's impressive dining room. The vision would not fit. Until yesterday, Mary had been quite sure one day Elizabeth Trevelyan would sit in her place, wearing the rubies that Haydn King had acquired on his travels.

Love for her son, even if it was only a lukewarm one, did not blind her to his temperament and his faults. Julian might set himself on a course that could be disastrous. Silas, of course, would never, could never, countenance such a connection. Why, oh why, could Julian not fall sensibly in love with Elizabeth? Or even Alice?

Her musings came to a halt when the door opened quietly. She looked up and saw the head housemaid, Ruby, bobbing a curtsey.

'Yes, Ruby?'

'If you please, madam, Mr Merridew sent me. He says Mr King is looking for you.'

This in itself was unusual. Something must be wrong. She glanced at the little gold fob watch she always wore, it was a few minutes to three o'clock. She nodded gently and handed over the list.

'Very well. You must finish this, Ruby. And come and see me later with it.'

The library door was ajar and as Mary went through the hall, Silas called her.

'Mary, come in here.'

His voice was not loud but she sensed the anxiety. Her husband was pacing up and down holding a letter.

'What is it?'

'Sit down, my dear, I have something to tell you.'

A foreboding caught her and she glanced keenly at him. 'Julian?'

He stopped pacing and his look was grim. 'Did you know?'

'I know…something is going on between him and—'

For the first time she could remember, he interrupted her, 'That saves me a lot of unpleasantness. I have told him he will marry either Elizabeth or Alice…or go to India.'

'India!' The catch in her voice did not escape him.

'Yes. The alternative is much more attractive. Elizabeth is a nice girl, she'll fit in well here. Most suitable. Whereas India…'

He did not finish the sentence and she swallowed.

'Silas, you don't think he might…do anything silly?'

Her husband suddenly came and sat beside her, clasping her hand in his, the letter falling to the floor.

'He has done something…which I hope will not be fatal.

A cold hand pressed on her heart.

'Fatal! Surely not.'

'The note he left is very short and to the point. He informs me that he cannot live without that woman. Apparently, she feels the same and he intends to inform Mark Goldburg of their feelings for each other and…take her away immediately. He has some plan to live abroad.'

The enormity of it took a moment to absorb and she did not move. When she spoke again, her voice was perfectly steady.

'Silas…'

'My dear?'

'Suppose she does not feel the same way? Perhaps he was just a distraction.'

Mary did not expect her strait-laced and moral husband to reply and when he did, his voice was quiet. 'I will go to London by the early train tomorrow and call in Cadogan Square on some pretext, though it will be awkward as they've just been here. I can at least see if she is still there.'

'Has he definitely gone?'

'The letter says he is following her at once and they will go abroad as soon as he has told Sir Mark. Don't tell the children yet.'

'No, of course not. Suppose he decides to marry Elizabeth after all?'

'Then this painful matter will never be spoken of again. I hope it will turn out that way, but I fear it will not.'

'My dear, I will go and lie down for a while. I have a slight headache.'

'Don't let this foolish young man upset you too much. It may yet turn out well, please God.'

In the darkness of her bedroom, Mary lay quite still. It was not a phase, she knew that well enough. Her son meant to marry that woman, if she would have him. There were few people in the world Mary thoroughly disliked, she had always tried to see the best in everyone. Sadly, Helene Goldburg was one of those people she knew had no merit at all. It was not just that she painted her face, or wore revealing clothes, many society ladies did that. Mary was not such a country mouse as to condemn her for that. No, there was something about her manner that made Mary feel uneasy. Greed, vanity, lust were words but somehow none of them covered what she felt instinctively about Helene Goldburg. She was the sort of woman who might even—awful thought—hit a servant if they stepped out of line.

The tea bell sounded and she rose wearily. She would give much to carry on lying here but the children would worry if she did not appear. How fortunate all the guests had gone. There were just the three of them sitting cosily in the small saloon they used for family gatherings.

'It's a bit flat now, isn't it, mother, with everyone gone?'

'Yes darling, parties have that effect, I'm afraid. Still, a little peace and quiet is refreshing. What have you two been doing today?'

'We went to the station to see people off, didn't we, Billy?' Grace's answer was a shade too quick and Mary guessed the person she had most wanted to see off was Major Simon Amory.

'Yes, then we came back here to change and Celia decided she wanted to walk up to High Point so we had lunch at The Risings.'

'Did either of you see Julian?' The words were out before she could stop herself.

A pause followed as they thought and Grace's answer was strained.

'No. Did you, Billy?'

'Saw him in the library talking to Sir Mark.'

Billy had no idea the effect his words would have on his mother. She felt her head begin to spin and the cup and saucer rattled in her hand. Grace was beside her at once.

'Mother, are you feeling alright?'

Mary closed her eyes for a moment, hoping the sick feeling would pass. She felt the cup being taken from her hand and a gale of cold air as her son began fanning her enthusiastically with a newspaper.

'Billy, stop that! Mother, do you want some smelling salts?' Grace was rubbing her hands and Billy waved the paper gently. Mary wished they would just go away and leave her in peace. A sick headache was beginning to pound her temples and she leaned back in the chair.

Into this scene of quiet desperation came Silas, closing the door behind him soundlessly as ever.

'What is going on?' The voice was not raised but his children stopped at once and gazed helplessly at him.

'Mother's ill and we don't know what to do.'

'I will sit with her. Leave us in peace for a moment.' Silas pulled a chair out and sat down next to his wife, picking up her hand gently.

The door closed behind them and Mary opened her eyes.

'Silas…Julian…'

'Do not fret, my dear. You should go and rest. I do not like to see you ill.'

'He spoke to…Billy saw him with Sir Mark…'

'Whatever happens, I will not have you ill with worry. Julian in not worth it.'

She sat up straight.

'Silas! Our son. The heir.'

'Promise me you will not distress yourself.'

The entreaty in his voice told her he was in earnest so Mary swallowed and returned the pressure.

'I promise. Julian… If he goes away with…her, what will you do?'

'Disown him. Billy will have to give up the army and learn to run the estate.'

Mary thought back to the day of his birth. The bells of the estate church had rung all day, Silas full of pride and happiness that beside her bed, a bonny boy lay in the cradle asleep. The future of the estate was secure, there would be Kings at Kingscourt into the next generation. She thought of the ancestors whose portraits lined the staircases, theirs had been hung only last year, the empty spaces for generations to come.

And all this, All...THIS, was to be thrown away for some painted...Jezebel. The word was hard but she did not flinch. That was what Helene Goldburg was and always would be.

Grace

Meeting Simon Amory for the first time at tea, she knew immediately that here was someone she wanted to know better. Not just because of his good looks—with two brothers, Grace had met plenty of young men, eligible and not—but there was something in his manner that drew her at once.

She had come straight in from playing tennis and wished at once that she had gone upstairs to wash and tidy herself. Why, today of all days, did she not? She had known they were having guests but how could she have known that Billy's friend would be...dashing?

Well, she would remedy that at dinner. She was one of the first to go upstairs to change and one of the last to come down. When she walked into the drawing room where everyone usually gathered before dinner, she could not resist a glance at him. He was resplendent in regimentals and she thought how very handsome he looked. She also saw the look of admiration in his eyes as he looked at her.

Her mother was strict about what was considered proper evening wear for young unmarried girls but Grace had stretched a point with the ivory-coloured evening gown that was almost new. She had resisted the temptation to do anything different to her hair, conscious that her mother would notice immediately. Beside Elizabeth and Alice, she looked more sophisticated, which was what she wanted. Beside Lady Goldburg, she looked a child.

At dinner, seated between her younger brother and Sir Mark, anything but general conversation was impossible but she was enjoying herself until gradually, she caught an undercurrent. Something was happening and Julian did not like it. Quite how she knew this was unfathomable but... Surely Lady Goldburg wasn't flirting with Simon Amory?

Grace did not like her. Naturally, she was polite to them both but somehow, she liked the husband better than the wife. That the wife was stunningly beautiful and gorgeously dressed had nothing to do with it. Grace looked at the expanse of bust being displayed, the ruby necklace that flashed with every breath and thought that for a lady, their guest was behaving like a slut. The last word brought her up short and caused her to spill her water. If her mother had guessed what she had just thought, Grace would be given a sharp reprimand.

As her mother began to assemble the bridge party, the younger people were all standing near the fire.

'What shall we do?' Billy threw at the others.

'Why not some music?'

'Good idea. Grace, will you play?'

'Yes, if you like.'

Simon was pleased to find she had a light pleasant voice and knew her range well, never attempting the impossible. Hugo had a good baritone and Celia also sang, the evening was over all too soon.

Sunday was filled with church and a walk around the grounds and after lunch, they made up a four for tennis. Grace, drawing Simon as her partner, glanced at him.

'Are you…that is…' She blushed slightly.

'I can play a casual game of tennis, if that's what you mean.'

'I'm sorry, I didn't mean to embarrass you.'

'You haven't.'

Sitting between sets and drinking lemonade, they chatted about anything and everything and soon found they liked each other. Grace felt she had never enjoyed a game of tennis so much.

The evening saw another dinner party with two more neighbouring families; once again, she was not sitting anywhere near him. The after-dinner entertainment was music for the younger guests and bridge and conversation for the older ones. Someone suggested a little dancing in the great hall and as they paired off, Simon asked her to dance.

His hand was out and she found herself in his arms. Under her sister's eye, she was decorum itself and was careful to dance with several other young gentlemen. This might be a small evening party but she didn't want any criticism to spoil her evening.

And all too soon, it was Monday morning. Billy was taking him to the station and as her mother made no objection, she decided to go as well.

Saying goodbye was hard but she felt that, if her mother had been there to watch, no reprimand would be heard. Grace had said all the proper things, but he took her hand and said he hoped they would meet again.

He had been one of the first to leave after breakfast and on her way to Kingscourt, she was full of pleasant thoughts, mostly to do with him. She ran lightly up the stairs intending to change into her old tweed walking skirt and jacket. The sound of a door lightly closing made her glance along the west corridor and then stand very still. Her brother was coming out of one of the bedrooms and he looked…why, he looked as if he had been rolling around in bed with his clothes on. He did not see her standing just to his left, he turned the other way and went along the opposite corridor. With a sudden horrid suspicion, Grace went soundlessly to the door Julian had just left. The brass nameplate told her whose room it was.

She went to her room and sat on the bed. Should she tell her mother? No, she couldn't even begin to imagine having that conversation with her. Talk to her brother? She had never been close to Julian and how could she even start? A tap on the door roused her and Celia popped her head in.

'Hugo and I are going to walk up to High Point and I thought you and Billy might like to join us, then we can all have lunch at The Risings.'

'Celia, did you notice anything at dinner last night?'

'What about, infant?' Though there were only five years between them, Celia—being married—was apt to treat her as a child.

'Well…Julian…or anything.'

'Out with it, Grace, you know I'm no good at riddles.'

'At dinner last night, Lady Goldburg…'

Grace plunged in and reeled off in a great hurry everything she had seen or surmised.

'…and he had been in her room this morning before she left. When he left, his clothes were all rumpled as if he'd been—'

'That will do, Grace.' Her tone was sharp but the next thing she said, more gently, surprised her sister.

'My dear, a man sows wild oats. With women. It means nothing.'

Grace returned her sister's gaze without flinching, feeling for the first time as if she were the elder.

'You don't know Julian at all. If he fancies himself in love, and I believe he does, he will want her with him.'

'That's impossible and he knows it. She is a married woman. He will marry Elizabeth or Alice and settle down to run Kingscourt.'

'But how could he go to her room? What will Mother say?'

Celia put a comforting arm round her sister.

'We can't mention this to anyone. Mother would only be upset and they've gone now so we should just forget it. You were mistaken, I'm sure.'

The calm conviction in Celia's voice was no comfort to Grace. She knew Julian's selfish ways all too well—what he wanted he got.

Her mother's indisposition at teatime gave her fresh concern. So her mother knew too. Nothing else could explain her normally serene parent being so agitated. In the sleepless night that followed, Grace saw it all clearly—the reason for Lady Goldburg's flirting with Simon Amory, Julian's hostility, going to her bedroom. Julian was capable of anything to have what he wanted.

Grace knew and loved Kingscourt with every breath in her body and until this weekend, she had taken it for granted that Julian would succeed her father and keep the estate just as it was. If he ran off with anyone, nothing would ever be the same. Lady Goldburg would never be a country lady as her own mother was, looking after the tenants and visiting the sick.

The next day brought Elizabeth and Alice, calling to ask if Grace wanted to go shopping with them to Exeter. Her mother was happy as Louisa Trevelyan had offered to chaperone the young people and between the high spirits of Alice and the temptations of the shops, she forgot it all for a while.

Simon

He had not realised quite how wealthy the Kings were. When they had first become friends, it had been very much Simon, older and more worldly wise, who had been the one to impress. Billy, immature in many ways, had followed admiringly in his wake.

The minor skirmish on Christmas Eve 1899 in which Simon saved the life not only of Billy but also his senior officer had been told and retold by all the newspapers until it bore no relation to what Simon knew had really happened. He found himself a hero, mentioned in dispatches and much photographed.

So when, a month later, he was wounded in another action, Simon found himself being hailed yet again as a fine soldier. The shot to his leg had damaged his knee badly and his commanding officer, mindful of the spectacle a wounded hero would make and the effect on morale, had him sent back to England to convalesce once he could walk on crutches.

That had been eight months ago and he had still not been recalled to duty. Once back in England, invitations had been showered on him and all were eager to meet the dashing young man who looked such a fine figure in his regimentals. Simon occasionally smiled to himself as he thought of all the eager young ladies who were so very anxious to hear of his exploits and so very solicitous of his wound.

The letter from Billy announcing that he would be home on leave for a month in September had been a welcome surprise and the invitation to stay at Kingscourt had been gratefully accepted. Simon was beginning to find adulation and attention wearing.

He was a career soldier—his only idea since he was a child. Having no great means to rely on—his father had been a gentleman farmer with a few hundred acres in Kent—Simon had begun the hard way, as a junior subaltern. His father's sudden death and his decision to sell the land had been a timely one and enabled him to buy a commission and leave him a small yearly annuity. It had been enough to keep him in a moderate lifestyle and pay his mess bills, though not to hunt as often as some of his brother officers.

Someone like Billy King, young, well-born and obviously from a wealthy family, was the last person he would have thought to be a friend and yet they became like brothers, despite the ten-year age gap. Listening to tales of life at Kingscourt, he thought it unlikely there was much brotherly love between Billy and Julian—his older brother very much the heir and brought up accordingly. As an only child, he listened with interest to childhood tales, always Billy and his sisters with only occasional mentions of Julian lording it over them all.

In the horrors of the South African campaign, it helped to imagine a welcoming old house, a family rooted in the land. Simon discovered to his surprise and horror that he had no appetite for killing his fellow men. It was an unsettling thought for someone who knew nothing but soldiering.

His much praised bravery—where had that come from? His ancestors had been gentlemen farmers, he had never been raised on tales of heroic military exploits.

It was a soldier's duty to go where his superiors told him to and carry out their orders but in the dark night his soul experienced after Spioenkop, Simon knew he could not kill again. The Medical Board's decision last week that he must be invalided out was welcome news but his future looked uncertain. He loved the army and it had been his life for fifteen years; suddenly, the world outside the regiment seemed remote and frightening.

His thoughts drifted to the King house-party, the family and their guests. The Goldburgs were as mismatched a couple as he had ever seen. He was alright, talking intelligently about the war; she was a painted lady. The Trevelyans looked exactly what they were, a typical county family, the girls were pretty and talked without flirting too much. His host and hostess he liked at once. Silas King was very well informed on the war and his wife ran a well-ordered household and had a beautiful daughter.

Grace King. He saw her again in his mind's eye, the vivid blue eyes, fair skin and graceful manners. He would like to know her better. How on earth did he think any opportunity to see her again would happen? He would be leaving the regiment very soon and although he might write to Billy, their lives would not touch again.

'Anyway, how would I stand a chance with Miss King of Kingscourt?' The sigh took him by surprise and he didn't realise he had spoken aloud.

'Did you want something, Major Amory?' His batman was staring at him.

'No thanks, Wilkins. That will be all for now.'

'Very good, sir. I'll lay your mess kit out later and the Brigadier will expect medals.'

As the door closed quietly behind Wilkins, not for the first time Simon wondered how his man always knew what was happening. He had been told the Brigadier's visit was confidential. Still, the other ranks always had their ear to the ground.

He stared into the fire and looked back on fifteen years of always knowing his place in the world and where he was going. What exactly was he going to do when the army cast him adrift in what would be, to him, an alien world? What did a decorated officer who had never known anything but soldiering do for the rest of his life?

Picking up the newspaper, he looked at the front page and read some of the adverts.

Perhaps I should advertise, he mused. *Ex-officer, not fit for much, seeks employment.*

Helene

When Fraulein Helene von Steine had been introduced by her guardian to Sir Mark Goldburg, she had immediately decided this was the man she would marry.

Helene had been 'out' in society only a few months but had already seen that the type of young man she was expected to marry would not be to her taste at all. A very rich and rather elderly Jew suited her far better. They would travel and see the world, far from the dull straightjacket that was Vienna. A quiet look through her uncle's papers had revealed quite how rich her suitor was and in a short time, she had persuaded her guardian that she really did like him enough to marry him.

A modest wedding had taken place, followed by a ceremony at the synagogue. Helene, not believing in either religion, had gone through it all thinking only of the dresses she would buy. On her wedding morning, when her betrothed had sent her a box containing the jewelled corsage he hoped she would wear, Helene knew she had picked the right man and sailed through the day with a radiant smile, which puzzled the older ladies who were firmly convinced she was only marrying for money and position. By the happy look on her face, they almost believed she loved her much older husband.

Practiced as she was in the ways of men, Helene knew that her husband wanted her—and despised himself for it. His visits to her were always the same—he asked his valet to inquire from her maid if she was well enough to see him. The answer was always yes and after her maid had left, he would appear in an elaborate dressing gown. He would sit on the side of the bed and chat for a few moments and then he would take off the dressing gown and climb carefully into her bed.

What followed would be exactly predictable and when he had finished, he would climb carefully out of bed, put on his dressing gown and retire to his own room. These visits were never mentioned by either of them but somehow, she knew he was disappointed there was no child.

She had taken great care that there should be no child; she did not intend to ruin her figure and miss out on a season for the sake of an heir to Mark's millions. That he was extremely wealthy she never doubted; her expenses were never questioned and the jewels he lavished on her were truly worth a king's ransom. He was a friend of the Prince of Wales and Helene, in that first heady blush of marriage, had ambitions to become that gentleman's mistress. With all the consequence that position implied.

To this end, she had first tried to make a friend of the poor deaf princess, although female friendship was not to her taste and she rather despised a woman who put up with her husband's mistresses all her married life. This had not worked any better than her overtures to the prince and it had taken a long time for her to understand why. She had not produced an heir for Mark and that had been enough for any desires her husband's friend may have felt to be ignored. The princess's rebuff she didn't trouble herself over.

She had told Mark when they married, three years ago, that she would not tolerate being made a fool of. She never denied him when he came to her room and she expected that to be enough for him.

That it was not enough for her she knew, and took action accordingly. Providing everyone was discreet, there were opportunities for a lady with a boring husband to amuse herself. Helene may not have had any female friends but she had many acquaintances and they all had country houses to which a clever woman could be invited alone. To be sure, she had no grand country mansion in which to return hospitality but their entertaining in town was lavish in the extreme and this summer, they had rented Coombe Florey to see how country living might suit them. It had not suited her at all and she was happy to return to town for the season.

Nevertheless, Coombe Florey had led Julian to her. She knew that her husband and Silas King were doing business together and Mark had indicated he would like her to invite the Kings and an invitation was duly sent. At the last moment, Silas King cried off and asked if his eldest son could escort his mother instead.

Meeting him for the first time over the tea cups, she thought him a personable young man but no different to a dozen other eldest sons she knew. He was good-looking enough, smartly dressed, ready with compliments. However, when their fingers accidentally met, she felt a tremor go through her and as their eyes met for a fleeting second, she knew they would be lovers.

It had taken some organisation to have her husband entertained in one part of the country and herself and Julian King invited somewhere else, but she had done it. The first night he came to her room, she had been overwhelmed. This young man was so entirely different to any of her other lovers. He had taken her roughly in his arms and pressed his lips ardently to hers. For one ecstatic moment, she thought he would take her on the floor but suddenly, he lifted her lightly—something her husband had never and could never do—and laid her gently on the bed. Not a word had been spoken; she could only hear his quick breathing.

That night had been the start of a very passionate affair and she had used every device in her extensive repertoire to give him pleasure and keep him wanting more.

In the beginning, it had been a delightful game, as the beginning of all her affairs always were, but just lately, she had begun to feel something was missing. A little spice was needed, and she had decided Simon Amory would fit the bill very well. And if…well, it would be a diversion, a new sensation, to have two lovers and a husband all at the same time.

She had seen the jealous glint in Julian's eyes when she had been talking to Simon Amory and his words came back to her now. He was beginning to be just a little too possessive so maybe it would be time to end it, such a pity. But there were always more young men in the world to appreciate her charms.

Helene studied her profile intently. Was that a wrinkle? She peered harder and decided it was not a wrinkle. She would have a long bath and try her new face treatment.

The thought never crossed her mind that her husband, so astute in business as to make a great fortune, might know about her activities. She was used to coaxing and cajoling men, finding just the right moment, just the right note, to get what she wanted. If she could have read her husband's mind that Sunday evening at Kingscourt, she would have had a very unpleasant surprise.

Mark

Mark Goldburg was remembering the first time he had seen her, at a very grand ball in Vienna. How lovely she had been; even though dressed as every other young unmarried girl was, she had stood out in the crowd. He knew her guardian slightly and had engineered an introduction to her. Dancing sedately with her that evening, he had decided he would marry her but Mark was no fool—Helene had married him for his money and social standing; he had married her because—fool that he was—he loved her.

He knew of his wife's "friendships", could have unhesitatingly revealed the names of all her lovers including those men of lower social station with whom she had enjoyed a "warm regard". He was not blind to her foibles but he did not intend to be made a fool of publicly. Provided she remained discreet and within certain bounds, he would—though at some cost to himself—turn a blind eye.

Her friendship with Julian King was known to him and this weekend, he had covertly watched the young man. Instinct told him that here was a situation that needed careful handling. Until last evening, he had been ready to swear that to his wife, this young man was just that—another young man like all the others who had enjoyed her favours. The very fact that this particular young man had visited her under his own mother's roof had made Mark sit up and take notice. He knew the type of man Silas King was, and he would have wagered a good part of his extensive fortune that if he had found out what was going on, the situation could become unpleasant. Mark had no wish for that to happen, he and Silas King were in a business deal that could be lucrative for everyone if it all turned out in the way he planned; he did not intend that this should be compromised merely because King's young fool of a son had become infatuated with his own wife's well-displayed charms.

For a second, he wished, irritably, that she would not wear what he privately termed "that goo" on her face. She was beautiful enough without it. *That was the trouble*, he reflected, *she was too lovely*. Men lost their heads over her, as he had, but the difference was he had been willing to treat her honourably and give her his name, not just take her body for pleasure.

He sighed deeply and stared unseeing into the blazing fire in his room. Mark Goldburg loved England with a passion but he saw that they must be abroad for at least a year now. His wife and this foolish young man must be distanced from each other for long enough to allow whatever feeling he entertained to die. That Helene might feel anything, Mark very much doubted. He knew his wife too well to believe her capable of any deep feelings other than self-interest. Still, he would miss "this green and pleasant land" very much.

Now he would have to plan a non-existent business trip and calculate how much money to put aside. He knew his wife would be perfectly capable of spending as much on clothes in Paris as he was presently paying for the house in Cadogan Square, which he had leased when they married. And what to do with that house? If they were abroad some time, would it not be better to give it up and stay a year in Vienna? He had a very grand house on the Ringstrasse but Viennese society bored him, it was so very rigid, so much insistence on "quarterings". They had a way of making him feel very much an outsider while being so very polite. English society could be rather strait-laced but was much more liberal in its attitudes. He had several close friends like himself, interested in money and making more of it. That particular talent of his had brought him to the notice of the Prince of Wales and he had been invited to Sandringham and Marlborough House several times.

It had amused him in an abstract way to watch his wife trying so artfully to ingratiate herself with both the prince and princess. He knew quite enough about the way Edwardian society operated and could have told his wife at once that she would not be successful, but at the time, it had been a diversion to watch her.

He roused himself from a pointless reverie—whatever he did, it was never pointless or profitless—and stood up, moving slowly towards the connecting door to his wife's room.

He knocked quietly. 'Helene?'

'Mark, I was just going to sleep.' Her tone was a little sharp, he noticed.

'My dear, I have some news and as you may not quite like it, I decided to tell you at once.'

For a second, as she looked at him, he could have sworn he saw a glimmer of fear but it was too transitory to be sure.

'Tell me then.'

'We will be leaving for the Continent almost immediately. For an extended period.'

She was silent for a moment. 'Where exactly are we going?'

'To Paris first, then Vienna and possibly Zurich. We will be in Paris at least a week and I think it is time you had a new wardrobe.'

Her face lit up and she clapped her hands.

'A week in Paris for shopping! How lovely. When shall we leave?'

He smiled at the childish delight on her face. 'Very soon. And perhaps we shall have Christmas in Vienna.'

She smiled happily at him.

'Then I shall see Uncle Viktor again. He will be so pleased; we can have a proper Viennese Christmas together.'

She lay back on her pillow and smiled happily. Mark smiled back but mentally, the calculating part of his mind thought, *Yes, my dear, we shall have Christmas and New Year in Vienna and next year, I shall expect a son.*

He was as sure as it was possible to be that, on his wife's part anyway, this young man was just an agreeable bedfellow. Quite what his wife meant to the young man was another matter and one he did not concern himself too much about. He would do whatever it took to safeguard his most precious possession.

Chapter 1

Grace stayed the night at Nether Bassett and arrived at Kingscourt in time for lunch the day after the shopping trip to Exeter. John Trevelyan had sent her home in his carriage and she was almost at the house when the station dogcart passed her going the other way.

Merridew made his stately way to the carriage and she glanced at him quizzically.

'Guests, Merridew?'

'No miss. Mr Beades arriving to see your father.'

Grace stopped and the glance became a question. Mr Beades was the family solicitor but she had never met him; her father always went to Gray's Inn. And why had he not consulted Mr Beades on his recent trip to London?

The butler said no more and she went into the house and upstairs to change for lunch. When she came down, only her mother and Billy were in the saloon and, calm as ever, her mother asked how she had enjoyed her trip.

'Very much. Will you come up and see what I bought?'

'Later, my dear. There are only the three of us for lunch.'

'I thought…that is, Merridew said Mr Beades was here. Is he not going to join us?'

'No, they will have a tray in the library.'

That in itself was unusual; her father loved his lunchtime meal and never missed it if he were at home. Something was definitely wrong, though her mother seemed calm enough.

Grace wandered around restlessly after lunch; she felt something momentous was about to happen and wondered why everyone else seemed unaffected. She was in early for tea and sitting with her mother when the tray came in, followed by her father and Billy who looked as if he had seen a ghost.

As soon as the door closed behind Merridew, her father went to stand in front of the fireplace, a sombre look on his face.

'I have something to say to you all, but we will wait for Celia and Hugo.'

Grace was surprised. 'I didn't know they were here.'

'I sent for them.' Her father's face gave nothing away.

As if on cue, her sister and brother-in-law came in and Grace knew at once it was something about Julian. Her father had not moved from his position; he did not kiss his daughter and shake hands with Hugo as he normally would. Instead, he swallowed the cup of tea his wife handed him, coughed and began.

'This is as painful for me to say as I am sure it will be for you to hear. Julian…' the name evidently said with some difficulty, 'has decided to go abroad. Consequently, I have been with Mr Beades today and made certain changes to the running of the estate. Billy will be selling his commission and gradually take over running Kingscourt Estates.'

A silence followed until Celia said uncertainly, 'But Daddy, if Julian has only gone abroad, why must Billy leave the army?'

Silas King gazed at the far wall before speaking.

'Celia, my dear, your…that is, he is disinherited. Billy is now the heir and your only brother.'

Billy, who had not spoken or moved at all, suddenly interrupted, 'Dash it all, guv, he is my brother. Can't turn on him like this.'

'Anything that happens now has been brought on by his own actions.'

Grace spoke rapidly, her eyes never leaving her father's face, 'Julian has eloped with Lady Goldburg, hasn't he?'

'Did you know anything about this, Grace?'

Under her father's stern, she felt uncomfortable.

'Not exactly. That is, not for certain. She…seemed to be flirting with Major Amory and Julian didn't like it. Anyone could read his face. Then, when he put a shawl around her shoulders, he…his fingers seemed to—'

'That will do, thank you, Grace.' Her mother's normally serene tone was sharp.

Celia's hard unforgiving voice cut across the room, 'I can hardly believe Julian would be so…foolish. But you have done the right thing, Daddy, and Billy will do a much better job running the estate.'

'I hope you will all help Billy settle down to his new duties.' Silas paused, put his fingers into his waistcoat pockets and glanced at each in turn before speaking again.

'We've had a hard knock but will present a united front to the world. This matter will not be discussed outside this room, one name will never be mentioned again. There remains one more duty to perform. Billy, please ring the bell.'

Scarcely had the ivory bell pull beside the fireplace rung when Merridew appeared, almost as if he had been listening for the summons.

'Merridew, the family Bible, if you please.'

No-one moved in the few moments it took an impassive butler to return carrying the huge Bible, which Grace had last seen when her niece was born. In solemn silence, the book was placed on the table. Silas seated himself and calmly reached for the pen. The others watched as one entry was scratched out, the book closed and the butler once more removed it. As the door closed behind Merridew, Celia half turned to her mother.

'Mother, would it be alright if we dined tonight?'

'Of course, my dear. You know you are always welcome.'

As her eldest daughter went out quietly followed by both her husband and her father, Mary King moved at last. She sat beside her youngest daughter and put a hand on her shoulder.

'It is very hard, my dear, but I believe your father did the right thing. Now, we must all help Billy.'

'He couldn't...he wouldn't marry her, would he, Mother? Surely not!'

'We cannot speculate now. It is of no consequence to us what J—what he does. We have our lives to lead and we shall.'

Billy had not moved or spoken but he laughed shortly.

'So I am to be sacrificed on the family altar! Julian always had everything as heir, and I got what was left. Now everything is changed, no doubt the guv will require me to marry Elizabeth Trevelyan to keep everything nice and tidy.'

'William, I will not have your father spoken of in that manner.' The soft voice was as cold as ice cream.

'Billy's right, Mother, though perhaps not in the way he expressed it. Julian was spoilt and arrogant and always got his own way.'

Mary was silent for a moment and then said gently, 'You have a lot to understand so I will overlook these remarks. Naturally, you will never say anything like them ever again to anyone else or each other. As your father said, we present a united front to the world and that means ignoring everything that has happened.'

'But I can't ignore it, can I, Mother? My life is turned upside down. Here the guv tells me I am to leave the army, which is all I've ever wanted to do and all I'm cut out for. I can't run this place, wouldn't even know where to start. Estate'll go to the dogs.'

'Mother, do we know for certain that Julian has gone with…her?'

Her mother looked surprised.

'Your father knows, my dear. It is not for us to question him.'

Grace looked unconvinced but her mother's raised hand silenced her.

'Now children, I have let you run on like this because it was better only I hear it. You must put it all behind you now, as your father and I have to. I see it is nearly time to dress for dinner, so we must bustle about.'

Dinner was a somewhat melancholy meal and afterwards, with everyone gathered in the saloon for coffee, Grace attempted to play a few notes on the piano. She had little enthusiasm but it saved her having to talk to anyone. Celia and her mother were talking about the harvest festival while Merridew served the coffee but when he had departed, everyone was silent. Silas, in his favourite position in front of the fire and smoking his much-anticipated after-dinner cigar, glanced from one glum face to another.

'Well, we are miserable tonight. I suppose it is to be expected after everything. However, we must make an effort.'

Grace half turned on the piano stool and stared hard at her father.

'You are being unjust, Father. How can any of us behave as if nothing is wrong when…well, one of us is not here?'

'Grace, we are the family now. Please remember this situation is not of my making and I like it as little as the rest of you. I offered…him…two choices. He rejected both.'

Celia's voice, curiously flat and unemotional, seemed loud in the silence.

'You don't need to explain…or apologise, Daddy.'

Mary stirred and coughed slightly. Silas glanced at her but she would not meet his eye.

'Children, if you are to understand why your father has done…what has been done, you must know everything.'

His heart missed a beat. How much did she know? Surely she couldn't know he had…and under her own roof!

His wife's calm voice reassured him and his momentary anxiety disappeared.

'It was time for him to settle down, marry and ensure the future of the estate. He could have married Elizabeth or Alice…or any other suitable young lady. We would have been delighted to welcome another daughter. When your father talked to him about it, he said he was in love with a…a married lady. They intended to live abroad and marry when she was free.'

The silence stretched uneasily until Grace, who was still looking at her father, spoke, 'He made up his mind while she was here.'

'What makes you think that?' Her mother's voice held a hint of warning but her daughter missed it completely.

'I saw him look at Sir Mark when we were coming out of the stables…it was not a nice look. Contemptuous…and a little…pitying. Horrible.'

She shuddered and her father cleared his throat.

'Yes, well, that is in the past now. We have, I hope, cleared the air by talking in this way. Whatever…he does is his affair. It is as much of a heartache to me as to all of you. But we, the family, will recover.'

There was another long silence, broken only by the logs crackling in the fireplace and he turned and applied the poker vigorously. When he faced his family again, his face was flushed, though whether from the fire or something else was hard for Mary to decide.

'I have been giving some thought to the help Billy will need. I hear from a friend that Major Amory is to be invalided out of the army, so I propose to invite him down here for a chat. See if he would be consider being our agent. He could help Billy and it would be good to have another young person around.'

Three faces immediately changed.

Billy broke into a pleased grin and a hearty 'Simon coming here. That's great.'

Grace said nothing but coloured slightly.

And Mary, glancing from daughter to husband, realised at once how much pride Silas had swallowed with this one gesture. He had always prided himself on not needing an agent to manage his acres and on the fact that he knew every one of his tenants personally.

'That is a very good idea. As you see, children, your father has arranged everything.'

Silas half smiled. 'No, my dear, it may not work out. We must see. The young man may not want to live here, he may have something else in mind.'

Billy at least was in no doubt.

'It will work, Father. Simon will be delighted to live here, because he really enjoyed his weekend.'

Grace was following a different train of thought. She would see Simon Amory again, quite possibly very soon. Inwardly, she smiled.

***

In the following months, Billy's prophecy came true. Before the family could well adjust to the change of heir, Simon Amory was in residence in a house in the grounds and Billy had resigned his commission and was home for good. Simon and Billy, already friends, began the daunting task of running Kingscourt. Silas, watching over them carefully, was satisfied that the estate would be safe.

His younger daughter he also watched. That she had feelings for the newcomer was plain but he was pleased to see that she behaved with propriety. That was only to be expected, of course, he reflected, after her mother's teaching.

At Whitsun, he decided to give a party and sought out his wife to discuss his idea in some detail, Luncheon was over and he presently found her in the small sitting room she used during the day.

'Mary, my dear, I hear the Trevelyans are back. They will have some tales to tell.'

She nodded gently. 'Perhaps you should ride down the valley and pay a call, Silas.'

'Yes, I will.'

Their own private "scandal" had soon been overshadowed by a greater and more public one when, in the previous November, Alice Trevelyan had eloped with a penniless subaltern. Silas had been much shocked for she was undoubtedly his favourite of the two sisters. John Trevelyan had enlisted his old friend's help in the affair but the couple were married and on their way to India by the time they reached London. Unable to face the county, Louisa had swept Elizabeth off to the Continent for a tour of some months, with her own brothers as chaperones.

Mary missed her old friend. Frequent letters were not the same as comfortable weekly chats about servants and dogs (and daughters), which they had enjoyed for two decades.

'Silas.' Mary paused. Though she had been married to him so long, she could not always tell what he was thinking.

'Yes, my dear?'

'Everything is going well, isn't it?'

He eyed her carefully before replying.

'Yes, it is. Billy is settling down and young Amory is more than capable.'

She glanced down at her hands, bare save for the wedding ring.

'I believe Grace is forming an attachment.'

'To Amory, yes.'

She glanced at him sharply.

'Do you approve?'

'Yes. If he asks for her hand, I will not refuse, though I should think he has little means.'

'That doesn't matter. Hugo is not rich and as a second son will not inherit, but we made allowances for that.'

'The young people must work out their own feelings, my dear, and we must just wait and see.'

A knock at the door and an apologetic Billy peered in.

'Sorry to disturb you, Mother. May I have a word, Father?'

His father sighed. 'Must it be now, Billy?'

'If you could spare the time.'

As the door closed silently on husband and son, Mary sighed. It would be agreeable to see old friends again but Silas had no idea how much organisation was involved. True, she would have Grace, and Celia at a pinch, but they needed guiding. She was always in overall charge. Mentally, she began her first list. The pain in her side that had begun to niggle several weeks ago was ignored. A little strain, that was all. She would not exert herself too much, the girls could do quite a lot of it.

A tap at the door and Alice, her personal maid, came in with an envelope and an air of agitation.

'A telegram, mum.'

Mary took the envelope calmly. Her family were all here so it could not be bad news and she opened it. It took several minutes for the message to sink in.

Julian ill, maybe dying, far from home. Her mind was in a whirl: what could she do? Silas would never permit her to go—yet he was still her son. Suppose he died?

A slight cough recalled her thoughts.

Could she tell Silas? Would he do anything? No, of course not. Only one person might help her.

'Alice, I want you to deliver a note to...Major Amory.'

'Yes mum.'

She concentrated.

'And I want it done...' She paused. How to say without her husband's knowledge?

She scribbled a hasty line and sealed the envelope.

'Alice, do this yourself. Find a discreet way of passing it to Major Amory, and say nothing to anyone about the telegram.'

'That'll be difficult, mum. You know what young Billy's like, be all over the county by now.'

'Well, we shall have to hope not.'

The girl bobbed a curtsey and was gone. Mary could trust her, Alice had been with her for years and was totally devoted. Simon Amory was the proper person to go, he would leave at once and go to...where was that telegram? She hunted around her desk. Grand Metropolitan Hotel, rue de Roi, Dieppe. The manager deeply regretted troubling her with news of her son's malady but they could not allow a sick person to stay in the hotel—*so bad business, after all*, Mary thought cynically.

She folded the small piece of paper and hid it in the pocket of her skirt. Then, trying to be calm and collected, she went to look out anything she could think of that might be useful to take to a sick person.

Sooner than she expected, he was there and as he sat down, Mary took the telegram from her pocket.

'Major Amory, no doubt you will think it strange to be summoned in such a...surreptitious manner.'

'Mrs King, you sent for me, and by the way Alice gave me your note, I wondered if it was a matter of some delicacy.'

'Please read this.'

'You wish me to go to France and bring him home. Without Mr King knowing.' He did not question, merely stated the fact.

'Yes.'

'When he finds out what I have done, my position will be...difficult.'

'No, I will tell him I asked you to go.'

'He would never trust me again. Certainly never see me...never mind.'

Mary gave him a long appraising look.

'You mean, he would never see you in the light of a suitable husband.'

The blue eyes shot a look at her.

'You know how I feel?'

'My dear Major Amory…I shall call you Simon now…of course. I will speak to my husband, never fear.'

Simon did not look convinced. He sighed and, as was his habit when bothered, smoothed his hair several times.

'I will go and make arrangements.' He stood up and squared his shoulders. 'I will telegraph as soon as I find him.'

'You will need money. I have a little—'

'No, I have sufficient funds.'

A small pang of conscience was swallowed immediately. After all, he was practically family and who else could she ask?

'Simon…Godspeed and…bring him home safely for me.'

On impulse, she stood and kissed his cheek.

'I will.'

The door closed and she sat by the fire, gazing into the flames and remembering Julian as a small boy, the escapades, the times Billy had taken the blame for him, how they had indulged him, Perhaps that was the root of his present problems—he had been spoiled.

Well, she had been as much to blame as Silas for that.

Somehow, she must have nodded off because when she woke, Grace was kneeling beside her, a face full of concern and patting one hand.

'Mother, are you alright?'

'Yes dear, of course.'

'You look tired.'

'Nonsense, I am perfectly well.' A glance at the clock showed it to be nearly tea time and she firmly removed her daughter's hand.

'Ring the bell please, my dear, and let us go into the saloon. It is tea time.'

Tea was shorter than usual for Silas and Billy did not appear, and Simon Amory was already gone.

As the final gong sounded for dinner, Silas came into the saloon and found all his family there, only Simon Amory missing.

'Can I get you a drink, Father?'

Billy was at the small drinks tray, which was all Mary would permit.

'No, thanks. Where is Amory, do we know?'

Grace spoke quietly, 'He has sent no message, so I expect he will be here soon.'

Mary swallowed nervously before going to her husband and putting a hand on his arm.

'May I have a word in private, Silas?'

He looked surprised but nodded. 'Of course, my dear. Grace, Billy, you two go into the dining room. We will be in presently.'

After the door had closed behind two surprised children, Mary fixed a look, half-apologetic half-defiant, on her husband.

'Major Amory will be away a few days.'

He frowned. 'Unlike him to go off without a word. How did you know?'

'Because I have asked him to do something for me.'

'Am I to know what?'

She tried to speak calmly but her voice trembled.

'I have had a telegram that...J...Julian is dangerously ill, maybe dying...in France. Simon has gone to help him.'

In the first flush of anger, Silas missed his wife's use of a Christian name.

'No! I will not have anyone helping...that... ' His voice shook with anger as he struggled to be calm.

Tears welled in her eyes.

'I am surprised...and disappointed in you, Mary.'

'Whatever faults he has committed, Silas...and maybe it was more a case of him being led astray than anything else—he is our son.'

'Billy is our only son. You were very wrong to involve someone—anyone—in this. I shall speak to Amory when he returns.'

'Please, Silas, I beg you...please forgive Simon. He went because I asked him to. I must know that everything is being done for...that everything possible is being done.'

The silence stretched into minutes and she began to feel uncomfortable. His face was a mask, nothing to help her gauge his mood.

Finally, he moved uneasily.

'Very well. It is done now and cannot be changed. But not a word of this to Grace or Billy. And Mary...' he stared at the wall opposite, '...this is only to ease your mind. Ask no help of any kind from me. You must manage this affair on your own. I wish to hear no more of it.'

Impulsively, she took his hand and held it to her cheek.

'Thank you.'

He cleared his throat and moved his hand.

'Very well, let us go into dinner.'

***

The next few days crawled slowly, trying to keep up appearances to everyone, unable to speak of what was most on her mind to the one person who knew. Endlessly wondering when she could expect to hear from France, Mary waited anxiously for every post. Resolutely, she ignored the worsening pain in her side.

At last, Alice one morning handed her a small buff envelope.

'Has anyone else seen it?'

'Don't think so, mum. No-one was in the hall when I saw Billy.'

'Thank you, Alice. You may go now but I may need you to go to the village later.'

Feverishly, she tore the envelope open; her breath seemed caught in her throat.

'Condition grave. Rendering all assistance. Letter following. Amory.'

She read it through once more before finally letting go her breath. Now that Simon Amory was there, she was relieved.

Two more days passed until she heard more. Silas and Billy were out and Mary and Grace were finishing breakfast, Mary trying unsuccessfully to eat some toast. Alice came in quietly with the post salver, which was normally brought in by Merridew.

'The post, Mrs King.' One glance showed a foreign stamp and Mary took it at once.

'Thank you, Alice. Grace, I am not to be disturbed.'

'Very well, Mother.'

She missed the surprised look her daughter gave to her retreating back, unaware that she had spoken sharply. All that mattered was here was news of him. And quite a lot of news too, for the envelope was bulky so she would need time and quiet to take it all in.

The door of her sitting room closed and Mary hastened to her favourite seat near the window. Normally, the magnificent view—sweeping lawns and far-off parkland—merited a thoughtful and approving look; today, she hardly glanced at it.

With trembling hands, she broke open the envelope. Five pages of closely written script began. 'My dear Mrs King, having at last some time to myself while Julian sleeps, I hasten to write an account of my journey.'

She read on, so absorbed she could have been with him every step of the way. His hasty journey to the continent—'I took only a small holdall and the valise you so thoughtfully provided'; how he found Julian—'the Grand Hotel sadly does not live up to its name, being squalid in the extreme'; his military training—'I took it upon myself to rent an apartment and have Julian moved. I have hired a manservant and consulted the best doctor here.'

She had picked well when she had chosen him, Mary thought absently. But back to the letter.

'His condition is very grave, the doctor does not disguise his anxiety. I must tell you, Mrs King, that his constitution is severely impaired. He has been neglecting himself in a serious way. When I first saw him, he was delirious—raving like a madman—and all the time only one name on his lips. I think you may know who so I will not distress you by writing it.'

Mary blinked away a tear. That wicked, wicked woman. She had brought a fine boy to this. A devout woman all her life, Mary found herself hoping that Helene Goldburg would somehow be held accountable for all the unhappiness and suffering she had caused.

A knock sounded quietly at the door and her daughter's head appeared cautiously.

'Mother?'

'I said I was not to be disturbed.'

'Aunt Louisa and Elizabeth are here and I thought you would want to see them.'

'Very well.'

She folded the letter with a heavy sigh and put it carefully into the small purse she always carried. It would be pleasant to see her old friend again but she desperately wanted to finish her letter. She rose carefully, ignoring the stabbing pain.

Louisa Trevelyan looked well and greeted her old friend warmly. Elizabeth and Grace were soon deep in an atlas and Mary sat next to her old friend.

'How are you, Mary?'

'Well enough, Louisa.'

'Travel has improved Elizabeth and we are both well. You, on the other hand, look tired. What is it?'

Mary sighed again. 'I am a little weary, it is true. And I have a slight strain in my side, which is painful.'

It was a relief to talk to a dear old friend.

'You have consulted Jenkins, of course?'

'No, there has been so much going on. Louisa…' she glanced across at the girls but they were absorbed and she continued rapidly, '…Julian is ill, maybe dying, in France. I asked Simon Amory to go and make sure he has…everything he needs.'

A warm hand reached out for hers as she blinked away a tear.

'Julian! Oh my dear, I am so sorry. Silas knows?'

'Yes but he does not approve. He will not have the boy mentioned. No-one else knows.'

'What news do you have?'

'I was just reading the letter when you came.'

Her friend settled in the chair. 'Then of course, you must continue. I shall sit quietly here.'

Not for the first time—but never so wholeheartedly—did Mary bless her old friend for being so understanding. The letter seemed to burn a hole in her bag as she took it out and unfolded it.

The last paragraph was alarming and reassuring at the same time.

'He has stabilised somewhat now and does not rant and rave. The fever seems to be passing. However, the doctor says he has no strength to call on—he looks malnourished and has obviously been drinking heavily. If we can only get him over this and keep him stable, he may have a chance. I am not optimistic though and I will not tempt you with false hopes. We must just wait and pray. I hope everyone is well and send my regards to your family.'

Mary saw in this last sentence what he meant and silently vowed that after this was over, he would marry Grace if she had anything to do with it. Slowly, the letter was folded and put away with a heavy sigh. With a start, she remembered Louisa, observing the large landscape over the fireplace as if she had never seen it before.

'My dear, I am neglecting you. Please forgive me.'

'Nonsense. How is he?' She lowered her voice cautiously.

'Not good. The doctor has no hope of recovery apparently.'

'A foolish young man, as my daughter is a foolish young woman. Why cannot one's own wisdom be passed on, I wonder?'

'I never thought Alice would be…well, so lost to any sense of duty to you and Sir John. Do you have any news of her?'

'John has received a letter from young Roberts' colonel. He seems a decent enough young man, though penniless. Certainly his colonel speaks very well of him and says he has the makings of a good officer. Perhaps we were premature in our assessment of him, though I don't see how. A young man who could take a gently reared girl away from all her family and friends—and to a climate like India! They will be gone several years, I believe.'

For a moment, the two old friends were silent and then Mary spoke quietly, 'Louisa, I should be obliged if you would—that is no-one knows about this so—well, Silas would not like…'

'Of course not, my dear, that is understood.' She paused before speaking again, 'I always hoped Julian would marry Elizabeth. It would have been so comforting to us, knowing that Nether Bassett would be safe.'

'And I will admit that I always hoped to see Elizabeth at the head of our dining table wearing the King rubies. Such a sensible girl and so mature, she is a credit to you.'

Her friend flushed. 'Thank you. Maybe I tried harder with her, as the eldest, after I knew there would be no son. That has been my greatest sorrow, no-one to carry the name. And Elizabeth will be a very considerable heiress. I worry about fortune hunters.'

Mary straightened up suddenly.

'I never thought of the cost! Louisa, how on earth does one go about sending money abroad?'

The two friends gazed at each other. Though both ran large houses and had generous allowances, the mysteries of banking were just that to each of them.

'Why would you want to send money abroad, Mother?'

Mary and Louisa became conscious that their daughters had stopped talking and caught their last remarks.

Mary was speechless but quick-thinking Louisa saved the day.

'We were talking of our expenses, my dear. Travelling involves so much expenditure, you know.'

'Yes, I suppose so. Mother, Billy is coming in and it is almost lunchtime.'

'We must go, Mary. Our visit has been too long, please forgive us. Come along, Elizabeth.'

As they left, Grace glanced across at her mother.

'Is everything alright, Mother?'

'Yes, my dear.'

Billy came in then and whatever Grace had thought to say, the opportunity was lost. Her brother sat down with a studied air of nonchalance, which meant he had something to say.

'Mother, did I see Lady Trevelyan's carriage?'

'Yes, my dear, you did. They have been back a day or two.'

'I suppose they had some tales to tell.'

Grace answered quickly, 'Elizabeth certainly did. She has been to Rome and Venice.'

'Perhaps you should invite them to dine one evening, Mother. So we could hear all about it.'

Grace started hard at her brother. 'Now why would you want to hear all about it, Billy?'

'No reason, just being neighbourly.'

'We were thinking of having a small dinner party soon, and it will be very agreeable to hear all about their adventures. How nice of you to suggest it, Billy.'

No more was said but her maternal mind jumped to an obvious conclusion. If Billy had seen Louisa, he must also have seen Elizabeth, and Mary would be the first to admit—though she had not had much time to talk to her—that foreign travel had given her a more polished air. *She looked remarkably well*, Mary thought to herself, *and very attractive*. Perhaps…she dared hope…Billy thought so too. Hence his sudden eagerness to see them again.

She moved slightly in the chair, trying to find a comfortable spot to ease the pain. Maybe she should consult Jenkins, after Simon had brought Julian home. For back to England he must come, whatever Silas said. And she had still not resolved the question of how to spend money abroad.

The door opened and her husband entered with his usual measured tread.

'Well, my dear, I hear we have visitors.'

'Father, Elizabeth has been to Rome and she looks wonderful.'

'Does she indeed?'

'Yes, and Billy has suggested we invite them to dinner so we can hear all about it.'

'So we entertain.'

'To be sure. A small dinner party, I think. I wondered whether to wait for…well, until Major Amory is back so we can have even numbers.'

Grace saw her father's face harden slightly and knew that something was wrong, and it had to do with Simon Amory. Yet he must be coming back, her mother had said so.

'It will be so pleasant to see our old friends again, my dear, we do not need to wait.'

The butler coming in to announce lunch put an end to the conversation and it was not mentioned again. Mary knew she must talk to her husband about sending funds to France but she dreaded it. Still, it was necessary, and as soon as lunch was over, she decided to speak while her nerve held.

'Grace, Billy, I'm sure you have things to do.'

They were gone at once and as the door closed, Silas glanced at her.

'I want to talk to you about…'—even now she could not say one name—'…Simon Amory.'

'What about him?'

'He will need money. I have some put by but I don't know how to send it.'

For a moment, he continued smoking and gazing into the fire, then he rose, threw the rest of his cigar into the fire and leant against the mantelpiece, his face half turned away from her.

'I told you I will have nothing to do with this…mission of his.'

'I don't want you to. I merely wish to send some money to France.'

He stood quite still for some time and she held her breath until he spoke again.

'Very well. Give me his direction and I will arrange it.'

'Thank you.' She rose and crossed to him, put one hand on his arm and gently kissed his cheek. That he was surprised was apparent for she did not normally indulge in displays of affection such as this even when they were alone.

He patted her hand and half smiled. 'If it eases your mind, I will do it.'

'I want to know that I have done everything I can… If…well, if anything happened, I should have a clear conscience.'

'You…all of us…having nothing to reproach ourselves with. But I will arrange the money for you.'

She leant against him for a moment, trying to steady herself as a wave of pain hit her side and made her shudder.

'Are you alright?'

'Yes, it's nothing.'

'Mary, tell me.'

He put an arm round her and made her sit down, staring hard into her face.

'You look ill.'

'A slight pain. Nothing.'

'We must have Jenkins.'

Another pain came, stronger and fiercer than before and she leant back and half closed her eyes.

'I was going to consult him, Silas, as soon as Major Amory was back.'

He rang the bell vigorously and his butler appeared as if by magic.

'Merridew, send for Dr Jenkins. Find young Alice and send her to Mrs King. Immediately.'

'Silas, don't fuss. It's just a strain, that's all. I've been overdoing it.'

'Nevertheless, Jenkins will see you. I can't have you ill, my dear.'

He had been holding her hand as he spoke but as the maid came in, he let it go and turned to the fire.

'Alice, your mistress is feeling unwell. She will go and rest until Dr Jenkins arrives.'

'Yes sir.'

In the silence of his wife's departure, Silas King gazed into the fire long and hard. He thought fleetingly of his eldest son and wondered what the young fool had been doing but that was insignificant beside the fact that his wife was so obviously ill. Why had he not noticed it before? *Too wrapped up in his own affairs*, he scolded himself silently.

Silas was a man of his time—a woman's place was at home and Mary had more than fulfilled that role. She had run his home, reared his children, entertained his friends—but more than that, she was his haven, his refuge against the world. So long as he could go to her room every evening and shut the door so that it was only the two of them, nothing else could touch him.

Now, in an instant, he had seen all that threatened. He was so lost in thought he did not hear his elder daughter come in and he started as she spoke.

'Daddy, what's the matter? I hear Jenkins has been summoned to Mother.'

'Yes, my dear, your mother is unwell. I fear she has been doing too much. We must take great care of her.'

He held out a hand and Celia, concealing the anxiety she felt at his words, took it warmly.

'I'll stay for a few days if you like, so she can rest.'

'Thank you, my dear.' He held onto her hand as if it was a lifeline and they stood just so until Merridew came to announce the doctor.

'Celia, would you take him up please?'

She complied willingly but when the doctor had gone into her mother's room and quietly closed the door, Celia ran back downstairs. She went into the library, wrote a hasty note to her husband and asked Merridew to have it taken to The Risings at once. Then she went back to her father and they sat side by side in silence, waiting for the doctor.

To Celia it seemed like hours, to her father only seconds, before the portly Welshman who had been the valley's doctor for nearly thirty years entered the room quietly.

As each one looked at his face, they knew it was very bad news indeed.

***

The next few minutes seemed like a dream to Celia when she looked back in later years. It was as if she were an onlooker, not a player. She saw the doctor come in, her father stand up to face him, herself sitting motionless on the sofa. Her father's voice, rough as she had never heard it, seemed to come from a great distance.

'Well, Jenkins, let's have it.'

'Mrs King is very ill.'

'What is it?'

'A tumour. Very advanced. I should have been called weeks, month ago. Now, there may be very little I can do.'

'Operate?'

'I want to consult—with your approval, of course—Stephen Clift. A very prominent man, an expert in this field. Has some advanced theories on treatment for this kind of illness.'

'Send for him. In the meantime?'

'I have given her something to help the pain, make her sleep. She is to have complete rest, no worries of any kind.'

'My daughter is coming to stay.'

'Excellent. I will be in touch.'

In the silence that followed, Celia saw herself thank him for calling, see him out. When she returned, her father had not moved and she went to him and put a comforting arm through his.

'Daddy, why don't you go and sit with Mother for a while, until she falls asleep?'

For a moment, she thought he had not heard but he turned suddenly and looked at her, his face brightening.

'Yes, I will. You can look after everything, my dear.'

He went obediently out and Celia put a hand to her brow and tried to think. So much to be done—she would need more clothes, to instruct her own servants, to speak to nanny about Maryjane, think about what her mother might need, tell Grace and Billy. The last thought moved her quickly and she rang the bell sharply.

'Merridew, where are Mr Billy and Miss Grace?'

'I believe Miss Grace is out riding, Mrs Phillips. Mr Billy is in the gun room.'

'Very well. My mother is very ill and Mr Hugo and I will be coming to stay…' she paused before carrying on, '…indefinitely. You will have to take your instructions from me. Dr Jenkins will be coming back and we shall have to think about nursing…and so on. Please let the staff know.'

The old butler bowed.

'I am sorry Mrs King is indisposed. We will do everything we can to help.'

'We shall all need to be as quiet as possible, particularly the maids.'

When he had gone, Celia squared her shoulders and went towards the gun room. How much to tell him? All…or a little?

Grace crossed the hall just then and Celia decided to get it all over with.

'Billy, Grace, I need a word.'

'Celia, I didn't know you were here.'

'I shall be here for a while. Mother has been taken ill.'

'Ill? Mother's never ill. What is it, a cold?'

Celia sighed. 'Much more than a cold, Dr Jenkins says. She may have to have an operation.'

'Operation? What for?'

'A tumour.'

Billy grabbed her hand and held it hard. 'She will be alright though? She will recover?'

'Too early to say. We must be strong, little brother—because Daddy is taking it badly.'

Grace began to cry then. 'She can't die, Celia, she can't!'

Billy came to stand beside his sisters, one arm around each of them.

'Now we must be very strong and help Daddy through…whatever comes. So, we must try and be as normal as possible and not worry him. Agreed?'

Celia held out her hand, small finger crooked the way they always had and with a watery smile, Grace hooked hers around it. Billy put his underneath in the old childish pact that had suddenly become more serious.

It was Billy who broke away first and cleared his throat.

'I'll speak to…damn, I forgot he was away. The estate staff report to me anyway and Celia, you can look after the house. Grace, you could try and help mother—do whatever you can.'

'Yes, I will. But Billy—do we know where Simon is? He should be here to help you, all of us.'

'Gone to see an old friend on the Continent was all the guv said. And come to think of it, he went in a dashed hurry too—never even said goodbye. I must try and find an address and write to him.'

A knock at the door announced Merridew, impassive as ever but clearly struggling.

'The doctor is back, Mrs Phillips.'

'Very well, I will come at once.'

For them all, the remainder of the short day passed in a blur. Somehow, everything carried on but the house was silent, waiting.

Silas did not leave his wife's room and would eat nothing. Grace, Celia and Billy gathered in the saloon for tea by force of habit, Celia longing to have Hugo beside her. Her husband arrived soon after and they went into dinner silently, sat before food they could not eat and very soon withdrew, by unspoken agreement, to Mary's sitting room. When Merridew came in with the coffee, Celia told him quietly that they would not be having any formal meals until further notice. There was no point.

Two days crawled slowly by with the servants tiptoeing around, the young ones looking scared and the older ones sorrowful. The tension built up so much that Grace felt she would scream if something did not happen soon. In the end she went into the grounds, as far from the house as possible, and cried her heart out in the woods. She was walking slowly back from the house when she saw Billy coming out of the stable entrance, waving frantically to her.

'What is it? Is Mother worse?'

'Here's a letter for her, and it looks like Simon's writing.' Her brother gazed at the envelope and frowned. 'Perhaps we should open it.'

'Oh no, we can't. How could we explain it to Mother...when she is better.' Grace looked distressed.

'Let's ask Celia.'

Celia was practical. She took one look at the letter and opened it quickly, taking out several closely written sheets.

'There is an address anyway. Somewhere in Dieppe. Now...My dear Mrs King, I write with further news of J...Julian.'

She broke off and gazed steadily at her brother and sister. Their puzzled looks reassured her that they were as much in the dark as she was.

'You will be relieved to hear that he is much improved and the doctor thinks with time he will make a complete recovery. Mentally, he is much changed, and physically, I do not think you will recognise him.'

She stopped suddenly and screwed the pages up.

'So, Julian is ill and Mother knew. And Simon. Well, that's not on. He's not coming back here. Ever.' Billy's voice was cold.

'Now Billy, don't get upset. Of course, he won't come back here. He couldn't; Daddy disinherited him, remember.'

Celia's soothing voice calmed him somewhat but he took the pages from her hand and threw them into the fire.

'Billy, you fool, that's Mother's letter. We need the address.' Grace was quicker than her sister; she grabbed the fire tongs and extracted the blazing pages. When Celia had stamped on the flames, very little was left but at least they had an address.

Billy turned away looking like a sulky child and banged the door on his way out.

'I could strangle him sometimes,' Celia remarked calmly as she sat down to write a note.

Grace wandered aimlessly around the room once or twice before saying disjointedly, 'I'll go and see if Mother...or Father...need anything.'

'Don't mention the letter' her sister said quickly.

'Of course not. I'm not a fool, you know.'

Celia began to compose a note, which took several attempts. She liked Simon Amory, saw that her sister was more than a little in love with him and wondered… Why? Why was he in France helping…well, someone as little worth helping as…the person who had been her elder brother.

Celia saw everything in black and white and as soon as her father had made his announcement, she had cast Julian out of her heart. This had not been difficult for she had never been able to love him as Billy and Grace did.

That Simon Amory, whom she had always thought entirely honourable—that he should have gone to the assistance—in however large or small a way—of an outcast was beyond her.

Grimly, she signed the note formally with no warmth of tone and dropped it on the hall table for posting. Then she turned back to read some of the letters that had been arriving daily since news of her mother's illness had become public knowledge. She would have to answer them all eventually, but not today, and please God, they would not have to be bereavement letters.

Chapter 2

In the nightmare month that followed, Mary King's condition worsened. The great London surgeon came, shook his head gravely and said there was no point in operating as her condition was too advanced. Silas rarely left her side and Billy and his sisters struggled to run the huge estate.

Usually, every July, there was a great banquet at Kingscourt in honour of Haydn King who had revived the family fortunes so spectacularly in India.

'Well, the Kings Feast will not happen this year,' Billy spoke gloomily to his brother-in-law.

'No-one would expect it, Billy.'

Grace came into the office just then and her stunned look alarmed the two men.

'Grace, what is it? Mother!' Billy spoke sharply.

'No, she's asleep. Billy…we have a visitor.'

'Well, get rid of them. We can't be entertaining…' he paused and stared hard at her. 'It's Julian! I won't have him here. Nor Amory.'

His sister's face crumpled into tears and Hugo Phillips, glancing at his brother-in-law, wondered anew at Billy's total lack of comprehension. He obviously had no idea his sister loved Simon Amory.

'Now Billy, calm down. I will go and speak to them.'

'Not even over the doorstep. Neither of them. Understand?' Billy spoke to the closing door for Hugo had already gone.

Grace began to shout at him, 'He's your best friend. He saved your life.'

The youthful face hardened. 'Julian left a mess and I've had to give up everything because of him. And Simon is actually helping him.'

Grace stopped crying and stared at him.

'Somehow, I've lost both my brothers. Well, I shall go and speak to…Major Amory.'

The door banged behind her but Billy did not move, only continued to stare at the far wall.

Grace crossed the hall swiftly and went outside. Hugo was standing at the carriage door and beside him the tall figure of Simon Amory. At the sight of him, her heart missed a beat. She went very slowly down the steps and heard Hugo's words before they saw her.

'I'm sorry, Amory, you really can't see anyone.'

He turned in surprise as he heard the slight rustle of her skirts but Grace ignored him and held out both hands, smiling up at him.

'Major Amory, have you come to see my mother?'

He took her hands reluctantly but answered the smile and when he spoke, it was at random. 'I certainly hoped to, Miss King. But I do not think it will be possible. I really...must see about...getting, well, going to my cottage. Perhaps I may call later?'

'You may certainly call on me, Major Amory.'

Grace spoke quite steadily but she did not miss the stony look on Hugo's face. Well, what did she care, all that mattered was that he was back.

He stepped into the carriage and waved her goodbye as they rolled away. She and Hugo stood side by side at the bottom of the steps watching until it had disappeared. Then she turned sharply and ran up the broad shallow steps. Merridew was hovering and Grace spoke baldly, 'Merridew, if Major Amory calls, it will be to see me. And I will always be at home.'

'Yes, Miss Grace.'

'I am going to see Mother now.'

Luck was with her; the chair her father usually occupied was vacant and Grace tiptoed quietly to the bed.

'Mother...' It was a whisper but the eyelids fluttered. 'Julian's home.'

Her mother's lips curved slightly. 'Julian! Bring him up.'

'Billy sent him away. I think he will be at Simon...Major Amory's cottage.'

'You love Simon.' It was not a question and Grace caught herself sobbing.

'Yes, and now Billy is being so hateful.'

'Quietly, my dear. Do not upset yourself. Send Billy to me.'

'But Mother—'

'Quickly, before your father returns.'

Grace was downstairs in a flash but her brother had not moved.

'Mother wants to see you.'

He was gone and Grace sat down in the comfortable padded chair Silas used and tried to sort out the jumble in her mind. Simon was back! That was her only thought, and he looked tired and strained. If he had been looking after Julian, it was no wonder but suddenly Grace wondered if it had been a good idea to tell her mother they were back. After all, they had agreed she mustn't be worried. What would her father say? And Celia?

Before she had sorted all these ideas, Billy came in and he did not look pleased.

'So you told on me. Thanks.'

'I knew Mother would be pleased to know that Si…Major Amory is back. And that…well, everything is alright.'

'So now it seems I must swallow my pride and feelings and welcome back my disinherited older brother. Like the prodigal son.'

Grace took his arm. 'No Billy, you don't even have to see him. He can just go and see Mother and then leave.'

Her brother stared at her for a moment before turning away.

'No, I won't see him, whatever happens. All this is his fault and I'll never forgive him. Never.'

But later that evening, it seemed Julian would not see his mother after all. Celia had a short note saying the journey had exhausted him and he would be in bed for a few days.

Celia sat with the note in her hand and glanced at three solemn faces.

'Now the question is…do I tell Daddy?'

Her husband frowned. 'We must. He hardly ever leaves mother Mary so he would be bound to see him.'

'I agree, we must tell him.' Grace nodded.

Billy smoked his cigarette silently. In the old days, such a thing would never have happened, and certainly not in front of his mother or sisters but in the last few weeks, so much had changed in their lives no-one even remarked on it.

Finally, he spoke, head wreathed in a cloud of smoke but his face set.

'Don't look at me. I'm having nothing to do with this. Someone else can tell the guv.'

'I will. But not tonight, in a day or two. After Major Amory writes to me.'

Celia spoke firmly and there the matter stayed until their mother's condition worsened.

Grace, sitting by the bedside while her father took a short walk, was alarmed to hear her mother's breathing grow slowly worse. Celia, when consulted, said they must call the doctor and gather the family.

'Should we tell Father about—' Grace got no further because the door opened quietly.

'What don't I know?'

Celia took his hand gently. 'Daddy, we must tell you…Julian's back. And he's—' She got no further.

'No. Not here.'

Grace spoke softly, 'Mother knows he's here. She wants to see him.'

'No. He is not crossing the threshold.'

He went to his wife's room, leaving the sisters to gaze at each other.

'Well, I don't see how we can go against Daddy.'

'No. If Mother wants…anyone, she can ask.'

Celia stood irresolute in the hall for a moment before going to find her husband. All she wanted at this moment was to be with him.

***

The room was dark and close. Mary lay inert on the bed, the sheet barely rising as she clung to life. Beside her, Silas perched on the edge of a chair, holding the thin hand in both of his as if willing her to live. Celia and Hugo were on the other side of the bed and Grace and Billy at the foot.

They had remained so for hours, or minutes, no-one knew. Eventually, the eyelids fluttered open and Mary stared puzzled at each of them. Her lips moved soundlessly and her husband bent forwards.

'Julian?' The name was a feeble whisper.

Silas straightened up and replied, 'We are all here, Mary.'

'I want to see Julian.'

Four pairs of eyes looked at Silas King and waited. Finally, he spoke very slowly, 'Celia, send a message to Hunter's Cottage.'

'Yes Daddy.'

Grace took the opportunity to slip out of the room as well. She was not sure she wanted to see her brother but she most definitely wanted to see Simon Amory and in the end, she went to the office, which gave a clear view of the drive and waited. After what seemed an age, an old pony and trap came up the drive and she sped out to meet it.

'Are we in time?' Simon's voice was anxious.

'Yes.'

He turned to help a figure out of the trap and Grace, glancing back, had a shock. This tall gaunt wreck could not possibly be her brother? He stepped gingerly down from the carriage and took Simon's arm.

'Hello Grace.' A ghost of the old Julian appeared briefly.

'Julian, there's not much time.' Her voice was cool, she could not forget everything he had done.

Slowly, they mounted the stairs but at the top Julian was exhausted, leaning on Simon and breathing heavily.

Grace stopped before her mother's room and hesitated before softly knocking. As if waiting for a signal, the door opened and Celia came out followed by Billy and Hugo. No one spoke or even glanced at the two men standing nearby.

Finally, Silas came out. He walked like an old man and looked hard at the man who had been his eldest son. Then he turned and walked away down the corridor.

Simon led Julian into the room and was about to leave when a whispered voice from the bed stopped him. 'Simon.'

He came back at that and stood at the foot of the bed, in exactly the same place Grace had occupied.

'Thank you.' A thin hand moved slightly and he moved to the side of the bed to kiss it gently.

'It was an honour to be asked, Mrs King.'

'You are a fine man. Grace will be happy with you.'

The hand fell back onto the bed and he knew it was time to leave them alone. As he reached the door a faint 'Julian' followed by something like a sob made him go very quickly. He could not bear to witness anything too intimate and he closed the door with a snap.

Grace was hovering in the hall when he came out. 'Major Amory.'

'Miss King.'

He took her outstretched hand and held it. 'How are you?' He felt compelled to ask very quietly.

'So tired. I suppose after the first shock, we have adjusted to the idea that...Mother will not be with us much longer.'

He was silent a moment, staring into space. 'A great lady, your mother.'

'To me she will always be just...Mother. But how will we manage without her? Father will be...difficult.'

To no-one else could Grace have voiced this thought, which had been with her for days now. But somehow, she knew he would understand.

'He is devoted to her but he will have all of you, the family, to help and stand by him.'

The unspoken thought hung in the air. There was one who would have no-one to stand by him through the long night ahead.

The door opened and Julian stumbled out.

'Grace, fetch the others—she's...not very long...I think...'

His words were disjointed and Grace turned abruptly to summon everyone else.

'Julian, we must go.' Simon's voice was gentle but compelling, the sight of the ravaged face before him shocking. He put an arm around the wasted figure and they moved slowly towards the stairs. As if they knew he was leaving, Celia and Hugo appeared followed by Billy.

Simon, settling himself into the driving seat of the old trap, glanced up at the great house, its darkened windows somehow pathetic. The next time he came here, its mistress would be gone. He sighed heavily as the old pony ambled away and glanced at the silent figure opposite.

'You were in time, thank goodness.'

'She's dead now.' He spoke with finality. 'Nothing more to say.'

'Your mother will be much missed. Not just by her family but all the estate. Everyone will feel a gap in their lives.'

'I'm so tired, think I'll go to bed.'

Simon helped him upstairs and left Phipps to undress him. The effort exhausted him so much that he sat down beside the sitting room fire and promptly fell asleep. A loud knock at the door roused him and he stared sleepily around. When he opened the door, it was to Billy, Mary King's errand boy. Simon was amazed to see it was broad daylight.

'From Miss Grace, sir.' He held out a small envelope.

'Thank you.'

'She said I was to wait for a reply.'

'Come in then.'

The note was very short. 'My mother died early this morning. Grace King.'

Simon took a sheet of paper from his desk and scribbled an even shorter reply: 'My sincere condolences to you all. Amory.'

As the door closed behind Billy, a creaking board overhead announced Julian was up. Simon went slowly up the stairs and knocked on the door.

'Julian?'

'Who was that?'

'A note from your sister.'

'Mother?'

'Yes.'

For a moment, he paused, holding the razor in his hand.

'As my father would say, I've made my bed and I must lie on it.' He sighed.

'We all make mistakes, Julian, and we pay for them. You are recovering your health now.'

'The price was too high. Helene Goldburg was not worth it.'

Simon drew a sharp breath for it was the first time the name had been mentioned when he was rational.

'Do you want to talk about it? Sometimes it's better to say it out loud and move on.'

'No, I don't.' He turned away and looked out of the small window, his face unreadable.

'Alright. Feel like breakfast?'

'No, not just now. Think I'll go for a walk.'

Simon did not quite like the look in his eyes and as the door closed, he called to Phipps, the manservant he had engaged in France and who had been happy to stay with them.

'Phipps, Mrs King died early this morning.'

'I am sorry, sir.'

'Mr Julian is naturally upset. I don't want to intrude but we must know that he's…alright.'

The man nodded. 'I understand perfectly, Major Amory. A discreet distance.'

Simon nodded gratefully. What a treasure he had been, this quiet self-effacing man who had answered his brief advertisement, come with no references but his manner.

There was some mystery, Simon mused to himself, a past that did not bear too much looking into. Well, they were all prisoners of the past in one way or another.

It was several hours before Julian returned and Simon had just put a kettle on the fire to make some tea. Long experience of campaigning meant he was never obliged to wait for a servant to do things for him and he had laid a small tray and was just going back to the sitting room when Julian came back.

'Good walk?'

'Yes. Cold now though. Is that tea?'

'Yes, in a minute. Take your coat off and sit down.'

Julian sat in front of the blazing fire until the kettle began to steam and presently, Simon handed him a cup of tea.

'What I said this morning, I meant it, you know.'

What was that?' Simon took a long drink of hot tea.

'Helene Goldburg was not worth the price I paid. Being estranged from my family, not to be here when Mother…all for that.'

'You couldn't have known that. Now you are wiser.'

'I was prepared to marry her. None of that backstairs stuff they indulge in. Creeping into bedrooms at midnight, then back to your own before the maid brings tea in. I wanted her as my wife, to have my children. Grow old together.'

There was pain in his voice but Simon glimpsed a weary acceptance of the situation. 'Some things are not meant to be.'

'No, she wanted that old man, jewels, dresses, his millions.'

Curiosity compelled Simon to ask the question he had vowed he would not ask. 'What happened?'

The silence lasted so long Simon thought he had overstepped the mark but Julian began at last in a quiet sad voice.

'I wrote to him, after the house party, told him the whole story. That I loved her and was prepared to marry her.'

'What did he say? How did he react?'

'I went to London the next day, called at Cadogan Square. I was told they had left the country. I didn't know what else to do so I stayed in town until someone told me they were in Paris, staying at the Ritz.'

'You called there?'

'I left my card but nothing happened. Finally, I saw in the newspaper they were going to the opera so I went. Awful rot it is but I sat through the whole thing, watching her. In the interval, all the men were going to her box, kissing her hand and paying her compliments.

'And he sat in the corner like a spider, smiling and watching her all the time. He never took his eyes off her.'

'Did you go and pay court?'

'No, I wouldn't be part of that circus. I found out they were going to the de la Tousselles ball so I wangled an invitation and turned up. Asked for a dance with her but she treated me like a stranger. Do you know…I went up and kissed her hand…looked her in the eye. Simon, we had been…lovers, you know. And she as cool as if it was our first meeting.'

He shook his head in disbelief.

'I was too shocked for words. Everything we had been…had enjoyed together…it was nothing. And he came up right behind her and put his hand on her arm like a snake coiling around her.'

'Did you say anything? To either of them?'

'No, I felt I had to get away at once. The room was so hot and everyone was smiling and happy. I could have murdered them all at that moment.'

A silence settled, which Simon felt he couldn't break and it was Julian who eventually continued, 'I went back to my hotel, started drinking. Then I ran out of money so I thought I had better come home. I made it to Dieppe and the rest you know.

'If you keep dwelling on it all the time…it's not healthy.'

'I know. She was my obsession. And because I've always been used to having my own way and getting everything I wanted, it never occurred to me that I wouldn't get her.'

'Do you know your father has disinherited you?'

It was a rhetorical question so he did not expect an answer. 'Disinherited me? He can't.'

'He has. Billy sold his commission and came home to run the estate. I'm the estate manager.'

Julian spoke slowly. 'So I have nothing. I was coming home but now I see there is no home and nothing to come back for.'

'Billy, Celia…no-one wants you back.'

'My father must hate me very much.'

'Your mother doesn't. When she had the telegram from that awful little hotel manager, she sent me to see what I could do.'

In a rare moment of acute perception, Julian half smiled.

'Yet I was never her favourite. The oldest son with all that means but never anything more.'

'What will you do now?'

'Go away, I suppose. As I have no-one to worry about me, I can do as I please.'

A knock at the door announced Billy with another note.

'Your sister writes that everyone is coping. A quiet interment is planned with only family and the Trevelyans.'

'My father wanted me to marry Elizabeth.'

'Did he?'

'He thought it would be a suitable match. Keep the estates together.'

Simon had heard much local news since he had come back and he sipped his tea before speaking, 'Alice ran off. Eloped with a subaltern and is in India.'

'Little Alice. She was a great favourite with my father. And…how is Elizabeth?

'She has been abroad with her mother.'

Julian rose abruptly. 'I'm going to have a rest. See you later.'

Simon remained a long time sitting by the fire, dreaming of Grace King. Finally, he got up and went to look out of the window. From here, the big house was not visible but he looked at the trees and saw through them to the great house, now mourning its head.

He half smiled to himself. Did being in love make one poetic, or philosophical? Certainly, he would never have had such a thought before coming here.

Part of that was Grace but a bigger part was her mother. Mary King had always been motherly. He thought if his own mother had lived, that was how she would have been.

Perhaps that was part of her charm, her warmth of manner. That was all gone now, would soon be laid in the King family vault with all the other ancestors.

'I'm getting morbid.' He must have spoken out loud and a voice answering startled him.

'Sir?'

'Oh Phipps, there you are. Is it time to eat?'

'I was coming to ask what you wanted me to do about a meal, sir. Especially as Mr Julian has gone out.'

'Gone out? Where?'

'He left some moments ago, sir.'

'Well, get your coat and follow him.'

The man disappeared and Simon stood for a moment before deciding to go out as well.

Just now, he had a feeling Julian must not be left alone.

***

Grace felt she was living in a nightmare from which she would never wake. How many times a day did she think 'mother will know'? How many times did the remembrance of her loss strike her heart?

All this made more unbearable by her father's naïve astonishment that he was suddenly alone. It was soon apparent to his children that their father could not—and possibly never would—come to terms with his loss. In their different ways, each of them suddenly found many duties and responsibilities that overshadowed their grief.

Celia, struggling to run Kingscourt, wondered enviously how her mother had always managed to look so serene. This enormous house was draining all her energies and every day was exhausting.

Billy, trying to run the huge estate single-handedly, could not find time to mourn his mother, his every moment was taken up with business.

Grace, on the other hand, had little to do. She wandered around aimlessly, missing her mother constantly and wondering about Simon Amory more and more. When would he come back? Never? How long would Julian stay?

The day of the funeral dawned cold but bright and they walked slowly behind the coffin on the short journey to the church Haydn King had built with his Indian riches. Grace, muffled in mourning, saw the leaves fall and the rich colours of a late autumn. Her mind seemed to take in every detail with clarity. She could not, would not, think what was at the head of the procession, could not look at the heavily polished coffin, carried reverently by the older estate workers and with every inch covered in flowers.

She saw Simon though, standing beside the Beggars Oak, dressed in mourning and holding his hat. Silas, leaning heavily on his son's arm, did not even raise his head so she doubted he had noticed. Of Julian, there was no sign.

The short service was soon over and Grace watched in a trance as her mother was carried into the family chapel. Somehow, it was all so final, a chapter of her life suddenly ending with the closing of the crypt door.

It was as they were turning to walk back down the aisle that she was almost sure she saw Julian slipping out of the door. Her father gave no sign of recognition to anyone in the congregation until he reached Simon and then he stopped.

'What are you doing here, sir?' The voice was weak but aggressive. Simon half bent his head but replied steadily.

'Paying my last respects to a very great lady and a true friend, Mr King. She will be much missed.'

Silas said nothing to that but after a pause, he walked slowly away.

As Grace passed by, she gave him a brief half smile and her lips formed a 'thank you'.

Simon waited until the church emptied before going to the altar and saying a short prayer. As he turned to go, Julian slipped in through the vestry door and came to join him.

'I'll leave you in peace,' Simon half whispered and went away as quietly as he could. As he left the church, he was surprised to see young Billy waiting for him.

'Yes Billy?'

'Mr King's compliments, sir, and he will see you at four o'clock.'

That was not precisely what Silas King had said but Billy had not worked for Mary King without learning a little diplomacy.

Simon nodded. 'Thank you. Tell him I will be there.'

Punctually, as the clock struck four, Simon knocked on the office door and was called in. He found Silas sitting in a chair by the fire and Billy seated behind the imposing rent desk.

'You sent for me, Mr King?'

Simon waited patiently, he was used to waiting for superiors to make up their minds and he did not fidget, merely stood, hat in hand.

'Major Amory, my wife tells me...told me she had asked you to go to France.'

'Yes sir.'

'That...errand is now discharged. Billy needs your help to run the estate so I shall expect to see you at your desk on Monday.'

Simon waited. Obviously, this was not all.

Billy spoke quietly, 'Where is he, Simon?'

There was no point pretending not to understand and his reply was also quiet.

'At my cottage. A temporary arrangement until he regains his strength.'

Silas did not move his gaze from the fire.

'He has regained his strength now and must leave.'

Simon hesitated before answering, 'He is…not strong.'

'Well enough. He must go now.'

Simon saw there was nothing more to be said and he let himself out without another word. Grace had evidently been watching for him and she crossed the hall.

'Major Amory.'

'Miss King.'

'I hear you are coming back.'

'Your father wishes it. How are you?'

She half smiled. 'Missing Mother. But I hope we may be able to regain some…normality now. How is…' She could not finish.

'He is of course much distressed at his…your loss. He was grateful to have the chance to say goodbye.'

'Yes, that was quite proper.' Her generosity of spirit surprised him. He knew that Billy, Celia and their father were implacable where Julian was concerned. Hugo Phillips was a bit of an unknown quantity.

'He will be leaving soon.'

'Father wouldn't want him anywhere near. Nor would Billy. I expect…I expect I shall see you next week then.'

Celia's quiet entry into the hall reminded Grace of the proprieties and she extended her hand to him on her final words. He took it for a moment.

'Until next week then.' He turned and was gone, leaving her staring at his retreating back.

Celia, from that brief glimpse, saw genuine affection on both sides. Well, he was agreeable, a distinguished officer and her father thought well of him. *Grace could have done worse, much worse*, she thought. *He hasn't declared himself though and maybe he won't because we are in mourning.* Celia's thoughts ran on as she gazed at the list in her hand.

Certainly, thinking of possible love affairs was more agreeable then trying to run this great place, especially when she was feeling a little off colour.

Simon walked slowly back towards his cottage, his thoughts all of Grace. He had loved her for a long time, not quite from the first moment he saw her but certainly very soon after. He had never bothered much with the opposite sex; in his younger days, he had little money and his way to make in the world.

If he had ever thought about the kind of wife he would look for, he supposed someone in his mother's mould, even though she had died when he was twelve. There was a good social life in the army but most of the regimental daughters, though pretty and polite enough, were very strictly controlled by their mothers. Once posted abroad, there had been no time to think of women in the horrors of a war and he had put the thought away.

Back in England and feted as a hero, Simon had met a great many young ladies but none had tempted him until he saw Grace. He knew that she was the only one for him, if only he could pluck up courage to ask.

His thoughts had run on and all too soon he found himself outside the cottage and his own affairs paled beside the task he now had. Somehow, he had to tell Julian he must find somewhere to go.

He sighed as he let himself in and put his hat on the hall stand. It was unlike Phipps not to come out and see if he wanted anything and he went into his little sitting room and lit the lamp. As the light flared, he saw an envelope lying on the table and opened it. The spidery writing leapt off the page.

'Amory, it's time for me to move on but not before I thank you for saving whatever was left of me.

My sister can be a little terror but she is a loving girl at heart.

I hope I may sign myself—your friend Julian.

P.S. I have taken Phipps—thought you wouldn't mind too much. He wants to be about the world.'

For a moment, he was too surprised to do anything but stare at the paper stilt in his hand. Then he refolded it and put it in the drawer of his desk. Perhaps this way was best—no unpleasant interview, no leave taking, just to go. Maybe somewhere, Julian could make a life, find some happiness.

Happiness—now there was a word. He fell to thinking again about Grace. He wanted desperately to propose marriage and he pulled out his small account ledger for the hundredth time and began once more to go over his assets. He could afford to marry, not with life's luxuries but certainly with some degree of comfort. But would that be enough for Miss King of Kingscourt?

'I suppose I must see about finding someone to look after me.' Mentally, he listed all the qualities he looked for in a servant and wondered where to find such a paragon.

'Perhaps I should have a word with Mrs—' He pulled up on the last word. That avenue was closed forever and he was at a loss.

The next morning, word of a certain person's departure having obviously got around, Billy rode over to talk over some business. Before he started, he handed Simon a letter.

'Came last week. Return address on the back.'

Simon turned the envelope and read, 'Alfred Wilkins, c/o Mrs Johnson, 4 The Ramparts, Plymouth.'

He tore the envelope open and read it aloud.

'Listen to this. Mr Amory sir, I take the liberty of writing and hope this letter finds you. I have now left the army and am in need of employment. I hope you will remember me, sir, as a loyal man, diligent and resourceful. If you have need of such a man, sir, please feel free to call on me. At present, I am staying with my sister.'

Billy smiled. 'Wilkins. Always wondered where he got those bananas.'

Simon met his eye, they both began to laugh and somehow, the ice was broken.

Billy glanced at him shrewdly. 'Well, you'll need someone to look after you. He could be the right person. Now to business.'

It was a relief to put everything behind him and talk about the estate, Simon reflected. He had discovered a love of all things rural that he had never experienced as a child. Managing the King estates was absorbing and they made a good team.

At lunch later that week, everyone seemed rather silent and Simon, glancing at the empty chair, suddenly felt a melancholy remembrance of all the happy times he had enjoyed at this table. And he was a relative newcomer. How must all the others be feeling?

Silas, who seemed to have shrunk since his wife's death, sat the head of the table with an almost untouched plate of food before him. Celia looked pale and drawn and Billy was only toying with a potato. Only Hugo and Grace seemed to have any appetite.

As the servants cleared away, Celia, who appeared rather edgy, spoke sharply, 'I'm sorry my poor efforts at housekeeping don't meet with your approval.'

'It was an excellent meal, Mrs Phillips, thank you,' Simon spoke sincerely and she half smiled.

'Yes Celia, you did well.'

'Cee, it was lovely, really.' Hugo and Grace broke in at the same time.

'Well, I try. It is difficult and time consuming running this house. Goodness knows how mother managed.'

Silas looked hard at her. 'Your mother always had everything under control.'

'Yes Daddy, but it takes a lot of effort.'

'You are doing well. Until Billy marries and we have a new mistress.'

All eyes instantly turned to Billy who flushed and began spluttering.

'I say, look here, guv, dash it all, can't marry just anyone.'

To at least one member of the family, it was obvious that Billy had formed an attachment and Celia smiled. Please God, it would happen soon and she would be free to go home, and let it be very soon if what she suspected was true. If she was going to have another baby, running this great house would be impossible. Grace would have to fill her shoes, that was all, and she could retire to The Risings and rest.

She would have been very surprised to find her husband's thoughts running on much the same lines. Hugo also suspected his wife might be 'in an interesting condition' and he did not relish the idea of her trying to run the house and also have proper rest. He would speak to her father if necessary. After all, Silas was a parent himself and would understand.

Celia rose from the table wearily and went towards the door. As Hugo rose, he glanced across at his wife, just too late to stop her falling in a dead faint.

Grace let out a scream. 'Celia!'

It was Simon who reacted the fastest. He leapt up and crossed the dining room and was out of the door calling for Merridew. Hugo went to his wife and began to loosen the high-necked blouse she was wearing. Billy, Grace and their father sat as if turned to stone. Suddenly, a babble of voices erupted.

'Grace, come and help me!' Hugo almost shouted.

At the same time, Simon called into the hall, 'Merridew, send for Dr Jenkins at once. Mrs Phillips is unwell.'

'Celia, don't you feel well?' Silas sounded plaintive.

Celia's eyes fluttered open to see her sister's anxious face peering at her and feel herself pillowed on her husband's shoulder.

'What happened?' Even to herself, her voice sounded far away.

'You fainted. Don't worry, we're taking you to bed.' Hugo's voice, just above her head, sounded vaguely comforting. *I must have a talk with Hugo*, she thought dimly.

Very soon she was tucked up in bed with a hot water bottle and Dr Jenkins fussing over her, for she had always been his favourite. He confirmed her suspicion and Hugo, sitting silently by the bed, raised her hand and kissed it.

'So now, young Celia, you will take things easy. Rest and sleep.'

'That's all very well, doctor, but how on earth can I do that when my father expects me to run Kingscourt?'

'I will speak to Mr King.'

'I will speak to your father.' Husband and doctor spoke at the same time. She would not be convinced.

'Well, who else is going to do it? Grace can't.'

'We'll manage, Cee, don't worry. Just rest for now.'

Hugo rose and shepherded the doctor to the door. On the landing, he spoke in a low tone to the doctor, 'I'll speak to my father-in-law. I was going to anyway. Is there any danger?'

'None at all, my dear young man. She's young and strong, but rest she must.'

'She will, I'll make sure of that.'

He went down to the small sitting room that, in the days following Mary King's death, her husband had almost constantly used, and knocked gently on the door.

'May I have a word, guv?'

Silas, sitting in his wife's favourite chair beside the fire, looked up.

'How is Celia?'

'Resting. She's going to have a baby.' Hugo had not meant to say it so baldly. Silas smiled for the first time in weeks.

'Good. I am pleased for both of you.'

'The point…is she needs to rest.'

'Yes, she must.' Her father appeared to miss the point completely.

'Therefore, someone else must take over responsibility for this house.'

Silas gave him a sharp glance under frowning brows. 'Someone else? There is no-one else.'

'Grace will have to. I am sorry, guv, but my wife must have rest and quiet, not exert herself. I will take her back to The Risings as soon as possible.'

Hugo spoke politely but firmly.

'Grace is not up to it.'

'She will have to be, my wife's health comes before everything.'

Hugo let himself out quietly before he forgot the respect due to his father-in-law. Grace would just have to take over, however unprepared she was.

In the end, the person who solved the problem was Louisa Trevelyan. On the day following Dr Jenkins' visit, she came to see Silas and was closeted in the sitting room with him for a long time.

When she came out, everything was settled. In a very short time, Hugo took his wife home and Elizabeth Trevelyan came to stay at Kingscourt for an indefinite period. The reason given was that she was keeping Grace company but the reality was she was going to show Grace the way to run a large household.

Louisa Trevelyan, ramrod straight on the sofa, had plainly spoken to Silas.

'I always told Mary it was a great mistake not to involve your girls more in the running of this place. But she always preferred to do everything herself. Now, both my girls…that is, Elizabeth…can give orders and know what's to be done.'

'What's your point, Louisa?'

'Let Elizabeth stay here for a while. Grace is an intelligent child, she'll soon learn how it's all done.'

So one cold but bright November morning, the Trevelyan wagonette, loaded with trunks bearing European stickers, rolled slowly up the drive, to be followed an hour later by Elizabeth herself, splendidly mounted on a bay mare.

Billy, who happened to be in the stable yard, turned quickly as she cantered in.

'Well, Elizabeth!! How are you? Splendid horse.'

'Hello Billy. I'm fine, thanks. Do you like Princess?'

'A very nice piece of horseflesh. Sir John chose well.'

As he spoke, Billy took the reins and led the horse to a mounting block. As he turned to help her down, Elizabeth dismounted gracefully and took his outstretched hand.

'It is a long time since we last met.'

'Yes indeed. How was your trip?'

'I enjoyed it. Travel does broaden the mind, so many sights and experiences. But I am happy to be back home. There's no place like England.'

She glanced appreciatively over the broad expanse of rolling hills that rose beyond the stable yard.

'I have always thought so. When I was in South Africa, I used to lie at night under the stars and though I knew it was the same sky and the same stars, somehow, it was not home.'

From under her veil, Elizabeth glanced at him steadily.

'That is exactly how I felt. Even in Venice, where we enjoyed a moonlit gondola ride, it was not Devon.'

'How strange we should think alike.' They were walking slowly, arm in arm, towards the house when Grace spied them from an upstairs window and waved her handkerchief energetically.

'Elizabeth, how lovely! I'll be down in a moment.'

They all arrived at the front door together and Grace took her friend upstairs immediately to wash and change. For a moment, Billy stood in the hall watching the graceful figure until it turned a corner into the east wing. He was pleased to find that his first impression of her was right—she had benefitted from going abroad. He had always thought her somewhat quiet and plain, she never said much and deferred to her mother in what he always thought showed a lack of spirit. *Certainly, she was not plain now*, he thought, remembering the radiant face as she alighted from her horse. The thought of being under the same roof for a while was intriguing.

By the time everyone was downstairs for lunch, in some indefinable way, the mood of the house had lifted. Their new guest did not put herself forward in any way but somehow, the conversation flowed and even Silas managed a smile or two.

Grace had always liked her although there was a slight age gap, for Elizabeth was more nearly Celia's contemporary, but they were soon fast friends and Grace was listening to a vivid description of the Grand Canal.

After dessert, Merridew entered with the coffee tray, the door closed quietly behind him and Elizabeth turned to Grace.

'May I go for a walk, Grace? I need a little air.'

'Yes, of course. Would you like some company?'

'Yes, that would be lovely. Please excuse us, gentlemen.'

The three men rose and Billy opened the door to let them out. In their absence, the three men sat on drinking coffee, each pursuing a different train of thought.

I wish I was going with them instead of being cooped up in the office with Simon, Billy thought irritably.

Travel has definitely improved that girl, mused Silas.

Simon, who had joined them for lunch, was also thinking, *I should like to walk in the garden with Grace instead of being cooped up with Billy.*

***

Three months passed quickly, during which time Celia blossomed and Grace and Simon and Billy and Elizabeth became couples. Silas, beginning to be more his old self, watched these love affairs being played out and was pleased, wishing only that his wife had lived long enough to see it.

Christmas arrived and went quietly, though the village children had their usual party and presents, it was hosted by the vicar and none of the Kings attended. Elizabeth Trevelyan seemed completely at home and the great house ran as smoothly as ever.

Billy's February birthday drew nearer and Grace and Elizabeth were planning a small dinner to celebrate when Louisa Trevelyan turned up.

'Mama, how nice to see you.' Elizabeth dutifully kissed the soft cheek presented to her.

'Aunt Louisa, how are you?' Grace hurried to kiss the older woman.

'Well, my dears, and pleased to see you both looking so well. How is everything?'

'We are planning a birthday dinner for Billy.'

'Goodness yes, that is very soon. He will be…' Louisa Trevelyan calculated rapidly, '25. How time does fly.'

'We thought family…yourself and Sir John as his godfather. And Simon Amory.'

The older lady nodded. 'Most suitable. Now, Eliza, after this you must think of coming home. Your father misses you'

'Home!' Both girls spoke together.

'Yes indeed, for you have been here above four months. I am sure Grace will cope very well now.'

Elizabeth invited her mother to stay for lunch but it was a somewhat muted affair and when Louisa announced that her daughter would be going home soon, Billy for one was thunderstruck.

'Oh but, I say, we've grown quite used to her being here. Almost another sister for Grace.'

'Well, Sir John misses her, he likes to hear her play after dinner.'

Billy was tempted to say that he would miss her playing after dinner but closed his mouth abruptly. One could not be rude to a guest under your roof, least of all a lady.

He soon went to work off his bad temper by shooting rabbits and was vigorously taking pot shots in the Spinney when Simon caught up with him.

One glance at the thunderous face before him caused Simon to tread warily. 'Catch anything, Billy?'

'One or two. Beastly sport anyway.' As it was one of his favourite pastimes, Simon was surprised.

'Anything happened to upset you?'

'No. Yes. It's nothing. Lady Trevelyan talks of taking Beth home.'

'Ah.'

'What does that mean?'

'Nothing.'

'Yes it does. You said 'ah' in a knowing way.'

'Billy, anyone with half an eye can see you have…formed an attachment to Miss Trevelyan. Naturally, you dislike the idea of her going home.'

'Formed an…well, yes I have. I love her if you must know.'

'So what's the problem?'

Billy bent and fiddled with his gun before straightening up, his face flushed.

'Not sure of her feelings. Might not have me.'

Simon thought privately that even if the young lady were only half-hearted, her parents would have been more than encouraging.

'You'll never know if you don't ask.' His friend smiled and Billy half turned and on a sudden impulse handed his gun to Simon.

'Shan't be long.'

As he walked away, Simon half shouted 'good luck' before disappearing into the woods.

Billy walked fast, anxious to find her while his courage was high. He had no difficulty for she was just waving the Trevelyan carriage off and stood on the steps of the house framed in the open doorway.

He waved his hat energetically.

'Beth! Hi, Beth!'

She smiled as he dashed across.

'Billy, there is no need to shout, I am not hard of hearing.'

'Are you doing anything right now?'

'No, as you see, mama has just left and I was going to have a few moments to myself.'

'Have them with me instead.' Billy took her arm in what he hoped was a gentle but masterful way and steered her towards the conservatory, conveniently placed to provide lovely views of the gardens, which at the moment looked like a winter wonderland. Beth sat down quietly and arranged her skirts before folding her hands carefully.

Billy paced up and down once or twice before coming to sit beside her. 'So, you are going home soon.'

'Yes.'

'Will you be sorry?'

'In many ways, yes.'

'How many? Will you miss us?'

'Billy, what are you asking me? Yes, I will miss you all even though I only live down the valley. Kingscourt is such a welcoming house, it casts a spell on you and makes you feel as if you never want to leave.'

He took one of the small hands in both his own and drew a deep breath.

'Then don't ever leave, Beth. Stay here…and marry me. I love you so much and the thought of you leaving, well…it's too awful.'

The last words came out in a rush and he gazed down at the hand imprisoned in his, feeling that if she said no—or worse still, laughed—he would surely die.

'Billy.' It was whispered and he looked up at once. 'I love you.'

'Then you'll marry me? Now?'

She did laugh at that. 'Not right now, but yes, I will marry you.'

He slid an arm around her waist and kissed her. When she finally came up for air, Beth smoothed the hair from his face and smiled lovingly at him.

'I was so hoping you would ask but never quite believing you would.'

'Why shouldn't I want to marry the most beautiful girl in the world? Let's go and tell Father.' She detained him a moment.

'Wait Billy, let's just have this day to ourselves. I know everyone will be pleased but—just for now—I would like this to be our secret.'

'I could never refuse you anything, my darling. Anyway, I had better speak to Sir John and see about a ring. You do want a ring?'

'Yes, please.' She kissed his cheek lovingly.

The news of their engagement was met with joy, and much coming and going between Kingscourt and Nether Bassett followed. Billy was anxious to marry at once but mourning and Celia's condition meant that in the end, a quiet June wedding was planned.

Beth, wearing Mary King's opal engagement ring in a new setting, went home for one last Easter to work on her trousseau and Celia's son, John George, was born in April.

And it was in the middle of one of their usual weekly meetings that Silas decided to tackle his agent.

'A wedding is an expensive business.'

'Yes sir, marriage is indeed an expensive business.'

'Ever thought of it yourself?' The gaze was quizzical.

Simon paused a moment, unsure of himself, but Silas himself filled the breach.

'It seems to me, young man, that you have formed an attachment to my younger daughter.'

Simon gazed at him in amazement.

'How on earth did you know?' For the first time in many months, Silas King found himself laughing and gasping for breath. He could not stop laughing and tears were running down his cheeks as he put a hand on the younger man's shoulder.

'I doubt there is anyone on the estate who doesn't know. Have you spoken to Grace?'

Simon bent his head slightly.

'No sir, I'm no catch for Miss King of Kingscourt.'

'I assure you that circumstance would not weigh with my daughter—any more than it does with me.'

'You mean, you would give us your blessing?'

'Yes. Now go and find her and let's have two weddings instead of one.'

Simon rushed to the door but the older man laughed again and Simon turned to look back at him, framed by the great stone fireplace that had always dominated the rent room.

'After all, two weddings are cheaper than one!' Silas laughed again and this time, Simon smiled too.

He went into the hall and saw Merridew just leaving the morning room.

'Merridew, is Miss King in?'

'Miss Grace is upstairs, Major Amory, in the linen closet.'

Simon frowned. This house was so large that even now he found himself at a loss.

'The linen closet?'

'Yes sir. If you are not familiar with the room, it is just off the main landing, four doors along on the right.'

'Thank you, Merridew.'

He crossed the hall in three strides and took the stairs two at a time, leaving the butler gazing after him with a very knowing look. *He must do it now*, Simon told himself, while his courage was high and Silas King's words echoed in his head.

He tapped gently on the door and heard her call 'come in.'

The linen room was large, every wall lined with cupboards and shelves and in the middle a desk at which Grace sat alone, a ledger in front of her and sheets of paper scattered everywhere. She looked confused.

'There you are.'

'Yes, and not sorry to be interrupted. I am trying to work out how much linen we will need for the wedding.'

Simon closed the door and went to the window. The back of the house looked towards the stables and outbuildings and he wondered whether he should try for a more romantic setting than this.

'Fancy a walk?' She shook her head.

'I really must work all this out. How tiresome of people to want to marry.'

'You'll think differently when it's your turn.'

Grace put her pen down with some force and gazed at him.

'That's not likely to happen now, is it? I've hardly been away from here…since Mother died.'

'You might have already met…that is, someone you know might care for you.' Grace stood up abruptly and joined him at the window.

'Even if someone did, I think…oh never mind, it's hopeless anyway.'

Simon knew whatever he said now would settle his future forever so he took a deep breath and plunged in.

'Grace, I've never been good at saying how I feel about…anything. I love you dearly and I'll be the happiest man alive if you say you'll marry me.'

She did not move or speak for a moment and Simon found he was holding his breath. Then she turned suddenly and at the expression on her face, he gasped.

'You do love me! I hoped…but I wasn't sure.'

She moved to kiss his cheek but Simon caught her chin and kissed her awkwardly on the lips.

'Then you are…fond of me?'

'No, Simon Amory, I am not fond of you. I adore you. Absolutely besotted.'

He laughed and kissed her again.

'Then you'll marry me, of course. Very soon.'

And so, one beautiful Tuesday afternoon in June, Silas King escorted his youngest daughter to the chapel and remembered his own wedding day over thirty years before with bittersweet nostalgia. He thought perhaps his old friend Sir John, following behind with Elizabeth, was probably thinking the same.

Neither of his daughters resembled their mother but as Beth King turned to her husband, he saw echoes of his wife in that serene happy look.

His younger daughter, all excitement, was laughing as Simon, trying to lift her veil, found it became hopelessly entangled in the buttons of his dress uniform.

'Simon, stop! You'll tear it.'

Celia bustled over and her new brother-in-law smiled.

'Well, I would like to kiss…my wife sometime soon please.'

'Hold still for a moment. Grace, stop laughing.'

'I can't. From here, it looks as if Simon is wearing the veil and it's so funny.'

Everyone began to laugh until the vicar coughed and Celia at last freed Simon.

So married life began in a glow of amusement for the Kings and the Amorys and, so it seemed to Celia, continued all summer. In July, the Kings Feast was held with the usual lavish party, and in September, both brides announced they were 'expecting'.

Silas, already Maryjane's favourite person, looked forward to an heir to the estate and Grace and Simon hoped for a fine healthy baby. Grace had told her husband she wanted their child to be born at Kingscourt and her father was so delighted that a suite of rooms in the west wing was speedily refurbished and they moved in. Simon was the first to admit to himself, privately, that of course his own cottage would have been far too small but sometimes, just sometimes, he would like to be master of his own house.

The end of the year saw a festive Kingscourt, celebrating all the usual Christmas traditions with one or two new additions thrown in. As the church bells rang, everyone looked forward to a very happy year.

Chapter 3

It was a cold late January afternoon when Hugo rode over to say that Celia had caught a cold and would stay home. It was just beginning to rain and, oh by the way, he had brought some newspapers and magazines to read.

They both seized on the magazines but Grace soon abandoned hers and took up a newspaper.

She read the notice twice before saying to her sister-in-law in a hushed tone, 'Beth!'

'What is it? Are you alright?'

'Listen.'

The fire crackled as Grace cleared her throat.

'To Sir Mark Goldburg of London and Vienna, the birth of a son Tobias on 10th December.'

Both girls were silent for a moment and the paper dropped from Grace's hand. Her sister-in-law reached across and looked at the paper herself.

'Oh Grace, you didn't see the next notice.'

'What is it?'

'Goldburg, Helene (nee von Steine), wife to Mark, mother of Tobias. Fell asleep peacefully on 10th December, aged 33 years.'

'Then she...why, she died in childbirth.' Both girls looked fearfully at each other.

It was Grace who spoke first. Beth was pale and she began to shiver but Grace, following her own train of thought, did not notice.

'Do you think we should tell everyone?'

Her friend's silence made Grace glance across and one look at Beth's face made her tug the bell impatiently.

Nanny soon had Beth in bed and Grace was obliged to tell Simon, who had come back in time for tea.

'Should we tell everyone, Simon?' He held an ice cold hand in his and shook his head.

'No, it can do no good. Now Grace, promise me you won't let this…this news worry you.'

'But Simon, she was…well, she must have died when her son was born.'

Possibly, but remember this, we have no details. It could have been anything. Grace, you must not dwell on this. Promise me.'

She smiled wanly. 'I promise. After all, women have babies every day and survive.'

'Yes, they do. So, no worrying.'

'Will you go and see how Beth is please?'

He came back with a sober look. 'Beth's taken it badly. Billy is beside himself with worry and even nanny thinks perhaps we should call the doctor.'

'Oh no! Simon, she must be alright. If she…well, I could never forgive myself.'

Grace had a troubled night and Simon was beginning to be worried himself when Billy caught him up at breakfast.

'Simon, can you manage the tenants' meeting today? I'm going to keep Beth company.'

'Of course. How is she?'

'Nanny thinks we should have the doctor if she doesn't buck up. She's calm but doesn't want to eat. Grace?'

'Had a bad night but she's having breakfast.'

'Damn that filthy foreigner. First my brother, then mother and now…he shan't have my wife and son.'

'You know then?'

'Beth told nanny. Why on earth did Hugo bring those papers anyway? We don't need news like that. We're quite happy as we are.'

'Beth will be alright, just a shock, that's all. We have to remember they're both in a delicate condition and not quite themselves.'

'Yes, I suppose so.'

Billy sighed and trailed off and Simon went to the tenants' meeting.

Beth made a recovery of sorts and was soon downstairs again, though very pale. She and Grace did not mention it again and Silas took to scanning all the newspapers as they arrived—just in case.

Billy's February birthday passed quietly and a month later, his daughter was born.

The estate bells rang the customary four times to announce a daughter and Silas, viewing his new grandchild for the first time, put into her hand the silver comforter that Haydn King had acquired.

Beth, exhausted and disappointed not to have a son, lay in the best bedchamber attended by nanny and a nurse specially hired by Billy.

Grace, coming to see her the next day, thought she looked lifeless and hoped silently that her turn would be easier. The labour had been long and painful and Beth knew she would have to do it all again for a son.

'Beth, your daughter is lovely.' Grace kissed the cold cheek.

'Yes, but a son would have been better.'

'Billy won't care as long as you're alright and she's healthy. What are you going to call her?'

'We were so sure it would be a boy, to be called John Silas.'

Grace looked again at her small niece peacefully asleep.

'Doesn't she look just like Mother!'

'I did wonder but thought I must be mistaken. We should call her Mary.'

'Mary Elizabeth.'

Beth closed her eyes wearily.

'Yes, if you like.'

Grace patted the cold hand gently. 'I'll leave you to rest now.'

She went out quietly and sought Nanny, placidly folding nappies in the next room.

'Nanny, I'm so worried about Beth. She seems…so lifeless.' Grace kept her voice low.

'Now Miss Grace dear, she's had a baby. A few weeks rest and she will be her old self, you'll see.'

But Grace did not see her sister-in-law alive again, for the next day her own labour started. Within a few hours, Grace, propped up on pillows, had her son put gently into her arms by Nanny, watched by an ecstatic Simon. Nanny tactfully left the room and Grace gazed at the little screwed up face topped with a wisp of fair hair and put her hand on his head.

'Beth's baby is definitely prettier.'

Simon smiled. 'I don't care. You are fine and he is perfect, what more could a man ask? Grace, I am the happiest man in the world.'

He kissed his wife's hand where it rested on his son's head and she caught her breath.

'We are lucky, aren't we? And I feel alright, really I do. How's Beth?'

Simon hedged. 'Very happy to be an aunt.'

'We ought to think of names. Your father's name was Edward, wasn't it?'

'Yes, Edward Patrick. Are you thinking of calling him after the parents?'

'I don't know. Or something Simon after his father.'

'I will not have my son called Something Amory. It's impossible,' he said firmly.

She smiled. 'Idiot.'

A light tap at the door announced her father. 'Hello, my dear, may I come in?'

'Of course, Father. Here is…your grandson.'

Silas eyed the little bundle cautiously.

'Well, hello little… What are you calling him?'

'Something Amory, my wife suggests.'

Silas glanced at his son-in-law for he had discovered that this husband and wife were fond of teasing each other.

'Really? It's original, I suppose.'

'We had a list but it's difficult. How did you pick names, sir?'

'That was easy. William, of course, for my own father. How about one of the saints?'

Grace frowned. 'He doesn't look as if he will be a saint.'

'He's only a few hours old, he doesn't look like anything yet.' As ever, her father was practical.

Another tap announced Billy.

'Hello, come to see my nephew. How are you, Grace?'

'Well, thank you. How is Beth?'

'Tired. Sleeps a lot. Is this the chap? Let's have a look, Father.'

He peeped at the little face and in that instant, the baby woke up and saw Billy. What could have been a smile made his uncle laugh.

'Good Lord, he looks just like old Roberts. Simon, do look.'

'So he does. Grace, how about Robert?'

'Robert Simon Amory. I like it.'

Silas smiled and said formally, 'Welcome to the family, Robert.'

Nanny appeared at that moment to find a room full of men.

'Out, all of you. Don't you know she needs rest. And Mr Silas, you should know better.'

The severity of her voice embarrassed Silas. Only Nanny could get away with calling him 'Mr Silas' in quite that tone.

'Sorry Nanny, we'll go now.'

Sorry Nanny.' Simon and Billy spoke together as Nanny shoved them firmly out of the room.

It was the next day before Grace was aware that something was wrong. Quite how she knew was impossible to say but there seemed to be whispers and doors opening and shutting quietly.

At tea time when Simon came in with a glass of milk for her, Grace tackled him. 'Something's going on.'

He sat down and gently took her hand. 'How are you, darling?'

She would not be side-tracked. 'I'm fine. What's going on?'

His face did not alter but she knew something had happened. 'Dr Jenkins has been out, as Billy was so worried.'

'What's the matter? The baby?'

'No, it's Beth. She seems to be getting weaker.' Simon held his wife's hand before kissing it.

'Oh Simon, but…well, she'll be fine. Nanny said so. It is exhausting.'

'She will be alright, of course.' But he did not sound convinced.

But she did not get better and three days later, with her parents at one side of the bed and Billy at the other, Beth King died.

Grace was the only person who did not know how near death she was and no-one could bring themselves to tell her and at last, it was left to Louisa Trevelyan.

Billy, his head buried in his wife's lap, was sobbing uncontrollably and Silas and John Trevelyan stood by the fireplace with bent heads. Louisa watched as the doctor covered her daughter's face.

She rose stiffly and moved slowly towards the door, for her knees were arthritic and every movement was an effort. With one last look at the still figure and Billy's bent head, she opened the door and went down the passage.

Grace's room was at the end of the west wing, overlooking the gardens at the back of the house. She tapped quietly and Grace's 'come in' was lively.

'Aunt Louisa, how very nice to see you. Did you come to visit my son?'

'Hello my dear, how are you?' She bent and kissed Grace's cheek before straightening up.

'I'm well, thank you. Please do sit down.'

The knees creaked but the face did not alter. She was as ever ramrod straight, head erect as Grace held out her hand.

'Oh my dear…' She took the outstretched hand and in that moment, a tear trickled down her cheek.

Grace, looking at the expression in the grey eyes, knew. She clasped both hands around the cold one.

'Beth's gone. So quietly, just slipped away.'

'She was my sister and I loved her. I'm going to miss her so much.'

The whisper was too much for a grieving mother and Louisa broke down and cried.

***

Grace and Celia sat in the shady arbour overlooking their mother's rose garden. Maryjane was in the old hammock reading and Eliza was playing quietly, watched over by Ruth, the newest of Nanny's nursemaids.

'Oh look, here comes Aunt Louisa's carriage.'

'It must be nearly tea time then.' And they both laughed together.

In the decade since the dreadful days after Beth's death, a pattern had evolved, so gradually that none of them knew how until it was settled, that every week Aunt Louisa drove to Kingscourt to have tea and see her granddaughter, accompanied punctually once a month by her husband.

In the aftermath of his wife's unexpected death, Billy had developed a shell none of them cared to try and break; he did not mention his wife's name and for a long time refused to see his daughter. Beth had been gone three months when he took their wedding photograph to Exeter and had several portraits taken from it. These were now in all the principal rooms at Kingscourt.

Silas was slightly bent with rheumatism now and a little deaf but he doted on his grandchildren and greeted their regular arrivals with enthusiasm. He had never recovered emotionally from his wife's death but gradually, the sharp brain began to focus again and he still took an active part in running the estates, these days from the estate office. Celia now had two more children, for she had unexpectedly given birth to twin boys five years earlier. The boys, Frederick and

Edward, were always known as Ed and Fred despite Fred being the elder by a few minutes. They were lively scamps, into everything and a constant terror to the nurserymaids, who ended up either leaving or becoming their slaves.

Grace had a daughter, Eliza, and it seemed sensible that all the cousins were brought up together in the extensive nurseries. There was plenty of room for everyone and Celia and Hugo spent a lot of time at Kingscourt.

The sisters were always pleased to see visitors, even Aunt Louisa who had little news beyond their small family circle. They turned to walk across the vast expanse of green, which was their father's pride and joy, to greet their aunt.

The carriage drew slowly to a halt as the Trevelyans' aged coachman judged the distance from the main steps within an inch, and his young assistant leapt down to open the door.

'Hello Aunt Louisa, how lovely to see you.'

'Well girls, you will not say so. I have bad news.'

Instantly, they were all concern.

'You look quite upset, aunt. Come and have some tea.'

'Presently, presently. I need to talk to you both, away from long ears.'

Much mystified, they retraced their steps to the arbour and sat down. It took a few moments for the older woman to compose herself and her face flushed as she cleared her throat.

'Is Sir John well, aunt?' Celia's gentle tone soothed her.

'Yes, that is, he is quite agitated.'

She paused. 'There is no easy way to say this. I have had a letter from Alice.'

'Alice!'

Louisa gazed into space until Grace ventured to say, 'Is she alright? Still in India?'

'She is in South Africa now. Her husband died three years ago.'

All three were silent for none of them had ever met the young subaltern who had eloped with Alice. In fact, nothing had been heard of them until now.

'Apparently, he did very well in the army. He was a captain at his death so Alice is not too badly off. And she will have a pension.'

'Is she…coming back to England?' Grace almost said home but decided against it.

'Yes.'

'Forgive me, aunt, but why has this news distressed you? And why will it upset us?' Celia was direct.

'Because she writes she has met someone…they will be married by now. He is very rich, a trader of some kind.'

'Yes, and…?' They looked at her impatiently. Really, she was so long coming to the point!

Louisa cleared her throat and glanced from one to another.

'She is marrying Julian.'

'Julian who?' For a moment, they were puzzled but Celia was the first to realise the enormity of this news.

'Daddy and Billy must not know.'

Louisa took her hand and held it, all the while gazing at her intently. Celia had always been her favourite, the one most likely to be an ally.

'The…couple are coming back so everyone will have to know.'

'No, not here. Aunt, they can't come back after…everything.' Grace was outraged.

'My dear, we must get used to the idea. They will come back to England and while they may not be invited here—'

Celia interrupted fiercely, 'They will never be invited here. Daddy wouldn't allow it.'

'No, nor Billy. He's never forgiven J…well, he wouldn't hear of it.'

An idea popped into Celia's head and she glanced in horror at Aunt Louisa.

'Aunt, you wouldn't, couldn't, invite them to Nether Bassett surely? Sir John wouldn't.'

Louisa smiled sadly.

'You forget, my dears, Alice is still my daughter. We have no-one else now, just you and Marybeth. Though I didn't approve of her eloping, I should like to see her again. The problem, of course, is her husband.'

Grace spoke abruptly, 'Surely she doesn't want to be forgiven?'

It was her sister who answered, 'In some respects, Alice could come back here; even though she did elope, they married. But to remarry such a…'

Nothing seemed bad enough to say about her new husband and Celia trailed off. Grace, remembering her duties as a hostess, rose and said, 'Come, let us have some tea.'

They walked across the lawns silently and went into the drawing room through the open windows. The grand saloon that overlooked the gardens was only used for entertaining but Grace murmured quietly, 'We'll have tea in here.'

Celia rang the bell and Merridew appeared silently and bowed.

'We'll have tea in here, Merridew, just tea, nothing more.'

'Very good, madam.'

Aunt Louisa had recovered herself somewhat and began again.

'We must be discreet at present, girls. For how long, I don't know. Soon everyone will be gossiping about it. Perhaps it will be announced in the newspapers.'

Celia shuddered. 'How horrible, to have the family talked of. Everything raked up. Things better left.'

'Shall we tell Father?' Grace was uneasy at the thought.

'I don't see how we can.'

'I don't see how we can't. He's bound to find out.'

The tea tray came in and they talked of other things until the door closed but before they could begin again, Billy walked in. In appearance, he had changed very little, only the hair at his temples was grey now and the outgoing personality had closed up. He did not "chat".

'Would you like some tea, Billy?'

'Thanks.'

Celia had her usual cup of tea and then went to supervise the nursery tea, Aunt Louisa decided to go home and Grace saw her out. Billy was still drinking his tea when she came back and said calmly, 'I'm off to the nursery. See you later.'

She went hurriedly upstairs and into the nursery. 'Celia, we need to talk this through…'

Too late, she saw her father and stopped speaking. Her sister, busy with mugs, sighed and Grace sat down next to her son.

'There you are, Bobby, drink it all up now like a good boy.'

'Grandpa must have his too.' Marybeth held a mug out to Silas and smiled.

With good humour, he took the mug and drained it in one go. Grace marvelled at how this—to them as children—rather stern and distant parent could be so easily handled by these small children.

Celia shot her a warning glance to be quiet and Grace obediently did so, though her mind was full of only one subject. What on earth had possessed her to come in without realising her father might be there? Silas would come back to her remarks as soon as they were alone, she knew that all too well.

'Grace, you haven't heard a thing I've said.' There was mild rebuke in her father's voice.

'Sorry Father, I was miles away.'

'Yes you were. We are planning an expedition that Marybeth is going to lead.'

'Where to?'

Her niece spoke importantly, We are going to the Spinney. It's a long way to walk but I can 'cos I'm older. The twins can walk too and Eliza can have the trolley.'

'I won't go in the trolley like a baby!' Eliza's voice wavered and she was on the point of crying.

'Marybeth, I have told you before to pronounce words correctly. Repeat after me…"because I am older".'

Nanny's voice was definite and, after a pause, Marybeth said with exaggerated patience, 'Because I am older.'

Grace was amused. 'When exactly is this great expedition to take place?'

'Tomorrow.'

Celia intervened, 'Not tomorrow, I'm afraid, children. It's going to rain.'

'That doesn't matter.' Marybeth was impatient.

'Yes it does, my dear. We had better wait until a fine day.' Silas tried to keep the peace.

'No! I want to go tomorrow.' Celia saw a tantrum coming on and swiftly removed the jam dish from the table.

'You will have bread and no butter, Marybeth, for answering your grandfather in that tone.'

Her niece's mouth set in the sulky line they were now familiar with and Celia sighed inwardly. She would have to curb Marybeth's habit of assuming everything would always fall out the way she wanted or her niece would grow up like—she pulled shortly. Now why should she think of him?'

Her father spoke quietly, 'We must do as your aunt thinks fit.' He said it with an exaggerate wink at his granddaughter and she smiled.

'If you say so, grandpa.'

'If we wait until Saturday, Marybeth, uncle Simon and your father can come as well. You know, the more people you have on an expedition, the more important is the leader.'

'Oh yes, uncle Simon and Daddy can come too. On Saturday.'

She folded her small hands and smiled angelically.

The nursery party broke up soon after and Grace went to change for dinner. She was fixing her hair when a tap on the door announced her sister, already dressed and obviously annoyed.

'What on earth made you rush into the nursery like that?'

'I don't know.' Grace smiled ruefully. 'I'm trying to behave normally but it's like waiting for a bomb to go off.'

The door opened quietly and Simon came in. He kissed the top of his wife's head and smiled at his sister-in-law.

'Hello Celia, what scrape has my wife gotten into this time?'

'Hello Simon, nothing at all. I had better make sure Hugo is ready. See you later.'

'Your bath is ready and I think Wilkins has laid out your clothes.'

'Won't be long.'

She gazed into the mirror reflectively. Quite how long she sat there, Grace didn't know but it seemed only a few seconds until Simon came in to take her downstairs. She glanced at him again and her face softened. Time had dealt kindly with him and he was handsomer now in a mellow way that youth did not give. His hair was still as dark and glossy and long hours riding the estate kept him trim.

'We do make a handsome couple,' she mused as he opened the door and she temporarily forgot her own problem as they went slowly along the corridor and, arm in arm, down the grand staircase old Thomas King had installed at such expense.

The evening sun streamed in through the huge stained-glass windows that family tradition said came from the old cathedral when it was demolished nearly a hundred years before. Down the left side of the wall hung portraits of the ancestors, most faded with age, and at the bottom were the double portraits of Silas and Mary and Billy and Beth, the last painted from their wedding photograph. *It was odd*, Grace thought, that the evening sunshine always caught Beth's face. In the rosy glow, her face seemed alive as they passed by.

'Dearest Beth, I still miss her, Simon.'

'She went too soon. It makes me aware what a very lucky man I am.'

He raised her hand and kissed it.

'Come on, you two, old married people shouldn't act like lovers.'

Billy came up so quietly Grace was startled.

'Goodness Billy, you gave me a fright.' Grace wondered if he had heard them talking.

Her brother's face remained inscrutable as ever but as Grace and Simon went into the saloon, he turned, as he did every night, for one last look at his wife.

'Goodnight, my love,' his lips formed the words and his eyes lingered lovingly on the beautiful face, becomingly framed in glossy ringlets and wearing the King rubies.

'Billy, are you coming?' Simon's calm voice carried across the hall.

'Yes.'

He closed the door and presented his usual blank face to the assembled company.

Grace, tense but trying to appear calm, poured herself a small drink and sat as far away from her father as possible, trying to be invisible.

The usual small talk followed, Merridew announced dinner and they proceeded into the dining room. When the meal was over and the ladies went to the saloon for coffee, she sat down with a sigh of relief. The evening was soon over and Grace counted the minutes until the bedtime candles were handed around.

The tradition at Kingscourt was that the head of the family stood at the foot of the stairs and as each person collected their candle, he wished them a formal goodnight. Privately, Billy thought this ridiculous as the house had been electrified the year of his...the year of Marybeth's birth. However, his father clung obstinately to the practice and he could do nothing.

Grace kissed her father and said, 'Goodnight Father, I hope you sleep well,' as she always did.

'Goodnight, my dear. We must have a little talk, shall we say tomorrow at 11 in the library?'

She smiled weakly. 'At 11 then.'

After a very bad night, Grace presented herself, as requested.

'My dear, I believe you have something to tell me.'

She swallowed hard. 'No, it's nothing really.'

'Shall I be the judge of that?' Her father's voice did not change but Grace felt exactly as if she were five again, caught in some forbidden act.

Oh, for goodness sake, I'm a married woman with two children and I run this house, mentally, she scolded herself for not being more...well, more.

'No, it's not something I can tell you. Maybe not at all.'

He hesitated before speaking, Were you going to tell me Alice Trevelyan has remarried?'

Grace choked. 'How do you know?'

'It was brought to my attention. How did you find out?'

'Aunt Louisa had a letter from Alice. Her husband—the army one—died. She has remarried a very rich man and maybe they will come here.'

A thin smile was her father's answer and Grace carried on, 'So, of course, Aunt Louisa and Sir John are upset. Aunt said naturally she would like to see Alice again but she wouldn't want to see anyone else.'

Grace stopped, her emotions conflicted. Relief to have it out in the open but what would her father say? How would Billy react?

'My dear, on one point you may be easy. Even if they are in the county, they will never come to Kingscourt.'

'No, that thought never entered my head. But Father, what about Billy?'

'Ring the bell, my dear, and call for your sister. We will have a little chat.'

Celia was adamant. 'I don't want to see either of them. Ever.'

'My dear, there is nothing to stop Alice going to Nether Bassett while Sir John is alive. When it comes to Marybeth, naturally that is a different matter.'

'Someone must tell Billy.'

'At tea today, I shall announce it, just as a piece of news that does not affect us at all.'

Alone in her sitting room later, Grace said pensively to her sister, 'I don't dare think how Billy will react but, Cee, Simon grew quite, well attached to him.'

'I see what Daddy means. If we are calm and uninterested, what else is there to say?'

'I suppose so. What can he hope to gain by coming back? Does he want forgiveness?'

'No-one in the family could forgive him. His disgrace caused mother's illness and death. The anxiety she felt for him, remember when he came on the night she died?'

Grace remembered that her only emotion apart from worry over her mother had been wild joy to see Simon again. Impossible of course to admit that. She nodded.

'He...the sorrow he caused. And after all, Grace, who knows if the news of...well, that woman...preyed on Beth's mind. When her time came. She was always highly strung and prone to worry over the smallest details.'

'I remember.'

'Do you seriously think Billy could forgive him?'

'No. And of course, you are right that this is just a piece of news concerning a stranger.'

They were all gathered in the library for tea when Silas came in. This was unusual because it was his custom to have a nursery tea with his grandchildren most days.

As he came in and sat down, Grace handed her father his cup of tea silently. It was for him to announce the news in his own way.

He drank the tea slowly before putting the cup and saucer down. Still no-one had spoken and he stood up, back to the fireplace, and calmly folded his arms across his chest.

'Well, I have some news, though it doesn't really concern us.'

Simon, sensing a certain change in tone, put his cup down and went to sit by his wife. Hugo did the same as Billy helped himself to a large slice of cake.

'It is only a small thing—Alice Trevelyan has remarried. She may be coming to Devon at some point.'

He glanced at his daughters but they remained silent. Billy was busy demolishing cake and it was left to Simon to ask the obvious question.

'Do we know who she has married, sir?'

'Yes. Once, I might have called her daughter.'

Hugo and Simon were quicker to work it out than Billy. When it finally dawned on him, he choked. Simon crossed the room and slapped him on the back.

'Drink some tea.' Celia's practical voice was not raised and Billy took a generous gulp of hot liquid.

'Father…' Billy half rose but Silas put up a hand to silence him.

'As I said, it doesn't really affect us, it's just a small piece of news. They may not visit Devon at all.'

Under his father's calm gaze, Billy subsided into the chair. Celia, feeling that the subject was exhausted, turned to her father.

'Daddy, I meant to ask you—'

She got no further for her brother interrupted recklessly, 'Does he think to play happy families then?'

Silas was stern. 'I cannot think what you mean, Billy. As I said, it really doesn't concern us.'

His face softened a little and he dropped a hand on his son's shoulder.

'This news causes us no problem, my boy. They are strangers to us, nothing. If they were to visit Devon, we shouldn't see them at all.'

Billy's racing heart slowed down. He said no more on the subject but as he dressed for dinner that night, one idea revolved around in his brain. The man who was responsible for the death of his mother and indirectly his wife, whose actions had so dramatically changed the course of his own life, was coming back to England.

That man had once been his adored older brother. How would he feel when he came face to face with him again?

***

Two weeks passed uneasily and as the one thought uppermost in everyone's mind was the one that could not be discussed, tempers became a little frayed.

Life continued its usual pattern, the Trevelyan carriage was at Kingscourt every week but still there was no news of the couple. By now, of course, the county knew and many were the sly hints that Celia and Grace endured. They began almost to wish that the couple would appear for, as Celia said to Grace one afternoon as they drove back from the village in the pony and trap, it was like sitting beside a bomb with a very long fuse.

Grace, expertly steering the pony around the final bend before home, was unhappy. 'I know father said they probably wouldn't visit down here but if they did…it would be awkward.'

'Has Simon mentioned it?'

'Only to say he hopes that J…they have found happiness. Simon always had sympathy for him, you know. He thinks…he did not see where his actions would lead.'

'Really?' Celia was unimpressed.

'Simon told me what he said after they came back here. When mother was dying. He said she wasn't worth the high price he paid.'

Celia glanced at her sister sharply.

'He said that, did he? Then perhaps, in some small way, he does understand.'

Dinner was a somewhat silent meal and Grace, pleading a headache, went to bed early.

At breakfast the next morning, Billy toyed with some porridge before announcing abruptly that he would go and see about the marquee being erected and Simon tried to eat and failed. He didn't like friction in the family. He found an ally in Hugo.

'Simon, shall we go along to Potters Wood and try for a few rabbits?'

'Good idea.' Simon was a little surprised, for Hugo wasn't much of a shooting type but he was pleased to have some company and they saddled up and rode off in quiet companionship.

'We must try and make the best of it, I suppose,' his brother-in-law remarked practically.

'Yes but I don't like it, Hugo. The girls are upset and...well, maybe the guv knows more than he lets on.'

In the years since his marriage, Simon had taken to using Billy's nickname for his father and he said it now in a tone of unhappy surprise.

'No, old chap, he wouldn't deceive us. Not father Silas.' Hugo was shocked. 'Besides, what else was there to tell us?'

Simon considered. 'Nothing, I suppose. Grace is most unhappy. Suppose they come back here? What then?'

'Nothing,' the other said calmly. 'We don't know them, the girls won't pay calls and they'll never come here or to Nether Bassett.'

'But it will be awkward.'

'Not at all. Remember last summer when that actress took Highways? Did we know her? Did we acknowledge her?'

'Nooo.'

'No, not even when she came to church. We didn't know her so we didn't speak. This is the same.'

'I suppose so,' Simon agreed cheerfully and they spent a happy hour riding around the estate.

By the time they returned to the house, it was time for luncheon and it was a surprise to see the Trevelyan carriage drawn up outside. Another surprise greeted them in the saloon where not only Aunt Louisa but also Sir John sat drinking sherry.

Aunt Louisa they were used to but Sir John, since the stroke that had partly paralysed him two years before, seldom left Nether Bassett. There was only one topic of conversation: apparently, they had received a letter from Alice saying she would like to see her parents again and suggesting a hotel in Exeter where she would be staying.

Silas only murmured gently, 'You must do as you see fit, Louisa, but not him.'

Sir John was shocked. 'My dear old friend, of course not him. I am not even sure I wish to see her. Though I think Louisa does.'

His wife looked unhappy. 'I did think maybe I should like to...but it is impossible. Quite impossible.'

Grace spoke slowly, 'Then let us talk of something else, and as I see Simon and Hugo are here, it must be almost time to eat. Have you seen Billy?'

'No, my dear, he was going to see about the marquee for the Feast.'

He brought the subject up neatly and Silas followed his lead.

Grace said, 'We won't wait for Billy, Father, so let us go in.'

They got through the meal easily and the talk was all of the Feast. They were having coffee when Billy came in and shut the door noisily.

'You have missed luncheon, Billy, so I'll ask for something cold for you.'

Her brother glared at her before taking a newspaper out of his pocket and throwing it onto the table. 'I knew no good would come of this.'

His elder sister, fanning herself gently, only remarked, 'It's too warm to be excitable, Billy.'

'You'll be excitable when you hear my news. Did you know the old Williams place was for sale?'

'No, but I suppose it makes sense. After old Mr Williams died, his son didn't want to leave London. I hoped they might keep it for a weekend place but it is very large. They have been renting it though. That awful actress type last year.'

'Well, it's been bought.' Billy paused a moment before saying dramatically, 'By Mr and Mrs Julian King.'

Three pairs of eyes were instantly riveted on his face.

'Oh no!' Celia let her fan fall from a suddenly limp hand and Grace dropped her cup and saucer.

Louisa Trevelyan said calmly, 'Do you know this for a fact, Billy?'

'Yes, they've announced it in the newspaper for all Devon to read,' Billy spoke bitterly before throwing himself moodily into a chair and carrying on, 'Now they'll be all over the place and we shall be forever meeting them.'

Silas took a different view. 'They're nothing to us. We didn't call on that woman last year...what was her name? The one who rented it?'

'Fair Florrie, the toast of the music halls.'

Silas smiled. 'Yes, Fair Florrie. We didn't call on her either.'

Billy however was still angry. 'We'll still be seeing them all over the place.'

His father judged it time to change the subject.

'We have a party to prepare, so let me know how all the preparations are going.'

No-one felt they could mention it again when Silas spoke in that tone and the subject lasted until the Trevelyans called for their carriage.

As he escorted them out, he held Louisa's hand for a moment. 'If you wish to see your daughter, why not?'

'I do not think it is possible. Too much water has gone under the bridge for us to forget. In different circumstances, maybe, but it is not to be.'

Silas waved the carriage off with mixed emotions and turned to his son.

'Well, Billy, let us have a talk, just you and I.' And without waiting to see if his son was following, he led the way to the library.

***

A week later saw the Kings Feast and as usual, the whole county was invited. It was brilliant weather and Silas was ready early, watching the carriages rolling up the drive and seeing the family appearing to greet their guests.

He was talking to Sir John and several other old friends when he gradually became aware of an undercurrent, dimly at first but gaining strength. He excused himself and went to find his elder daughter.

She was in the large tent set aside for refreshments and he signalled to her quietly.

'Celia, I have the oddest feeling.'

'I know, Daddy. It's as if everyone wants to say something but they don't know how to.'

'It's spoiling the day.'

'Here's Aunt Louisa.'

The old lady advanced slowly, painful arthritic joints protesting every step of the way but back straight and face as composed as ever.

'Silas, Celia.' She extended her hand to her old friend and offered her goddaughter her cheek to kiss.

'Aunt Louisa, how are you today?'

'Older, my dear, definitely older. I must speak to your father in private.'

Celia disappeared and Louisa, glancing around to see that no-one was nearby, spoke softly, 'Silas, there is something we must speak of.'

He listened attentively, seeing from her manner that it was important.

'There has been speculation that…certain people might be invited today.'

He understood at once.

'Louisa, time has not changed my mind or my position. That young couple will never be invited here while I am alive, and I doubt Billy ever would when he is master here.'

'I thought you would say that. But…he is your son, Silas, as Alice is my daughter.' She sighed gently.

'Have you seen her?'

'I met her in Barnstaple, at the Railway Hotel.'

In that single sentence, Louisa revealed to him the depth of hurt she felt. Silas had known her nearly fifty years and for her to admit she had resorted to meeting a member of her family in a hotel seemed incredible.

'How was she?'

'I hardly recognised her. She is…I don't mean physically, she is a pretty young woman. But hard, Silas, brittle.'

He could think of no response to this so wisely stayed silent. After a moment, she resumed, 'But that is by the by. As I say, there has been speculation that all would be forgiven and forgotten.'

'Do they expect it?'

'Alice does not, at any rate. When we met, she gave me to understand that she wished to see me to apologise for her behaviour in eloping. She told me of her first husband; in other circumstances, he sounds the kind of young man Sir John would have approved of. Why they felt obliged to go off as they did she never explained, and I did not ask.'

'Did she mention her husband?'

'No. She asked the circumstances of Elizabeth's passing and I described Marybeth to her.'

The tent began to fill up and Silas, conscious that his old friend was standing on painful joints, took her arm gently.

'Let us sit down and have some tea. I see the Hopkins' coming in so they will join us.' She did not resist.

'Thank you, Silas, but remember, it is only speculation.'

Grace came in shortly afterwards and it was plain that something had been said and Silas, sipping his tea, caught several sidelong glances from people. He was irritated that a day he had looked forward to was being spoiled.

Should he say something? Make an announcement? Ignore it and pretend it wasn't happening?

Hugo, coming in with Robert Amory, came straight out with it.

'Hello sir, good day, isn't it?'

'Is it?'

'Of course, in the great King tradition. Everything just as usual.' Hugo gave his father-in-law a meaningful look. 'After all, there's nothing to spoil it, is there?'

'No,' Silas replied hesitantly.

His son-in-law, taller by a head, put a brief hand on his shoulder.

'You should say a few words.'

Silas frowned. 'I never make speech.'

'Today, it would be a good idea. Possibly with the children around you.'

Robert Amory tugged his trouser leg impatiently.

'Grandpa, when you are coming outside? We're missing all the fun.'

On a sudden whim, Silas took his hand.

'Right now, young man. Let's find your cousins.'

In the warm sunshine, talk flowed agreeably as people gathered in small groups across the broad lawns. Silas gathered his grandchildren together and began to walk towards the steps leading to the drawing room windows. To his left, he could see Hugo beckoning Grace and Celia and as he reached the bottom step, Billy and Simon appeared. Obviously, Hugo was engineering the scene.

Surrounded by grandchildren, his children ranged behind him, Silas looked down on a sea of faces and smiled. He raised his voice slightly.

'Ladies and gentlemen.' Conversation began to ebb away and an expectant hush fell.

'It is my great pleasure—as ever—to welcome so many friends to Kingscourt. You see in me a happy man, surrounded by a family to be proud of.'

Here, he paused and beamed at his grandchildren.

'I have five wonderful children—for Hugo and Simon are sons to me as well as Billy—and my grandchildren are the future of Kingscourt and Nether Bassett. There are only two other people who could make my happiness complete by being here today…' He paused and cleared his throat as an electric hush ran through the crowd. He resumed again in a warm loving tone, 'I refer, of course, to my most beloved wife Mary and dearest daughter Elizabeth. They are with us always in spirit.'

He waited a moment before changing tone.

'On behalf of my family and myself, I thank you all for coming together once again to celebrate a very special day.'

He stopped speaking and in the quiet that followed, as his listeners digested the meaning of his words, both daughters stepped forward and kissed him. Polite applause broke out and conversations resumed as Billy, Hugo and Simon all came to shake his hand.

Hugo, heartily shaking hands, murmured, 'Well said, sir,' and Simon, visibly moved, muttered thickly, 'Thank you for including me, sir.'

'Nonsense, I think of you and Hugo as my sons, the same as Billy. I am a lucky man.'

'When I was in the army Billy was like a younger brother to me. I never thought he really would end up my brother.'

'It was a blessed day when you married Grace. You two are happy and you and Billy make a good team running the estate.'

Simon flushed a little. Praise from his stern father-in-law was praise indeed for Silas never paid empty compliment.

They were making towards the tea tent when Mrs Hoskins came out. A garrulous old lady with a particular fondness for Silas. Once—and only once—Grace and Celia had teased him that she was hoping to become the second Mrs Silas King but he had silenced them immediately.

'Silas King, here you are. I have been wanting to talk to you this age.'

'I'll leave you now, sir,' Simon began respectfully, but his escape was blocked.

'No, young Amory. A good-looking man on each arm will take me back—only a short time, you understand—to the days of my youth when I was always knee-deep in men.'

She laughed suddenly and Simon began to laugh.

'Now Silas, I'm simply dying to know...' a pair of blue eyes fixed on him. 'Why are Julian and Alice not here?'

Both men stiffened and Silas stopped abruptly.

'Who, madam?' The ice in his voice would have given most people pause. Simon's heart missed a beat for he had only ever heard that tone once before.

'Don't poker up on me. Your son.'

'My sons—all my sons—are here today.'

The old lady smiled grimly. 'That will disappoint a fair few today. They came expecting to see a great reconciliation.'

Silas disengaged his arm and turned on his heel.

'Come Simon, we are awaited.' He walked off, leaving a surprised and embarrassed son-in-law to make his apologies and follow behind like a schoolboy.

The rest of the Feast passed as ever. If anyone felt disappointed at being cheated of a great reconciliation, no-one said anything and when the family gathered later in the evening after the last guests had gone, they all agreed it had been a splendid day.

'I was talking to Cooper earlier. You remember his son, young Albert, joined the army in '06.'

Billy was half listening. 'Oh yes, I remember. Wasn't there some talk of a girl from the village? He certainly went in a hurry.'

Simon half smiled. 'Yes, there were rumours, but she married a chap from the brewery in Exeter later that year and moved. Apparently, young Cooper is doing well. He wrote to his father that there are strong rumours of another war.'

Silas grunted. 'Another war. Where will that lead us I should like to know. Sky-high prices and no men to farm the land.'

'There has been a spot of bother abroad—a place in the Balkans called Sarajevo. Some archduke shot. Killed his wife too.'

'Poor man.' Celia was instantly sympathetic. 'Did they have any children?'

'No idea. Anyway, young Cooper thinks this means war. Says everyone's getting wound up.'

Simon spoke in measured tones, 'If the people who are getting wound up had ever been to war, believe me, they'd never want to rush into another.'

Billy agreed. 'That's true. We saw some sights, Simon. Best forgotten, eh?'

'Much better forgotten. Have a drink, Billy?'

'Thanks. Father?'

'Just a small one. Let's talk of something else, I've never cared for war talk.'

The conversation turned then but later, in his dressing room, Simon sat gazing into space.

His wife, coming to find him as it was so quiet, touched him gently on the shoulder. 'Are you alright, darling? You were daydreaming.'

He caught her by the waist and swung her around to sit on his good knee.

'Hey, what's all this?'

'I don't want there to be another war, Grace. War is hell.'

'I know, darling, you have always said so.'

A thought occurred to her as she smoothed the line across his brow.

'Simon, you wouldn't go?'

He smiled. 'Not with this knee. I was invalided out, remember.'

'That's a relief. And Bobbie is far too young, luckily.' Grace sighed. 'It's wicked of me to think that way, I know, but I couldn't stand my husband and son risking their lives. You've done your bit.'

He hugged her before looking her straight in the eye.

'If this war turns out as I think it will, Grace, a great many husbands and sons and fathers are not coming back.'

She gazed into his eyes, her own troubled. 'Will it really be so bad?'

'Yes, I think it will.'

The dinner gong sounded and she moved swiftly, one thought taking precedence over all.

'Heavens, I shall be late. This is your fault, Simon Amory, for keeping me talking.'

She hurried into her room, knowing her father's dislike of being kept waiting. Simon did not move for a long moment before sighing heavily. Then he went to dress.

No-one seemed to take much notice of the faraway murder of an archduke and his wife, but Celia was full of sympathy when the newspapers told her there were three orphaned children in Austria.

Simon wondered if he was the only one who took such a gloomy view; everyone else seemed more absorbed in their own concerns. Nevertheless, he could not shake off a feeling of foreboding.

Chapter 4

A week passed before the next news arrived and then, it seemed to Grace and Celia, everything happened at once. Ultimatums were bandied about, battle lines were drawn, armies mobilised and in their corner of Devon, war news took second place to the death, very quietly, of Sir John.

It was all over quickly and painlessly and they were all there to say goodbye and give what comfort they could to Aunt Louisa. Twelve-year-old Marybeth, as Sir John's only grandchild and heiress, suddenly became more important and began assuming so many airs and graces that Maryjane longed to hit her. At the funeral, in a moment of anger, she pinched Marybeth so hard during the eulogy that her cousin screamed in pain. Nanny, sitting behind with the nursery group, saw everything and lost no time in talking to Celia.

'I don't know what the answer is, Nanny.' Celia sighed unhappily.

'Send her away to school. She needs to meet girls her own age.'

'School! Do you think so?'

'Yes, it's for the best.'

Celia nodded unhappily and went to talk to Hugo but her normally supportive husband was not much help and in the end, she decided her daughter would take the suggestion better if it came from her grandfather.

Silas had been a doting grandfather since her birth but when he told Maryjane that she was going to school, his favourite little girl produced such a spectacular tantrum that he was shaken. This could not possibly be the same child, this girl shouting and screaming that she wouldn't go anywhere, she just wouldn't.

He rang the bell for Nanny but was told she was grown up now and didn't need Nanny any more. And Nanny, coming in almost at once, was affronted.

'You'll need me soon enough, missy, if you hurt yourself the way you did last summer when you sprained your ankle and you screamed as if your leg was broken.'

Maryjane shrugged. 'I was younger then.'

'And of course, you are so much older now.'

'I don't need you to look after me, I'm too big for the schoolroom.'

Silas spoke sharply, 'That is why you are going to school, Maryjane.'

'I won't. I won't!'

'Be quiet!' It was a voice Maryjane had never heard before and Nanny only once…a scene she did not dwell on. 'I will not be spoken to in that tone. Go to your room and stay there until you are ready to apologise.'

A sulky young girl flounced off to the door, Nanny following behind and he sighed. He would miss her dreadfully but Nanny had been adamant. Marybeth was the heiress to both estates and a considerable fortune and if Maryjane was being spiteful to her cousin, and Silas was quite sure Nanny would not lie, then it was better she went to school.

Sir John's passing caused another break in the family at Kingscourt in that summer of 1914, for Louisa Trevelyan found she did not want to live alone at Nether Bassett. She talked Silas into letting Marybeth go and live with her for an indefinite period.

'Come Silas, it's time the child began to learn about her inheritance. And she should leave the schoolroom now and begin to learn how to be a young lady. She will have a position after all.'

'What do you have in mind, Louisa?'

'She can start by learning from me running the house. Then she will need a governess. Dancing lessons, of course, and she begins to have some small talent for drawing, so art classes as well.'

'I suppose you are right. Billy, of course, must have the final word.'

His son, when approached, said what he always said when referring to his daughter. 'If you think it's best, guv, then of course, she must go.'

Silas became irritated. 'She's your daughter, Billy, you must have some say in her upbringing.'

'I'm sure Aunt Louisa will do everything that's proper for her,' Billy spoke in an off-handed manner and his father gave up. Marybeth, when told she would be going to stay with her grandmother for an extended period, took it all calmly. She had always spent a good part of her time with her Trevelyan grandparents so to be told that she would be living permanently at Nether Bassett was no great upheaval. The news on the other hand, that she was to have art and dancing classes, was greeted with enthusiasm.

She could not tell Maryjane, for that volatile young lady was at present in her room for something unspecified, which Nanny hinted darkly would be the ruin of her, but Marybeth could not resist lording it over Robert, John, Eliza and the twins. Ed and Fred, of course, couldn't have cared less. Airy remarks about dancing and art classes, governesses and being grown up were all tossed around in the schoolroom until finally, Nanny put a stop to them.

'Now Marybeth, that will do. You are going to be a companion to poor Lady Trevelyan in her sad loss. Naturally, you will still do lessons, which is why you are having a governess.'

Grace and Celia, discussing it at length, agreed it was the only solution. Still Grace sighed. It was all for the best, of course, but it would still break up the family circle. Her own darling Bobbie would be leaving to go to school soon and if, as Simon seemed to think, there would be a war, her calm and ordered life might be turned upside down.

She attempted once again to go through the household accounts but gave up when she added the butcher's bill three times and came out with three different amounts. Restlessly, she wandered around her sitting room aimlessly, fingering a photo frame here, a china ornament there. This was still, even after thirteen years, her mother's room. Nothing had been changed, the only additions were photographs of the children.

There were a great many of these, for Hugo had found the science of taking and developing photographs fascinating and all the family were victims to his obsession. Grace looked at the shots from the last Kings Feast—there was Bobbie aiming at the coconut shy and nearly hitting one of the dogs; Marybeth with an enormous ice-cream and Nanny, faintly disapproving, in the background; Simon and Billy at the butts. She stopped at the one of Maryjane and scrutinised it carefully. The child's face stared boldly at the camera in a very adult manner and Grace wondered for the millionth time who she took after. None of the Kings certainly and Hugo's parents were very placid and somewhat reclusive.

'This is getting me nowhere,' she said to the room generally. The small mantel clock, which all four children had given Mary King on her fiftieth birthday, showed it was nearly time to dress for dinner and Grace went slowly upstairs.

The next two weeks were a whirl of activity. The old luggage van trundled down to the station with Maryjane's trunks and she was escorted onto the train by her grandfather, a very different person to her now. At the school, he was closeted a long time with the headmistress and when he came out to say goodbye, he merely shook hands and told her to be a good girl. Then he was gone without a look and Maryjane looked into the face of the headmistress with a sinking heart. The eyes and voice were quite cold.

'No visits at present, Phillips, and one letter home a week, which I will read. The free time normally enjoyed by pupils, you will spend with my senior mistress who will try to instil some manners into you.'

The tone of her voice made it quite clear she doubted this would be any use. She clapped her hands sharply and a very tall girl with a face full of freckles knocked gently on the door and entered.

'Miss Clarke, take Phillips up to the dormitory and make sure she knows the rules.'

'Yes ma'am. This way, Philips.' The voice sounded friendly but outside the door, Maryjane was shocked and surprised to receive a very hard pinch on her arm.

'Now then, for the rules.'

Sudden anger blazed in Maryjane. 'I'll tell Mrs...' She received another pinch, if anything even sharper.

'You'll tell no-one. We know all about you. No privileges, no visitors—you've been very bad. But don't worry, you'll soon learn. The easy way or the hard way, it's all the same to us.'

All too soon, the van came back again for Bobbie's trunks but his first day was very different. His parents took the long train journey to Winchester and they stayed overnight in a hotel where he felt very grown up to be going to dinner with his parents. The next morning, they escorted him to school where he met some jolly-looking chaps and had an early lunch with his parents before they started on the journey back to Devon.

Heading back towards Kingscourt, Grace and Simon were struck with how quickly war fever seemed to be spreading. Already, there were young men in uniform to be seen here and there and a definite buzz in the air.

Simon was turning his thoughts to harvesting and winter pasture, Grace was already thinking about the next departure. Once more, a trunk came down from the attic and Marybeth set about packing her treasured possessions for the short journey to Nether Bassett. Celia and Hugo had come for a day or two and everyone was gathered on the lawn in the warm September sun one afternoon when a horse was heard galloping up the drive.

'Now what on earth—' Grace had no time to say anything more before her brother appeared around the side of the house, wearing an army uniform.

He strolled nonchalantly towards the group sitting under the old elm tree and paused. 'Hello. Everyone alright?'

A silence descended until he held his hands up in surrender.

'One at a time please! Guv?'

Silas stared hard at him but said nothing.

'Celia? Grace? You normally have something to say. Simon?'

'What on earth made you, Billy?' Grace spoke at last.

'Serving my country? You can understand that Simon, Simon.'

His brother-in-law was slow to reply and when he did, Billy was not pleased.

'No, I can't understand. This estate is a lot to run, I can't do it on my own.'

Billy was defensive. 'The army needs every able-bodied man; besides, it'll all be over by Christmas. I'll be back before you even miss me.'

His father spoke at last, 'If you think that, Billy, you are a fool. This war is going to be like no other war we've ever fought. The Germans have been looking for an excuse for a long time and now they have it. Over by Christmas! I seriously doubt it. Wouldn't be surprised if it went on for years.'

Hugo shook his head before speaking, 'Too late now, you've signed up for the duration.' He caught the sidelong glance his wife shot at him and shook his head again. 'Don't be alarmed Cee, I'm too old. Doubt they would take me with my eyesight.'

'I'll go and change before dinner. Don't want my uniform to upset anyone.' Billy stalked off and Simon, watching him dispassionately, said, 'young fool.'

His father-in-law replied grimly, 'Not so young.'

The mood of the day had soured suddenly and the party on the lawn broke up. Celia went off to the nursery to see the twins and Grace to have one last talk with Marybeth.

'What you said…about running the estate. After Billy's gone.'

Simon looked at him steadily. 'I meant it, sir. Dawley's a good man, steady and reliable and I go over once or twice a week, as you know. Then there's everything else here. With Billy gone, there'll be double the work and…just me.'

Hugo looked unhappily at both men before saying regretfully, 'I've never had much feeling for the land but if I can do anything, let me know.'

'Thanks Hugo, I appreciate it. We must all pull together. It will be a long war, sir?'

'Yes, it will.'

That evening, as a special treat, Marybeth had been allowed to dine with them and Billy, changed now into his evening clothes, escorted his daughter to the saloon and offered her a drink. Before his sisters could open their mouths, he turned to the small drinks tray and they saw that a jug of lemonade had been put out along with the sherry.

At the end of the meal, Grace eyed Celia, who at once took her cue and said gently, 'Now Marybeth, we will leave the gentlemen to their port and cigars.'

Billy glanced at his daughter and smiled. 'I'll see you tomorrow before you go to Nether Bassett.'

As the door closed, Hugo took a sip of his father-in-law's excellent port. 'You have had better luck with your daughter than I have, Billy. She's very sweet-natured and polite.'

Billy reached for the cigarette box and lit his favourite after-dinner smoke before answering, 'Can't say I had much to do with it. Mostly Grace, Celia, her grandmother.' His tone was off-hand.

'Well, if her mother were here now, she would be proud of her daughter.' Silas reached for the port and poured himself a small glass. He missed the look that passed over his son's face but Simon did not and he hurried to fill the sudden awkward pause in conversation.

When the men joined the ladies, Marybeth had already gone to bed and the two sisters were drinking coffee in a somewhat depressed silence.

'You look very glum.' Simon went to sit beside his wife.

'We were just thinking. Billy going creates another gap in the circle. In just a few weeks, four members have gone.'

Simon took his wife's empty coffee cup and placed it carefully on the table.

'Maybe Billy is right and it will all be over by Christmas.'

He had meant it to sound reasonable but Celia suddenly put her cup down with a bang and glared at him.

'And it might not. Billy might be killed!'

'Thanks sis, for caring so much about my safety.'

Billy stood in the doorway and Celia rounded on him, 'Yes, you go off and play at soldiers, Billy. Don't worry about looking after the estates or your daughter, we'll do it all for you as usual.'

He whitened. 'That's not fair, Cee.'

'What do you call fair? What you've been doing since Beth died?' she said it deliberately, meaning to hurt him and it did.

He came into the room followed by Silas and Hugo who had not heard Celia's last words.

'You are being unreasonable. I only want to go and serve my country. I've always loved being a soldier, you know that.'

'Yes, I know you did but you haven't thought what this will mean for the rest of us. Simon will have to run everything. How is that fair to him?'

'You'll cope, Simon, I know you can.'

'No Billy, I don't know that I can. Celia's right, you haven't thought it through.'

Grace, silently offering her father a cup of coffee, saw a rare family quarrel beginning. 'I'm sure we will all help Simon.'

'I know you mean well, Grace, but you've no idea what's involved. Billy does, and that makes his decision to enlist all the more indefensible.'

Billy looked around at his family, seeing in each face a look of puzzlement at his decision, and he suddenly turned to the door.

'I'm going to smoke outside so you talk about me in peace.'

If Billy had hoped that a little reflection would make his family see his decision in a different light, he was disappointed. The next morning, breakfast was a silent meal and later everyone gathered in the hall to say goodbye to Marybeth. As the Trevelyan carriage rolled away down the drive, Grace began to cry and Celia, an arm around her sister, took her into the morning room for a cup of tea and a chat.

Billy went off into the woods with his gun and Simon went to the stables to begin his rounds. Silas ambled around with no clear idea of what to do until he found himself in the estate office, everything neat and orderly as everything to do with his son-in-law usually was, and he began to wonder seriously how they would manage.

When Simon came back at lunchtime, he had a proposal ready.

'Been thinking about it since Billy…well, as he won't be around for much longer, how would it be if I go over to Nether Bassett once a week. I can see Dawley, and Marybeth too. Keep an eye on everything.'

Simon put his soup spoon down and eyed his father-in-law carefully.

'It would be a great help if you could, of course, but it will be a lot of…riding and with the winter coming on…'

'Are you saying I'm not up to it?' Silas queried.

His son-in-law had the grace to blush slightly. 'No, of course not.'

Grace rushed to her husband's defence. 'Simon was only thinking of you, Father.'

'Don't worry, my dear. I was planning on taking the carriage when I do go. I'm not such a fool as to ride in the depth of winter at my age.'

'It's much appreciated, sir, you know that.'

Billy, when told the plan at tea, smiled. 'Told you it could be managed. Give the guv something to do as well.'

In Billy's mind, it was all settled and he promptly asked Grace how long it would take to have all his clothes ready.

'Oh, about a week, I should think.'

'A week! Far too long.'

'Well, I have a great many other duties running this house, Billy. What's the rush?'

'I want to get over to HQ and start.'

Celia, who had been talking to her father, caught the last sentence and replied sharply, 'Then pack a bag and go now. We'll send your luggage on.'

He reddened. 'Now look, Celia, there's—' but at the tone of his voice, Grace interrupted.

'What a good idea. If you are keen, just take your night things and then telegraph me your address.'

He glowered at her. 'Keen to get rid of me.'

'No but I can't just drop everything to attend to you. This house doesn't run itself, meals don't just appear. I have to supervise many things you know nothing about.'

It was obvious to both his sisters that this plan was not at all what he wanted but, faced with them both, he could think of nothing else to say. His father agreed it was best if he went as soon as possible.

Simon, riding back into the stable yard, cross because he had missed tea, found a grumpy brother-in-law feeding his favourite hunter.

'Hello Billy, what's up?'

'Nothing.'

'Can't fool me, old chap, known you too long.'

Simon swung out of the saddle and tossed his reins to one of the stable lads. Billy fed his last carrot to Wellington and sighed.

'All I asked was how long Grace would need to get my stuff ready.'

'And how long will it take?'

'A week! I mean, how difficult can it be to pack a few things up?'

They fell into step together across the stable yard and out onto the main drive. The clock began to strike six and Simon waited a moment before replying, 'I suppose you want to be off now.'

'Yes, and Celia has made this suggestion…ridiculous, of course.'

'How ridiculous?'

'To take my overnight things and go now. They'll send my stuff later.'

They were almost at the main steps before Simon said carefully, 'If you are eager to be off, it's a good idea. Otherwise, well, a week isn't so long to wait. Give me chance to break the guv in.'

That drew a laugh, as he knew it would, and they went into the hall with Billy feeling less unhappy than he had. He knew he was being unreasonable but, dash it all, he loved soldiering. It had been the only thing he had ever wanted to do and but for that other business, he would still be with his regiment.

He went down to dinner in a better mood and at once apologised to his sisters.

'Being unreasonable, I see that now. Of course, I know you have lots to do so I'll stay until everything is ready. I'll ride over to Nether Bassett with you, guv, before I go.'

Silas inclined his head gently. 'Thank you, Billy, I shall be glad of your help.'

His eldest son-in-law shot him a sharp look but there was no mockery in the tone and only a slight smile curved his mouth.

As Billy handed the drinks around, Celia, taking her small sherry and sipping it, smiled at him. 'I will help Grace with your shirts, sewing and such. We must go through everything and see how much more you need.'

'Thanks Cee, I appreciate it.'

He spoke sincerely but if Billy could have read the minds of his family, he might not have been quite so sincere.

I suppose it's a small price to pay for family harmony. I do hope we have enough materials. Cee's thought ran along purely practical lines.

Young fool getting mixed up in this. The guv and Celia will take it hard if he gets killed. Hugo stared into his drink and pondered.

How can he want to through all that again? So much blood. That last moment before facing the enemy... Simon took his glass and tossed it off in one go, caught the look on his father-in-law's face and looked away.

I should have seen this coming. Of course, he would want to join up. If he's killed how will I face Mary? At least Simon can't go. Silas watched as Simon tossed off his drink.

Thank goodness for Celia. If I never have to pack another trunk, it will be much soon. I suppose we could turn his room out though and clean it properly. Grace put her untouched drink on the table beside her.

Merridew opened the door to announce dinner and they formed up as usual to walk into the dining room. The atmosphere at least was better and they chatted away, if not quite as happily as normal, at least tension was less, but two of them at least had no illusions.

Simon, talking to Celia about Bobbie's first letter home, knew he could never go to war again. The horrors he had seen in South Africa had taken him time to live down, even now occasionally when he was out hunting, an old memory would surface and he would have to fight a feeling of nausea. He would never understand how Billy could volunteer to go through that again.

Silas, listening to Grace talking about the vicar's visit tomorrow, was grimly aware that his son was about to set out on what he thought of as an adventure but which his father, who was better informed than anyone in the family suspected about world events, was convinced would turn into a war of unimaginable horrors. As the table cleared and dessert dishes were placed, Silas mentally shook himself and tried to banish his gloomy thoughts. For a few more days at least, his family was safe.

***

Grace had been right about her ordered world being turned upside down, for in the week it took her to organise Billy's trunks, the tenor of life in the big house changed forever.

Simon had three of the estate workers enlist and two of the maids were called home to help look after their families. As the servants and what was left of the family once again gathered to say goodbye, this time to Billy, Grace wondered pessimistically what would happen next.

Celia and Hugo left that afternoon and when Grace and Simon went into the saloon for their evening drink, only Silas was there. It seemed rather silly for three people to process into dinner and by tacit consent, Silas went first and they followed. The meal was, by their standards, quite short and afterwards Grace, leaving the two men to their port, spoke quietly to Merridew, 'In future, Merridew, shorten the table and lay the three places together. Mr King at the head and Major Amory and myself on each side of him.'

'Very well, madam.'

'We can always change it when we have more people. And we must have fewer courses.'

'Fewer courses, madam?'

'Yes, it's ridiculous cooking these huge meals just for us three. I'll talk to cook tomorrow. My father thinks there may be food shortages, or at any rate, prices will go up.'

That was the beginning of changes that came so fast that some days, Grace felt she could not keep up. There were days when she had her lunch-time meal alone, did not see her husband and father until the evening and struggled with the war fever sweeping the country and causing more footmen to enlist.

Merridew disapproved of her idea to close rooms off to save work for the remaining housemaids but in the end, even he had to agree. Her own small sitting room in the west wing, which had been decorated on her marriage, was dust-sheeted and closed. She now used the morning room, which meant she was at the centre of the house.

Christmas approached and with it, the first snowfall. It was unusual to have so much so soon and Simon was kept busy with Silas masterminding efforts to preserve the herd and feed them.

Grace was knee-deep in planning what she already knew would be a very poor Christmas by Kingscourt traditions. It was a dark day and the lights were already on when Bobby arrived home. He came to find his mother at once and she smiled as her son bent to kiss her.

'Mmmm, you're cold. Want some tea?'

'Later. Mother, I have…that is, I want to ask you something.'

He cleared his throat and leant against the fireplace, looking at the glowing coals intently.

'Mother, is it true I have another uncle?' His head came up then to stare at her and Grace found herself speechless.

'So it's true. I wouldn't believe it, but it seems I was wrong.'

'Who…told you?' She struggled for words.

'Berrow Minor. He's a beastly little worm and I told him he was a liar.'

Grace swallowed before beginning slowly, 'It's true you did have another uncle. Once, a long time ago.'

'What happened to him?'

'He…went away. Forever.'

'Like Aunt Beth?'

'Something like that, yes.'

'So we were both right. I'll go and wash for tea now mother, see you later.'

Well, they had always known this day would come. But how to tell the children?

Dinner was silent and no one protested when she suggested an early night. Alone in their room after Alice had brushed her hair, Grace turned to him.

'Simon.'

The tone of her voice warned him something was wrong.

'Out with it.'

She stood up suddenly and went to stand beside him.

'Bobby knows he has another uncle.'

'How?'

'Someone at school told him. I was so surprised I didn't know what to say.'

He put an arm around her and pulled her onto the sofa at the foot of their bed.

'What did you say?'

'That he had once had an uncle but he had gone away forever. He asked if I meant like Beth and I said yes.'

'We shall have to tell them eventually. Goodness knows what the guv will say.'

She nestled into his shoulder and sighed. 'I hoped they would never have to know.'

'That's impossible. But we must not let this spoil the holiday, which your father would never forgive.'

'No, he loves Christmas so much, more now than he did when we were children.'

The next day, Grace waited for her sister to arrive before springing on everyone the unwelcome news that Bobby knew he had another uncle. Silas, who Grace had been fretting over, took it surprisingly well.

'I'll talk to him, Grace, don't worry.'

'Yes but Father, if Bobby knows, the others might find out.'

Hugo was matter of fact. 'Who told Bobby?'

'Some boy at school.'

'That's not likely to happen to the rest of them. But I suppose we must at some point explain something about it.'

The grown-ups were all gathered in the library and Grace was about to argue further when Merridew put an end to the conversation by opening the door with a flourish. What looked suspiciously like a smile hovered on his face as he announced, 'Captain William King.'

Everyone jumped up as Billy, still wearing his greatcoat, bounced into the room.

'Merry Christmas, everyone.' He shook hands with his father as his sisters went to hug and kiss him.

'Where did you spring from?' Silas was pleased to see his son.

'How long have you got?' Simon shook hands, noting the tired eyes and surely he was thinner?

'Why didn't you let us know you were coming? I haven't got your room made up.'

Grace kissed him and went to ring the bell.

'I didn't know myself until last night. Got a weekend pass unexpectedly.'

Grace was already speaking to Merridew about airing her brother's room and laying an extra place at table, while Simon poured him a generous drink.

'Good to see you, Billy, marvellous that you could make it for Christmas.'

Billy swallowed the brandy in one gulp and grimaced.

'Have to leave after breakfast on Monday. Who else is here?'

'Aunt Louisa and Marybeth arrive this afternoon. Celia and Hugo. Just family.'

Simon eyed him intently. Billy seemed the same, yet different. Handing him another brandy, Simon spoke quietly, 'Is it bad?'

'I'd better to and wash for luncheon.' He would not say any more and Simon wouldn't bring it up again.

Dinner was a merry one, for Grace had gone to a lot of trouble despite shortages of staff and food. Billy noticed the only servants waiting at table were very young inexperienced girls. That would never have happened in his mother's day. Sitting with the men after dinner, he asked his father if everyone had joined up.

'Nearly everyone. Even those I thought too old. They've all been fired up to join the fun!'

There was an edge to Simon's voice that Billy did not miss.

'Fun! If only they knew.' Billy stopped, afraid he'd said too much.

'Is it so very bad?' Hugo quietly passed the port.

'Yes. Oh, they put a good face on at home to keep everyone happy, but it's hell.' Billy's face was open and angry. 'They've no idea what to do. The generals, I mean. They've just never seen anything like it and from way behind the lines, it's difficult—impossible—to make them understand. The men are so brave and trusting. They think there's some point to all this killing.'

Simon was silent, remembering his own state of mind all those years ago when he had first come here. In this bright room with a glowing fire and surrounded by family, a shiver went through him as he remembered the sights he had seen in South Africa. Strange that he could see all those bodies so vividly even now. If he carried on thinking like this, he would never sleep tonight.

His father-in-law, gazing into the fire, shook his head.

'It's a bad business alright. Over by Christmas, they said!'

The next day saw another, entirely unexpected, arrival. As Grace was supervising the maids, something she found herself doing more and more, Merridew came in holding the silver salver.

'A telegram, Mrs Amory.'

'Oh, for goodness sake, now what?' Grace took the small envelope and opened it. The look on her face said it was not good news and she sighed.

'Merridew, have Miss Maryjane's room prepared.'

'Miss Maryjane, madam?'

'There is influenza at the school and she is on her way home now.'

They were all gathered for afternoon tea when Maryjane finally arrived and to Celia, at least, there was a marked change in her daughter. Merridew opened the door and announced her quietly but the girl who followed him in, though to all outward appearances Maryjane, seemed to her mother a ghost.

'Hello Mother, Grandpa.' She kissed her mother and went to her father.

'So you have come home for Christmas.' Silas received her kiss calmly enough but his shrewd eye detected a certain hesitancy.

'Yes Grandpa.'

'Sit down then, and have a cup of tea. You must be cold.'

Maryjane took the cup and saucer her mother held out and carefully selected one of the small gilt chairs dotted around the room. In this way, she placed herself outside the family circle, holding the cup as if it were an expensive object she was afraid might break.

'So how is school, Maryjane?'

'Very good, thank you, aunt Grace.'

Celia began to talk to Grace and gradually, conversation picked up again. Still Maryjane sat quietly, watching her family, seeing only happy contented faces. How could they know how she felt, what the last three painful months had been like? She sat on, the tea cooling in her hands, frightened to move in case they noticed her, for if there was one thing she had learned in her time at school, it was this—if you sat perfectly still, sometimes people forgot you were there at all. It was safer that way.

All too soon it seemed, Aunt Grace was moving to the door and saying something about nursery tea. She would have to move now, become visible again. She waited until the room was nearly empty before going to the door. Merridew was just coming in to begin clearing away.

'It's good to have you home, miss.' He sounded sincere enough but the smile she gave him was bleak.

'Thank you, Merridew, though I doubt the rest of my family feel that way.'

***

The traditions begun years ago still held but the merrymaking was muted now, too many were wearing black armbands; the Christmas Eve carol service was much the same, though there were hardly any young men. The day itself was quiet, going to church and lunch were the main events and in the afternoon, all the children were allowed into the saloon to play.

The cousins played and Maryjane sat in the corner as far away as possible, but not apparently far enough away to escape her grandfather's notice.

'Well, Maryjane, if you are not going to play games, you can come and talk to me.'

Reluctantly, she came and sat on the small stool near him, to be cross-questioned at some length. Maryjane thought she had come off well, for some of the questions had been awkward, but he seemed satisfied enough. However, he was far from satisfied and the following morning, a long private chat with Nanny followed, the result of which was that just as Maryjane was going to wash for lunch, Nanny came in, full of curiosity.

For as long as Maryjane could remember, Nanny had always been a round plump figure swathed in a crackling white apron, her grey hair tucked neatly under a cap.

'Now my dear, let old Nanny look at you. I've hardly seen you since came home.'

Two arms were held out; after a moment's hesitation, Maryjane went to be hugged.

'Hello Nanny, how are you?'

'Rheumatism. Well, you are quite the young miss now, growing up.' The sharp eyes missed nothing but she continued to talk, 'Let me help you. Now roll those sleeves up or they'll get wet.'

The bruises were all too clear but no comment was made. She combed the long hair and braided it smoothly, talking all the while of the shortages the war was causing and who had joined up.

Perhaps she hadn't noticed, Maryjane thought optimistically. After all, they were mostly on the insides of her arms where a pinch hurt the most. She was cornered in the afternoon by her mother and aunt who asked a lot of searching questions.

She began to feel scared and sick, for they had all promised her that if she told…well, they would know soon enough and then she really would be hurt. To all the questions she made the same reply, yes she liked the school, yes the food was nice, yes she liked the girls. Celia and Grace finally stopped asking and she breathed again.

Monday came around and Billy took his leave of everyone, only his daughter held on to him a little longer than usual and whispered something in his ear before he moved out of her embrace.

When he had gone, everyone went their separate ways but Silas beckoned his eldest granddaughter to the study.

'Sit down, Maryjane, here by the fire.'

'Yes Grandpa.' She had automatically gone for a chair near the wall but he wasn't having that.

'It's time we had a little talk, you and I.'

She folded her hands in her lap and waited. The sick feeling coming back stronger than ever.

'Do you want to go back to school?'

This question took her by surprise and she blinked before staring hard at the wall.

'Of course. I like school.' It was said too brightly and his eyes narrowed.

'This is me you are talking to, Maryjane, and I've known you since you were born. Something is wrong and I want to know what it is.'

He waited as she stared down at her hands; the sick feeling was stronger than ever but she swallowed and tried to smile.

'There's nothing wrong, Grandpa, really. I like school.'

'Hmmmmm. Then tell me about those bruises.'

'I...I've been learning to play hockey.'

He did not reply and the silence stretched out until her nerves began to jangle. She was going to be sick, she knew it.

'Whatever it is, you can tell me. Maryjane, I won't be angry.'

Silas put an arm around her in what he meant to be a comforting gesture but he was not prepared for her reaction. Maryjane turned away and was violently sick. She was so ashamed she began to cry.

Silas was completely dumbfounded for a moment before ringing the bell.

'Merridew, ask Nanny to come in please, and find Mrs Phillips.'

As the door closed, he handed Maryjane a handkerchief and told her to wipe her eyes and blow her nose.

Nanny and Celia arrived together, one out of breath and one cross to be interrupted.

'Daddy, Merridew said you wanted me urgently.'

'Mr Silas, I'm not as young as I was and to send a message like that... Well, it gave me a turn.'

'Nanny, take Maryjane to the nursery and let her have a rest. Celia, my dear, Maryjane will not be going back to school.'

Maryjane hiccupped loudly and blew her nose before turning to her mother.

'I want to go to school, Mother, please. I like it!' She sounded desperate.

'Daddy, if she really wants to go back—' Celia caught her father's look and stopped.

He spoke softly, 'No she doesn't; what has happened to make you so afraid, my dear?'

His tone made her start to cry again and Nanny stepped forward and put her arms around the slim shoulders.

'Now then, Miss Maryjane, you just tell old nanny.' She cradled the bent head and began to rock her slowly to and fro. Presently, Maryjane stopped crying and her voice, muffled against Nanny's broad shoulder, came quietly to her mother.

'The girls...they'll think I told on them. They'll hurt me so much more when I go back.'

Celia stared at her daughter, appalled.

'Why didn't you let us know?'

Maryjane said wearily 'No visits, letters read by the headmistress.'

'Oh Daddy, what have we done?'

'We could not have known. It's over now and she will not be going back.'

'Now you come with Nanny and have some hot milk with nutmeg. You always liked that, didn't you? Come along now, like a good girl.'

Between Nanny and her mother, Maryjane was led upstairs and into bed. Before she drifted off to sleep, she began to cry again until Nanny told her severely that if she was sick again then she could clear it up herself. When Celia was sure her daughter really was asleep, she went to find her husband and have a good cry herself.

Hugo, as appalled as his wife, let her cry before saying practically, 'There'll be plenty for her to do here, Cee, what with the war. She can help you and Grace.'

'But Hugo, those bruises! She's not the same girl at all.'

'Give her time, she will be.' Above his wife's head, Hugo smiled but it was grim and he wondered just how much damage his daughter had suffered. The bruises, of course, would fade but mentally...well, they would have to wait and see.

On New Year's Eve, the whole family went, as always, to a special church service to which everyone in the neighbourhood was welcome, to give thanks for the old year and ask a blessing for the new.

The bitter weather made walking impossible and shortly before five, three carriages made their way slowly through the icy weather to St Michael and All Angel, the small Norman church maintained by the Kings.

Most of the congregation was already there and the family proceeded down the aisle, nodding to tenants and friends. For this special end-of-year service, the church was always full and Silas noted the same faces year after year, though rather older and greyer now.

He had escorted Louisa into the church and she sat opposite him in the Trevelyan pew with Marybeth. Silas seated himself carefully in the first pew surrounded by his elder grandchildren, daughters and sons-in-law behind and Nanny and the very young ones at the back. He followed the service closely but gradually became aware of an uncurrent behind him. Good manners forbade him to turn in church so he concentrated on his bible instead. This year, there were special prayers for everyone at the front, the list headed by Billy was very long.

The organ crashed into the final hymn and everyone gave a spirited rendition of *Onward Christian Soldiers* when Silas saw that the vicar was trying to catch his eye. He had known Barnabas Hall for nearly thirty years but he could never remember seeing him so—what was the word he was looking for? Silas mused to himself. Almost frightened.

The hymn finished, he rose and went to shake hands with his old friend but the words died on his lips as Barny Hall murmured softly, 'Let us have no trouble in God's house, I beg you.'

'Trouble? Why should there be any trouble?'

'We have two new faces here. Or more precisely, a couple known to us but not seen for a long time.'

In the same moment Barny Hall finished speaking, Silas, half turning, saw Louisa rise and turn to Marybeth. As if watching a play unrolling before him, Silas, standing rigidly beside the vicar, saw his old friend take her granddaughter's arm and begin what he knew would be a slow and painful walk back down the aisle.

He saw her catch sight of the couple near the door. She did not slow down but Silas thought he detected a certain stiffening of the back as she neared them. She would have to pass them, could not help but see them, and Silas held his breath.

He need not have worried. Her arm firmly in Marybeth's, Louisa passed by the couple as if they were invisible. Silas offered his arm to Maryjane and the family left the church and went to the carriages. It was a silent trip home and as soon as they had all gathered in the saloon, Silas, standing in front of the fireplace, spoke sombrely, 'It was bound to happen, I suppose. But today of all days.'

'What could they hope for? That we might acknowledge them?' Celia was incredulous.

Simon, attempting to be fair-minded, said calmly, 'We must remember it is a public service. They may have just wanted to attend.'

'No-one drives twenty miles in this weather for a church service.'

Hugo's voice was soothing. 'Celia, this is useless speculation. Let's just be grateful Billy wasn't here.'

Silas put his pipe down carefully before speaking, 'This…episode is over now, we forget it.'

The tone of his voice warned them all that the subject was closed and Celia at once began talking to Aunt Louisa while Marybeth dutifully handed around coffee cups.

At midnight, the family gathered to hear the church bells ring in 1915 and they all hoped the war would soon be over.

**

The first months of the war were a time for mourning. Telegrams telling the death of estate workers seemed to be never-ending and both sisters sincerely mourned young men they had known, farm workers or footmen. Grace knew it was very selfish to secretly thank God that Simon could not be called up but as the news worsened and casualty lists lengthened, she heaved many a sigh of relief.

Celia, having had a bad fright when Hugo went to the recruiting office, was relieved when, as he had predicted, her husband was refused on the grounds of his weak eyesight. Hugo salved his pride by joining the territorial brigade that was being formed of everyone who had been refused enlistment.

For both sisters, it was enough to have a brother to worry about and there was also Maryjane. She had not returned to school, Silas and Hugo had written a joint letter to the headmistress explaining she would be educated at home in future.

Thursday was Silas' day for visiting Nether Bassett and he set off early, well wrapped in the carriage and with a flask of coffee from his daughter. He always had lunch with Louisa and Marybeth, interviewed Dawley and returned home in time for tea. He had always been careful with his horses and as he grew older he disliked travelling in the dark, or expecting his coachman to do so either.

When he came back, his daughter sent in a pot of tea for him and then turned again to the list she was trying to compose of what they would need from Exeter. As the war went on, she found it harder to run Kingscourt as her mother had done. In the old days, they had always been completely self-sufficient making almost everything. That was impossible now with so few hands and most of them so inexperienced. Grace now bought soap, candles (though fewer of those now, of course, with Kingscourt electrified), even (how horrified Mother would have been!) butter and cheeses. She simply did not have the time or the resources to make them on the estate. *Thank goodness*, she thought for the hundredth time, for the housekeeper. Mrs Mills was a tower of strength.

She heard Simon's voice in the hall and Grace folded the list carefully, put it in her pocket and hurried out to greet him.

'Hello Simon, are you ready for some tea?'

He gave her a brief hug. 'Yes please.'

When the three of them met up for dinner that evening, Grace had no idea of the bombshell her father was about to drop.

The soup came and went. (Tinned, of course, in these hard days. *Oh Mother, forgive me please, but tinned soup! I doubt you ever had it in your life.*) The roast, though much smaller now for just three, was carved methodically by Silas and the slices were thinner. Everything had to go much further these days.

As she put a potato on her plate and Simon reached for the carrots, Silas coughed.

'So how was your day, Father? You haven't said anything about Nether Bassett. Is everyone well?'

There was a small silence during which she began to feel apprehensive.

'They are well. I have been thinking we should take in some convalescent, the way old Colonel and Mrs Forrester are doing at Deane.'

There was a moment of absolute silence before Grace reacted and neither her father nor her husband were prepared for it.

She rose abruptly, threw her napkin on the table and moved her chair noisily.

'Obviously, you think I don't have enough to do around here so finding a few more mouths to feed and look after is the answer.'

She flung the door open, nearly knocking Merridew off his feet. She went without a backward glance, leaving the men to look after her in dismay. Simon rose and muttered to his father-in-law, 'Told you it was a bad idea, sir,' before going after his wife. He went to his dressing room, took off his dinner jacket and put on his old smoking coat before going to knock gently at the door.

There was no sound.

'Grace?'

He opened the door quietly and popped his head around. She was sitting on the bed gazing at the far wall and she did not move when he came in and sat beside her, putting one arm around her shoulders.

She turned to face him and said fiercely, 'Did you know about this?'

He replied reluctantly, 'He mentioned it a couple of days ago. Grace, I support you on this.'

She put her head on his shoulders wearily.

'Oh Simon, he has no idea. Do you know that the soup we had tonight was tinned! Tinned! Mother would be turning in her grave but what else can I do? There is so little help these days, at least any help who know what they're doing. I have to watch them all the time, show them what to do. If not for Mrs Mills, I would have had a nervous breakdown long ago.'

He hugged her.

'I didn't know it was tinned, it tasted alright to me. But darling, you do so much around here and we never thank you enough. Shall I tell the guv he's out of order?'

'Yes. And that you think I have enough to do with very little help.'

Before going down to breakfast the next morning, Grace wrote a note to her sister, who arrived mid-morning full of fury.

'He's wrong, Grace, and I'll support you all the way.'

Lunch was strained until Silas said quite suddenly, 'Maryjane seems to be getting on well enough now.'

Since her return from school, Maryjane had been cycling into the village every day and having lessons with the retired school teacher who still lived next to the school. She had her meals in the nursery with the twins and saw her parents only when they visited Kingscourt. Outwardly, she was submissive and when she did join them for tea, which was usually when her parents were there, she still sat in a distant chair and never spoke unless spoken to.

Celia was taken aback by the sudden turn of the conversation.

'Yes. Old Miss Parkes says she is an intelligent child and applies herself to lessons quite diligently.'

Silas put down his knife and fork slowly.

'It's time we thought about her future. She can help Grace, start learning about running a house as Marybeth is learning to run Nether Bassett.'

Grace shook her head.

'Father, Marybeth must learn to run a large household. There is no necessity for Maryjane to know any of that.'

'She needs to know a certain amount though and I'm sure she could be a great help to you, Grace.'

'The fact remains that I would still have to supervise her. In the end, it takes more of my time. Time I don't have.'

The silence was broken by Merridew coming to clear the table. Eventually, Grace took her sister upstairs to have a long talk in the privacy of her bedroom. They talked around in circles until deciding to have tea in the nursery.

They were just in time to see the young nursery maid setting out the cups and watched as bread and butter was handed around and cups of milk poured. Celia looked again at the twins, could hardly believe they were nearly seven. And Eliza would be six this year. Where was the time going? She had a moment's pain that her mother never saw these grandchildren, how she would have doted on them.

Maryjane as ever sat quietly at the table but, during the merry tea that followed, Celia suddenly realised with dismay that her father was right. Her daughter was nearly sixteen and should not be having nursery teas. Marybeth was two years younger but was already behaving like a young lady, though she had a governess so still did lessons.

Celia was in a thoughtful mood as she dressed for dinner and when her husband arrived, she poured into his sympathetic ear the whole tale as he dressed.

Hugo had always been a listener and as his wife unburdened herself, he bathed and dressed. His valet, Jenks, volunteering almost at once, had not been replaced and Hugo was perfectly happy looking after himself.

He was tying his tie when his wife finished and she caught his eye in the mirror. 'What do you think, Hugo?

She waited, knowing he was sifting the matter in his careful way.

'On one point, your father is right, Cee. She can't stay in the nursery much longer. Maybe there is something in what the guv says—she could learn to run a household. There must be things she could do for Grace.'

'Yes, perhaps,' his wife spoke slowly. 'Only, well, you know, Hugo…it will seem to Grace as if I'm siding with Daddy.'

'We are only agreeing that Maryjane should come out of the nursery. Nothing more.'

Celia threw her arms around his neck.

'Oh Hugo, I knew you would understand how I felt.'

She kissed him.

'Hey, you'll undo my tie and it looks halfway reasonable.' But he smiled as he returned the kiss.

At dinner, no-one seemed particularly talkative, so Simon and Hugo tried to keep up some semblance of normality by chatting about the platoon Hugo was attempting to drill.

'I tell you, Simon, I'm no good at it. I'm sure they all laugh at me behind my back. After all, what do I know about army life? I've always been a civilian.'

Simon grinned. 'When I was a new lieutenant, I was always convinced that my men were looking down on me. I thought that way for a very long time.'

'What happened to change their minds?'

'Joubertskop.'

Hugo shook his head. 'That can't happen for me.'

The plates were cleared away and dessert laid, the servants withdrew and Silas accepted a cup of coffee from his eldest daughter. Since the war, certain customs had been suspended, one of which was the gentlemen withdrawing after dinner, and now the five of them sat together until Grace abruptly said she had a headache and would retire.

On the way upstairs, she remembered her sister's words.

'Grace, have you thought of this? Kingscourt may be too remote for a convalescent home.'

Her sister was amazed.

'What do you mean too remote? We have the railways and…well, everything.'

'Just wait and see.'

A month went by and Grace began to feel relieved. Perhaps Cee was right and it would be impractical for Kingscourt to take convalescents but she soon stopped worrying about wounded soldiers when they each received a panic-stricken message from Marybeth that aunt Louisa was ill and getting worse.

Grace took the shortest time to give Merridew some hasty instructions and say a hurried goodbye to her father before setting out for Nether Bassett. She arrived at the same time as the doctor and he was upstairs examining his patient while a visibly upset Marybeth tried to explain what had happened.

She was making no sense at all when Celia arrived and immediately took charge.

'Now Marybeth, my dear, calm down. Aunt Grace and I need to understand exactly what has happened.'

Marybeth blew her nose and tried to stop crying.

'She had this cold last week and I told her she should rest. It was so cold and I thought if she stayed in bed, that would be best. But she wouldn't listen and she got up and dressed and came downstairs…' She began crying again.

'Gently, my dear, we must wait and see what the doctor says.'

The stairs creaked as Doctor Jenkins came slowly down to find three anxious faces looking up at him.

'I should have been sent for sooner.'

'She wouldn't let me. I wanted to but she wouldn't let me.'

'Don't upset yourself, Marybeth. What's your view, Dr Jenkins?'

'A severe chill and I am worried it may turn to pneumonia. There are things to be done at once and I need to see the housekeeper.'

'Of course. Grace, we had better fix up a bedroom for us to share, we shall be here a while, I think. And send notes to Hugo and Simon.'

Grace's mind was in a whirl as she and Marybeth went upstairs. So much to be done and Father must be told as soon as possible.

It was a week before the crisis passed and Jenkins pronounced himself satisfied with his patient.

Louisa Trevelyan, sitting propped up on pillows and trying to drink a little broth, smiled weakly.

'If I had listened to Marybeth, none of this would have happened. The child told me to rest but I was obstinate and wouldn't.'

'That's beside the point now, aunt, we are happy to see you looking better.' Grace smiled at her aunt as she took the empty bowl away.

The older woman sighed. 'I'm sorry to have been such a burden on everyone. You two have enough to do without looking after a silly old woman.'

'We're happy to do everything we can, Aunt. And Marybeth has been a marvellous help.'

Her granddaughter blushed and preened. 'I only did everything you taught me, Grandma.'

The fact that the elderly housekeeper had done most of it without prompting was conveniently forgotten.

Chapter 5

In the end, of course, her father had his way and Kingscourt offered to take convalescent officers. As Silas remarked blandly, naturally there could be no question of them taking other ranks.

Grace did not find it easy organising rooms not only for convalescent officers but also for nursing staff and several times she came close to tears trying to manage with inexperienced staff. Finally, she decided the officers would just have to make do and she promoted Patty to head house parloumaid, once she stopped dropping trays and breaking china. Grace could only be grateful her mother's very best Sevres dinner service, bought for great-grandmother's wedding, was safely packed up in the attics.

This made what happened next all the harder to bear. Grace was upstairs when she found Patty and the two girls who came from the village every day to help with the cleaning. The linen room door was slightly ajar and as Grace passed by, she caught enough of Patty's conversation to make her stop and listen.

'…And he went out to India and made a fortune. He married Lady Trevelyan's youngest daughter.'

Molly was agog with excitement. 'Why don't they ever mention him?'

'Because he was disi…dsi…disgraced. They live at Crossways now.'

Mary said timidly, 'I don't see what this has to do with us.'

Patty was impatient. 'I'm trying to tell you. They're going to America. Business trip he says. Business, my foot. I know the real reason why they're going.'

'Go on, Patty, you couldn't.'

'Oh yes, I do. I know for certain, sure and positive why they're going. Now you'll be asking how I know.' Patty was full of self-importance and only needed Molly egging her on to talk.

'Well, our Jim, my youngest brother, he helps deliver post and telegrams and stuff. And he's been delivering certain things to Crossways.'

'What things?'

There was a long pause before Patty' voice, full of suppressed excitement, whispered, 'White feathers.'

For a moment they were silent and then Mary murmured, 'But that means people think... he's a coward.'

Grace judged it time to intervene.

'Who is a coward, Mary?'

All three girls started and Patty in particular looked very guilty.

'No-one, Mrs Amory.'

'If you have time for idle chatter about no-one, then obviously you haven't enough to do. I'm sure Mrs Mills can find you all some extra duties.'

Mention of the fearsome housekeeper was enough to send them scurrying off and Grace closed the door quietly behind them, leaning against it with a puzzled frown.

Julian a coward! It seemed incredible. She had heard, of course, that women who had lost husbands and brothers at the front had been handing white feathers to any man not in uniform but—Julian! He would have been the first to volunteer, wouldn't he?

Who knows now? she murmured quietly to herself. Perhaps he had changed more than she had realised in the long years since they had been growing up together. Why wasn't he in uniform?

She pondered the question all afternoon until tea time brought her husband back. As always, the tall figure striding towards her made Grace's heart beat faster and she thought again how well uniform suited him. He had joined Hugo's defence force though his time was so limited that sometimes, they came to Kingscourt to drill so that he didn't lose valuable time travelling.

Perhaps it was as well he was in uniform, she reflected, otherwise, would other women be handing her husband the dreaded white feather?

She got no opportunity for a private chat until they retired after dinner and as the door finally closed behind her maid, Grace curled up on the bed and watched her husband folding his shirt. She half smiled at his careful placing of cuffs, though it had been her idea last year to try and lessen the amount of washing they had to do. He had quite literally taken her at her word.

'Simon...'

'Yes, my darling. You are going to tell me something.'

'How did you know?'

'I have been married to you long enough to know that particular tone of voice. Out with it.'

'I overheard something today.'

He finished folding the shirt and sat next to her on the bed.

'Eavesdroppers don't usually hear anything good about themselves.'

'This wasn't about me. You know that some women are handing out white feathers to men not in uniform.'

He grimaced. 'Yes and it's misguided. There may be many reasons why a man isn't in uniform. Lionel for one.'

Lionel was Hugo's nephew and had tried several times to enlist only to be refused each time. His short-sightedness, one recruiting officer told him bluntly, meant he was likelier to kill his comrades than the enemy; finally, the troop had taken him on as a quartermaster so that all he did was paperwork.

'Well, I heard today that one person in particular has received several.'

'Someone we know?'

She paused and took a breath. 'Julian.'

'Julian!'

She nodded. 'Yes, and so he's going on a business trip to America.'

He put his arm around her and Grace snuggled into his shoulder. Above her head, his voice was reflective, 'I wondered why he hasn't enlisted.'

'Could he be unfit?'

The head shook slightly. 'Doubt it. That business was years ago. Physically, he should have made a complete recovery.'

'Perhaps he's scared.'

Grace could not see her husband's face and so missed the look of sick horror as he closed his eyes. There had been times since this war began when he thanked God he could not serve because he was running an estate and producing food. He could imagine the horrors even though Billy must have glossed over some of them.

'Best thing for them to do then, go away.'

He stroked her hair gently and when he began to kiss her, Grace forgot all thoughts of Patty and white feathers.

The next morning, Simon was up and gone early, leaving Grace to breakfast alone with her father. Another leisurely custom that the war had ended was married women breakfasting in bed and Grace used her time over the toast to work out what she needed to do during the day.

'Simon was out early.' Her father buttered his toast methodically.

'Yes.'

'He worries too much. We are coping well.'

She sighed. 'He does worry, Father, about all kinds of things.'

He gave her a sharp look. 'And have you been worrying him about anything?'

Grace was surprised. 'Now why should I be worrying him?'

'I can't tell. But young people these days, you must always share all your worries with each other. In my day, we kept things to ourselves. I wouldn't have dreamt of telling your mother if there were problems with the estate. That was my worry, not hers. Different now.'

Grace had a twinge of guilt. Should she have told Simon about—

The door opening interrupted her thought and Merridew came in quietly.

'Mrs Amory. Mr King...'

'Yes, Merridew?'

'I am sorry to disturb you but Nurse Todd reports that one of the officers is missing.'

'Missing!' Grace and her father spoke at the same time.

'His bed has not been slept in and no-one has seen him since cocoa last night.'

Grace put her napkin down and stood up. 'We had better organise a search, Merridew, find out who saw him last. Who is it?'

Merridew's face was grave as he answered, 'Captain Allen.'

'Oh no!' Grace glanced at her father before going to the door.

'I suppose it was only a matter of time before we had a problem. And it would have to be Captain Allen.'

As the door closed behind her, Silas felt her unspoken disapproval. As if this was all his fault somehow. He drank his second cup of coffee in thoughtful silence, his mind on Captain Roderick Allen.

Perhaps it had been a mistake to agree to take him. The doctors had assured him that mentally the trauma he had gone through was quite over but Silas had doubts. Roddy Allen had been wounded trying to save three men on a reconnaissance mission, they had been trapped in no man's land under heavy fire and he had crawled out to try and guide them back. They had all ended up spending the night in a shell hole, the night sky lit by tracers and with bombs exploding all around them. By the time they got back to their own lines, Roddy Allen had been wounded in the leg and shoulder and severely shocked.

When he arrived at Kingscourt, he was very quiet, speaking rarely and keeping very much to himself. He had lately taken to long solitary walks in the woods and he was the only officer who did not attend Grace's weekly tea parties when they all gathered in the saloon and played games and sang songs.

Grace managed to find six helpers and they spread out and began to search the gardens but in the end, it was Maryjane who found him and walked back to the house with him. Grace heaved a sigh of relief when Nurse Todd came to tell her the captain was eating his lunch and seemed quite normal.

'Where is my niece now?'

'In the kitchen having a glass of milk, madam. She is quite the heroine of the hour.'

Grace made her way down the back stairs and entered the kitchen in time to see Maryjane cut herself an enormous slice of fruitcake.

'Well, Maryjane, we are very grateful to you. How on earth did you know where to find him?'

Maryjane drank some milk before replying, 'I have seen him going into the woods several times so I had an idea where to start. After that, it was quite easy to follow his trail and I found him by Keeper's Lake.'

Grace was silent, thinking of the deep dark waters of the lake.

'What was he doing there?'

'Just standing. Leaning against one of the trees and looking at the water.'

Grace stared at her niece in horror.

'He wasn't going to…do anything?'

There was a pause as Maryjane shook her head.

'When I went up and spoke to him, he responded quite normally. I told him it was almost lunch time and we walked back talking about birds.'

'Well, I'm pleased you did find him, my dear. Now I must go and tell your grandfather that Captain Allen is alright and you have been very helpful.'

Maryjane drank her second glass of milk, thanked Mrs Mills politely and then escaped to her room. She had not told her aunt the whole truth and she did not intend to. Roddy Allen had not been quite normal when she found him and there was a desperation in his eyes that she recognised. Here was a fellow sufferer and Maryjane knew that the merest hint he was not quite normal would mean him being sent away. She did not intend that to happen.

***

Quite how it happened Grace never worked out but gradually, it dawned on her that her niece was spending time with the officers. Of course, the child was making herself useful, playing cards with them and reading newspapers by the hour. Everyone seemed to like her but was it suitable? She stored in her mind that she must have a serious talk with her sister on Celia's next visit.

Celia came over the next day and after the exchange of news, Grace poured out her fears into an incredulous ear.

'I don't see why you are worrying, Grace.'

'But it's so…unsuitable. Surely she shouldn't be spending so much time with them.'

'Is she being useful?'

'Oh yes, only last week Nurse Todd said what a little treasure she was. All the officers seem to like her. And I told you about Captain Allen, didn't I?'

Celia gave her a hug. 'I think you are worrying about nothing but I'll have a chat with her.'

Grace had to be content with that. She considered—and rejected—telling her sister about Julian. It was only gossip after all.

While the men planned running the estate with far less manpower than they were used to, and the ladies struggled to keep up a semblance of pre-war lifestyle, Maryjane continued her usual round of lessons, talking to the officers, reading aloud to them, playing card games. But all the time, she kept a special eye on Roddy Allen. She had recognised in that moment by the lake a kindred spirit, someone who had been through a similar experience. *It couldn't have been the same, of course*, she thought, he would never have been bullied. But there was something in those eyes…something he was very much afraid of.

Maryjane tried hard not to speak to him any more than she did the other officers and it was a shock when her mother summoned her for a "chat".

She was scared, mentally going over everything she had done in the last few days. Had she done something wrong? The old Maryjane would have shrugged it off, the new one worried until she felt sick.

Her reading, normally calm and precise, was becoming erratic as her mind focussed on this new worry. She was sitting in the great hall by the fire and several officers were lounging around but the only one really listening was

Roddy Allen. Maryjane faltered once, corrected herself and glanced up from the paper to find a pair of sympathetic eyes fixed on her.

'What's the matter?'

She swallowed. 'Nothing.'

'I know that look. It is certainly not nothing.'

She swallowed again. 'My mother wants to talk to me.'

'Is that so terrible?'

'I…no, I suppose not. It's just…well, she doesn't…that is, I don't…I live here.'

He was looking at her, the fixed wooden stare she knew so well but he only said slowly, 'Best thing is to blank your mind. Square your shoulders, look straight ahead and meet whatever's coming.'

Maryjane winked away a tear. 'I can't. I'm so scared I'll be sick. In fact…I was sick once, all over Grandpa.'

He did not smile and the fixed stare never wavered. 'Everyone is, at least once. Nothing to be ashamed of. Anyone who tells you different is a fool.'

Maryjane looked at him with renewed respect.

'Were you scared?'

A long pause followed, broken by some of the officers on the other side of the hall laughing at something. The log in the great fireplace split, sending a shower of sparks everywhere and Maryjane held her breath, waiting for him to tell her to mind her own business. Finally, he nodded.

'Yes. Still am.'

She breathed out cautiously and glancing around to see that no-one was nearby, burst into a confidence, 'I find the best way is to be invisible. You just sit quietly and not draw attention to yourself; that way, you get by.'

He looked at her as if seeing her for the first time and suddenly smiled. In that instant, Maryjane fell in love forever.

'I must remember that. Now you had better go and see your mother. Remember, square shoulders and look straight ahead.'

She stood in confusion, thinking in that moment he must have seen into her heart, but he only continued to smile pleasantly and she flushed scarlet, stammered something and went off to find her mother.

Maryjane, her mind a jumble of thoughts, found her aunt Grace in the little sitting room.

'Hello aunt. Mother sent for me.'

'I know. She'll be here in a minute so come and sit by me. What have you been doing today?'

Mentally, she squared her shoulders and looked into the fire.

'I had a French lesson this morning, and history. Then I had lunch and sat in the hall and read the newspaper to the officers.'

'Nurse Todd tells me you are becoming indispensable.'

Was that what this was all about? the girl thought. *Do they think I spend too much time with the officers? With him?*

The door opened quietly and Celia came in.

'There you are, Maryjane. I looked in the great hall but Captain Allen said you were looking for me.'

Maryjane became cautious. 'I don't spend all my time with the officers, Mother. Only reading to them in the afternoon and sometimes playing cards after tea.'

'Just so long as you don't spend all your time with them, I am satisfied.'

Maryjane came out of the sitting room and stood for a moment, back to the door, before making a decision. She went very quietly across the great hall and sure enough, he was still sitting in exactly the same position, he sat sometimes for hours on end without moving.

She moved quietly as always but he caught the slight footstep and looked across at her. 'Was it bad?'

'No. Do you want to play cards after tea?'

'If you have time.'

'I have time.'

She went off to the nursery in a much happier mood than she had been for a long time.

***

The summer of 1915 was an unhappy one at Kingscourt. War news was constantly depressing and Silas was not alone in dreading checking the casualty lists. There seemed no end to the dead and wounded and everyone grew used to wearing black. Grace had long since used up all her supplies of good quality prewar black material, for she could not in all conscience refuse any tenant's request to grieve for their son in the proper manner. It was hard enough for them to know that their missing son or brother was buried 'in some corner of a foreign field', worse that there would be no funeral to attend.

Billy seemed well enough, his letters were cheerful and he had been promoted. The day he was mentioned in dispatches was a red-letter one for the whole estate, one of the few happy moments. The newspaper with its full account was passed around so many times it quickly became tattered.

Silas himself rode over to Nether Bassett to take the news to his granddaughter but was disturbed to find Lady Trevelyan still in bed at nearly noon.

'She had a bad night, Grandpa, so I told her to rest today. She will be down for tea.'

Marybeth seemed calm enough and Silas marvelled at her new-found poise.

'Very well, my dear, then I shall stay for luncheon and perhaps see her later.'

'Of course. I will just ring for Hawkes and order you some sherry. I want to hear all the news of Daddy.'

The elderly butler came in with the sherry tray.

'How are you, Hawkes?' He took the small glass and eyed the old man carefully.

'Mustn't grumble, sir. And it is a pleasure to see you looking so well.'

'Everything going smoothly?'

'Yes sir, though the food shortages are worsening.'

Marybeth smiled. 'Hawkes, they are dreadful and you know it. Grandpa, you have no idea what we are reduced to. Grandmother shakes her head over some of the dishes but what can we do?'

Luncheon passed pleasantly enough but afterwards, a message came down that his old friend would like to see him. He was ushered upstairs and into her bedchamber. Louisa was propped up in bed, her face nearly as white as the sheets. Though they were old friends, the proprieties were rigidly observed; in the corner, her maid, who was nearly as old as Louisa, attempted to be invisible.

Silas took her cold hand in his and kissed it.

'Louisa, my dear, I don't like to see you in bed.'

She did not answer at once and he seated himself carefully in a chair.

'Silas, you must take the child back to Kingscourt.'

A fear began to grow in his heart. He ignored it.

'Is she unhappy here?'

'No but this is my last illness. I shall not recover.'

He was aghast. 'Of course, you will. Years left in you yet. Never heard such nonsense.'

She raised a hand imperiously. 'This is my last illness. I've had enough, Silas, and want only to be with John.'

He could think of nothing to say so kept silent.

'Do you remember when we first met? At the ball at Tivenor Park?'

'Good grief, that was a long time ago. Yes, I remember.'

'I wondered for a long time if John preferred Mary but you got in first. For me, it was always him from the first moment. How well he looked in evening dress, so handsome.'

Silas frowned, remembering. 'Mary wore a white evening dress and she carried a bouquet of lily of the valley. You were wearing…pink.'

She smiled faintly. 'Cream, and I carried pink rosebuds.'

'John loved you from the first.'

'Yes, only I was the quiet one, Mary was always so lively.'

'Lively, yes she was. When I first saw her, she was surrounded by men. I thought I'd no chance.'

'Everything turned out perfectly though. Silas, Marybeth cannot stay here when I'm gone.'

'No, but all this talk of dying, Louisa—'

'Old friend, I would say this only to you. My time is near. Prepare her.'

She spoke with finality and closed her eyes. Silas rose quietly, kissed the cold hand again and went out without a backward glance. He would not see his old friend alive again and his heart was heavy. Downstairs, his granddaughter was waiting.

'Marybeth, we should have a nurse here.'

'I can manage, Grandpa.'

'Not if your grandmother gets worse.'

'Is she going to get worse? But a nurse! Grandpa, you know she dislike strangers around.'

He had an idea. 'I'll speak to Nurse Todd, she may know someone. Leave it with me, my dear.'

He climbed into the carriage and drove away, waving his handkerchief as she grew smaller in front of the rambling old building and at last the carriage turned and hid her entirely.

His thoughts ran on. So much to think of; if Louisa really were...*no, I won't think like that. She's depressed, we all are. All this bad news from France. She'll recover. Needs a tonic, I expect.*

But Dr Jenkins, when consulted the next day, did nothing to calm his fears.

'Mr King, I won't disguise from you that I am seriously alarmed. She seems to be fading away.'

Silas began to feel seriously alarmed.

'Should we have a nurse, do you think? My granddaughter is alone there.'

'Yes, for I fear she will not last the month. A nurse by all means and I think your granddaughter must be told.'

In the dreadful week that followed, Silas had one piece of good news. Nurse Todd did know of someone who could come to Devon at very short notice and was a qualified nurse.

'She's my cousin, Mr King. An excellent nurse and especially good with elderly patients. Her last post was just such a one as Lady Trevelyan, died last month. My cousin had decided to take a few weeks' leave before seeking her next post, but she could be here by the weekend.'

'Yes please, Nurse Todd, arrange it. Now I will have to break the news to my granddaughter.'

Silas, supported by both his daughters, drove to Nether Bassett and broke the news to Marybeth. She was so greatly upset and cried so bitterly that he began to fear she would be ill. His daughters took a different view.

'Of course, she's upset, Daddy. Stands to reason. Why, Aunt Louisa has been more like a mother than a grandmother to her.'

The luncheon gong sounded at 1.15 as usual but seemed oddly muffled. It was the first of the orders Grace gave very quietly that morning. When Marybeth came in, her eyes were red but she seemed composed enough as she sat down next to her grandfather.

'Now Marybeth, this news is very upsetting,' Grace began as soon as the soup was handed around.

Everyone nodded in agreement.

'I thought...she would always be here.' Marybeth choked.

Silas was bracing. 'Nonsense, my dear, none of us can be here forever.'

Grace spoke as if her father had not spoken, 'We must not let her see we are upset or it will only upset her. So we must make her last days as peaceful as possible and keep our tears for...after.'

Marybeth sat up a little straighter. 'I suppose so. But Grandpa, life without her will be…I can't imagine it.'

He patted her shoulder.

'When we love someone very much, we can't begin to imagine life without them. It seems hard now but we shouldn't wish her to linger if she is in pain.'

Marybeth gazed out of the window at the rose garden, which was her grandmother's special pleasure. She heard her aunt say quietly, 'Is there anything we can do to cheer her up a little?'

Suddenly, she said, 'I shall pick her a bouquet of roses, Aunt Grace. All her favourites.'

When he was finally alone, Silas sat a long time gazing at the photograph Hugo had taken at the Kings Feast in 1910. There had been several prints made of it and both Kingscourt and Nether Bassett had framed ones in all the rooms. How happy they all looked, a united family. Mentally, he ticked off the empty spaces if that same photograph were taken now—John, his oldest friend and long dead, Louisa about to follow him. Ah well, no good to dwell on all that now. Time to be practical.

A sharp pull on the bell brought Hawkes.

'Hawkes, a nurse is coming to look after her ladyship and one of my daughters will also be here permanently.

The old man shot him a sharp look from under bushy eyebrows.

'Will her ladyship…that is, if a nurse is coming…' He trailed off uncomfortably and Silas knew it was time to be honest with this old family retainer.

'You are right, Hawkes, her ladyship will not be with us much longer. We must do everything we can to make her comfortable so you might let them know in the servants hall to be as quiet as possible.'

'Yes, Mr King.'

He shuffled out quietly before taking his handkerchief out and loudly blowing his nose. Then he straightened up and went through the green baize door to the kitchen to tell the few remaining staff the news.

Celia and Grace tried to think of everything to be done.

'We can shut some of the rooms, less work for the servants. We'll need a bedroom for us, we can take it in turns to come over. Also, some nice light food for Aunt Louisa. The nurse will need feeding as well.'

Grace drew out the small notebook she always carried these days and made notes. Celia spoke sombrely, 'One of us will have to be here all the time. I'm afraid you'll have to take the first shift as Hugo will be back tomorrow. I'll go to Kingscourt and pack some things for you.'

Grace nodded. 'Thanks Cee. Can you take a note to Simon for me?'

'Yes. He won't be surprised, not after Daddy announcing so dramatically last night that we were both required today.'

They smiled slightly for it was unlike their usually calm father to be dramatic.

Louisa Trevelyan did not linger over her last illness and within a fortnight of the nurse arriving, she was gone, peacefully in the night. Marybeth, gazing at the face next morning, thought she was just asleep. The nurse had smoothed pillows and sheets and the thin white hands were neatly folded across her breast.

'Very peaceful she looks, Miss Marybeth. God rest her soul.'

Marybeth looked at the large vase of fresh roses she had placed on the table yesterday and wondered idly if they would last until the funeral.

'I should like to have said goodbye.'

'Not to be, miss. She knew you were here and that comforted her.'

'What were her last words?'

'She said thank you as I helped her into a more comfortable position. I asked if she needed anything else and she said 'only to sleep.' I turned down the lamp and sat with her until she was asleep.'

Marybeth somehow could not look away from the still figure in bed. The nurse, used to grief in all its forms, was practical.

'We must let your aunt know, she should be up by now. And send news to Kingscourt.'

'Yes, I suppose so. Nurse, could I have a few moments alone with grandmother please?'

The older woman eyed her tactfully.

'Very well, miss. I'll tell your aunt.'

She went out, told Celia and then after what she judged the right time, went back into the room. The girl had moved to sit beside the bed and was holding one cold hand in both hers. There was no sign of tears or hysteria and the nurse was relieved.

'Now miss, time for you to go and see your aunt. And change.'

Nurse Blake was a stickler for the conventions. Her patient had died, it was proper that the family should don mourning at once.

By the time Silas and Grace arrived, everything was done. Louisa had been redressed in her best gown and granddaughter and aunt were wearing black. Silas hugged his granddaughter before going upstairs for a final goodbye to his old friend. Grace and Celia carried Marybeth off to the morning room for a cup of tea and there, at last, she broke down. The three of them clung together and cried.

Silas, coming in quietly, almost retreated before such hysterics but Celia saw him and broke away.

'Don't go, Daddy.' She dried her tears as she spoke. 'We all feel better for that but we must be practical.'

He looked at his eldest daughter with renewed respect. Celia was getting more and more like Mary with every passing year and she could always be relied on in a crisis.

'As to practicalities, my dear, we were somewhat prepared for this. I have telegraphed Billy, left a note for Simon and sent a messenger to Hugo. We have only to wait for…the funeral director.

At that word, Marybeth broke down again and this time, her grandfather put his arm round her.

'There, there, my dear. Better to cry now, get it over. Must be strong in front of the servants.'

A watery sniff was all he got in reply.

'I don't suppose any of us will want lunch. Grace? Daddy?'

They both shook their heads and Celia, sitting down, said, 'We will just sit here quietly then.'

In the time it took for the black carriage to arrive, Grace and Celia said their goodbyes to their aunt. Simon arrived just as the coffin was being carried into the hall and raced upstairs ahead of it for a few moments with someone he had looked on as a second mother. He kissed the cold forehead and whispered a soft 'God bless' before going downstairs.

He went at once to find his wife and popping his head into the morning room, found her with Marybeth.

'Grace.' He took her hand.

'I'm so glad you got the message.'

'Had to come back. Charger threw a shoe. Nearly threw me too.'

'Are you alright?'

'Yes, but I shall have to find another horse for a day or two. No-one around to go to the smithy. Marybeth, my dear…' He went and kissed her. 'I'm so sorry.'

'Thank you, Uncle Simon. I'm going to miss her. And I wish Daddy were here.'

'Doubt he'll get leave. Still, your grandfather has telegraphed.'

'I'll be home later, Simon. In time for dinner I hope.'

'I'll see you later then.'

Celia, coming in with her father, glanced at Marybeth and then at her father before sitting down. Silas took up his favourite position in front of the fireplace and coughed.

'Well, Marybeth, your grandmother has left us now. It's time for us to go back to Kingscourt.'

She raised red eyes to him. 'Very well, Grandpa. I'll tell Hawkes.'

'My dear. I think you misunderstand me. You will of course return with us.'

'No!'

The one word took everyone by surprise.

Grace exclaimed sharply, 'My dear girl, you—'

Celia shook her head at her sister and went to sit beside her niece. 'Marybeth, be sensible. You can't stay her alone.'

'I won't go. This is my home.'

'You are too young to live alone. It will be more practical for you to come back to Kingscourt.'

'I want to stay here.' The baby face set in a look Silas recognised as a child trying to get its own way.

'Well, you can't. Your father is away in France and I stand in his place. He wouldn't agree to your living here alone.'

'I shall ask him.'

Practical Celia took over. 'Write to him by all means, but a response might take a week. In the meantime, you must come back to Kingscourt.'

A noisy sniff was her niece's only reply.

'Of course, we understand your feeling but I for one would much prefer to have you with me just at the moment—you can help me through my grief at losing such an old and dear friend.' Her grandfather's tone was sympathetic and Grace wondered again how very good her father was at saying just exactly the right thing to his grandchildren.

'I'll order the carriage now. Marybeth, you should think about putting some night things together.'

Celia was calmly practical but it was Grace who said, 'I'll do it for you, Marybeth. You stay here with Father.'

'We'll go for a short walk around the garden then. I need some fresh air.'

Silas offered his arm courteously to his granddaughter.

By the time a small valise was packed, the carriage was drawing up at the front door and Marybeth, still occasionally sniffing, was handed in by Silas. As the carriage rolled away, she turned and gazed sadly at the house, which somehow already looked forlorn, missing the person who had loved and cared for it so many years.

'When shall I see you again, my dear old home?' Marybeth's tone was desolate and Silas judged it was time to be brisk.

'Nonsense, my dear, you are being maudlin. Of course, you will see it again very soon. Naturally, the procession must go from here and people will gather afterwards. This was Louisa's home and must be the setting for the last events.'

'I suppose so. I hadn't thought of it that way.'

'You're upset, we all are. Daddy is right as usual and of course, Nether Bassett will be the centrepiece of the funeral.'

'I wonder if Daddy will come home.'

'Don't count on it. We haven't seen him since Christmas and there's no indication that he's in line for any leave.'

***

In that, Silas was wrong and on the morning of the funeral, a weary and travel-stained Billy turned up.

Marybeth, catching sight of him as he came into the hall, flew downstairs and flung her arms around his neck. He kissed her briefly before gazing into the white tear-stained face.

'Daddy, I must talk to you. Grandpa says I must live here and I can't. I won't. You must help me.'

'May I have some tea before anything else, please?'

Belatedly, she remembered her manners.

'I'll ring for Merridew.'

'Thanks. Where is everyone?'

'Upstairs getting dressed.'

He took the stairs two at a time until he reached the bedroom wing and went along to his old room. Opening the door, he found it all exactly as he had left it so many months ago. The only thing missing was the framed photograph of Beth, which he always carried with him. He stood for a moment at the window gazing down on the stable block and beyond to the rolling hills of Exmoor.

Then slowly, he turned and looked around, memorising every last detail. His reverie was broken by a gentle tap on the door and Merridew entered quietly with a tray.

'Merridew, good to see you. How are you?'

'Well, thank you, Master Billy. And very happy to see you, though under such sad circumstances.'

On impulse, Billy held out his hand and after a slight hesitation, the old man took it.

'Billy? Merridew said you were here. How are you?' His father's voice was followed by his father coming in.

'Hello guv. I'm fine, thanks. You?'

'Good you made it. How long have you got?'

'Forty-eight hours. Told them I had papers to sign regarding Aunt Louisa.' He grinned suddenly, the old Billy briefly reappearing.

'Seen Marybeth?'

'Yes, when I arrived.'

'The funeral is at noon. The carriages are leaving here at 10.30. You will be in the first carriage with myself and Marybeth.'

'I'll just wash and have a cup of tea. With you shortly.'

The funeral was so well attended that the crowd spilled out into the churchyard and Billy, walking solemnly at the head of the procession arm in arm with his daughter, was touched at the sea of faces, many with tears in their eyes. He had known, of course, that his mother-in-law was well respected but she always seemed to live such a retired life that the amount of people she knew was a surprise.

The carriages waited at the church gate and Billy handed his daughter in, waited for his father to be seated and then climbed in and slammed the door. No-one spoke during the short journey to Nether Bassett but he was uneasy. The look in Marybeth's eyes as she spoke when he first arrived told him an unpleasant scene could be ahead and he disliked unpleasantness. Besides, his leave was so very short and he had not left one war to walk into another.

During the reception that followed, he had no difficulty in avoiding her for every room seemed full of people and as he had not been home for so long, everyone wanted to talk to him. One old face after another kept popping up until he knew almost word for word what they would say. Yes, Lady Louisa would be very much missed. Yes, he was glad to be home, even at this sad time. Yes, the war would be over soon.

His face stretched into a mask, forever smiling. The same inane unanswerable questions.

It was Simon who finally rescued him. A Simon who had been watching his brother-in-law closely all morning.

'I'm afraid I must take Billy away, Mrs Hawkins,' he spoke courteously to a sour-faced lady in full flow. 'His time is limited and we have estate business to settle.'

The black plumes in her hat waved vigorously as she nodded.

'Of course, young Amory. Look after yourself, Captain...ah...Major King.' She noted the new pips that had been shoddily sewn onto a uniform, which looked grubby. Louisa Hawkins turned away with a sniff. Goodness knew what the General, departed these twenty years, would have made of a soldier who turned up to his mother-in-law's funeral looking like a ragbag. And with half the county here too! Her only son's weak heart had meant he was unfit to fight but he had joined Hugo Phillips' troop and drilled diligently. She had seen to it that his uniform was always perfect, his father would have expected nothing less.

Meanwhile, the object of her silent criticism was in the small library with his brother-in-law, comfortable with a large glass of whisky.

For a moment, it was quiet before Simon spoke, 'Is it very bad?'

'Yes. How did you know?'

'Recognised the look. Had it myself after Spioenkop. Too much killing. Just closing your eyes makes you see blood.'

'What saved you?'

'Coming here. Grace.'

The younger man grimaced. 'That road is closed to me.'

Simon stirred uneasily. 'It's been a long time, Billy. You might...after the war...meet someone.'

Billy did not move or raise his voice. 'Beth is and always will be my wife.'

'Then you must find something to hold on to. Marybeth. Kingscourt.'

'It's difficult, Simon. How difficult you'll never know. Sending them over the top into machine guns. Telling them to walk. Walk! And we at HQ sit on our fat backsides and move little toy soldiers around on paper maps.'

There was nothing Simon could find in reply and they sat on in silence, hearing the hum of people outside. They would have sat on for hours but they were interrupted.

'There you are. I've been sent on a scouting party looking for two chaps who are AWOL.'

Hugo's curly head, only slightly grey, came around the door.

Reluctantly, the two men stood up and went back into the hall where tables were laid with food. Almost as soon as he entered, a small hand tugged at Billy's sleeve insistently.

'Daddy, I must speak to you alone. It's absolutely vital.'

The uneasy feeling grew.

'We can't now, dear. Too many people. Perhaps later.'

'No, not later. Now.' His daughter raised her voice and several people turned curiously. Rather than have a scene, he decided to face it.

'Alright. Come on.'

They went back into the small library where as a child, Sir John had allowed him to build bridges and forts with fat books from the shelves. As he shut the door and turned, his daughter spoke quickly, 'I want to come and live here. But Grandpa and my aunts say I'm too young.'

'Of course, you can't live here.'

'You've already spoken to Aunt Celia. She says I have to live with Grandpa.'

The threat of tears was not far away and Billy began to look uneasy but the door opened quietly and Grace came in.

'Billy, your absence is being noted. You must come back.'

He shrugged. 'My daughter was insistent on a chat so I obliged.'

Grace, glancing at her niece and seeing tears forming, sighed. 'Marybeth, your father will not agree to this nonsensical scheme. Of course, you can't live here alone.'

'I won't be alone. The servants—'

'I never heard such a thing. Of course, the servants don't count. You will listen to your grandfather and aunts.' Her father's tone was impatient and Marybeth let the tears fall.

'I knew it! You're all against me. Why can't I do what I want?'

Her father sighed and turned to his sister.

'Grace, see if you can talk some sense into her silly head. I'm going back to the guests. Marybeth, once and for all, I do not give my permission for you to live anywhere but at Kingscourt.'

The door opened, muted noises came into the library before the door closed behind him with a determined click. Grace faced her niece and tried to keep her temper.

'My dear, you must see that we cannot have this conversation just now. It is neither the time nor the place. Our guests are waiting and we must say goodbye. Will you come?'

'No. I want to…oh, what's the use. You have no idea how I feel.'

'Suppose the three of us discuss it later? You can explain how you feel.'

The quiet reasonable voice calmed her somewhat but the tears still flowed. Her aunt sighed before going to the door.

'Very well, I will tell everyone you are too upset and have gone to your room.'

Grace made straight for her sister and related, as briefly as possible, what had happened. Celia glanced at her brother but Billy's expression gave nothing away.

'If we must have the scene, better when everyone has gone. Oh Lord, here comes Louisa Hawkins.'

'Well, Grace, where is your niece?' The sharp eyes were hard.

'She is rather overcome, Mrs Hawkins. I have advised her to rest. She will be sorry to have missed you.'

The older woman gave an audible sniff. 'Don't foist that May story on me. I'm not that gullible. Showing her airs already, is she? Should nip that in the bud now.'

Celia and Grace were both painfully aware that once that kind of story did the rounds, Marybeth's reputation would suffer.

'Nothing like that, I assure you. Marybeth was most sincerely attached to her grandmother and feels the loss greatly. And in one so young, it is naturally difficult to adjust in the way we can,' Celia spoke quite deliberately and looked the older woman in the eye.

Louisa Hawkins wavered slightly. Perhaps she had misunderstood that look on Billy's face as he had come out of the study. Still, the girl would bear watching.

Billy went back to his regiment the next morning before most of the household were awake. He disliked goodbyes and tears, everyone kissing him, wishing him well. He had taken leave of his father the night before and that was enough.

He mounted his horse and rode off down the avenue, someone would collect Captain from the station later. At the end of the drive, something compelled him to look back, seeing the house rising out of the early morning mist. He felt a tug at his heart; perhaps Simon was right and this was what he needed to hold onto.

For a long moment he gazed, imprinting it on his mind, before turning and riding away. He did not know his daughter, clad only in a nightgown and with a shawl around her shoulders, was watching from the old night nursery. It gave an excellent view of the front of the house; somehow, she had known he would rise early to avoid her.

Chapter 6

One lunchtime a week later, Grace and Celia were coming downstairs together when Grace missed her footing and took a tumble. She lay awkwardly, winded for a moment, as Celia tried to help her up.

'Are you alright? Here, lean on me.'

Grace stood up gingerly and held her side. 'Ouch! That hurts. And I feel a bit giddy.'

'Come back upstairs and lie down.'

Celia, ever practical, got her sister to bed and undid her collar before ringing for Alice.

'I'm alright, Cee, really I am. Don't tell Simon.'

'Just have a rest for a while and I'll send you up a cup of tea.'

Celia, going downstairs thoughtfully, rang the bell. Merridew was much slower these days and he took so long to answer that she began to wonder whether going to find him would have been quicker.

'Merridew, there you are. Miss Grace has had a fall so send for the doctor. Also, have a cup of tea sent up.'

'There's no-one to send, madam, other than one of the lodgekeeper's children.'

'Alright, do what you can. And don't forget the tea.'

The family for lunch was just Celia and her father but it was so unlike Grace to miss a meal that Celia, caught on the hop by her father, made a clumsy excuse for her sister and immediately regretted it.

Silas might be slower with age but his mind was still agile.

'What's the matter with Grace?'

'She's...I'm sorry, Daddy, but she didn't want me to mention it. She had a fall earlier and is going to rest for a while.'

'A fall? How bad?'

'Not a fall really, more a slip on the stairs. But it winded her and I told her to rest for a while.'

'Sent for the doctor?'

'Well…yes, I have.'

Dr Jenkins, arriving in the middle of the afternoon, examined Grace and came into the library with a beaming smile. Silas, glancing at his face, was relieved.

'Well, Jenkins, what is it?'

'Too early to say—ask me in about six months or so.'

The old man was puzzled. 'Six months…'

'Yes, I should say six months. Should be a New Year baby.'

'Baby!'

'Not a word to anyone yet. The happy father must be the first to know.'

The happy father, coming in for a cup of tea to be greeted with the news that his wife was resting after a fall, took the stairs hastily and raced into the bedroom, to find her sitting on the daybed.

'Grace, are you alright? Merridew told me the doctor's been.'

His wife did not move and he went to sit beside her.

'Grace?'

'Simon…I have something to tell you…'

Her eyes were full of tears and he knew a moment of blind panic but the soldier he had been took over and he held her hand and waited.

'I'm…that is…we're going to have a baby.' The last words came out in a rush and she began to cry.

'But my darling, why cry? I'm delighted.' He put both arms around her.

'Are you?' She looked at him in surprise.

'Yes, aren't you?'

'Well, the war and everything…'

'My love, I'm delighted. Now stop crying because when we tell everyone, I want my wife to look radiant.'

Silas did his best to look surprised and everyone else was genuinely pleased. Celia, ever practical, told her sister, 'Both Maryjane and Marybeth will be able to help, just when you need to be resting more.'

On being told news the next morning, something like resentment welled up in Marybeth. Why had Mother died when she was born, leaving her to Aunts Celia and Grace? All they said was she was too young to live at Nether Bassett

Without a chaperone. It was all rubbish. She would have the servants. She stared out of the dining room window for a long time, looking at her situation from every angle and suddenly, the solution flashed into her mind.

Of course! Why had she not thought of it before. There was someone here who could live with her, someone to keep her company and go riding with. Of course, it was true Maryjane was little—well, odd—quiet and all that, but she just knew they would get on together.

As soon as she could, Marybeth hurried along to her cousin's room.

Her gentle knock went unanswered and she repeated it loudly. Hearing no answer, she put her head cautiously around the door and breathed quietly, 'Maryjane?'

She was putting on her hat before cycling to the village and her tone was not welcoming. 'What do you want, Marybeth?'

'I want to talk to you.' Marybeth carefully closed the door.

'Well, get on with it.'

'I want to live at Nether Bassett. It's my home after all.'

Maryjane eyed her uneasily. 'I can't help you.'

'Yes, you can. It's all so beautifully simple. They say I'm too young to live alone—alright then, I won't be alone. You'll come and live with me.'

The last words came out in a rush; by now, it was obvious that her cousin wasn't going to simply agree.

She was not prepared for Maryjane's reaction. 'No, I won't!'

'But Maryjane, it'll be great. We can do what we like—'

She got no further because Maryjane raised her voice in sheer panic, 'I won't. I'll tell Mother I want to stay here.'

She seemed on the point of hysteria and Marybeth, scared someone would hear, tried to speak calmly, 'I realise it's all a bit sudden but when you think about it—'

'No! I won't go. I'll tell Grandpa I don't want to go.'

Her voice was rising and Marybeth spoke hurriedly, 'Yes, well, alright...don't get so excited. Maryjane, calm down. Anyone would think I was suggesting...'

Maryjane was crying, wild sobs shaking her body. 'Please stop crying. I'm sorry I even suggested it.'

Her words had no effect and she was too young to recognise hysteria when she saw it. Maryjane would not stop crying and in the end, her cousin's worst nightmare came true—the door opened and Aunt Grace walked in.

'Maryjane, are you… Good gracious, whatever is the matter?'

'She won't stop crying, Aunt.'

Grace stepped to the washstand, picked up the jug and threw the contents straight into her niece's face. The effect was magic—the crying stopped and Maryjane looked at her in amazement.

'Now what on earth is going on?' Grace handed a towel to her dripping niece and regarded Marybeth with curiosity. 'Whatever did you say to cause this outburst?'

Marybeth opened her mouth with no idea of what she was going to say but her cousin was ahead of her.

'She wants me to live with her at Nether Bassett, Aunt. But I won't go.'

One glace at her niece's face told Grace everything and she put an arm around Maryjane and hugged her.

'Of course, you are not going. Now change out of that wet blouse and go for your lesson. Marybeth, you will come with me.'

Grace led the way downstairs but instead of turning left at the bottom to go to the morning room, she crossed to the library and went in, motioning Marybeth to sit down.

'Wait here until I come back.'

Marybeth sat down and wondered what was going to happen now. If only Maryjane hadn't been so silly. How could she possibly have known that her cousin would be so silly about a perfectly reasonably suggestion? She had always thought her quiet and dull, spending too much time with the officers or hanging around with Nurse.

Her thoughts were interrupted by the door opening and her grandfather came in followed by both aunts. *Now for it*, she thought.

'Marybeth, what is this I am hearing? You want to live at Nether Bassett with your cousin?'

'Grandpa, I want to live there, it's my home.'

'Your father refused permission, therefore you cannot.'

The tone was final and he went out quietly, his tread firm and measured as always, leaving behind two very relieved women and one very unhappy young lady. Grace was the first to break the silence; she went over and put an arm around her niece and hugged her.

'Marybeth, I know how much this means to you but truly, you couldn't live there alone.'

'It's my home.' Marybeth's lip trembled.

'Yes, but for the moment, it will be closed and you will live with us until the war is over and your father comes home.' Celia's voice, calm and practical, seemed to her sister sound common sense but to her niece, it was anything but.

Marybeth shook her aunt's arm off and gave way to noisy grief and hysteria.

'You just want me to stay here forever with all of you. I'll never forgive you for this—not Maryjane or Grandpa or any of you. If you think—'

She got no further for the door opened and Nanny came in.

'What a commotion! I declare they can hear it in Exeter. Miss Marybeth, you stop right now.'

Another burst of tears followed and Marybeth began again.

'I won't be quiet. I want to go and live at my own home. I will live there and no-one can stop me. It's…Oh!'

The slap was not hard but it was enough to stop her and she gazed wide-eyed at Nanny.

'Young ladies don't tell their elders what they will and won't do, miss. I thought you had better manners than that after all my labours with you, and what Lady Louisa would think to hear you ranting on I'm sure I don't know. You are making an exhibition of yourself and that I don't allow in my children.'

There was silence for a moment until Grace once again put an arm around her niece.

'Now my dear, you really are being unreasonable. Wait until your father comes home and the war is over.'

Nanny gave her a long measuring look before turning to the door. 'Perhaps what you need is a spell back in the nursery.'

'I'm not a child anymore.'

'Come with me and stop behaving like one.'

The door closed and Celia and Grace were left shaking their heads.

'Where do you suppose she gets that temper from? Beth was always so placid.'

'It's not so much temper, I think, as wanting her own way.'

'How did Maryjane take it?'

'That's the interesting part, she was quite hysterical. I had to throw a jug of water over her.'

Just for a second, Maryjane's mother tried to imagine her silent daughter behaving so dramatically and then she shook her head.

'I wish I was closer to her but somehow I feel she holds me responsible for sending her to that school. And we couldn't possibly have known what would happen to her.'

'Darling, of course, you couldn't. She seems alright now, you know, Nurse Todd told me she couldn't possibly manage without her.'

'I suppose so. Shall we go into breakfast or couldn't you face it after that scene?'

'Oh, coffee will be good and perhaps eggs and toast.'

After breakfast, the sisters went into the morning room and began to look at the accounts. Even Celia agreed that the costs of running the house were staggering. 'And when I think what Mother would say if she could see the corners I have to cut, well, she would be horrified.'

Celia shook her head. 'It's the war. Food is expensive and with staff shortages, sometimes we only have soup and a main course.'

'Oh Celia, I had no idea it was that bad!'

Grace patted her elder sister's arm but Celia shook her head and smiled. 'We are not starving, idiot! It's just that for two people, it seems so wasteful to have so many courses.'

They sat for a moment remembering the lavish hospitality their parents had taken for granted before Grace shook herself.

'This is getting us nowhere. At least this year, there will be no King's Feast, not so soon after aunt Louisa's death. Even Father couldn't expect it.'

Her sister smiled. 'You never know with Daddy. Let's go up to the nursery and see how the brood are'

They enjoyed a happy hour and Marybeth, after sulking in her room for some time, decided to put a good face on and go back downstairs. Only Maryjane could not shake a feeling of impending doom.

***

She had been shocked at her cousin's suggestion because in the instant Marybeth had spoken, Maryjane could see the life she had made for herself falling apart. She couldn't, couldn't leave now; if she did, she would never see him again. The knitting needles did not lose their rhythm but her mind could not leave the idea alone. After all, both aunts and grandfather had said it would not happen, she must take courage from that.

Maryjane knew for certain that she loved Roddy Allen and could never love anyone else but she knew that everyone would consider her far too young to know her own mind. They would think he was too old for her. *He's not old, not at all!* Her mind ran around this idea, as it had done for months past, since that day in the library when he had looked into her eyes and smiled.

She had made it her business to find out how old he was and as much as she could about him, and to that end, she had made a friend of Nurse Todd and listened to her ramblings about all the other officers, none of which held any interest for her, until she got to the man she really wanted to know about. Maryjane knew about his invalid mother and much younger brother and that they had moved out of London at the beginning of the war to a small rented cottage in Kent. She also knew that his mother had not once been to see him since he had been at Kingscourt, her indifferent health being her excuse.

That doesn't excuse her not writing though, she thought to herself so often. *His brother writes every week.*

The door opened quietly and she glanced up to see the object of her thoughts hesitating in the doorway.

'Captain Allen, is anything wrong?'

'No, no...nothing. Just thought I would see if you were alright.'

He still hesitated in the doorway and Maryjane sat up straight and put the knitting down.

'I am quite alright, thank you. Why did you think I might not be?'

'Just wondered. Hadn't seen you this morning. Thought you might be...indisposed.'

'No, I...that is, there was something.'

His mouth moved in what might have been a grimace.

'Your aunt threw a jug of water over you.' The bald statement took her by surprise.

'Yes, she did, but I was being hysterical at the time. No doubt I deserved it.'

'Care to talk about it, man to man?'

Her heart gave a great leap of joy, he was making her his equal.

'My cousin Marybeth wants to go and live at Nether Bassett. She can't live alone, of course, and she wanted me to go with her.'

He frowned. 'She's too young surely?'

'That's what Grandpa and the aunts say. When she suggested it, I was upset.'

'Hence the jug of water?'

'Yes.'

For the first time, he smiled. 'I should like to have seen that.'

Maryjane, meeting his eye, laughed. 'Yes, I think you would.'

'Anyway, just thought I would make sure you were alright. Will you read as usual after lunch?'

'Yes, of course.'

He went back into the hall and shut the door quietly. Maryjane sat, the knitting untouched in her lap, thinking. Somehow, with this simple conversation, they had crossed a boundary; nothing would be the same again and suddenly, everything was new and different. There was no possibility whatsoever of her going anywhere now.

She picked the knitting up, did a few stitches, put it down again, stood up and wandered around the room. Somehow, she could not sit still and finally decided on a walk. Perhaps fresh air would clear her mind.

While Maryjane wandered idly towards the statue of Diana, which one of Haydn King's sons had erected, her cousin was chatting to several of the officers on the terrace and doing her best to be charming. She succeeded so well that at least one young man began to wish he could have a much longer convalescence.

After a difficult interview with her grandfather, who had told her she could help out more instead of complaining, Marybeth had decided to be as charming as possible to the young officers. Who knew what might come of that?

It was shortly after this momentous talk that Roddy received a letter from the War Office telling him he would be resuming active service and the first person he looked for was Maryjane. He found her in the hall, weighing parcels.

'Leaving!' She stared at him in shock.

He grimaced. 'Apparently, I'm fit enough to resume active service.'

'The doctor will never let you go.'

'He'll have no choice. I am to go to London and be examined by the War Office doctors.'

She began to feel sick. 'When?'

'Next week.'

He paused awkwardly and Maryjane swallowed hard and willed herself not to cry and definitely not be sick.

'Miss Phillips, that…er…Maryjane…'

He paused again but Maryjane, caught up in her own misery, missed the note in his voice. She stared at the floor fiercely and told herself firmly to act normally. Roddy Allen, vividly aware that at any moment someone might walk through the hall, squared his shoulders.

'Anyway, just thought I would let you know.'

He went to the sitting room that Grace had made over to the officers when they first came to Kingscourt. Maryjane gazed into space for a long time before turning to look around the hall as if she had never seen it before, then very slowly she went to find him.

When she opened the door for a moment, she thought the room was empty but then she saw him standing by the cabinet of Indian curiosities she had always disliked. Very quietly, she closed the door and took a tentative step.

Quite how she knew her whole future depended on this conversation, she never knew but it was her one certainty.

'Captain Allen…I was wondering…'

Her turn to pause. How to word it without sounding as if she were begging? Well, in a way she was.

'When you have to…' She swallowed hard. '…leave us, would you keep in touch?'

He was standing very still, hands in his pockets, staring at her. 'Keep in touch?'

'Yes, write to…my aunt and she could let you know all the news.'

This isn't going to work, Maryjane thought desperately.

For another moment, he hesitated and then carefully walked the few feet that separated them. He was so close she could have reached out and touched him.

'Or you could write to me with all the news.'

Somehow she found the courage to look him in the face, not difficult because he was not much taller than her, and what she saw made her heart turn over. He liked her, he really liked her.

'My mother would say it's not appropriate.'

For a moment he said nothing but then he smiled, a smile that joined the two of them in a conspiracy.

'You'll have to write to Fuller and Armstrong as well. Safety in numbers.'

'Are they leaving too? I didn't know.'

'Not for another two weeks, but you've offered to write to all of us when we leave. Send us news and home comforts.'

'Alright, I will.'

He held out his hand and Maryjane took it shyly; it was the first time she had touched him. A thrill ran through her like an electric current and their eyes met for a long moment.

'I shall write first…Maryjane…and no doubt your mother will read them all.'

'I understand.' And she did. Nothing must be said of an intimate nature, not even anything personal but she didn't care. It was enough that they would keep in touch—she would know how he was.

He dropped her hand suddenly and became impersonal again. 'Are you reading after lunch?'

'Yes.'

She left the room walking on air. It was enough—for now—to know she would not lose contact with him. Quite how he talked her parents around she never knew but the next day her mother found her in the library, knitting as usual.

'Well, Maryjane, your father and I will be going back to The Risings after lunch so I thought we should have a chat now.'

'Yes Mother.' She laid the knitting down calmly, fighting sickness pangs.

'I hear you have volunteered to write to one or two of the officers when they leave us.'

'Yes Mother, if you have no objection.'

'No, none. They need some sense of home and they have all enjoyed their time here. Naturally, your aunt or I will read the letters first.'

'Of course.' She had to hide the smile carefully. Roddy had been right.

'Just leave the letters open and give them to me, if I am here, or to aunt Grace when I am at home.'

'Yes Mother, thank you.' Maryjane picked up her knitting again and Celia, after a moment's hesitation, stood up. Why, whenever she spoke to her daughter, did she feel so…inadequate? Maryjane was always so very polite, such an obedient child, but why did her mother always have the feeling that there was a whole life below the surface of which she knew nothing?

Lunch passed quietly but when Maryjane went into the officers' sitting room as usual to tell them she would be late reading to them, no-one was there. She went back into the hall puzzled and found Lt Fuller standing by the front door.

'Miss Phillips, I came to say goodbye to your parents. I hear you will be writing to us.'

Maryjane nodded. 'Yes, I am. My parents are going home now so I am bidding them goodbye, which means I will be late reading to you all.'

One of the doors opened quietly and Roddy came into the hall.

'Miss Phillips, just came to say goodbye to your parents.'

All at once, she saw his scheme—he had suggested this.

So when Hugo and Celia came downstairs, there was a whole party waiting to shake hands and say goodbye. Maryjane watched as officers thanked her parents politely for allowing their daughter to write to them. *A master stroke*, she acknowledged to herself. What had he said—safety in numbers?

Later in the afternoon, finding him the only person listening to the newspapers, Maryjane took a chance.

'That was your idea, to say goodbye to them?'

'Yes. Fuller is so grateful to you for offering to write—he is smitten with your cousin.'

'Marybeth? And Lt Fuller? It's a novel idea.'

'I'm sure it will come to nothing as he's a younger son and she's an heiress. But he thinks he will hear from you about her.'

'You were right, my mother says my letter will be read either by her or aunt Grace.'

He nodded. 'Bound to be. Can't blame them.'

'Captain Allen...'

'Roddy.'

She smiled. 'Roddy, when I do write to you...you'll let me know how you are? I mean, how you really are, not just a polite phrase.'

'Yes, I'll let you know. Look here, I've jotted down a sort of code. One for you and one for me.'

She took the paper and looked at it thoughtfully as he explained.

'Yes. I see. I think. They look innocent enough but I'll know it means something else. How clever.'

He shook his head. 'Not really. Basic stuff you are taught in intelligence.'

'I didn't know you were in intelligence.'

He shrugged. 'Don't mention it.'

'Alright. Which day...that is, when...'

'Next Wednesday. After breakfast.'

She swallowed hard. 'I'll see you off. Make sure the others do as well.'

All too soon it seemed, Wednesday came, and although they had said a private goodbye the day before, she shook hands with him along with everyone else and wished him well. As the carriage rolled down the drive, Maryjane wondered how long it would be before she heard from him.

***

Marybeth had thought that her aunt having a baby would make very little difference to her life but she very soon found out differently. Her aunt began to rest more and she found that running Kingscourt, even under supervision and with Maryjane to help, took all her time and energy.

Christmas came all too soon and between them, the cousins managed a feast of sorts, though compared to previous years, it was a poor show. Billy did not come home and Grace spent a lot of time resting in her room.

Maryjane was always busy "making comforts for the troops", though there was only one soldier on her mind, and Marybeth wondered how her aunt managed to took so calm while trying to run a household this size on a limited staff.

It was a cold and very dreary late January day and the cousins were in Grace's sitting room in front of a large fire. Marybeth was absorbed in endless lists and Maryjane was knitting a pair of socks and planning phrases for her next letter to Roddy.

Alice, who had been parlourmaid for a year and had at last acquired some dignity and authority, came in quietly.

'Miss Marybeth…'

'Yes, what is it, Alice?'

'I think you should send for the doctor, miss. For Mrs Amory.'

Both cousins shot up at once.

'Is she…that is…is the baby coming?'

'Not quite yet, miss, but we should be prepared. And perhaps Mrs Phillips could be sent for.'

Maryjane looked at her cousin. 'Shall I write to Mother?'

Marybeth looked somewhat distracted. 'Yessss, I suppose so. And we should tell Grandpa.

Maryjane sat down calmly enough to write a note but her mind was busy as ever. Marybeth had looked…almost afraid. Of course, she remembered, Marybeth's mother had died when she was born. A phrase came to mind and she noted it carefully in the little book she always carried and privately called 'phrases for Roddy'.

Dr Jenkins arrived promptly and found Nanny already in front position—after all, as she was forever reminding him, she had delivered three generations of King babies and she knew a thing or two!

To her relief, Marybeth found she had very little to do with the birth of her nephew beyond organising hot water and towels and making sure two maids were available. In fact, the whole process was so efficiently managed by the doctor and nanny that the proud father, hurriedly summoned by a flustered Marybeth, arrived at tea time just as his son was being born.

The next day, the cousins went to see the new arrival together and inspecting the wrinkled bundle lying snug in the cradle where six generations had previously slept, each had very different thoughts.

Maryjane thought she might like to have Roddy's children and hoped it was fairly painless. Marybeth couldn't imagine ever having any and thought that her new nephew looked like one of the prunes that Nanny made them eat. Aunt Grace looked pale and tired and she couldn't imagine herself in that position. They both said all the right things and were very soon shooed out by nanny and went downstairs to the sitting room.

'He looked all wrinkled.' Marybeth screwed up her face.

Her cousin did not smile. 'He'll grow into his skin. Wonder what they'll call him.'

The proud father, gazing at his son in wonder, was all smiles.

'Who is my clever girl then? Grace, I love you.'

'Are you happy to have another son?'

'Of course. Names?'

'What about Edmund, for your father?'

'Edmund for mine…Silas for yours…Amory. I like it.'

Silas King, on being told his new grandson would bear his name, was content. The family was pulling together, Mary would have been proud of them. Now he would have nothing for her to reproach him with when they met again. Silas was very sure they would meet soon, for his age was telling now and most mornings were an effort. He concealed his weaknesses as best he could for he disliked fuss and the war news helped him. Everyone was so wrapped up in their own concerns they took his presence for granted and if he was a little slower, well, no-one seemed to notice.

Grace, spending less than the usual time in her room after the birth of her son, came downstairs one afternoon for tea and noticed at once that her father was subtly changed. She watched him covertly before tackling her husband.

'Why didn't you tell me about Father?'

Simon eased his boots off and wriggled his toes. 'What about him?'

'He's not well, anyone can see that.'

Her husband sat up suddenly. 'He seems alright to me.'

'Just look again and tell me that tomorrow.'

The next day Simon took a sharp look at Silas and admitted with a shock that his wife was right, there was something up with the guv. Quite what he couldn't put his finger on but certainly he was…well, older suddenly.

Billy arrived unannounced for two days' leave and Simon took the first opportunity to ask him direct.

'The guv?' Billy seemed surprised but stopped and thought. 'Yes, now you mention it, he does seem…'

'Older.'

'Well yes, I suppose, but that's to be expected surely?'

'I suppose so, but he's always been so active.'

Billy stretched out in front of the fire and stared into the flames. Simon, stealing a sidelong glance at his brother-in-law, noted the grey hair and tired eyes. Before the silence became noticeable, he coughed.

'How's everything going?'

For a moment he thought Billy had not heard but at last he turned to face him. Simon had a quick glimpse of eyes full of sick horror before the usual bland phrase came out.

'Another push should do it.'

'Billy, don't try to fool me. I've seen that look before—once had it myself. Things are worse than you are letting on.'

His companion made no answer for a moment but poured a stiff whisky.

'The sheer waste, loss of so many young men, good men, it's folly. The Bosch are better equipped and we send men to walk over the top into the machine guns. Sometimes, I feel sick of it all—and the wounded and maimed…' Billy took a generous gulp of whisky. 'Simon, the next generation won't thank us for this. What we're putting them through is criminal.'

Billy did not raise his voice and somehow, his tone made it all much worse. Simon took a sip of his drink before speaking.

'Sounds far worse than any experience I had. But when I came here that first weekend...'—he smiled in reminiscence—'...I only thought how good it was to see people with the correct number of arms and legs.'

Billy's face was a mask. 'You more than anyone else could begin to understand some of what I've seen. We have to be cheerful, of course, for morale back home. But I wonder if people do see through that, because the casualties don't go down.'

Simon nodded.

'I know. Nearly every family on the estate has lost one, some of them two, sons. How much longer, do you think?'

Billy stood up, suddenly restless. 'Top brass think one more push. I don't. Another year. Even two.'

Simon was appalled. 'Two more years! I don't know much longer I can go on trying to run two estates and if the guv is...well, couldn't help me, I'd be lost.'

Billy did not seem very interested in Simon's problems.

'Then of course, we have the new recruits. They send them with hardly any training and expect them to just fit in. I tell you, Simon, sometimes I think we should just chuck it—'

The door opened and Silas came quietly in.

'Chuck what in, Billy?'

His son's face became remote.

'Nothing guv. Just telling Simon some mess gossip.'

His father came to the fire and stood in his usual position, facing his son.

'Well, perhaps you would care to share it with me too.' The look was sharp but Billy did not flinch.

'Not really, wouldn't interest you at all. Now I haven't seen my daughter yet, or my new nephew so perhaps, you'll excuse me.'

The door closed with a click and Simon wondered how much Silas had heard and how much he guessed. Was Billy about to say we should surrender? He instantly started a conversation.

'We shall have a family dinner tonight, guv.'

'Yes. How do you think Billy looks?'

'Tired, and there seems no end in sight. Maybe one more push will do it.'

Silas glanced at him. 'Do you think so?'

Simon sighed. 'I can't believe it will, no. By the by guv, did you hear that Mrs Jackson has lost another boy? The youngest, Alf.'

'No, I hadn't heard. Two now, isn't it? I think the eldest died early in the war. Alf worked here for a while.'

'If it goes on much longer, we'll run out of young men. Then they'll be looking at old relics like me.' He spoke at random but it was evident it had crossed his father-in-law's mind as well because his reply was a little too quick.

'No, we couldn't spare you. Who would run the estates?'

'You could, sir.'

'Too old now. Can't be done. You must stay here.'

Later that evening, looking along the dining room table at his family, Silas felt quietly proud of his children, though he could never tell them in words. It was good to see everyone gathered and chatting quite like the old days. Two new additions were here now—Maryjane and Marybeth had been allowed to join them, for, as Celia so sensibly remarked, it was only fair to let them join family meals given their age. So both young ladies, hair very self-consciously up, joined the procession into the dining room.

The talk was general and no-one mentioned the war. In honour of Billy's recent birthday, instead of dessert, a large cake came out and amid applause he blew the candles out.

'Speech! Speech!' His sisters cried in unison.

'Not much of a one for speeches. Still, it's good to be here and have everyone gathered around. I'll give a toast—to us, the King family. Our good health.'

He raised his glass and everyone joined in but Simon caught a thoughtful look—was he wondering if this would be the last family gathering?

The rest of Billy's leave was soon over and though he sat and listened while Simon and his father talked of the estate, Simon doubted he heard very much—or was even interested—in their problems.

***

The bitter weather did not ease and Simon was hard-pressed to keep the farms going. His temper was not improved by a visit in March from a man Grace later dubbed "Major Foodshortage".

It was a cold rainy day, the mist hung heavily over the valley and everyone was lingering around the breakfast table when their visitor was announced.

It was unheard of for visitors to be ushered into the small room that Grace had made the main dining room when they were alone. It was small and easy to heat, also near the kitchens so more convenient for everyone though certainly not grand or imposing.

Merridew was laid up with a severe chill and Daisy, the young inexperienced and very nervous new housemaid, obviously overwhelmed by authority in a crisp uniform, opened the door and announced breathlessly, 'A Major Smart to see you, mum, to—'

She got no further as the visitor calmly walked in. He was tall and lean with a chilly manner and cold grey eyes. He took in the family at a glance—Grace and Celia in mourning for Hugo's young cousin killed on Christmas Eve, Silas methodically finishing his toast and Simon, already wearing riding boots ready for his day's work.

For a moment, no-one spoke and then Grace, remembering her duties as lady of the house, rose and held out a hand.

'I am Grace Amory, Major Smart. We do not receive guests here, let us go into the drawing room.' She spoke calmly enough but inwardly, she wondered—had he brought bad news of Billy?

The major shook hands briefly and as his cold gaze rested on her, Grace shivered.

'Mrs…Amory. Who runs this estate?'

Simon rose, eyeing the visitor warily. 'What can I do for you, Smart?'

His voice was clipped and Grace, who knew her husband well, saw him change instantly into the officer he had been.

Major Smart was carrying a thin briefcase (Grace said afterwards that everything about him seemed thin) and pulled out a thin file.

'My information tells me you have close to 20,000 acres here. There must be a lot of land capable of better production.'

Simon eyed him with dislike. 'Certainly there is.'

'We must have more food produced. What are you doing about cultivating that land?'

'Nothing.'

'Why not? Everyone must pull their weight if we are to win…Major Amory. You have just admitted you are hampering the war effort.'

Grace opened her mouth to reply angrily but Silas spoke sharply, 'I suggest if you want more production, you give us the manpower to achieve it—Major Smart.'

A cold eye rested on him. 'And you would be…?'

The question hung for a moment before Silas spoke equally coldly, 'Let us have no games here, sir. That paper you are holding tells you very well who I am.

My son and heir is currently at the front, one of my sons-in-law is in the local militia, his cousin was killed on Christmas Eve. My other son-in-law, Major Amory here, is trying to keep two estates and more than 20 farms going single-handedly. There can be no question—real or imagined—of any of my family hampering the war effort.'

'Nevertheless, there must be more land cultivated if we are not to have food shortages and—'

He got no further. Simon put his napkin down and went to kiss his wife.

'Standing here arguing is definitely hampering the war effort. Grace, my dear, I'll see you later.'

'Be careful riding, there's been a hard frost.'

'I'll let my father-in-law talk to you, Smart. He knows more about this estate than anyone.'

Silas rose stiffy and walked to the door.

'We will talk of this in the study, Smart. This way.'

Nothing more was said and at lunchtime, Grace was just sitting down with her father when Simon returned.

'How did you get on with Smart, guv?'

'I think Major Smart is under no illusion about our capacity to help the war effort.'

He said no more and Grace dismissed it from her mind.

***

Maryjane soon settled into an easy correspondence with Roddy Allen but she never forgot to leave the letters open on the post tray and there came days when Merridew came to ask her if she wanted to send the letter, because her aunt had been so busy the letter had not been read.

She always smiled and said yes please but still Roddy had said they must be careful and so she continued writing in the code they had now developed into a sophisticated form of communication.

One day when the post came, her mother, who happened to be staying the night, saw the letter. 'Are you still writing to the officers, Maryjane?'

Instantly, she was on her guard.

'Yes Mother. Aunt Grace reads the letters.'

Her mother looked at the envelope and opened it.

'Hmmmm, Captain—no, I see he is Major Allen now.' She read on while Maryjane held her breath.

'He seems to be quite optimistic.' Her mother passed over the letter and she took it carefully. She knew she must read it under her mother's gaze but would have rather been alone with her phrase book.

She tried a small diversion. 'Did you have any post, Mother?'

Celia, glancing through envelopes, nodded. 'A letter from Mrs Hawkins. Probably another list of grumbles. Really, the woman has no idea we are at war.'

Maryjane seized the moment to put the letter away in her pocket. She must retrieve the envelope. In her room, carefully hidden at the back of the wardrobe, were all the letters he had written placed in a chocolate box and scented with lavender.

'Do you need me for anything else, Mother?'

'No, my dear. What are you doing today?'

'Aunt Grace wants Marybeth and I to inventory the linen cupboards. And then I read to the officers after lunch. Aunt Grace was talking about the Kings Feast.'

'Good gracious, she surely doesn't want to do that?'

Celia was surprised but her sister, coming in shortly after, was defensive.

'I thought it might cheer everyone up. Goodness knows, we could all do with a bit of fun.'

'But Grace, the organising, the food. It's a bit impractical.'

'Father thinks it's a good idea and we didn't have one last year because of Aunt Louisa.'

Celia frowned. 'He would. Men have no idea.'

'I thought we could ask the convalescent officers from Deene as well. Make it more a tea party with entertainment. Something a little different from the usual Feast.'

'Not all day then?'

'Heavens no. Just the afternoon. Maryjane can play the piano and the twins can do a sketch.'

'I suppose so.' Her sister still sounded doubtful.

Maryjane, having escaped to her room as soon she could, opened the letter. The contents made her go through it twice, in case she had misunderstood. He would be in England in July! He wanted to see her! At lunchtime she listened as usual to the conversations flow but said little. Mention of the Feast gave her an idea.

'We must make a list of the officers—from Deene as well—to invite.'

'Aunt,'—Maryjane hesitated—'Major Allen said he will be on leave in July. He's going to see his family and said he might call on us as well.'

'Invite him then by all means,' Grace spoke calmly but Maryjane's heart was pounding.

As soon as she could, she made some illegible notes in her diary before going to read to the officers. Would she see him again soon? It was the one thought in her mind all the time she was reading to the officers.

Going to wash her hands before tea, she gazed in her mirror. Her hair was up now and her face rosy from the summer sun. Would he think she was pretty? As pretty as Marybeth? Oh, for goodness sake! Mentally, she shook herself. They had been writing to each other for months and in all that time, not a romantic word had passed between them, but she loved him and would never love anyone else. She was seventeen now but would grandfather and her parents think she was too young to know her own mind?

She sat daydreaming until a knock on the door roused her. She grabbed a hairbrush and called 'come in.' Her cousin came in and closed the door sharply.

'So we are to have the Kings Feast.' Marybeth was abrupt.

'Yes, why not?'

'Ridiculous. So much work and for what? To entertain a few officers.'

Marybeth put down the hairbrush carefully. 'And to give everyone a little fun, brighten them up.' Unconsciously, she echoed Aunt's words.

Maryjane's room looked towards the stable yard and two officers were looking at the horses. Marybeth, pacing about, halted and looked out of the window. 'So we'll have to work like slaves for what?'

'Don't exaggerate, cousin. And you are always complaining we never have any fun.'

Her cousin flounced out without a word and Maryjane sat turning the conversation over in her mind. What had made Marybeth so grumpy between lunch and now? And she had looked particularly at the officers coming back from their walk.

Like a flash it came to her—one of the officers had proposed. She reviewed all of them one by one and settled on Lt Cooper. He had been 'making eyes' at her cousin for ages but how could he have proposed without speaking to uncle Billy first? And uncle Billy was in France. She must get Marybeth on her own.

The opportunity happened sooner than she thought and very soon, Marybeth found herself in the linen closet with her cousin barring the door.

'What's the matter, Marybeth? And don't tell me nothing.'

Her cousin sat in the chair and propped her elbows on the table, something Nanny had always told them not to do.

'I've had a proposal of marriage.'

I knew it, her cousin thought, before asking calmly, 'May I ask who?'

'Lt Cooper. You said he was sweet on me and I didn't believe it.'

'I hope you told him to speak to uncle Billy first.'

'I accepted, of course.' The blue eyes were defiant.

For a moment, Maryjane was silent; this needed carefully handling. She sat in the chair opposite. 'A proposal! How exciting.' She hoped she sounded more enthusiastic than she felt.

Her cousin eyed her warily. 'I didn't think you would say that.'

'A proposal is exciting and you know what we're supposed to say if it happens. But he was wrong not to speak to uncle Billy—or even Grandfather—first and ask permission to court you.'

Her cousin stood up so quickly the chair fell backwards and Maryjane found her shoulders gripped hard.

'Don't you see, he's my ticket out of here. Once married, I can go and live at Nether Bassett and no-one can tell me what to do.'

She spoke eagerly and her cousin, seeing the determined look in her eyes, knew trying to reason was no use. She made her voice calm. 'They'll never let you. You're underage.'

The next words took her breath away.

'Don't tell anyone. We're going to elope.'

Chapter 7

Maryjane paced up and down anxiously. Oh, to be able to talk to Roddy! But it would take a week for a reply and anything might happen before then.

What to do? She went downstairs with a heavy heart.

She had no idea what to do next or even who to talk to and she was frowning as she came slowly into the hall. The library door opened and her father came out.

'Father…'

'Hello Maryjane.'

Looking at him almost for the first time—the kindly smile, twinkling eyes, greying hair. She could talk to him.

'I must talk to you. It's important.'

'Sure you wouldn't rather talk to your mother?'

'No, definitely you.' She must do it now, while her nerve held.

'In the study then.' Hugo looked nervous. Surely girls were a wife's department?

Five minutes later, his face grim, he stopped her. 'Wait here.'

Maryjane sat still and wondered if she was doing the right thing. What would Roddy say? Should she tell him?

The door opened again and her parents and grandfather came in.

'Now Maryjane, tell me once again.'

Hugo's voice was calm but she was conscious of all eyes on her and knew a moment of panic. She didn't like being the centre of attention.

'Square your shoulders and look straight ahead.' She heard his voice as clearly as if he had been sitting next to her.

She took a deep breath and began.

'…and she said they were going to elope. She's desperate to…'

She stopped, suddenly aware of how this might hurt them.

Her mother's voice was unsteady, 'She's desperate to what?'

There was a long silence but she had come this far.

'To leave here, have some fun. She says we never go anywhere or see anyone. She said...when she's married, she can live at Nether Bassett and no-one can tell her what to do.'

Hugo moved to sit beside his daughter and dropped a kiss on her head.

'I am proud of you, Maryjane, you have behaved entirely properly.'

It was the first time she could ever remember him praising her and she flushed.

'Maryjane'—her grandfather spoke quietly—'will you go and find Lt Cooper and tell him—no, bring him here at once. Not a word to anyone.'

'Yes Grandpa.'

It was easy enough to find him but more difficult to get him to the study discreetly and she was glad to shut the door behind him and go to her room. For once, code was impossible and she wrote an open letter to Roddy full of details and exclamation marks. By the time she had folded the pages and slid them into an envelope, it was so bulky she had no idea how she could post it.

The gong sounded for tea and she went down to find her aunt coming out of her sitting room.

'Maryjane, where is everyone?'

'I think they're all in the study.'

Merridew appeared with a maid and the tray just as everyone else came out of the study and as usual, they all gathered in the saloon.

'Thank you, Merridew, we'll help ourselves. Maryjane, my dear, I'm sure you can pour for us.'

This was an honour and she coloured slightly as she moved to the table. Celia told Grace in a very audible whisper what had happened. Silas took a sip of tea before saying quietly, 'Lt Cooper is packing. He will leave tomorrow morning. Marybeth is in the nursery.'

'We must have failed her somehow, Cee. Both girls have been told how to respond to a proposal. And how on earth did she think they could get to Gretna Green undetected?'

'What did he say, Daddy?'

Silas smiled grimly. 'Not much after I made it clear exactly what I thought of a man who makes love to an underage girl.'

'So he will leave. What about her?'

'She will stay in the nursery with Nanny for now. And if you two think you've failed her, that's nothing to how Nanny feels. She is shocked beyond words.'

Maryjane coughed. How that would hurt her cousin—to be with the babies! Hugo, passing his cup for a refill, smiled at his daughter.

'And this—a family scandal—has been avoided because you had the courage to come and tell us.'

Silas put his cup down slowly.

'Yes, my eldest granddaughter knows how to behave properly.'

'We must have let her down though, Cee. It was so hard, losing Beth, but we did our best. Didn't we?'

'Yes, we did. I'm sure I don't know what to do now.'

Hugo turned to his wife. 'We must tell Billy.'

'No! Not just now.' Simon spoke without thinking and Grace looked at him sharply.

'Why not just now Simon?'

'She's his daughter. It should be his decision.' Celia sided with her husband.

Silas came to his rescue and not for the first time.

Simon silently blessed his father-in-law.

'Simon is quite right, we shouldn't bother Billy. Not least because his comment would be "Do what you think best".'

Grace and Celia smiled because it was exactly what he would say, given the chance. He had never taken much notice of his daughter.

'But Father, this is so very serious.'

'My dear, how can we put this in a letter? We can't have the censor reading it. We'll talk about it on his next leave.'

Silas spoke in the tone that meant he had made his mind up and they changed the conversation but on Maryjane, his words fell like a stone. She had never thought that anyone other than her aunt or maybe her mother would read her letters. She couldn't send the letter now hidden in her glove box at all. She sighed before remembering that he was coming for the Kings Feast. It would have to wait until then.

'Maryjane, I'm sure you have things to do.' Her mother's voice cut into her daydream.

'Yes Mother. I'll leave you to ring for Merridew.' She went out quietly, leaving her mother gazing at the door.

'Why can't Marybeth be more like her? She's growing up.'

Her husband, not usually critical, surprised her. 'Spoiled. Indulged since her mother died as we all tried to make up for that loss.'

'Yes, well, we must think of an answer but not now, later.' Simon dismissed his niece with a wave of his hand.

Maryjane carefully marked off the number of days until she could reasonably expect to see Roddy, but when she wrote, it was impossible not to tell him, as vaguely as she could, that something had happened. She had no reply, which was unusual because he was usually so punctual in answering but before she had time to fear the worst, he turned up.

She was in the Great Hall reading to the officers as usual when Merridew came in.

'Yes, Merridew?'

'Major Allen has arrived miss.'

She gripped the newspaper and found her voice.

'Please excuse me, gentlemen.'

He stood hesitantly in the entrance hall, still carrying his old attaché case, and it was all she could do not to run up to him. In front of Merridew, a handshake and exchange of greeting was all she could do.

'Merridew, please let my grandfather and aunt know we have a visitor. Major Allen, let us go into library and perhaps you can stay for tea.'

'Thank you, yes, I should like to. I found I could leave earlier than planned and hope to enjoy some time with…you all.'

He opened the door for her, noting the new hairdo and rosy cheeks.

'You look suddenly very grown up.'

She blushed. 'Do you think so? I've so much to tell you…oh wait.' Quickly, because she was afraid of being disturbed, Maryjane fished the bulky letter out of her knitting bag. She had taken to carrying it around with her in case an opportunity came to put it in the post.

'You must read this to know it all. I couldn't use code and couldn't send it either.'

He looked at the envelope soberly before putting it in his case. 'Tell me in one sentence first.'

She moved to sit down, still afraid someone would come in.

'Marybeth tried to elope with one of the officers.'

He sat down opposite, obviously shocked, and then someone did come in.

'Ah, I heard we had a visitor. How are you, Major Allen?'

'Very well, sir, thank you. I hope you are?'

Silas waved a hand. 'Getting old. My granddaughter has been entertaining you?'

'Miss Phillips had been telling me about the Kings Feast.'

She smiled inwardly. That was something she had written about weeks ago.

'A little light entertainment will do us all good. Make some money for the troops too. Glad you could join us.'

'I have two days, sir, and on my way to see my mother, I thought I would call and see you all.'

'Maryjane, my dear, ring for tea please.'

'It's a little early, Grandpa.'

'Never mind that, I want my tea. I expect our guest could do with a cup too.'

The gong sounded, everyone gathered and, though it seemed an endless wait, Roddy schooled himself to make polite conversation. He wanted very much to read his letter.

When the trays arrived, he was surprised to see Maryjane presiding over the teapot and neither her mother nor her aunt seemed to find anything unusual in this—they simply took the cups handed out by Simon.

Finally, when he had drunk the polite two cups, Roddy could wait no longer.

'Thank you for tea, Mrs Amory. I hope you'll excuse my leaving now but I must see about a room in the village.'

Silas stared in amazement. 'Staying in the village? No, we can't have that. Grace, I'm sure the major could have his old room.'

'Certainly, Father. I'll organise it.'

'Thank you. My bag is at the station so I'll walk down for it.'

Her grandfather, with a sly look at Maryjane, said, 'Perhaps you would go with the major, my dear, and see if there are any parcels.'

Before anyone could object, she was gone and very soon back with her hat on but as they began to walk down the drive, she asked the one question on her mind.

'Roddy, the letter I gave you…do my letters…that is, are they read by the censor?'

She glanced sideways at him.

'Whatever put that idea into your head?'

'Something Father said.'

There was a long pause before he replied, 'No, our letters aren't read. You know what my unit does, and we're honour-bound not to write anything that might be misinterpreted. I suggested the code mainly for your family.'

She smiled with relief. 'That's alright then.'

The walk to the village included a stop for a certain letter to be read and on the return trip, the whole topic was so thoroughly covered that by the time they were at the front door, Roddy said he thought they had spent quite enough time talking about her wilful cousin.

'Don't you think she's pretty?'

'I suppose she is, in a chocolate box kind of way, but only certain men fall for that package.'

'Do you?' The question was out before she knew it.

'No. I like'—he glanced at the glowing face—'another kind of beauty.'

It was lucky that Merridew was in the hall or her blush would have been his downfall.

'I must go and dress. I'll see you later, Major Allen.'

Opening her wardrobe and looking at her few dresses, Maryjane suddenly longed to wear the cream dress that she had, with much labour, made over. The Kings Feast was to be its first outing so she would not be able to wear it tonight. She put on the plain much worn green dress and sighed at her reflection in mirror.

She was about to go downstairs when she heard a sound somewhere to her left and, turning sharply, saw a hand beckoning her to the old east wing that had been closed up last year.

'Roddy!'

'Shhhh. Come here.' He was in the corridor behind the curtain screen, still in his uniform. He took her hand gently.

'Maryjane, do you know what I thought when you wrote that something had happened? I thought someone had proposed to you. That you were going to be married.'

She blushed. 'Me! Oh no.'

'That's why I came down now. Thought it best to know at once if you…well, if there was someone…'

Hardly daring to breathe, she risked looking at him, although it was rather gloomy to see much. Afterwards, neither of them were sure how it happened but they seemed to be holding each other tightly, kissing as if they couldn't stop. The sound of the dinner gong brought them back to reality with a jolt.

'You'll be late, Roddy.'

'Not me, ready in a jiffy. You go on.'

She put a cautious head out and seeing no-one about, went back to her room and gazed into the mirror. She looked exactly the same except a friendly cobweb had nestled in her hair. He must love her to kiss her like that.

The second gong caused her to hurry downstairs, trying to calm down. It was a quiet family dinner, no different to any other, and yet to her, it was very different and she couldn't help stealing a glance at him when she thought her mother wasn't looking. The rest of the evening passed with no chance to speak to him and the next morning, she was early to breakfast.

He was already there talking to her uncle but Simon was soon gone; she glanced shyly at him on her way to the buffet. What had seemed natural the night before in a dimly lit corridor might not seem quite the same in the cold light of day and Maryjane was apprehensive.

She turned to see if he wanted more coffee, murmuring softly, 'Roddy—'

She got no further, his arms were around her and she was kissed.

'Good morning, dearest girl.'

'Then last night…you really meant it.'

'Of course, you goose. Why…Maryjane, you didn't…you couldn't think I was just amusing myself?'

'Well, I wondered if you…if you…' She blushed.

'Whatever you wondered—I love you.'

The careful phrase her mother had taught Maryjane for just such an occasion went right out of her head. 'I love you too.'

The morning flew by and at lunchtime, Maryjane said to her mother, just arriving for lunch, 'Do you need any more help with decorations for the Feast, Mother?'

Boxes were coming in behind Celia and she nodded. 'We need more streamers.'

So after lunch, they sat in the hall with several other officers and a mountain of paper, scissor and glue, fashioning some bunting. As soon as the others moved away, he whispered quietly, 'Maryjane. I've been thinking about us.'

She flushed at the word 'us'.

'I'm going to approach your father and say how very grown up you are, and quite the prettiest girl in the world…'

She blushed. 'Am I?'

'Yes, and I shall say that I like you and would like to know you better.'

Quite how she managed to carry on calmly gluing streamers, Maryjane didn't know, but across the room several officers were painting a banner so she couldn't feel quite alone with him.

'Then what?'

'I'll ask permission to write to you properly with no-one reading the letters.'

That evening, dressing for dinner, she was summoned to the library by her parents. She knocked and entered quietly to face her parents and grandfather with a fast beating heart.

***

'You sent for me, Mother.'

'Maryjane, my dear, we have something to tell you.'

She sat down as calmly as she could and folded her hands.

'You have been writing to Major Allen.'

'I write to several officers, Mother. The letters are left open for you or aunt Grace to read.'

'Do you like the major, my dear?' Her father's voice was studiously blank.

Like him? I'm madly in love with him. Maryjane wanted to shout back. Instead, she nodded and murmured, 'He seems agreeable.'

'He is quite taken by how much you have grown up since he was here last. And he has asked for permission to write to you on a more personal basis from now on.'

Maryjane looked at her hands silently. Her father, anxious that there should be no misunderstanding, came and sat next to her.

'Maryjane, you must understand that when a girl's father is asked for that kind of permission, it can lead to a proposal.'

'Marry Major Allen?'

'Not if you would dislike the idea. No-one would force you to do anything you didn't like.'

Her mother spoke hastily and her grandfather said calmly, 'Of course, you are young to be thinking of marriage at the moment.'

She cleared her throat and looked directly at her grandfather before saying, 'I should like to know him better, Grandpa. He seems agreeable and intelligent.'

'Then we shall give him permission to write to you.' He smiled.

'And as a beginning, you may sit next to him at dinner.' Her mother also smiled.

'Thank you, Mother and—' The gong interrupted her and it was a happy girl who sat down to dinner next to the man she loved. The talk was all of the Feast and she tried very hard to talk just as much to her uncle, sitting on her other side, as to Roddy.

When it was a family-only dinner, her aunt expected the gentlemen to smoke in the great hall but tonight, she seemed to have forgotten they had a guest and as the family walked through the Great Hall towards the saloon, Roddy touched her elbow, gave a ghost of a wink and mouthed 'It's alright.' She nodded and he said aloud, glancing at the streamers already up, 'Do you sing, Miss Phillips?'

'No, that is, very badly. I play the piano a little.'

They were engrossed in talking and somehow ended up sitting together.

'Have you ever played duets?'

She was surprised. 'No, I've never been asked.'

'Shall we try now just to see if it would work?'

They made one or two mistakes but finally managed a tune, to everyone's applause.

He was far too polite to talk only to her and later that evening, Hugo said to his wife, 'Allen seems a nice chap. Likes Maryjane.'

Celia sighed. 'I never thought of her marrying so soon.'

Hugo laughed and kissed her. 'They're not even engaged yet.'

Grace and Simon were also talking about the new couple.

'Of course, he's older than her but perhaps that's good. Maryjane's so quiet.'

'Pity Marybeth can't be more like that.'

'She's Billy's problem and if he says you and Celia must do what you think best he'll be told she's his daughter and his problem.'

***

The Kings Feast of 1916 was, compared to those before the war, meagre in the extreme.

There were still treats for the children but instead of the usual buffet, a small afternoon tea was served. There were very few young men visible, only convalescent officers and a few unfit local lads. The concert that followed was pronounced a success, not least because of two additions to the programme.

Major Allen and Miss Phillips did a duet of popular melodies and at the end, the major organised an impromptu sing-along involving everyone, even dignified Mrs Haskins and stiff-necked Mrs Hill.

These two notorious ladies, taking their leave of Celia and Grace as joint hostesses, were almost kind in their praise. For the family, now automatically including Roddy, it was a relief when it was over.

Celia surveyed the Great Hall with its limp streamers and rows of disorganised chairs and sighed. 'So much to do now, putting everything back.'

'Leave it until tomorrow, Cee.' Grace was fanning herself languidly.

'No, we can do some now. Maryjane, let's start putting the music away.'

Silas handed her the scores and nodded to the major.

'Allen, you can help.'

'Yes, of course, sir. I'm afraid tomorrow will be my last day. I have to leave on Monday.'

'Monday?' Maryjane, although he had told her already, was dismayed.

'I must be in London by 11 am on Tuesday.'

Silas glanced at his daughters. 'If that's the case, we won't work you too hard—we'll have a picnic after church.'

His eldest daughter stared in amazement.

'Daddy, you can't be serious. Having a picnic on a whim—the work involved for a start.'

'Now my dear, no extra work. We can take the rest of this food and go…I know, Tom's View and have lunch there.'

Roddy looked a question at Maryjane.

Silas would not be put off. 'It'll be a treat for the children and it's some time since I saw it.'

Grace rose slowly. 'Then I had better talk to cook. Celia, come and help me.' Between the sisters, this was a code for 'Father is the limit sometimes' and Celia took the hint.

When they had gone, Roddy spoke to Silas, 'Don't make a fuss on my account, sir. Quite happy to help putting things back.'

'No, we must have a little trip on your last day.'

'I'll take the afternoon train on Monday then.'

After dinner, alone in her room, Maryjane could not settle, her mind going round and round the thought that he was going back to France. She might lose him!

The next morning her mirror told her she was heavy-eyed and white-faced. Before going into the dining room, she tried pinching some colour into her cheeks but the only person in there was her grandfather.

'Good morning, Grandpa.'

He gave her a shrewd look. 'Not so good, I think. Did you sleep at all?'

'Not much.'

'We haven't pressured you over Allen, have we?'

'No, I…like him.'

There was a pause before he spoke again.

'Then you are worried about him going back to France.'

'Grandpa, he…might not come back.'

Her grandfather stood up, joints creaking but ignoring the pain and put a hand on her shoulders before whispering to her, 'My dear, Major Allen is an intelligence officer. He will be nowhere near the Front.'

'How did you know he was in intelligence, Grandpa?'

'Maryjane, if one of my granddaughters is writing to an officer, don't you think I would make discreet enquiries about that officer?'

'I suppose so. Grandpa, nothing improper has ever…'

The hand on her shoulder tightened. 'Of course not. I never imagined it would. But I think you write in code?'

Her silence answered the question.

A noise in the hall made him say, 'Everyone will be coming in now. Drink some coffee.'

She managed two cups but couldn't eat anything and did not see the sharp look Roddy gave her as he sat down.

By the time church was over and they arrived at Tom's View, she felt better. They were sitting under the tree with the children running around everywhere but Roddy, glancing around, saw they were alone.

'Maryjane, are you alright? You looked tired at breakfast.'

'I am tired. I didn't sleep very well.'

'Second thoughts?'

'No, never. It's just that…if you go to the Front, you…might not come back.'

If they had been alone, he would have kissed her but all he could do was press her hand.

'My dearest girl, I won't be at the Front. Don't worry about that. I'm usually behind the lines.'

'You are?'

'Yes, but I'm vain enough to be pleased at your concern. I love you.'

'I love you too but I'm worried about you.'

'If you keep looking at me like that, I shall have to kiss you and then your mother would be shocked and your grandfather would say I was a bounder.'

She smiled. 'Grandpa knows.'

'Knows what?'

'That I love you, that we write in code. He told me you are an intelligence officer.'

He gave a sharp look at the old man, innocently playing with the youngsters.

'Your grandfather knows a great deal.'

'There's never been anyone who could deceive him.'

'I must have a talk with him before I leave.'

'Roddy, if I don't have a chance before you go…you will be careful?'

'I'll be careful, my love.'

He never told her of the talk he had with Silas before he left, but in the months that followed, several small boxes were sent to Major Allen from a famous firm of London grocers. There was never a note but Roddy, dutifully sharing them around the officer's mess, knew exactly where they came from.

***

The summer passed, the war dragged on and autumn brought unwelcome news. It seemed Major Smart had not forgotten them after all and Silas was incandescent with rage to receive a letter telling him that Kingscourt would be allocated twelve detainees to help them farm the land.

Simon, coming in early for lunch one day, was summoned to the library.

'Let's have the big estate map out, Simon.'

Mystified, Simon rolled out the large map onto the circular rent table.

'Now read this letter I've just had.'

While Simon carefully read the letter, Silas peered at the map.

'This field here, marked with a red dot. That's the marsh?'

'Well remembered. I doubt if even Major Foodshortage could make that land productive. It's fenced off, naturally, because of the cattle, but still very wet and marshy. Slightest shower and it's a morass—probably as bad as the mud in Flanders we read about.'

Silas scratched his chin and pondered.

'My father always meant to drain it off, we got as far as looking at expensive drills to begin work.'

'What happened?' Simon was always interested in the history of the estate.

'My father died and I inherited. With a young family and several bad harvests, I couldn't undertake such an expensive project. It was abandoned.'

He looked carefully along the line of the Exeter Road.

'There are three small barns, dilapidated, I seem to remember. We can put the detainees up in those.'

'I could ride over and check them out. They're roofed, I think, but guv…surely they'll need better…well, a more—'

Silas cut him short. 'No. If they come here, that's where they'll stay. I have women and children to think of. Can't have the house full of foreigners. Won't have it, whatever Smart thinks.'

So one cool October morning, a shabby group of men huddled in the back of an army wagon arrived at Kingscourt.

Merridew, shuffling into the book room to tell Silas, received a sharp command, 'Tell them to drive around to the stable and I'll meet them there.'

Sometime later, the nervous young army driver looked at him unhappily.

'Mr King, sir, your…er, detainees.'

'Very well. Wait here while my carriage is harnessed and I'll lead the way. Who is the senior person?'

From the huddle in the back of the wagon, a figure moved.

'William Frietel, sir.' He sounded English and Silas was momentarily surprised.

'Very well, Frietel. You are going to Oakley's Bottom, there are three barns quite suitable with basic cooking and lavatory facilities. My son-in-law, Major Amory, who runs the estate, will see you later about your duties.'

Silas climbed stiffly into his carriage and led the way to the edge of the estate. The barns had been patched up and he eyed them critically.

'Frietel, a word.'

'Yes sir.'

'What kind of men are they?'

'All English-born sir, most of German extraction but two Italians. They all love England and don't understand why they have been detained.'

'What did they do before the war?'

'Two teachers, three lawyers' clerks, three hotel waiters, three cooks.'

'Professional men then. Not sure how they'll manage on the land. Yourself?'

'I was a lecturer, sir, at Oxford.'

'Hmm. We could have done with experienced agricultural workers but we shall have to see how you get on.'

William Frietel gestured helplessly. 'We are no traitors, Mr King. We are English.'

When Silas, in a sombre mood, arrived back at the house, his eldest granddaughter was in the hall. The smile she gave him was, for her, almost carefree.'

'What are you up to, my dear?'

'Hello Grandpa. Weighing a parcel for Lt Foster. Shall I ring for some coffee for you?'

'Yes please. In the book room. And I want to see Simon as soon as he comes back.'

His son-in-law, coming in just after, was summoned to the book room.

'Well Simon, the detainees have arrived.'

'That was quick.'

Simon poured some coffee and sat down. He had inspected the barns and made sure they were weatherproof and had some basic conveniences but, listening to his father-in-law, he wondered just how much supervision a bunch of non-agricultural workers would need. He either spoke his thoughts aloud or Silas, with his usual uncanny knack of knowing what people were thinking, had followed his train of thought.

'I'll ride over with you tomorrow and try and get them started. I know it's not ideal and the women will need to be warned to keep away them there. That includes the maids.'

To everyone else, it was only a piece of news, soon forgotten, but Silas gave precise instructions to Mrs Mills and Merridew regarding the maids and to his own daughters about his grandchildren.

'At least they're well away from the house.' Unconsciously, Grace echoed her father's thoughts. 'Just more work for Simon, as if he didn't have enough to do.'

***

For Maryjane, endlessly knitting socks for the troops, endlessly writing coded letters, endlessly worrying about Roddy, the winter seemed to drag slowly. Sometimes, she wondered how she could look so very normal and feel so very old.

At least her letters were now private, sealed by her and put in the posting box in the hall but the dark November days were depressing and Marybeth, still in the nursery with Nanny, was sharp and cutting to everyone.

Towards the end of that dreary month, Kingscourt heard the news of more casualties on the Somme; Grace, accompanied by a sober Maryjane, again visited mothers and tried to help where she could, but as they drove the old pony and trap home, both shed a few tears.

'I don't know what to say to any of them now. I can't imagine their pain, though I'm a mother too. Is there no end to this suffering?'

For once, Grace spoke bitterly. She was exhausted by so much grief.

'Mrs Potts was showing me the photograph of Albert taken when he enlisted last year. Apparently, he lied about his age.'

'So many of them do, Simon was telling me They're all anxious to go and teach the Huns a lesson.'

'It seems the other way round at the moment and they are teaching us.'

Maryjane spoke cynically, for the officers she read to liked hearing the war news followed by sport. So she read far more of the newspapers than her aunt or her mother and comments made by the officers helped her read between the lines of official reports.

Her aunt sighed. 'Nearly two and a half years and there seems no end in sight.'

Maryjane felt like crying herself, forever worrying about Roddy being safe whatever he said about not being near the fighting, but she was a realist and what they needed was something to look forward to.

'Aunt Grace, Christmas is almost here and we need to start planning We are only depressing ourselves like this.'

'You are right, of course. If I don't start to look more cheerful, Simon will know at once something is wrong. I can never deceive him.'

Maryjane hoped with all her heart that Christmas would bring Roddy and a proposal but he had no leave and merely said he hoped to see them all in the New Year. Someone did turn up on Christmas Eve though, just in time for the teatime carol service.

Silas, shaking hands with his son, smiled broadly. 'Good to see you, Billy.' Simon was pouring him a large drink and his sisters were hugging and kissing him.

During the buffet after the service, Billy glanced around several times and once at Maryjane but he said nothing After all the tenants had gone and the family were alone, he asked where his daughter was.

'Thought she might have been at the buffet.'

His father's stem voice cut across the room, 'Marybeth is in the nursery.'

Billy frowned. 'Nursery? But she dined with us last time I was here.'

The silence was deafening.

'Well, what?'

'Billy, we didn't want to…couldn't write and tell you in the summer but…well, it's a sort of punishment. Marybeth tried to elope with one of the officers, they were going to Scotland to marry.'

'Elope?' He frowned again. 'But she's only 15.'

'Yes. Maryjane told us and we avoided a family scandal.'

Billy hardly heard. 'So what have you decided to do?'

'Do? You are her father and it's time you took responsibility for her.' For Hugo, this was being bluntly to the point and his brother-in-law blinked.

'I've other things to think about. The war and so on. You must decide.'

'No, Grace and I have done enough.' His elder sister was firm.

'I say, guv, you must see my position,' he appealed to his father.

'No I don't. Marybeth is your daughter. Since her mother died…' At this, Billy flinched but his father carried on, '…you have shelved all your parental duties onto your sisters. They have their own children to look after. She's your daughter, start behaving like a father.'

His father's voice was cold and Billy looked at a united family front. He stared into the fire for so long that eventually, Celia spoke impatiently, 'Oh for goodness sake, just tell her to behave.'

'But after all…a girl…'

Words failed him as he looked glumly at his family before his brother-in-law spoke quietly, 'Billy, she tried to elope. When we asked her why she said wanted to have some fun.'

Argue though he might, the next morning after breakfast, he did go to the nursery, Nanny was overjoyed to see him and kept him talking until he was forced to say he wanted a word with his daughter.

Marybeth came in cautiously, trying to gauge his mood. 'Daddy, how lovely to have you home for Christmas.'

'Never mind that. What's this I hear about an elopement? Marybeth, what were you thinking?'

'But Daddy, you don't know what it's like here. There's no fun, we never go—'

She got no further.

'Fun? Have you noticed there's a war on? Young men not much older than you are dying every day and all you can think about is having fun!'

Marybeth began to cry. 'But it's so dull here…'

Her father's voice was edgy. 'There's no time to think of yourself in a war.'

She cried harder, hoping to soften him. She had no idea it was doing the opposite for he hated scenes and female tears.

He stood up suddenly and straightened his belt. 'A fine Christmas leave this is turning into. Well, it's time for church so I will wait downstairs for you. Don't be late.'

Nothing more was said about the subject but on the last day of his leave, Simon suggested a ride around the estate and at last saw him jolted into surprise.

'Let's ride towards Oakley's Bottom and see how everything's coming along.'

'Oakley's Bottom? What on earth are you doing with that worthless bit of land?'

Simon sighed. 'I wrote to you about it. We had a visit from someone in the War Office who said we hadn't enough land under cultivation. I explained we didn't have the manpower so we've ended up with detainees.'

'What was the War Office thinking? Who did you see?'

'A Major Smart. Thin chap, glasses, chilly look.'

'I wonder if you mean Brigadier Smart's son—Alex, I think. He's not fit for fighting so they put him in the Commissariat.'

'No idea. He came here one day and practically accused us of being unpatriotic. The guv soon sorted him out but it was only temporary. Anyway, they must have somewhere to sleep so we kitted out the barns for them.'

His brother-in-law frowned mightily. 'What was the guv thinking? Detainees! Rabble and scum! Shouldn't have to take them on.'

'We didn't have a choice, Billy. Can't be accused of being unpatriotic now, can we?'

'I'll see what I can do about them.'

'I doubt you can do anything, old chap.'

Before he left, Billy had at least made up his mind about one problem. He told his father that Marybeth would have a governess to teach her how to behave properly, and asked Silas to find a suitable one.

Maryjane smiled at that. She would have to be an impressive governess to teach her cousin anything. But she very soon had other things on her mind, because on New Year's Eve, her grandfather called her into his study and gave her a present.

'It's beautiful, Grandpa, but it must be very valuable.' She gazed at the beautiful ivory inlaid writing box.

'It was your great-grandmother's when she was young, and I thought as you write so many letters now, you might like it.' This was said with a smile and, for Silas, almost a wink.

The box now had pride of place on her dressing table and bulged with letters. As she heard the church bells ringing in the new year, Maryjane said a silent prayer for Roddy to come home safely.

***

The year came in bringing snow and bitter cold winds. January became February and still Roddy did not mention any leave. In March, Maryjane celebrated her eighteenth birthday and felt quite grown up. The day was marked with a special birthday lunch attended by everyone, even the younger children, and in the afternoon, a telegram arrived.

When Grace, chatting with Celia in her sitting room, saw the youngest Hopkins boy cycling up the drive, her heart missed a beat.

'Celia, the Hopkins lad is cycling up the drive. Must be a telegram.'

'Please God, not Billy,' her sister whispered.

Merridew did not knock the door and at last curiosity overcame them and in the hall, they found a very happy Maryjane holding the telegram.

'Mother, Aunt Grace, I've had a telegram from Roddy…I mean, Major Allen.'

'That's good, my dear. I thought it must be bad news.'

The girl's smile faded. 'I never thought of that. How selfish of me. I am just so pleased to hear from him.'

Celia couldn't resist hugging her daughter. 'Of course you are, my dear. You love him.'

Maryjane blushed.

'It's alright, Maryjane, you have been writing to each other a long time.' Aunt Grace smiled.

'Sometimes a long courtship is better before a proposal.' Her mother nodded.

Maryjane escaped at last to her bedroom and began to write a letter but she was interrupted by Merridew.

'Miss Maryjane, the new governess is here.'

Maryjane could hardly wait to go downstairs but whatever she had expected, it was not Helen Field. She was a plainly dressed middle-aged woman but with a distinct twinkle in her eyes. Grace and Celia had already met her for Silas, struggling in unfamiliar territory, had insisted both his daughters be involved in the whole process.

'I hope you didn't find the journey too tedious, Miss Field.' Maryjane shook hands.

'No, not at all.'

'Tea will be along presently. Here are my mother and my aunt.'

After a cup of tea, Helen Field declared herself ready for anything and Maryjane went to the nursery to fetch her cousin with interest. This could be amusing, given Marybeth's often-aired views on governesses.

Celia made the introductions and Helen Field covertly examined her new charge. Inwardly, she sighed; she recognised the type at once.

'Marybeth, this is Miss Field, your governess.'

'I don't need a governess, I'm a grown up.' A sulky girl sat down with a bang.

Her aunt's tone was sharp. 'Then act like it. A grown up welcomes a guest and shakes hands. Miss Field, on behalf of our family, I must apologise for my niece's bad behaviour.'

Marybeth flushed but stood up and shook hands. Helen Field spoke as calmly as if nothing had happened, 'How do you do, my dear?'

Grace rang the bell and Merridew appeared so quickly he must have been waiting in the hall.

'Merridew, show Miss Field to her room.'

'Very good, madam.'

As the door closed behind him, Grace faced her niece.

'Marybeth, you will not disgrace the family again. I hope I won't need to tell your grandfather about your behaviour to a guest.'

Marybeth sighed with exaggeration. 'I'll go and apologise, Aunt Grace.'

The door closed behind her and Grace shook her head sadly. *How could Beth's daughter have turned out so selfish?*

But by the time summer came again and Silas began talking of the Feast, they had to acknowledge that Marybeth did seem more helpful and less prickly. The sisters, talking to the governess one sunny May morning, were full of praise.

'I don't know how you did it, Miss Field, but my goodness, what a change!'

Helen Field blushed a little. 'Not at all, though she was spoilt.'

'Because her mother died when she was born, we have all indulged her since. A mistake, I see now.'

'Maryjane has been telling me about the Kings Feast.'

Celia sighed. 'Yes, Daddy wants to do it this year. So much work, Miss Field, you wouldn't believe.'

'What is it? It sounds quite exciting.'

Both sisters tried to explained, in a disjointed way, exactly what the Feast was.

'Well, this year, you will have Marybeth and myself to help as well.' The practical voice was exactly what Grace wanted to hear.

'Oh yes, you will be roped in for all sorts of things. When Daddy makes his mind up to something, there's no stopping him.'

***

Two weeks before the Feast, Maryjane had a letter from Roddy saying he was coming home on leave and had something important to ask her. For a whole day, she hugged the secret before telling her mother.

'You look very happy, my dear.'

'I will be happy to see him, Mother.' She did not tell her mother the rest of her news but Celia, glancing shrewdly at her, guessed.

'He may propose when he comes. Think about that.'

In the end, it was her grandfather she told. She was in the library, reading the letter for the hundredth time, when he came in slowly. As he eased himself into a chair, his joints creaked painfully.

'Maryjane, I hear we are to have a visitor.'

'Yes Grandpa.' How he always knew what was going on was a mystery, but he always did.

'It's a long time since you have seen him.'

'Almost a year. I did hope he would come at Christmas but he couldn't.'

'When he comes, he will have something to tell you.'

Her heart missed a beat. Surely he wouldn't have told her grandfather first?

'My dear, your major has been awarded a DSO.'

'How do you know?'

'I know, that's all.'

Maryjane burst out. 'But in his letter, he only…said he had something to ask me, not tell me. And I thought perhaps he was going—'

The old man interrupted her, 'Yes, I think he will ask you to marry him. Will the answer be yes?'

'Yes, oh yes.'

He smiled. 'Then I shall see you walk down the aisle. Come and kiss your old grandpa.'

Two weeks dragged slowly but one bright morning, Maryjane was watching for the station taxi and he did not disappoint her. Before lunch, he was standing in front of her, smiling.

'Roddy.'

'Maryjane, just as beautiful.'

'Come and say hello to Grandpa, he's longing to see you.'

Silas did not rise as they went in and Maryjane had a sudden moment of perception, seeing how frail he had become.

'Major Allen, good to see you.'

'How are you, sir?'

'I get by. Maryjane, give us a few moments, will you please?'

Disappointment rose in her but she tried to smile as she closed the door quietly. The doors into the garden were open and she went outside into the sunshine. Old Batch, the gardener, was pottering around and she went to see what he was doing.

'Morning, Batch.'

'Morning, Miss Maryjane. You'll be wanting some flowers for your major's room, I expect.'

She stared in amazement. 'Batch, how did you know?'

A ghost of a wink and he smiled. 'Easy to see, miss, for anyone with eyes. You come with me and we'll pick some together.'

The next time she saw Roddy, he was having a chat with her mother.

'Major Allen was telling me he can stay for a day or two after the concert, my dear.'

'Grandpa wants us to do another concert.'

Celia glanced at them both before saying, 'Then I suggest you go and have a chat about that before lunch.'

They were gone before she had finished speaking and Celia sighed, remembering her own happy courtship.

Roddy and Maryjane, wandering around the rose garden, had a happy hour talking over his visit to the Palace, what the King had said and how the Queen had looked.

'But why did you get the award?' She was fascinated.

'A bit of intelligence work I did. Just fitting pieces together really. Led to a major breakthrough.'

'You didn't write to me about it. If Grandpa hadn't told me, I wouldn't have known.'

'I think your grandfather has a friend in the War Office The award hasn't been announced because they can't say what it was for. You—and your grandfather—are the only ones who know.'

She felt immensely proud of him in that moment, and young enough to feel a thrill that no-one else knew.

'I am so proud of you, Roddy.'

He looked sheepish. 'Nothing really. Couldn't get any leave and had time on my hands so I had to do something.'

'It's been so long since I've seen you.'

'I know. Sorry about that. We are so short of staff and there's so much to be done.'

She was about to say something else when the stable clock chimed one and she stood up quickly.

'Lunch in half an hour. We'd better go and wash.' He held her hand a moment longer.

'Maryjane, can I speak to you in private, before dinner?'

'Oh yes, I mean, of course.'

She could hardly eat and long before tea, she went to find her mother.

'Mother, can I wear my new dress tonight?'

Her mother frowned. 'It's only a family dinner, my dear.'

'Yes, but…well, it's Major Allen's first night here and he may…that is…he might…'

She stopped, blushing and gazing at the floor as her mother had a flash of insight.

'He has asked for a private word before dinner. And it will not be a refusal if you want to wear your new dress. Of course you can, and I will send Watkins to dress your hair.'

Maryjane was not normally impulsive but she kissed her mother and smiled. 'Thank you.'

Emily Watkins had been her mother's maid since before she was born, and Maryjane was a little afraid of her but she was pleased as well. Her mother always looked so well turned out and if, with Watkins' help, she could look her best tonight, that was all she wanted.

By the time the dinner gong sounded, Roddy Allen was on his knees in front of a Maryjane suddenly grown up, wearing her new silk dress and with her hair beautifully arranged by her mother's maid, who somehow now did not seem quite so terrifying.

'Yes, oh yes, Roddy.'

He was up and had his arms around her before she had finished.

'I love you.' *A kiss.*

'I love you too.' *Another kiss.*

'And I have something for you.' With another kiss, he produced a box. Inside was a diamond ring.

'For me?' She gazed in awe.

'Of course for you.' He slid it onto her finger and was about to kiss her again when the second gong brought them down to earth. By the time they went into the library, everyone was assembled and every eye turned to them. Obviously, their news was out.

Celia was the first to kiss her daughter. 'Congratulations to both of you! Maryjane, you have a ring!'

'Yes Mother.' She proudly held out her hand for everyone to admire it and wish them well. She did not notice her grandfather having a quiet word with Merridew but when dinner was over and the dessert cleared, champagne was produced.

Silas rose stiffly as glasses were passed around.

'My dear family—I know Hugo will forgive me for making this announcement—tonight is a very special occasion for two reasons. First, our dear Maryjane, my eldest granddaughter, is engaged to be married to Major Roderick Allen.' He nodded to the happy couple before carrying on, 'And I am proud to announce that Major Allen has just been awarded a DSO by His Majesty.'

There were gasps all around and applause as Silas raised his glass.

'The toast is Maryjane and Roddy. We wish them long life and much happiness.'

Roddy winked at her as everyone drank and Maryjane looked at the sparkling diamond, felt Roddy's solid presence next to her and was happy. She was going to be married!

The rest of the evening passed in a daze and although she went upstairs as normal, somehow she knew sleep would not come tonight.

Her mirror next morning showed only a happy face and she dressed quickly and hurried downstairs, wondering what they would do today. She was crossing the hall when he met her cousin.

'Good morning, Marybeth.'

Since Helen Field had been there, her cousin had changed somewhat, not so sharp as before but now she smiled disagreeably.

'Roddy Allen! I suppose you couldn't catch anyone better than that old man? I only hope he makes love better than he writes letters!'

A cold feeling came over Maryjane.

'What do you know about his letters?'

With a malicious smile, Marybeth sneered. 'I've been reading them, that's how I know. Talk about dull, I nearly fell asleep over them.'

Chapter 8

Just for a moment, the old sick feeling came over Maryjane, to be swiftly followed by a slow anger. Her cousin, watching her face closely, was disappointed to see only a blank look. She had expected something more.

Before Maryjane could say anything, however, an ice-cold voice behind her said, 'Go to your room, Marybeth.' Helen Field was furious.

'But I haven't had any breakfast...'

'To your room now, miss.'

Marybeth trailed away towards the stairs but turned to her cousin with a face full of spite. 'Did you really think I'd let you get away with telling on me and Lt Cooper to everyone? I've been planning how I could pay you back for ages.' Her normally pretty face was contorted with hate.

Her cousin simply stood in the middle of the hall staring blankly at her. Marybeth, angry because she couldn't get a response, went upstairs without a backward glance.

Helen Field, staring at the white face, gave her a push. 'Go into breakfast, Miss Maryjane. Some coffee will make you feel better.'

For a long moment, Maryjane stood immobile before going to the dining room. Roddy and her grandfather were already there and she went to the sideboard for some coffee but her hand shook so much that she spilled it. Roddy, coming up behind her, took the coffee pot and looked into the white face.

'What is it, my love?' The low tone was too much and she began to cry.

'Someone has upset you.' His arm was around her shoulders before Silas's precise voice interrupted.

'What has happened, Maryjane? Come and talk to me.'

'Go on, talk to your grandfather.' Roddy was mopping up the mess.

She sat down, drying her eyes and blowing her nose. There was a pause before she answered, 'Marybeth has been...has been reading my letters, Grandpa. Things only I was meant to see!'

Roddy had a moment of panic wondering if he had said anything he shouldn't, before remembering with relief that they had decided to keep to the code even though the letters weren't read.

Silas put his toast on the plate and took her hand. 'Now, you will have some breakfast, this is an order. Allen, see to it.'

'Yes sir, I will.'

He rose stiffly and rang the bell. 'I will deal with this.'

When they were alone, he compelled her to eat an egg and some toast and she began to feel better.

'Roddy, she's so…such a spiteful girl. She said she'd been plotting since I gave her and Lt Cooper away, as she puts it, and spoiled her chance to elope.'

'My dear girl, you couldn't do anything else. Of course, she could not marry, Cooper was a bounder even to think of it. There are names for men like him.'

'I wonder what Grandpa will do.'

'Whatever it is, she will deserve it. Now, as we have had some breakfast, I suggest a walk, so go and put your hat on.'

By the time they came back, it was time for coffee and everyone was gathering in the library, Silas in his favourite position in front of the empty fireplace.

'Ah, Maryjane and Allen. Did you have a good walk?'

Once again, Maryjane wondered how he knew just where everyone was and what they were doing.

'Yes Grandpa. It's going to be beautiful for the Feast.'

Maryjane both longed and dreaded to ask about her cousin but her mother got in first.

'So, Daddy, what are we to do about her?'

'I'm not even going to ask Billy as we know what his response will be. She must go away to school, of course; she will not attend the Feast and will spend all her time in the schoolroom with Miss Field.'

There was a silence, broken at last by Hugo who glanced at his daughter, 'How are you, Maryjane?'

'I'm alright, Father, it was just such a shock to know what she had been doing, And last night had been so happy.' She looked at Roddy who shook his head.

'School might teach her something, though I doubt it. Now, shall we talk of something more pleasant? We need to do some practicing for the concert.'

At once everyone began to talk and Roddy, catching the older man's eye, saw him nod slightly.

By the next morning, everyone was full of the Feast and Marybeth was largely forgotten, out of sight and out of mind in the nursery. To everyone Grace and Celia, as joint hostesses, gave the same message. Such a shame, everyone agreed, that Marybeth had been struck down so suddenly with influenza and of course, her governess would stay with her.

They soon had something else to think of because Hugo, standing with his wife and her father, made the announcement of Maryjane's engagement to much applause. The happy couple were congratulated and the ring was inspected before the concert began but naturally, the star turn ended up being the new couple playing duets.

The day ended happily and Roddy, now automatically included in the family gatherings, had a long conversation with his prospective father-in-law before church on Sunday. He came into the hall smiling and found his bride-to-be supervising the younger children.

'All have your bibles? Fred, straighten your tie.'

'Are we ready?' He glanced at the two young lads who would be his brothers and smiled. 'You two will like my younger brother very much.'

For the family, the following weeks after he returned to France were full of school prospectuses and Celia and Hugo found themselves deputed by Silas to find somewhere suitable.

'I'm too old to be going around the country You two must do the best you can. And make sure it's far enough away so that she won't be wanting to come home too much.'

So off the two went, not entirely happy but willing to do their bit. Privately, they thought it would be a waste of time and money but they had to do *something* with Marybeth and perhaps, as Hugo pointed out, being one among many would wake her up to a few realities.

***

In September of that year, Marybeth, her trunk packed and with her uncles to escort her, went to the school Celia had picked. The further north they travelled, the less Marybeth liked it—so bleak and nothing like Devon, she hated it already. The school building did nothing to improve her mood and the headmistress, starched and prim, was waiting in her study. It was obvious that she knew exactly what had happened because once Simon and Hugo had departed, she turned to Marybeth.

'King, you must learn the rules of my establishment.'

'I am Miss King of Kingscourt.'

'No, here, you are King.' She rang a small bell on the desk and immediately a tall freckled girl came in.

'Here is Miss Jones, our head pupil. This is King, our new student.'

'Yes ma'am. Come along, King, to your dormitory.'

'Dormitory! I want a room of my own. I demand a room of my own.'

Miss Jones stood silently as the headmistress rang the bell again and a large woman dressed in uniform came in.

'Matron, this is King, the new pupil; she is demanding a room of her own.'

Matron sneered. 'A room of her own? Very well, ma'am, we shall see to it. Come this way, King.'

Marybeth smiled inwardly. That had not been difficult; if she could just question everything and demand her rights, she would be alright. They walked down a corridor or two and at the end of the second one, Matron took out a key and opened the door. Marybeth, with Miss Jones behind her, had no choice but to go in.

'Here you are, King, a room of your very own.' Matron gave her a shove and Marybeth tripped into the dark room just in time to hear the door shut and the key turn in the lock.

She felt her way along the wall and found a light switch, which illuminated a small bare room with no windows, just a bed and a washstand. The jug was full of cold water and under the bed was a chamber pot.

Marybeth suddenly realised she was in solitary confinement, a term she had heard but not understood until now. So angry was she that she took up the jug and hurled it at the wall, watching as water ran down the wallpaper. Now they would have to come and let her out.

As hour passed and no-one came; she was hungry and thirsty and now began to regret throwing the jug of cold water. When would someone come?

***

The family had scarcely cleared up from the Feast when the Battle of Passchendaele began and once more, everyone began checking casualty lists, dreading the arrival of young Hopkins with telegrams and trying to keep cheerful. This one last push would end the war, everyone knew that.

It was October before Silas received a letter from the War Office telling him that the detainees would shortly be moved elsewhere. Simon, reading it, commented briefly, 'Looks as if Billy has pulled a few strings, guv.'

'Well, for all the good they are on the land, whoever gets them next is welcome.'

It was a very cold November morning when an army wagon pulled up and the detainees were driven off to a secret destination. Simon, inspecting the barns afterwards, was surprised to find everything had been left in perfect order. All the blankets were folded, the kitchen and lavatory facilities had been scrubbed clean and the beds stacked neatly against the wall. He reported to Silas later on that he had been pleasantly surprised.

'They were alright, you know, guv, not their fault they weren't used to the land. They were willing enough to do what I told them, but they did need so much supervision that I'm not sorry to lose that task.'

The same day, Maryjane received a telegram, handed to her by Merridew, which made her turn pale. Something had happened to Roddy! She opened it quickly to know the worst but it was to tell her that he was going to see his mother and would stay at Kingscourt for one night.

She went straight to her grandfather, sitting by the fire in the book room, which he did a lot now as it was smaller and easier to heat.

'Did you know he was visiting his mother, my dear?'

'No, he said nothing, it's quite a surprise.'

'Well, we must just wait and see.'

They did not have long to wait because four days later, he arrived just in time for lunch.

'Roddy.'

'Hello, my dear, how are you?'

'Alright, very happy to see you. Would you like a drink?'

'After the journey I've had, a small brandy and soda would be welcome.'

She took him into the book room to say hello to her grandfather, who asked the question she longed to.

'What brings you down here so unexpectedly, Allen?'

'Visiting my mother, sir.'

'Very sudden visit.'

Maryjane handed him a generous drink and sat down beside him.

'Maryjane, my dear, you had better let your aunt and Merridew know we have another guest.'

She longed to stay just where she was but couldn't disobey the old man. Merridew had already laid another place and her aunt knew so she went back just in time to hear him say, 'My younger brother has been called up.'

'Filling the numbers killed at Passchendaele, I expect.' Silas was caustic.

'Yes sir. But it's not only that.'

The gong sounded and he paused. Silas stood up and took his granddaughter's hand. 'Tell us all shortly.'

Maryjane walked him to his seat and everyone greeted him. It was not until the soup was served that she looked at him.

'What else, Roddy?'

'My younger brother is my mother's darling. She's gone to pieces completely at the thought that he has to fight.'

'Understandable, I suppose.' Celia sipped her soup.

'Yes, but she sent a telegram demanding my presence to the CO. Very embarrassing.'

'She's not alone in having both sons in the army.' Grace put her napkin down.

'By the time I got there, she was hysterical. Told me I must pull strings to have it cancelled. She didn't care what, so long as he didn't have to go.'

'You can't, can you?'

'No, certainly not.'

'What about your brother?'

'Raring to go. Can't see why my mother is so…well, so frightened.'

Under the table, Maryjane squeezed his hand. Only she knew how little Roddy's mother cared about him.

'How did you leave her?'

'Sedated and the local doctor is keeping an eye on her. Our old housekeeper is there too. By the time she comes to, John will have gone; he's due at Catterick next Monday.'

As the coffee came around, Roddy turned to Silas.

'Hope you don't mind my just turning up, sir. I wanted to see Maryjane even if only for a day.'

'Of course not, come whenever you like. When do you have to leave?'

'After breakfast tomorrow.'

'Then we will have a little music tonight after dinner.'

He was gone the next morning soon after breakfast, though not so early that Maryjane was still asleep; she had been determined to say goodbye to him.

'Come back, Roddy.'

'I will.'

She watched the station taxi drive off until it was out of sight.

Christmas preparations were soon beginning and though it was, by King standards, a meagre one, everyone seemed to enjoy themselves. Maryjane had hoped Roddy would have some leave but he did not mention it. Someone else did turn up though, on Christmas Eve, just as the tenants were assembling for mince pies and carols.

Billy, happily shaking hands with everyone, did not immediately miss his daughter. Later on, when the tenants had all left and he did, it was to be told by his father of Marybeth's latest escapade and that she was at school.

'School! But I say…that's a bit much.'

'No, it isn't, Billy. Reading private letters is not something I would condone in anyone and in my granddaughter, it is inexcusable. And if we had asked you, your response would have been to do what we thought best. So we did.'

Billy drank the last of his whisky hastily.

'I'll admit that was wrong of her, but surely you could have done something other than to send her so far away.'

Maryjane coughed slightly. 'Uncle Billy, you have no idea what her character really is. On the rare occasions when you do see her, of course, she is on her best behaviour. If you had seen her, snarling at me that she had long planned to get even with me for ruining her chance of elopement…you would not have recognised her.'

Her uncle plainly didn't believe it and Silas, judging that the conversation would go nowhere, stood up.

'I refuse to spend the rest of Christmas talking about it. What's done is done and I hope that by Easter, when she comes home, she will be more amenable. Now, let us have a little music. The piano, if you please, Maryjane.'

The three days of Billy's leave passed quietly enough and as the new year chimed in 1918, Maryjane hoped that she would see Roddy soon. She did not know how soon, or in what circumstances until he turned up, unannounced, on what was Billy's birthday.

'What brings you here?'

'Do I need a reason to come and see you?'

'No, but I think there is something. Let's go and speak to Grandpa.'

The old man was sitting in his usual place beside the fire in the book room and he did not rise as they came in.

'Grandpa, Roddy is here.'

The shrewd eyes assessed him. 'Trouble?'

'My mother, sir. The doctor has summoned me.'

'Ah. And you have called in on your way to see her. Let us have some coffee. Maryjane, my dear, ring the bell.'

They sat for a while in silence before Silas spoke, 'Your last chance to see her?'

'I believe so. And we did not part on the best of terms so I have no idea how she will be. The CO was understanding. I have four days but then I must go back.'

'Call on your way back to France if you have time. Now you two go and be alone somewhere.'

When they were alone, Maryjane turned to him. 'Will she be awful to you?'

'I should think so. She resents me bitterly for not keeping John out of the war.'

'You couldn't do anything about that.'

'No, but my mother is very good at ignoring what doesn't suit her. And she still doesn't know about you.'

'Perhaps now that doesn't matter.'

'Perhaps not. John knows all about you though, I've shown him your photograph. He's delighted to think he'll have a sister.'

'When do you leave?'

'I'll take the night train from Exeter. I hope I'll see you again very soon.'

'I hope so too. Roddy, I hope it won't be too awful.'

He shook his head. 'Come and kiss me and we won't think about it just now.'

They had a very few moments together before Grace, having heard they had a visitor, put her head into the library.

'Roddy.'

'Mrs Amory, just a flying visit, I'm afraid.'

'Your mother, yes. Father has just told me. Staying for lunch?'

'Yes, thanks. I'm taking the night train from Exeter.'

He was gone after lunch and back two days later, having seen his mother one last time.

'She died quite peacefully in the end, the doctor had sedated her very heavily. I've had to leave the housekeeper to make all the arrangements but I've seen to it that she has enough money. Had a chat with the vicar too.' He told the family over a cup of tea.

'What about John?' Maryjane asked.

'I'll write to him while I'm here if I may, though there's nothing he can do. He's already in France.'

Once more, Maryjane asked him, 'How long are you here?'

'I can stay tonight and then go in the morning, if that's alright?'

Grace nodded. 'Of course, it's alright, Roddy. I'll see about your room now.'

The family dinner was quiet, Roddy already wearing the black armband Grace had provided. His letter to his brother was already in the post and he left early the next morning but at lunchtime, Celia, coming over in the old pony and trap, met the young Hopkins lad delivering a black-bordered telegram.

'It's alright, Albert, I'll take it to the house.' She was proud her voice did not waver but for a moment, her eyes could not focus on the little envelope. Was it Billy? Surely it couldn't be Roddy?

She blinked and saw it was addressed to Roddy. His brother!

Celia spurred the old pony a little more and as soon as the door opened, she jumped out and threw the reins to Merridew.

'See to it, Merridew.'

The old butler, used to Miss Celia going around to the stables and seeing to it herself, was shocked but she had no time to notice his outrage. Whenever anything happened, the one person they all went to was Silas and she found him in the book room.

'Daddy, a telegram. For Roddy.'

The old man held out a gnarled hand. 'We must read it, of course.'

He glanced at it as she waited impatiently.

'Is it John?'

'Yes. Killed yesterday morning. Find Maryjane for me, would you please.'

Maryjane shed a few tears for the brother-in-law she would never know and then sat down to write the most difficult letter of her life to his brother. For once, she did not write in code and Silas refolded the telegram and put it with her letter.

'Roddy has no-one now, Grandpa, only me.'

'He has all of us, Maryjane, our family is his family now.'

When Roddy answered Maryjane's letter, he sent another to her grandfather that led to a long conversation between them.

'So Maryjane, Roddy writes to me asking my advice. About his mother's cottage.'

'Why, Grandpa?'

'It is rented, you see, and what should he do? Keep it on? Or let it go?'

She considered. 'His mother…John was always her favourite. Roddy always felt excluded.'

'I gathered that from something he once said. Always a bad idea to have favourites. Remember that when you have a family, my dear.'

She blushed. 'I will, Grandpa.'

'This decision will affect you greatly. Do you want him to keep the cottage?'

'It will have so many bad memories for him. His mother only moved because she wanted to be as far away from the war as possible. Perhaps he should let it go.'

'Then I shall write to him and say that. My dear, you will live in London when you are married.'

'London? How do you know?'

He smiled. 'I know.'

Nothing more was said, Roddy let the cottage go and at Easter, he turned up at the same time as Marybeth. For Maryjane, there was no question who to greet first.

'Roddy!' She went to kiss him, careless of who might be in the hall.

'Hello.' He returned the kiss.

'I had no idea you would be here so soon.'

'Lucky with the trains but I could do with a drink.'

Maryjane, greeting her cousin with a cool handshake, noted a change in the pretty face.

'How are you, Marybeth? Liking school?'

'Yes.' It was a whisper.

'Let's go into the saloon and I'll ring for tea.'

It was now quite natural for Maryjane to preside over the teapot and her grandfather, knowing in his own mysterious way that they had guests, arrived as well.

'Roddy, good to see you.' He shook hands before turning to Marybeth.

'How are you, Marybeth?'

'Well, thank you, Grandfather.' She sounded hesitant.

They were soon joined by Grace and Celia, eager for all the news. Grace soon went off to see about rooms and Celia began talking to Roddy, leaving Marybeth to her grandfather.

'Do you like school?'

'Yes, I like school.' She tried to smile.

'That's good. It will be pleasant to have some more family around the table for lunch. I shall look forward to hearing all about your days.'

The next morning brought Roddy to the book room for a talk with Silas.

'I'd like your permission to marry Maryjane, sir. At the King's Feast.'

'Excellent idea. You don't need my permission, young man, but we will need to speak of money and for that, Hugo should be with us. After dinner, I think.'

'Yes sir, thank you.'

He flew off to find his fiancée and tell her the news.

'Married at the Feast! Roddy, are you sure?'

'Why, do you think I've changed my mind?'

'No, of course not. But at the Feast?'

'Your grandfather thinks it's a good idea.'

'We had better tell my parents then, and Aunt Grace.'

'Let's wait until tea time when everyone is here.'

The announcement being made, Celia and Grace immediately began to start planning. Roddy, listening to what sounded like an alarming list, murmured to his fiancée, 'I thought of a quiet wedding.'

'It will be, I expect. Especially if we have it at noon, followed by the tea party, which is what we had last year.'

Marybeth, sitting with a cup of tea, began to be interested. She would be a bridesmaid! Chief bridesmaid, of course.

Dinner over, Maryjane watched Roddy disappear into the library with Silas and Hugo, to appear again later on and come and sit beside her. He had been apprehensive, going through his accounts over and over, trying to think how a prospective father in law would see his present position.

'How did you get on?'

'Alright. It seems I am marrying a young lady of means.' He smiled broadly.

'Me? I haven't got any money, only what Father gives me for pocket money.'

'Ask your grandfather, I think you'll be surprised.'

The next morning after breakfast, she duly went to the book room to speak to Silas.

'Grandpa, Roddy says I have money.'

'Yes, my dear. Your grandmother left it to you when she died, I have been investing on your behalf. It is quite substantial now.'

'I didn't know that. No-one told me.'

Silas took her hand. 'It was not in her will, just a wish that I honoured. You were, when she died, the only grandchild. Unless you are marrying a man who is a gambler or spendthrift, and I know for a fact Roddy Allen is neither, then you will be quite well set up, apart from what he has, of course.'

'And we will live in London?'

'I believe so, yes. But not a word to anyone else about it. Not yet.'

She nodded thoughtfully and came out of the room to meet Marybeth just coming across the hall.

'Maryjane, I'll be happy to be your chief bridesmaid.'

For a second, Maryjane looked as if she were seeing her cousin for the first time, before saying 'No' and walking off. She went to find her mother, already talking weddings with Grace.

'Mother…sorry, am I interrupting?'

'No, my dear, we are talking about your wedding. Come and sit down.'

'I thought perhaps we could be…married…at noon. Then a family lunch and the Feast later.'

'What a good idea. A quiet simple wedding. We really must see about your outfit.'

'There's something else…' She paused. How to say it without seeming petty? 'Marybeth thinks she will be the chief bridesmaid. She has already told me she is quite happy to do it.'

Glances were exchanged.

'And what did you say?'

'No. I don't want her. In fact, I was thinking Eliza could be a flower girl and no-one else.'

Her mother looked at Maryjane with respect. 'What a good idea. It is a wartime wedding, after all. And Eliza can wear the dress Daddy bought for her confirmation. One thing off the list.'

Grace nodded. 'Now we need to think about the trousseau.'

Maryjane blushed. 'How will we pay for it, Mother?'

Celia smiled. 'I've already spoken to your father, my dear. We know exactly how much he will give us, so we must be organised. A trip to Exeter, don't you think, Grace?'

'Yes, but first we need to check some of the trunks in the attics.'

'Why?' Maryjane had not known there were trunks in the attics.

'A lot of Mother's old stuff is up there, nothing to do with the dressing up boxes. We will go and have a look soon, see if there's anything we can use.'

Roddy left soon after and Marybeth, trying again to talk to Maryjane about bridesmaids, was rebuffed.

'It will be a wartime wedding, no fuss and frills. Eliza will be the flower girl and that's it,' Maryjane spoke coldly.

'But I want to do it! I could do it, you know.' Her voice rose.

Silas, overhearing this last remark, said quietly, 'It is the bride's choice, Marybeth. And she has chosen.'

'You don't want me to have any fun. You're all against me.' The old Marybeth was returning.

Maryjane said nothing, it was for her grandfather to speak and he did not disappoint her.

'Go to your room, miss. Now.' He seldom spoke in that tone and when he did, no-one disobeyed him but he reckoned without the demon in Marybeth.

'I won't! You can't make me,' she shouted at him, eyes blazing and clearly furious.

Two officers came into the hall to see what was happening but speedily left when it seemed a hysterical scene was about to start. Maryjane longed to slap her cousin but her grandfather was in charge so she went quietly into the saloon and picked up the soda syphon from the drinks tray.

By the time she came back into the hall, Marybeth was crying noisily. Maryjane stepped up to her and, with an apologetic glance at her grandfather, sprayed soda water liberally all over her cousin. The crying stopped at once but Marybeth glared at her with loathing.

'I hate you. I hate all of you.' By now, Grace and Celia were coming from the sitting room to see what the fuss was about and saw a dripping girl hurling insults at her cousin.

Hugo, coming in the front door, took it all in at a glance and even his wife was surprised what happened next. He walked calmly up to his niece and took her arm.

'Marybeth, you will go to your room and calm down. Then you will apologise to your grandfather for raising your voice in his house.'

Celia had never heard him use that tone of voice before, even when his own children had been naughty.

'I won't! You can't make me.'

He was steering her towards the stairs and she made an effort to shake off the arm but found herself held in a strong grip.

'If you resist, I shall put you over my knee and give you a good spanking. It's what you've needed for a long time and as your father is not here, I will be happy to oblige.'

He compelled her to walk up the stairs and promptly locked her in her bedroom, coming down and giving the key to his wife.

'Thank you, Hugo.'

'That's alright, sir. She's altogether too spoiled and it's time she had some discipline.'

'I thought the school would do that, but obviously not,' his wife spoke sadly.

'She will have to go back there again. Perhaps another term or two will do better. What was it all about anyway?'

It was his daughter who answered, 'She wanted to be chief bridesmaid but I refused.'

Three days later, two grim-faced uncles escorted her back to school after she had an unhappy interview with her family.

Her apology met with stony faces and both her uncles were clear that her behaviour was awful.

'I've enough to do running two estates without having to waste days on a wilful disobedient girl who thinks she can do anything she likes.' Simon's voice was bitter.

'I meant what I said, Marybeth. I have often thought you would benefit from a good spanking and if you carry on as you have been, you will have one.'

So off Marybeth went and everyone settled down to planning the wedding and the Feast.

Celia, Grace and Maryjane went off to Exeter, escorted by Silas whose old-fashioned notions would not permit his womenfolk to stay in hotels alone. They indulged in an orgy of shopping and Roddy, replying to Maryjane's letter written from the hotel, asked what had happened to his sensible fiancée as her last letter had been full of dresses, hats and parasols.

Home again and Maryjane still had dressmakers' visits to alter her grandmother's dresses, which her aunts knew would make good day dresses, the material was such good quality. Maryjane had doubts but seeing them finished in a more modern style, had to admit that her mother was right. Her wedding dress was also courtesy of her grandmother, a silk evening gown, which was made over by her mother and Watkins, with the aid of some old lace from another dress.

The dress was a secret even to her grandfather but when he saw her coming down the stairs on the morning of her wedding, Silas felt a tear in his eye. He recognised it at once.

'Maryjane, you look quite beautiful.'

'It was Grandmother's dress.'

'I know, my dear. I could tell you exactly when she wore it, but that is not a tale for today.'

It was a beautiful morning and Maryjane, riding in the carriage next to her father, was happy.

'Father, I'm so happy.'

'Of course you are, my dear. And I couldn't be prouder of you. Roddy Allen is a first-rate man, just the sort I hoped you would find. You will be very happy.'

Before the stable clock chimed one, Maryjane was Mrs Allen and champagne was circulating at Kingscourt. A family lunch followed, without Marybeth who was still at school but including, for the first time, ten-year-old Eliza.

Maryjane changed out of her wedding dress into her going-away dress and the happy couple went the rounds of officers and guests at the Feast. At four o'clock, they slipped away, having said goodbye to the family.

Maryjane, sitting in the carriage next to her husband, glanced back at Kingscourt before she remembered her mother's warning: 'Don't look back, Maryjane. Today, you look forward to your future.'

Maryjane saw her grandfather, small and wizened, framed in the doorway before she turned back to look at Roddy.

***

Silas went slowly upstairs after the Feast to his room. He felt tired but happy to have seen one more wedding.

An hour later, one of the housemaids went to his room with a cup of tea but there was no answer to her knock. She went in quietly, saw Mr King sitting in his chair apparently asleep and tiptoed to the table. She had just put the cup and saucer down when his head fell to one side and Patty, who had seen her own grandfather look the same, went downstairs at a run.

Merridew, when told, moved faster than he had for a very long time. One glance told him that his master was indeed gone and he wiped his eyes before going back downstairs. He went into his pantry and sat down, having poured a glass of port.

'God rest you, Mr King. It has been a pleasure to serve you all these years.' He tossed off the port and sat for a while.

The youngest and most inexperienced housemaid, finding his door slightly ajar, knocked and walked in and found the ruler of her small world motionless in his chair.

She rushed into the kitchen, shouting, 'He's dead. Mr Merridew's dead.' The staff stood silently as Mrs Hughes came in.

'What is the matter, Ruth?'

'Mr Merridew's dead. He's dead!' She began to cry but before Mrs Hughes could move, the door opened and Merridew came in.

'What is going on here?

Ruth stopped crying. 'Mr Merridew, I thought you was dead. You looked dead, sir.'

'I am very much alive, thank you, Ruth, but I must correct your grammar yet again. Now, why is everyone standing around? Is everything tidy upstairs?'

Like leaves in the wind, they scattered and Merridew went back upstairs to break the news to the family. He told Simon and Hugo, who went to tell their wives as gently as they could. Celia began to cry and Hugo put an arm round her. 'My dear, it was a quiet dignified way to go.'

'But I'm going to miss him so much, Hugo.'

'We all are, my love.'

Grace was also crying in Simon's arms. 'Father always seemed indestructible. I'm going to miss him so much.'

Simon unconsciously echoed his brother-in-law, 'We all are.'

Neither sister could face telling their children and it was left to two bewildered husbands to try and tell them. Nanny helped and somehow, a chocolate cake was produced that had them all excited, but for the two eldest, chocolate cake was ever after associated with something sad.

Grace had cancelled dinner but everyone still gathered quietly in the saloon. Hugo poured everyone a small drink and they toasted Silas each in their own way.

'I had better write to Billy.'

'And I will write to Marybeth's school. I suppose she will have to come home for the funeral.' Celia was doubtful.

'Perhaps there won't be enough time to go and come back with her before the funeral.'

Merridew came in quietly and approached Simon.

'Major Amory, can I have a word please, in private?'

Simon glanced at his wife before replying, 'Very well. In the library.'

When he came back, his face was puzzled. Hugo was the first to question him.

'Merridew has found several letters in the guv's room.'

'Who from?'

'No, who to. They are addressed to us. You, Hugo, me, Billy.'

'I don't understand.'

'I think we had better read them first. I'll have to send Billy's on.'

An hour later, two very shocked couples read and re-read Silas's last letters.

He had been very much to the point, as he always was where business was concerned. Marybeth's actions so far had convinced him that she was not suitable to be the heiress to Kingscourt and so, he had dramatically changed his will. They had always known that Billy would have both estates for life and that Marybeth would inherit after that. Silas had decided that Simon would inherit Kingscourt and Billy would have Nether Bassett.

Hugo, reading his letter with Celia looking over his shoulder, saw that his father-in-law had left him the whole parcel of land around The Risings so that, in his words, 'he would have a nice little estate.'

'Surely, the guv must have been…upset.' Hugo couldn't bring himself to say that he thought Silas might have been deranged. It seemed so out of character in one who had always maintained that the estate should be kept exactly as it was.

'Of course, we know Marybeth has been, well, outrageous but somehow I thought she would calm down as she grew up.'

Grace, answering her sister, was for once much nearer the truth than anyone knew, 'She has been spoiled, Hugo was right to say we had tried to make up for her mother dying so young. But I don't believe she will grow out of it. If something happens and she doesn't get her own way, then she becomes unmanageable.'

Simon agreed. 'Of course, she can't marry without Billy's consent yet, but she has tried to elope. She could marry someone who would bankrupt the estate.'

In Simon's letter was a direction from Silas and he read it now:

'As soon as anything happens to me, you will notify my solicitor, Mr Beades, at Lincolns Inn. He knows he must attend the funeral, and that the will must be read immediately after. Billy and Marybeth must also be present. This is my last wish and I trust you to execute it faithfully.'

'So, Billy doesn't know yet. And whatever will Marybeth say?' Celia was shocked.

Hugo, pouring himself another drink, said practically, 'Then you, Simon, must write to Mr Beades and let him know. I'll send a letter to Billy requesting him to come at once and Celia, you can write to the school. Should I send your father's letter?'

That point started a disagreement that ended only when they all retired for the night. At breakfast the next morning, they all agreed that the letter could wait until Billy arrived home.

Their other problem was that no-one knew where Maryjane and Roddy were. The happy couple had gone away for a few days somewhere so secret that only the bride's grandfather knew and there was nothing for the family to do but wait.

The couple duly turned up later that afternoon and as they were walking up the drive, Maryjane said, 'Something's wrong.'

'How do you know?'

'I don't know. Just, something is wrong.'

She very soon found out what was wrong and, for the normally placid Maryjane, she began to cry. 'Mother, I'm going to miss him so much.'

'We all are, my dear. It was such a shock. Only one thing comforts me, that it was quite peaceful. He didn't suffer at all.'

Everyone was in mourning and Maryjane went quickly to change and Roddy to don the black armband he had put off for his wedding.

The one topic of conversation was, of course, the will and how Billy would take it.

'Of course, it was for Daddy to decide the future of the estate. It's not entailed, after all. Hugo and I will have a small estate we never expected.'

'I shall have to see about an agent, I expect. Or someone to help me.' Hugo sounded glum.

'Time to think of that later, old chap. I may have to have an agent yet.' Simon was thinking of how much work there would be to do now that he was on his own.

Roddy coughed. 'I don't want to add to your problems but I do have to go back to France tomorrow night. Mr King said that…my wife…could stay here until the war is over. I hope that will be alright.'

'Of course, it will. I rely so much on you, my dear, to help with the officers. That will not change until they all move on.'

'I'm sorry you can't be here for the funeral, Roddy.'

'Only if I can swing a 48-hour pass. You don't know when it is yet.'

'No. We must wait for Billy and Marybeth. How long they will be heaven knows.'

Billy surprised everyone by turning up two days later without warning but there was no news of his daughter.

'Well, someone will have to go and fetch her,' Billy said bluntly.

'I can't, old chap. No time just at present. The good weather has caused us to begin some harvesting already.'

Hugo said wearily, 'Then I suppose I shall have to go. You could come with me, Billy.'

'I've had enough of travel, thanks.'

So Hugo went to collect his niece and was back with a young lady who looked rather indecently excited that her grandfather had died.

In the carriage coming home, she had rattled to her uncle about how she could come home now.

'I'm next in line, it's only right I be involved in running the estate now.'

Hugo kept silent, wondering yet again how she would take the news.

Mr Beades arrived from London and was put in the best spare bedroom; the funeral was as well attended as Aunt Louisa's had been and after the family settled in the library, there was the reading of the will. Just before that, Simon had put his letter into Billy's hand and told him to read it in private.

As Mr Beades seated himself, Billy came in looking very unhappy.

The last will and testament of Silas Haydn King, made of sound mind and body, fell like a stone on at least three of the family.

Robert Amory understood suddenly that one day, he would inherit the house he had lived in since he was born, and the estate it stood on. Merridew, standing quietly at the back of the room, heard the glowing words of his late employer followed by the bequest of a sum that seemed to him magnificent, together with a cottage for life on the estate. For Marybeth, struggling to understand the will, it was a disaster. She was disinherited!

Roddy, who had managed one day's leave for the funeral, watched her covertly. *Heading for trouble, that one*, he thought. *Will go off the rails*.

'I don't understand. Daddy, this estate is yours, and then mine. Grandfather can't do this.'

'The estate was never entailed, Marybeth. It was Daddy's to do with as he wished.'

'He must have been soft in the head. Why, he even left money to the butler! It must be overturned. Father, we'll contest it.'

Maryjane was nearest to her cousin and she stood up quietly, walked the few steps to her and calmly slapped the angry face.

'You will never say anything like that about Grandpa again. It was his estate to do with as he wished.'

'He must have been…confused. We can—'

'Enough,' Billy raised his voice. 'This is my father's decision and if I can accept it, then you must, Marybeth.'

'But surely—'

'No. We will still have Nether Bassett when I leave the army.'

The thought that crossed Grace's mind was one Simon had already had.

'You're not leaving the army, are you, Billy? Even when the war is over.'

'Now you mention it, no. Simon is doing a great job running the estates and I'm happy where I am.'

The lawyer, sitting forgotten, began to shuffle some papers in the deafening silence.

'If you think for one moment, I'm going to run your estate indefinitely then you are mistaken. Time you took responsibility for something, Billy. I'm running your estate and my wife and her sister are trying to bring up your daughter.'

'I'm busy with the war.'

'That's an excuse and you know it. You were quick enough to join up, in fact, you couldn't wait. The army, where there's always someone up the chain to take responsibility.'

'You know I'd have never left if it hadn't been for—' Billy stopped suddenly, realising all the children were agog.

His own daughter forgot her anger to say, 'I didn't know you were in the army before, Father.'

'Old history. Before you were born.'

Grace faced her brother. 'That's why Father did what he did. He knew you only ever wanted to be a soldier. That wouldn't help the estate at all. You expected Simon to keep on running everything and Celia and I to keep on looking after your daughter. Well, I for one, have had enough.'

'I can't look after her and be a soldier. She's alright here.'

Maryjane judged it time to speak, 'No, Uncle Billy, she is not alright. You are never here and have no idea what she's capable of.'

'Oh yes, the tantrums if she doesn't get own way, the casual disregard of everyone else's feelings. They don't matter because she wants to do something.' For Hugo, this speech was heartfelt. How many times had he told his own children to consider other people's feelings as well as their own? Because he didn't want them turning out like his niece.

'Mrs Amory, I really must be going in order to catch the train.' The dry lawyer's voice broke into the conversation.

'My dear Mr Beades, do please forgive me. I am neglecting you. Of course, you must go and we thank you so much for coming from London even though you have had to witness a most unpleasant family scene.'

Merridew had already gone to order a carriage and arrange for his case to be packed and it was an apologetic Celia who saw him to the door while Grace ordered everyone else to the nursery.

Robert sidled up to his father. 'Dad, can I drive with you to the station?'

'Yes, if you like. Let your mother know where you are though.'

Finally, it was Billy left alone with his daughter and he didn't like it one bit. She was still angry and he wasn't sure how he felt at all. Damn it, he had only ever wanted to be a soldier except for that brief eighteen months with Beth. He was being punished by his father once again.

'I don't want to go back to school, Father. I hate it.'

'Best thing for you.'

'I could live at Nether Bassett.'

'Of course you can't, you ridiculous child. Who would chaperone you? Who would run the estate? Doesn't look like Simon will. I shall have to find someone to do it. Just one more problem I don't need.'

Chapter 9

The funeral of the last of the old Kings, as everyone termed it, was a huge affair. By now, details of the will had leaked out and while people might have been shocked, amongst the older generation, no-one was surprised.

Marybeth, looking angelic in black, could barely bring herself to listen to some of the more pointed remarks made to her father.

'Off playing soldiers won't run the estate properly. Major Amory has been doing a first-rate job but now it's time for you to look after your own affairs.' Mr Hawkins' verdict seemed to sum up the general view. The only one of the family not present was Roddy, who wrote to say he couldn't have any more leave quite so soon but to his wife he wrote she should expect him within weeks.

So Maryjane settled once more into the routine she had before she was married and if it hadn't been for the ring on her finger, she might have thought she was still a single girl. She wrote long letters to Roddy, read to the officers and under Mrs Mills' supervision, was beginning to learn about housekeeping. It had been her mother's suggestion, made after Maryjane found a book by Mrs Beaton in the library.

Celia, trying to decipher the inscription, thought it must have belonged to her mother as a young bride.

'We don't know yet what kind of establishment you will have, Maryjane, but it's best to be prepared. Mrs Mills will be able to guide you and then when Roddy does come home, he will be surprised at how efficiently you can run a kitchen.'

Celia did not know how presciently she spoke for one cold September afternoon a week later, Roddy turned up. He was driving a little MG and Maryjane, hugging him tightly, asked how long he would be here.

'A few days. I've got some news.'

It took him an hour to say a proper hello to his wife and wash and change before tea. They were gathered in the saloon when he told them all.

'I'm coming back to London. Got a billet at the War Office.'

Amid general exclamations of joy, Maryjane said quietly, 'When?'

'I should be back about the last week in October.'

Hugo was astonished. 'But why are you coming home before the war is over?'

Roddy was aware that his parents-in-law knew something of what he did but he was still vague in answering, 'They think I can be of more use here.'

'But where will you live?' Celia as ever was practical.

'I've seen a nice little flat just round the corner from Whitehall. Maryjane, I'd like you to come and see it.'

'I've never been to London.' She sounded forlorn and Roddy, glancing at his mother-in-law, made a decision.

After tea, everyone scattered and Roddy went to his mother-in-law for a private chat. 'Mother Celia, when I go back to London, will you bring Maryjane, just for the day, to see the flat?'

'I should like that.'

'She's never been to London.'

'She's never been anywhere much, the war saw to that. But she's very sensible and for a while, she'll have to learn housekeeping, which will be a novelty. I'll give you a couple of months then see if I can come and stay for a day or two.'

'She's used to all of you around, lots of coming and going, and I'm worried how she will cope, but there's a nice widow who lives two doors down, not much older than her. I'll see if she can keep an eye on things, without seeming to.'

'Is your flat furnished?'

'No. We shall have to see about that.'

The next morning, he and his wife were summoned on a tour of inspection of empty rooms, of which there seemed an awful lot.

'Just pick a few pieces you like, Maryjane. Anything at all.'

'But Aunt—'

'No, really. We don't need any of this. I know some of it is hopelessly old-fashioned but you might find something.'

So they had a happy hour rummaging about and Maryjane, to her surprise, found a pair of Regency cabinets she fell in love with and some chairs, a mirror and a pair of wardrobes. Roddy spotted a small desk in the library and asked if he could have it.

'I don't think Father ever used it.' Grace opened the drawers, all empty, and nodded. 'One more piece of furniture gone.'

After lunch, they were taken to the linen closet and shown their wedding present.

'Grace and I have been sorting through all this stuff. Here is enough of everything to start you off.' There were damask tablecloths, napkins, sheets, pillowcases, and everything bore the initials MJA.

Maryjane shed a few tears. 'It's too much, with all the furniture.'

'Nonsense, my dear. You are the first one to be married so of course, we will help you set up house. Mrs Mills has been sorting kitchen items and there will be china and glassware.'

Roddy smiled. 'Thank you both. And the family.'

A small hand slipped into his. 'It's our family, Roddy.'

All too soon, she was waving him goodbye but then came the excitement of a trip to London with her aunt and mother. The flat was pronounced the very thing by all of them and Roddy took the opportunity to introduce the neighbour, Mrs James, who invited them into her flat for a drink and offered any help they might need.

A very good lunch at a café just off Whitehall rounded everything off and as soon as Roddy had waved his family goodbye at Paddington, he went straight to the estate agent and signed a lease.

Maryjane packed her clothes and possessions and her mother provided several large wicker baskets for the linen. Mrs Mills found two crates for kitchenware and just as they had finished packing everything up and wondering how to get it to London, a lorry and several young army cadets arrived. Roddy had arranged transport for the furniture and as she watched the van going off down the drive, suddenly to Maryjane, it was real. She was about to begin married life.

Marybeth, on the other hand, was finding that school was just about alright if she put on a front. She found that she could, with effort on her part, fool people. It was a lesson she put to good use and before long, she was popular with the girls. The headmistress, who saw her only as part of a larger group, wrote an excellent report to Celia who was so pleased she forwarded it to Billy. It seemed her niece had turned a corner at last.

The telegram from Roddy saying he would be coming down for the weekend and taking Maryjane back with him was joyously received and Grace planned a special dinner on the Saturday evening, which all the children could attend.

He arrived in his friend's car, spent a happy two days with his family and Sunday, after church, they set off, provided with sandwiches and a flask. Celia, hugging her daughter, whispered in her ear, 'Remember what I told you on your wedding day, Maryjane. Don't look back.'

'I won't, Mother.'

Hugo, shaking hands with his new son-in-law, also gave a few words of advice, 'Always ask her opinion if you have a problem, Roddy. She is the one person who will have your best interest at heart.'

Roddy nodded. 'I will, Hugo.'

They drove off happily. Maryjane did not look back and Celia, leaning on her husband, shed a tear.

***

The end of the war came as days old news to Kingscourt because bad weather came in and Simon was busy with the cattle. When they did hear at last, Grace, remembering the estate lads she had known who would not come home, said bitterly to Simon, 'I hope they think it was worth it.'

'They always do, my love, until the next time.'

She shivered. 'Please God, there won't be a next time.'

Christmas of 1918 passed quietly. Everyone thought they ought to be happy at the end of the war but somehow, they couldn't. Too many people were still wearing black and the carol service had far too many old men and not enough young in the congregation.

Grace had one surprise though, because Billy had evidently written to the school and told them to send his daughter home. He had not told his sister and so the arrival of Marybeth, escorted by an old servant from the school, caused a surprise.

'How are you, my dear? I wasn't expecting you.'

The sweet face smiled angelically. 'Father wrote and said I could come home now, Aunt Grace. He had a marvellous report about me.'

'Yes, I saw it. I had better see about your room, and some food for your escort.'

It was the day after the Boxing Day Hunt, once again sadly depleted owing to the war, when three more visitors arrived. Grace began to feel she was living in a hotel and complained to Simon, 'Honestly, has no-one ever heard of telegrams?'

Billy was the first to arrive, just in time for lunch and pleased to see his daughter looking so well. 'School has improved you, my dear.'

The smiled widened. 'Thank you, Father, I'm happy you think so.'

Roddy and Maryjane arrived after lunch to stay for new year. Marybeth, noting her cousin's new hairdo and the smart little MG they drove up in, was seething.

'Marybeth, I didn't expect to see you here.' Maryjane was cool, the handshake just a formality.

'Father had such a good report about me, so he says I've finished school now. And you live in London?'

'Yes, we do.' There was a definite barrier there and Marybeth set herself to get over it.

'I hope I shall be able to see your home soon.'

'Possibly. Maryjane, we should go and wash.' Roddy's voice was also cool.

No matter, the girl thought. *We'll see.* She had decided that she would not live at Kingscourt again and needed a plan.

Her father, when approached about what was to happen to her, was vague. 'Well, you carry on living here, of course.

'I would like to live with you, Father. Just the two of us.' The winsome smile was in evidence.

'Not possible, my dear, as I'm in France.

She had anticipated he would return now the war was over but he shook his head. 'No, I'll be staying in France. I'm going to be based at Versailles for the peace negotiations.'

France! Marybeth caught her breath. She wanted to go too but was now smart enough not to blurt that out. This needed careful handling. She went off to think.

The solution came to her as she watched Maryjane and Roddy playing with the youngsters. *I know*, she thought, *I'll go and stay with them. It's not that far to Paris from London.*

She had the chance to talk to her cousin later, having decided to go and have tea in the nursery. There, she found her cousin talking to Nanny and waited patiently until she could get talk around to a visit to London.

'Maryjane, I should love to see your home.'

'Would you? Mother said she would come and stay for a day or two soon, you could come with her. I'll find you a nice hotel to stay in.'

This was not starting well. 'Couldn't I come and stay at your house?'

'It's a flat, Marybeth, so not possible.'

Marybeth had developed a cunning she would not have thought possible and so said quite innocently, 'But you have two bedrooms.'

'Mother will be staying in a hotel so you could too.'

She didn't say why, with a spare bedroom, her cousin couldn't stay and Marybeth, scenting a mystery, was more determined than ever.

Later that evening, dressing for dinner, it suddenly struck Maryjane what her cousin really wanted.

'Roddy, Marybeth wants to come and stay with us in London.'

'Don't like the sound of that. Tell me.'

So his wife told him and his first reaction was definite. 'No, she's not coming to stay with us. I couldn't put up with her and I don't want my wife at her beck and call all day.'

Maryjane smiled. 'I don't think I could put up with her either. But I wasn't thinking so much of that as…you remember, she read my letters. She might see papers… Something she's not supposed to.'

Their small spare bedroom had been turned into an office because sometimes, he brought work home. Though Maryjane had a 'daily', she always checked it herself and made sure there was nothing to be seen.

'My discreet wife.' He laughed as he kissed her. 'But you are right, my love, she couldn't be trusted. And I for one don't believe this 'new' person.'

'You don't?'

'No. Leopards don't change their spots. She's using that pretty face and some charming ways to get what she wants.'

He thought so again during dinner as he watched her talking to her father. *I shouldn't be surprised if she goes off the rails and does something but so long as she's not anywhere near Maryjane, I don't mind.*

The new year was toasted in and before they left, he found the opportunity to let Marybeth know that while she and Celia would be welcome to come and see them, staying was out of the question. She pouted and went off in a huff but Roddy smiled grimly as he watched her. *Definitely ready to go off the rails.*

***

The first few months of the year were quiet as everyone tried to adjust to a world of peace. Those who had survived the horrors came home, some wounded, some not but all were silent and withdrawn. Simon, interviewing them to see how they felt about coming back, was shocked and sad. He had felt the same after his war but he needed to know now who would want to come back to the land and who would not. Only then could he try and make plans for the future.

John, thinking about his future, had told his parents he wanted to join the newly established RAF. Celia was stunned and inclined to think they should refuse, but Hugo took it more calmly and only asked his son to consider it very carefully. John did, but still ended up going to Officer Training Camp.

Talking to Hugo at Easter, Simon decided to look for an agent and Hugo had another suggestion, 'What do you think about the telephone, Simon?'

'I've not given it a thought.'

'Well, think about it. Be good for us all to keep in touch especially now Maryjane is in London.'

Grace and Celia didn't need much convincing and very soon Grace, could head her letters "Exeter 21". The end of the war meant other changes too, as the last of the officers went home or back to the army and Grace made a momentous decision.

Robert had announced that he didn't want to go to university, he wasn't academic. He did, however, want to go to Cheltenham Agricultural College, much to his parents' surprise.

'Look Dad, Mum, I can be more use to Kingscourt if I know about farming and stuff. I really don't want to go to university.'

They discussed it all but finally, his parents gave in. It was no good trying to force the lad to do something he didn't want to, Simon sighed. And in the end he would inherit the estate so he was right to want to understand what was involved.

After many interviews, they finally found a land agent, Jonathan Anderson. He came with such impeccable references Simon asked why he wanted to move from the estate in Kent he was currently running.

'Sir Philip's only son died, sir, on the Somme. Sir Philip has decided to sell up and live abroad.'

'You could work for the new owners.'

The older man shook his head. 'No sir, the estate is to be developed for housing.'

'Is that Homes for Heroes? I read about it. A beautiful estate, if I say it myself. Building housing—while necessary—will destroy it. I couldn't stay there.'

'No, I see. Well, I am happy to employ you here. A house goes with the position, just a small cottage on the estate.'

'I'm sure it will be suitable, sir.'

Simon grinned. 'It used to be my house, so I expect it will be.'

'Your house, Mr Amory?'

'I came to Kingscourt after the Boer War as land agent to old Mr King. Then I married his daughter and moved into the big house.'

They talked of other matters but Simon's good fortune led to Hugo also interviewing someone, a man who Jonathan Anderson recommended.

'I don't mind telling you, Simon, I was very nervous interviewing Johnson.'

'He knew quite a lot about your situation though. Anderson told him.'

'He understands exactly what I want, and Mrs Bates in the village has offered him a bedroom and sitting room and all his meals. So that's quite a relief to me as I was worrying about where he would live. Thought I might have to build him something on the estate.'

Simon frowned. 'Mrs Bates? Her only son was killed at Ypres and I always thought the shock of it killed her husband for he died a few months later.'

Marybeth also had news, at Easter. She had a letter from her father that caused her to go straight to her aunts.

'Father wants me to go and stay with him. In Paris!' She was so excited she missed the look that passed between the sisters.

'So he will arrange a chaperone for you, and somewhere to live. When do you go?' Celia was matter of fact and Marybeth began to feel angry.

'I don't know. He hasn't said yet. Isn't it enough that I am to go to Paris! Paris!'

Grace smiled. 'Yes, my dear, very exciting. Your father had better give us warning though because you may need new clothes.'

After Marybeth had gone to lord it over the nursery with her news, the sisters were relieved.

'Once she's gone to France, we shall have some peace. It's time Billy took responsibility for her.'

It was the beginning of April and Jonathan Anderson was having tea with Grace and Simon, something she had started as a way of getting to know him better. Robert was also present and she decided it was time to put her idea to them.

'So, I've been thinking about how we live now compared to when Mother and Father were alive. All that entertaining, all those rooms, all the staff.'

'You wouldn't entertain again, Mrs Amory?'

'Not on the scale my parents did, no. And so, we should think about knocking the bachelor's wing down.'

Robert choked on his tea and Simon stared at her, a scone halfway to his mouth so that the jam he had liberally spread on it fell onto his plate.

'Knock it down!' Robert coughed and drank some tea.

Grace was not surprised, it was a radical suggestion but Jonathan Anderson shook his head sadly.

'I've heard some estates are being sold up.'

'Well, that's not happening here.' Simon was quite determined but his wife carried on.

'No, but listen, I've been around that wing. There are nine furnished bedrooms upstairs and sitting rooms on the ground floor. They've been shut up ever since the war and I don't see us ever using them again.'

'But knocking down! Surely not.' Simon put his scone back on the plate.

'Simon, you know we manage now with far less maids, and no footmen at all. I don't need empty rooms that need cleaning and I certainly don't want them just shut up and left.'

'I see your point, of course, but knocking down seems a bit extreme.'

'Will you think about it?'

'Yes, I'll think about it.'

She was satisfied with that, because her husband, while a traditionalist in many ways, was also practical. Grace knew it was radical, that some of the tenants would think it extreme, but she was determined on it.

May brought another visitor, one who Grace had heard was back in the village. James had been one of their footmen, one Merridew had once told her could make an excellent butler in time. Merridew, coming into her sitting room with coffee, mentioned that he was back.

'How is he, Merridew? He wasn't wounded, was he?

'No, Mrs Amory. He wants to know if you would take him on again as a footman.'

'Ah. How do you feel about that?'

'As the opportunity has come along, there is something I should like to talk to you about, madam.'

Grace was not her mother and sometimes she took a liberty.

'Please sit down, Merridew. I insist.'

The butler perched himself stiffly on the edge of a chair and spoke with an effort, 'It has been in my mind for some time to retire.'

That she was shocked was evident. 'Retire, Merridew?'

'Yes indeed, madam. I'm not as young as I was but the late Mr King was so generous to me, giving me a house on the estate. Also, of course, there is Mrs Mills.'

What he was going to say next flashed into her mind. 'You want to get married.'

'It has always been understood, madam.'

'And do you think James would be a suitable replacement for you? Not that anyone could ever replace you, Merridew.'

'Kind of you to say so, madam. He is young, of course, but I always thought he had the makings of a good butler. The kind of life you and Major Amory will have will be very different.'

Merridew knew that the kind of large-scale entertaining Silas King had indulged in would not return because Grace had already discussed it with him.

There seemed no point in asking him to think it over, as it was obvious he had made his mind up and so Grace asked him to bring James in.

'James, how good to see you again. How are you?'

'Well, thank you, Mrs Amory.'

'Merridew tells me you are asking about a position as footman.'

'Yes madam. I have been discharged from the army now and am back living with my mother.'

'I have no footmen now, only maids.'

James Mostyn fiddled with his cap. 'You couldn't have just one footman, of course.'

Merridew was pleased that his young protegee understood the nuance.

'No, but I have another proposition for you.'

'Anything, Mrs Amory.'

'How would you like to be my butler?

An astonished young man glanced at Merridew.

'But...what about...Mr Merridew?'

Grace glanced at the older man. 'You can tell him, Merridew.'

The plan was agreed after Grace had explained that there would be no grand entertaining on her parents' scale and Merridew had promised that he would always be on hand for help and advice.

'And there will be no question of the Feast this year, as Father...it will be a year on that day.'

'He had such a presence, even for the staff, that the family must miss him very much.' Mostyn had always revered Silas King since the day, long ago now, when as a young lad he had come to the 'big house' and found it so very daunting. Sitting in the stable yard after supper one evening, head in his hands and feeling so very alone, he had felt a tap on his shoulder and looked up to see the master of the house coming to say goodnight to his favourite horse. The short talk that had followed had made such a difference and James had resolved to do his best and not disappoint his employer.

'It was a shock, yes, but at least it was peaceful. Now, we must see about you settling in and introducing you to the family.'

Grace was pleased to have solved one problem, but another loomed. Mrs Mills! However was she to find a replacement for the woman who had been her right hand during the war years?

While Grace fretted and Celia and Hugo made planned for spending more time at The Risings, Simon had a letter one morning that puzzled him. Jonathan Anderson, coming in with Robert after looking at a tenant's cottage, was handed the letter and told to read it.

'Doesn't tell us much, Major Amory. William Wright. A Cambridge college.'

Robert glanced at it. 'Wants a meeting. Something confidential to discuss. Sounds exciting, Dad.'

Simon looked at his diary and sighed. 'He had better come next week; make a note, Anderson. We'll say Thursday, and he'll have to stay overnight.'

He forgot about their visitor until the following week when, on Thursday morning, Grace had a telephone call from Hugo. Celia was not well and he had called the doctor.

'I'll come over now, Hugo. Robert can drive me.'

Going into the library to tell her husband, she found Jonathan Anderson and Robert.

'Robert, can you drive me over to The Risings? Celia's not well and Hugo has called the doctor.'

'Grace, we have a visitor coming to stay. I'm sorry, I forgot to let you know.'

'A visitor? Who?'

'Chap name of Wright, coming from Cambridge. I told him he could stay overnight.'

'I'll tell Mostyn but I really must go now.'

The doctor came and diagnosed influenza, which led to a minor panic and frantic telephone calls. Maryjane was told, John was warned not to come home from OTC and Grace told Simon he would have to manage their visitor himself.

Simon, greeting William Wright sometime later, thought that he looked vaguely familiar. *A typical academic*, he thought as he introduced his son and agent, *slightly shabby, a pocket full of what looked like books.*

Over coffee they chatted until Robert, consumed with curiosity, asked the question. 'We were most intrigued by your letter, Mr Wright.'

Their visitor swallowed the last of his coffee and smiled. 'It was a matter I felt could not be conveyed on paper.' His voice had a slight foreign twang and Simon began to wonder if he had met him before.

'Have we met before, Mr Wright?'

The older man smiled. 'I am not surprised you do not remember, Major Amory. I was here very briefly with some other men.'

At once Simon remembered. 'You were the detainees!'

'Yes. My name was William Frietel then but after the war, I decided to become more English and changed my name. I was sorry to hear about the death of your father-in-law. Mr King was very polite to us and we were well treated here. More so than in some other places we were put.'

Simon, remembering his father-in-law's determination to have them housed as far away as possible, had the grace to blush slightly. 'Thank you. It was sudden, but very peaceful. We always felt that you were all misplaced as agricultural workers. I seem to remember you were an academic.'

'I lecture in botany. That is why I have come to see you. Are you aware that you have a rare plant on your land?'

'No, tell us more.'

So William Wright happily launched on his favourite subject, explained all about wet meadows and Oakley's Bottom.

'I was lucky enough to see the plant when I was working here. It does not flower every year and as it is usually found only in calciferous open grassland, I cannot imagine how it can grow here. Your land is wet and marshy but definitely not chalky.'

Over lunch, he explained his mission. In Cambridge lived an elderly gentleman, wealthy and very reclusive with a great interest in rare plants. He had offered to finance an expedition to search wetlands and marshy areas to see if any rare plants could be found. William Wright, thinking of Oakley's Bottom, had approached this gentleman and talked to him of it. He had been asked to approach them and see if they would consider selling the land.

'No, it is part of the estate. We will not sell.' Simon's first quick decision was followed by a more considered view from his agent.

'How much land were you thinking of, Mr Wright?'

'The whole of Oakley's Bottom. I should think it covers about an acre. Our patron is prepared to pay handsomely should you decide to sell, but he does insist that the whole matter be kept quiet.'

'We should think about it, Dad. No point being too hasty,' Robert put his view.

'Let's finish lunch and then perhaps we could all drive over and take a look around. I'm sure Mr Wright will be able to stay the night.'

They drove out to the field in Robert's new car and looked around. William Wright was pleased to see his memory was exact and he pointed out the area to Jonathan Anderson. It was getting towards dinner before they arrived back, to find a message from Grace saying that Celia was getting worse.

For some time, Celia was very ill and Grace telephoned to give Mostyn some garbled instructions. It soon became clear this would not work and meals became haphazard. Mostyn, confiding in his mentor, said that the household organisation was going to the dogs. Quite how London heard of this no-one knew, but one morning, Maryjane turned up unannounced to 'help out'.

'It's very good of you, my dear.' Simon kissed her gently. 'Can Roddy spare you?'

'Don't worry, Uncle Simon. This is a family emergency after all, so of course, he said I must come. Now I must see Mrs Mills.'

Within a very short time, everything was back to normal and Maryjane, pleased to be back in her old home but missing her husband, organised everything just as her aunt would.

Grace, telephoning every morning, was grateful. 'It's such a relief, my dear, to know you are there.'

'How's Mother, Aunt Grace?'

'The doctor says she is no worse but I can't see it myself. Hugo and I are taking it in turns to sit with her but I'm not sure she knows we are here.'

Maryjane gripped the receiver and swallowed. 'I'll stay here until she is better, Aunt. Roddy is quite firm that I should.'

Billy chose this moment to ring and see if Marybeth could travel to Paris. Maryjane, struggling with the thought that her mother might die and missing her husband, was somewhat short.

'No, Uncle Billy, I haven't time to spare organising that. Mother is very ill and Aunt Grace is at The Risings. I'm here to run Kingscourt but as for anything else, it's impossible.'

Billy grumbled somewhat, 'I should have thought you would be glad to get rid of her as you've never liked her.'

'That has nothing to do with this. We are all worried sick about Mother, she might die, and no-one has the time to escort Marybeth anywhere. You'll have to make your own arrangements.'

The old Maryjane would have turned sick at the thought of saying this, but marriage and moving to London had matured her.

'Oh, very well.' He rang off in a huff.

Celia rallied and began to recover but Grace came home looking exhausted. Both husband put their heads together and decided it was time their wives had a holiday so Maryjane found herself being politely asked if she would stay another two weeks. Naturally, both sisters immediately said they didn't need a holiday but found themselves overruled because the hotel was already booked and Maryjane, not entirely happy, had agreed to stay and carry on running the house.

Before the sisters had finished packing, Roddy arrived on a weekend leave and Billy sent Marybeth's new companion, Mrs Rodgers, escorted by someone the family only heard about later. Maryjane and Roddy, on being introduced to the new companion, both had the same thought and compared notes as they dressed for dinner.

'She's not that much older than Marybeth. They'll get into all sorts of trouble. Billy won't bother supervising them too much,' Maryjane spoke soberly.

Her husband was pessimistic. 'I was surprised at how young she seems to be. Paris! Full of temptations.'

Mrs Rodgers did not improve on further acquaintance and at dinner that evening, she showed signs of a fondness for wine, which alarmed Simon. It was customary for the ladies to have a small glass of wine followed by water, something Mary King had established and Grace had always kept up. Mrs Rodgers, however, with a titter that was already beginning to irritate Simon, asked for another glass of wine.

'Such an excellent meal, Mrs Allen. It deserves to be washed down with this wonderful German wine.'

Mostyn, waiting behind her, ground his teeth. The woman was an idiot not to recognise the best French wine but he blandly refilled her glass.

Marybeth seemed in raptures over her new friend and told Maryjane that she wasn't taking too many clothes with her, Mrs Rodgers seemed to think some of her dresses were too out of fashion and she must buy some more in Paris. Maryjane, ordering trunks down from the attics, thought at least they would not have to wait too long before 'getting rid of her', as she phrased it to herself.

'What would you like me to do with your old clothes, Marybeth?'

'Give them to the poor, my dears. Such a treat for them.' Mrs Rodgers laughed.

'What a good idea. Yes Maryjane, give them to the poor.'

Maryjane waved them off with relief and turned to Roddy. 'She told me to give her old clothes to the poor. Such a treat for them.' She mimicked Mrs Rodgers' artificial tone so exactly he smiled.

'And will you?'

'Certainly not. Sometimes we send some meat, and eggs and butter if the older people are ill, but the tenants wouldn't thank me for trying to fob them off with clothes.'

So Maryjane packed all the unwanted dresses into two trunks and had them sent to the attics. Marybeth's bedroom was then turned out and spring-cleaned and she could report, when her aunt and mother turned up again, that everything was in order.

Grace, tanned and fit after two weeks of doing nothing, was especially grateful. Her mother, looking thin but much better, hugged her.

'Now my dear, time to get back to your husband. It has been wonderful of Roddy to do without you for so long but time now for you to go.'

Simon was the first of the family to hear Billy's arrangement for looking after Nether Bassett and he lost no time in discussing them at one of their Tuesday evening dinners.

These had been an idea of Celia's that every Tuesday evening, the sisters and their husbands gathered at The Risings for dinner and a game of cards.

'Apparently, his name is Snyder and he is Billy's new agent.'

Hugo, sipping his wine, asked the obvious question, 'Do we know anything about him?'

'Not much. He served under Billy during the war, Billy seems to think he can manage the estate.'

'Seems to think?'

Simon smiled. 'I have been talking to old Mr Haskins, the father of young William Haskins.'

Everyone smiled, because young William must have been at least seventy so no-one knew exactly how old his father was.

'Seriously, according to the old man, this chap Snyder has absolutely no idea how to run so much as a chicken coop. The estate, he says, will go to ruin.'

'I suppose Billy will say he has too much on to keep a close eye on anything.'

'Well, if he doesn't and old Mr Haskins is right, the estate will go to ruin. And it borders us, so I had better ask Anderson to keep a sharp eye on our borders.'

They had just settled down again when Simon received another letter from William Wright, asking him to Cambridge for a few days to meet the reclusive gentleman.

Grace, who had missed all the news, heard it all and was agreeably surprised. 'A rare plant! Whatever would Father have said? What does Mr Wright say?'

'That he is inviting us to Cambridge, he mentions Robert and Anderson, for a few days. His patron wants to meet us.'

'When shall you go?'

'In a week or two. There will be no Kings Feast this year as it is the anniversary of the guv?'

'No, not this year. Maryjane tells me she and Roddy are going to spend their first anniversary in Brighton so we shan't see them.'

At the end of June, Simon took his son and agent off to Cambridge for a few days and were met at the station by William Wright, who look them off to the hotel he had organised. Later that afternoon, he talked to them about his patron.

'Mr Chalmers, an intelligent gentleman with a great interest in plants. His library is quite magnificent. He wishes to meet you so I have arranged for you to go for lunch tomorrow.'

'Does he live alone?'

'No, his granddaughter lives with him. I will collect you at eleven and we'll drive over from there.'

The next morning, he was punctual and the four men drove to the Larches, a large imposing residence just outside Cambridge on the road to Kings Lynn. The butler announced them in precise order and Robert, going in behind his father, saw him shaking hands with a tall slim girl crowned by the most glorious red hair.

Robert, shaking hands politely, thoughts her the most beautiful girl he had ever seen. She offered them coffee but before it could be served, an elderly gentleman, reference book in hand, entered.

'Juliet, my dear, listen to this. This plant was mentioned in the transactions of the Linnean society, considered rare in 1815 and thought to be extinct. Orchis militaris—'

'Grandfather, we have visitors.' She smiled at him affectionately and Theo Chalmers shut his book at once.

'Forgive me, gentlemen. You must be Major Amory, who is so fortunate as to own the land where this jewel lives.'

Robert started slightly, it was so exactly what he had been thinking himself. He shook hands feeling dazed and mentally shook himself and listened to the conversation. That Mr Chalmers was an authority on his subject was not doubted, he quoted extensively without even looking at a book and after lunch finally asked the question, 'So, Major Amory, will you consider selling your land?'

Simon hesitated. 'No part of the estate has ever been sold, though my late father-in-law gifted about a hundred acres to my brother and sister-in-law in his will. I had never thought of selling any part of it.'

'Hmmm. Well, it is your choice but I am prepared to be quite generous, as Mr Wright knows. This plot of land is naturally not capable of cultivation, it is far too marshy and boggy.'

'No, my father-in-law always intended to drain the land when he inherited but there were one or two bad harvests and he had a young family, so such an expensive project was abandoned.'

'I must say I am excessively glad of it. This plant must be preserved in its natural habitat.'

'I will think about it seriously, Mr Chalmers, and may I let you know in a month or two?'

'Let Mr Wright know, and he will contact me. I should be glad if you would give it your most urgent and serious attention.'

They were waved off by Juliet Chalmers and Robert for one was sorry to say goodbye to her.

***

July passed and on the anniversary of Silas King's death, the family gathered at church for a small service and afterwards, they all had lunch.

Maryjane wrote that they had enjoyed their trip to Brighton and would Mother please come and see the flat now it was finished. Celia was soon on the telephone to Grace and arranging for them to go to London for a couple of days.

Marybeth wrote a rambling letter from Paris, full of the dresses she had bought and how many people she had met. There was very little about Billy and she did not ask how anyone was, nor mention the anniversary of her grandfather's death.

It was September before the family heard anything more of Marybeth and that was only indirectly. Mrs Hill, who Grace had never cared for but Mary King had always liked, went to London for a family wedding and picked up some gossip that she lost no time in relaying to Grace.

She invited herself to tea one afternoon and told Grace with relish all she had heard.

'Fast, Mrs Amory, is the only word to describe her. The tales I have been told would make your hair curl, and Mary King would turn in her grave at what her granddaughter has been up to.'

'What has she been up to, Mrs Hill?'

'This companion of hers, a widow. Doesn't act like a widow. Fond of a drink. And they have been going to parties and dances.'

'Marybeth was bored during the war because it was quiet and dull here, so maybe she is letting off a little steam.'

'Steam! It sounds to me as if she has become a flirt, and that's something that should be nipped in the bud. She'll never find a respectable young man if she has a reputation.'

So Grace discussed it all with Celia but they came to the same conclusion: it was Billy's problem and he must deal with it. They forgot all about it in the excitement of their London trip to see Roddy and Maryjane. The flat was perfect and they all had lunch together with Maryjane's neighbour.

Roddy took them to the theatre one evening and Celia and Grace went to see Buckingham Palace and 10 Downing Street. All in all, it was a very good visit and it was with some regret that they waved goodbye to Maryjane at Paddington and went home.

In November, Maryjane and Mrs James decided to go to the dedication of the Cenotaph and saw the king and queen. Roddy was working but had a full account of it all later, including what the royal ladies were wearing.

'Thank you for that, my love, I am most interested in what Her Majesty was wearing.'

Maryjane laughed. 'Alright, I know when my audience isn't interested. I shall tell Mother and Aunt Grace when we go for Christmas.'

Arriving on Christmas Eve just in time for the carol service, Maryjane at last had a rapt audience for her recollections of the day. Simon had been approached by some of the tenants who wanted a war memorial built in the village as they had seen in the newspapers so many towns and villages were doing. So many young men were not brought home and Simon felt it would be the right way to mark their lives, and so he and Hugo, together with one or two of the young men who had come back, formed a small committee to see how they could do it.

So that Christmas of 1919, there was plenty to talk about and as the new year was rung in, everyone looked forward to another year of peace.

***

In January, Grace at last got her wish and Simon agreed that the bachelor's wing should be demolished. He had walked around it with Grace and found, as she had, that there were so many rooms they would never use again, all dust-sheeted and depressing.

'I have to agree with you, my dear, I never gave it a thought. You are right to make this radical suggestion.'

'Thank you, Simon. I'm not just doing this at random or on a whim. You know we'll never reach the heights of Father's entertaining. I've no wish to, to be honest. There's more than enough room for us and for people to come and stay.

So Robert's 17th birthday in February saw a small party to celebrate and they decided that Easter would be the best time for the demolition to begin.

'We can give all the furniture to the cottage hospital or the village.'

Simon had made another decision, one that pleased his son immensely, though he would not admit it. 'As your mother has made a decision about the house, I have made one about the estate. We should go and see Mr Chalmers again and talk about selling Oakley's Bottom.'

'You think so, Dad? I thought so at once but it's your decision.'

'We need to talk to Anderson, and while we do, look at the estate map.'

Easter brought Roddy and Maryjane for a visit and to watch Robert ceremonially swing a hammer at the first window.

'The old bachelor's wing,' Roddy reminisced. 'That was my room, four along from the right.'

Maryjane laughed. 'So long ago it seems now. Aunt Grace was telling me she has been working like mad on the rooms. Apparently, she hired several ladies from the village and they have been sorting through the furniture and bits and pieces.'

He frowned. 'I remember my room was hopelessly crowded with loads of pictures on the walls and not enough space in the wardrobe to hang my dress uniform.'

'That was the old Victorian idea.' A more modern Maryjane thought of their own small flat, with just one or two pictures on the walls and no ornaments at all.

After Easter was over and letters had been exchanged, Simon, Hugo and Jonathan Anderson descended on Cambridge and arranged to meet the old gentleman. William Wright was happy to go along so Robert had the chance to meet Juliet Chalmers once again.

He was pleased to see that his recollection of her had been wrong; she was much more beautiful than he remembered. The estate maps were rolled out and gone over and William Wright, at the gentleman's suggestion, agreed to go once again to Kingscourt and look carefully over the side. The sum of money Mr Chalmers suggested seemed staggering to them, but he was quite firm about it.

'I wish everything to be done in a certain style, Major Amory, and am quite prepared to pay for it. Now, Mr Anderson, explain to me again about the boundaries.'

Juliet, going to ring for coffee, smiled at Robert.

'They don't seem to need us, Mr Amory.'

'I've already discussed it with my father, and he knows exactly how the land to be sold should be sectioned off. If your grandfather agrees, we will be able to sell.'

'I wish my grandfather could see it for himself,' she spoke wistfully.

'He seldom goes out?'

'No, not much. But I feel this would be so good for him.'

At that moment, an idea popped into Robert's head but he said nothing over coffee nor afterwards when they left.

When they were home and Grace had been told all about the meeting and that William Wright would be coming to stay for two days, she said exactly what Robert was thinking, 'Such a shame Mr Chalmers can't come and stay. To see what he is buying.'

'I did wonder, Mother…should we ask him to come and stay for a few days? I know he doesn't go out much but perhaps, if you wrote to him…'

Grace smiled at her son. 'It might be a good idea, Robert, but can I please get rid of the builders first and recover from the demolition works? At the moment, we are knee-deep in rubble and dust.'

'I never thought of that. Yes, of course, we can wait.'

The builders eventually removed themselves and the rubble and they were left with a very untidy-looking side wall and a lot of bare earth. Grace decided a herb garden would be just the thing. As a child she had loved looking at pictures of Elizabethan gardens and had found a book about alpine gardens in the library.

By now of course, it was June and time to be thinking about the Feast and so the idea of visitors was shelved. They had tidied up the odd-looking gable end wall but even so, during the Feast, they were all asked continually how much more of the house they would be demolishing. Grace had just endured Mrs Hill asking what she thought Silas King would say when Mrs Haskins approached her.

'Mrs Amory, such a lovely day and what a wonderful feast. Just like the old days.'

'Thank you, Mrs Haskins. Are you enjoying it?'

'Yes, my dear. It's such a shame this will be the last one for us.'

'The last one? Why?'

'We are leaving Old Barrow farm.'

Grace was shocked. The Haskins had farmed Old Barrow, which was on Billy's land, for at least three generations and it had always been the practice, since old Sir John died, that the tenants of Nether Bassett attended the Feast.

'Why? Are you ill? How is old Mr Haskins?'

'It's his decision but we support him. Ask Mr Anderson about it.'

She had no further chance to say anything but later in the evening when they all gathered for a drink, she took the opportunity. Jonathan Anderson and John Johnson had been at the Feast and were invited to stay for drinks afterwards.

'So, Mr Anderson, please explain to me why the Haskins family are leaving Old Barrow.'

Celia choked. 'Leaving! Are they ill?'

There was a silence before anyone spoke and it was Simon who answered, 'No, they're not ill. They can't farm any more, under the new regime.'

'What new regime?' Hugo asked calmly.

The agent coughed. 'The agent at Nether Bassett is putting in place a lot of new rules and of course, the older farmers are unhappy.'

Simon helped him out. 'When you run an estate like this, you always look a year or two ahead.'

'The thing is mother, Snyder isn't doing that. He's just looking at making the most money as quickly as possible. Also…' he paused '…he's moved into the big house.'

There was a stunned silence before Simon spoke slowly, 'Of course, there is no agent's house at Nether Bassett but still…'

John Johnson, who had never been heard to express an opinion, was scathing, 'Then he looks for accommodation in the village. I never heard of such a thing before. An agent living in the master's house.' His tone was shocked.

Hugo, full of food and geniality, looked at his agent and was satisfied. First-rate chap, Johnson, felt just as he should on the things that mattered. And Hugo knew he was happy in the village because he had taken the trouble to go and see Mrs Bates and make sure she was content with her lodger.

The enormity of the agent's action shocked everyone and put a damper on the rest of the evening. Soon after, everyone went their separate ways.

***

Grace had not forgotten Robert's suggestion and she wrote to Mr Chalmers inviting him to come and stay at Kingscourt. Before he could reply, Marybeth turned up with Mrs Rodgers in tow and by the time Mr Chalmers replied, Grace could only be relieved that he had refused her invitation.

All during September, both sisters heard tales of late night music blaring out and Marybeth declaring that the house was positively primitive and needed a complete make-over. Hawkes, Sir John's ancient butler, was told that he was positively gothic in his ideas and gave his notice. Very soon, Grace and Celia had maids in tears asking if they had any vacancies for maids.

The sisters, comparing notes, decided that there were so many things Marybeth was positive about. And what would she say about the agent living in the house?

Simon gave the answer to that one because, surveying his boundary with Anderson, they had met Mr Snyder. At least, they assumed it was the agent, but he did not introduce himself, merely grunted that this was private land and they were trespassing.

'This is my land, sir, and I am definitely not trespassing.' Simon's voice was clipped.

Immediately, the man's air changed and he touched his cap in a servile manner, which set Jonathan Anderson's teeth on edge.

'Beg pardon, Major Amory. I didn't know as it was you.'

'Now you do.' They turned the horses and cantered off and for a while, nothing was said.

It was his agent who eventually broke the silence, 'So that was Mr Snyder.' There was a world of scorn in his voice. 'Was it just my imagination, Major Amory, or did he look as if he had been sleeping rough?'

'I noticed that too. A certain air of...shabbiness. Didn't look as if he had shaved either. If he had been any kind of agent, he should at least have come and introduced himself to you. And also Johnson.'

'In fairness, The Risings' land does not border on Nether Bassett but you are right. In my last post, I knew each of the land agents who managed the surrounding land; indeed, we sometimes had dinner together to discuss all sorts of things.'

'As I believe you and Johnson do?'

'Yes, John and I have dinner from time to time. He does sometimes ask my advice.'

'Mr Hugo is not a countryman born and bred, as he would be the first to admit. My father-in-law's decision to leave him some land did throw him into something of a panic. It's good that Johnson has you to talk to.'

Telling this to Grace and Robert later, Simon summed it up neatly, 'It looks as if Marybeth has thrown him out. Anderson said he looked as if he had been sleeping rough.'

'Sounds like something Marybeth would do.'

The autumn wore on and one afternoon, a smart little car came up the drive in a cloud of dust, out of which stepped Marybeth and Mrs Rodgers, both dressed to the hilt. Grace, glancing out of her sitting room window, summed them up in a phrase her mother would have used: 'Totally out of place in the country dressed like that.'

Still, when they were announced, she had them shown into the saloon and tea was served.

'So Marybeth, how are you enjoying Paris?'

'Um…I'm known as Beth now, Aunt Grace.'

Mrs Rodgers gave her usual annoying titter. 'Beth is so much more modern, don't you think, Mrs Amory? Marybeth is so old-fashioned.'

Grace's normally warm voice was cold, 'The only Beth King I knew was my much loved and missed sister, Marybeth's mother.'

She had the satisfaction of seeing the companion blush but was pleased when Robert came in shortly after.

'Hello Marybeth.'

'Cousin Robert, how are you. Let me introduce my companion, Mrs Rodgers.'

Robert shook hands politely but thought that his cousin looked ridiculous. However, he tried to make small talk. 'So, is this the latest Paris fashion, Marybeth?'

She smoothed the silk dress complacently. 'Yes, isn't it lovely. So modern.'

'Certainly modern for around here.' Mrs Rodgers thought she detected a hint of criticism.

'Nether Bassett is certainly not modern. We have been quite shocked, haven't we, my dear, at how primitive it is.'

'Oh yes, everywhere so dusty and old-fashioned.'

'It has been shut up since aunt Louisa died, of course. The maids came here to help me so everything was covered up.'

'They're useless as maids. I've told them to smarten up their ideas or leave. I have an interior decorator coming from London soon.'

If she had hoped to shock her aunt, Marybeth could not have done it more completely. Good manners compelled Grace to carry on the conversation but as soon as the car swept off down the drive, she was on the telephone to Celia immediately.

'An interior decorator!' Her sister was dumbfounded.

'I know. I couldn't believe it either.'

But it seemed it was true and Mrs Haskins, paying a farewell visit to Grace, gave a first-hand account of the man from London.

'Mrs Amory, the suit he came in! I thought he was some Bond Street swell. And he walks like this.' Mrs Haskins minced across the room until Grace began to laugh.

'My William said there was a word for men like him. If he was a man.' Grace was not such a country mouse as not to understand the implication; after all, there was the author who lived just outside the village with his "friend".

Grace said goodbye with regret to Mrs Haskins and turned to thinking about next week's harvest festival and then it would be Christmas. Where was the year going?

She did not see her niece again but the village grapevine told her what happened next. The smart interior decorator had told her he could renovate the whole place but it would be cheaper to knock it down. The sum he mentioned was whispered in the village but Grace heard it and wondered whether that was why Mr Snyder was trying to wring every penny out of the estate.

Whether Marybeth wrote to her father, they never knew but apparently, Marybeth was summoned back to Paris. Everything was once again put into dust sheets and old Hawkes told to stay there and look after things.

With no-one to gossip about, the village once again settled down to the usual round of harvest festival and bonfire night. The Remembrance weekend also saw the dedication of the war memorial, the plaque listing the names in the country was the same.

Christmas was a quiet holiday, not the usual merrymaking they had enjoyed before the war.

Chapter 10

The new year of 1921 saw all the family gathered and it was quite like old times with so much coming and going. The Boxing Day Hunt was a great success and on New Year's Eve, Ed and Fred invited all the adults to a 'soiree' in the great hall at tea time.

They were lively boys and after the last of their antics, Hugo had decided it was time for them to go away to school. Fred was the elder by a few minutes but it was always Ed who got them into scrapes, he was a natural leader. After the incident with the gunpowder, their father told them sternly that enough was enough and they were going to school. They came home for the holidays but didn't seem very much tamed, though Fred was showing signs of being academic.

All morning, the hall had been 'off limits' to everyone and the boys and the estate carpenter were heard banging and hammering away. The sisters were having coffee in the sitting room but Grace was fretting.

'I hope they aren't damaging the floor or the panelling. Some of it is quite valuable.'

Maryjane, on a New Year visit with Roddy, was calm.

'Don't worry, Aunt Grace. Not only is Jenks with them but Roddy has been commandeered to help as well.'

Her mother smiled. 'Well, we can stop worrying then but I hope Roddy doesn't mind.'

Maryjane almost grinned. 'It was more a case of Roddy putting them in a position where they couldn't refuse. After Father had a word with him.'

The sisters began to laugh. 'How very like Hugo.' Grace wiped her eyes.

The 'soiree' turned out of be a mini theatre complete with arches and a backdrop, in front of which John, Ed, Fred and Eliza performed a comic play. When the curtain was pulled back to show the little theatre, Grace's eyes flew to the floor but Jenks had cleverly made some hollow casters for the base and

Roddy had suggested felt squares as well. The play was a great success and Eliza began to think that being an actress might be fun.

It was nearing Robert's birthday before Grace heard again from Juliet Chalmers. They had been writing to each other for some time before Grace found out she was fond of gardening and of course, she had mentioned her idea for a herb garden. The long letter was full of advice but reading it through the second time she was still puzzled. An idea popped into her head and at dinner that evening, watching her son, she mentioned it.

'I've had a letter from Juliet Chalmers about my herb garden.'

'How is she? And her grandfather?' Robert did not blush and hand and voice were steady as he spoke.

'She is well but the old gentleman has a cold that won't clear up. Anyway, her letter is interesting but some of it I can't follow. I was thinking of asking her to come down for a couple of days.'

Simon was doubtful. 'She might not want to leave her grandfather if he is ill.'

'No, maybe not. I'll reply and ask how he is and suggest a visit when he's better. I'm sure it won't be too dull for her and you can always drive her around, Robert.'

Her son glanced sharply at his mother but her face seemed innocent enough. His father, however, later that evening in their bedroom, was firm.

'No matchmaking, Grace.'

'I'm not. I do need some help and if I'm wrong, no-one will be any wiser.'

Old Mr Chalmers improved and though he didn't feel up to a visit, he was quite willing for his granddaughter to go and so the day before his birthday, Robert drove to the station to pick up their guest. She looked, in his eyes at least, quite as beautiful as ever but he maintained a studied polite air.

'It's good to see you again, Miss Chalmers. I'm pleased your grandfather is better.'

She smiled. 'Such a lovely part of the country, Mr Amory, I almost envy you. Cambridge is so very…flat.'

'No-one could accuse us of being flat. I know you are here to help my mother with her garden but if you have a spare hour and the weather holds, we could have a picnic.'

She considered gravely before he carried on, 'My cousin Maryjane and her husband are here for the birthday celebrations so we could make up a party.'

'That would be very agreeable but it depends how your mother and I progress in the garden. I told the porter at the station to be very careful with the large tin trunk. I hope he remembers.'

'Jenks will. His brother is our estate carpenter and they're both very good men.'

He said no more but when the trunk was delivered, to his surprise Juliet Chalmers said it should be left in the hall. He had assumed she had brought lots of clothes with her for what was a short visit.

After tea he discovered why, because their guest had brought some plants to begin Grace's garden. When the lid was opened, they saw eight plants, all packed in straw, and Grace was delighted.

'How very kind of you, Miss Chalmers. This will be a wonderful start for my garden. When can we see about planting them?'

'They really should be put somewhere to recover from the journey.'

'Mother, why not consult Batch? He'll be interested as well.'

So the old gardener was summoned and came into the hall just, he told his old crony Mr Williams later over a pint in the pub, as if he were a guest.

'Fair gave me a turn, I can tell you. All these years I've never been into the front of the house.' He took a long swig of beer.

'So what about these plants then?'

'Some kind of herbs, apparently Elizabethan.'

His friend said dryly, 'They must be pretty old then.'

But Batch was too full of his visit to be drawn into the kind of exchange they normally had and Ted Williams resigned himself to a half hour of gardening.

The morning of Robert's birthday dawned bright but cold and at his mother's suggestion, he took Maryjane, Roddy and Juliet Chalmers for a drive around the estate before they had lunch overlooking Tom's Field. Mrs Hughes, the cook Grace had with much difficulty found, had provided so much food that Roddy suggested a walk before they went back.

Roddy and Maryjane soon wandered off and at last, he was alone with her.

'How very kind of you to bring Mother a present. When will you plant them?'

'Grandfather said they would need a day or two so Batch is keeping an eye on them. We thought, perhaps tomorrow.'

'When will they begin to start...do herb gardens flower?'

'The plants themselves will be colourful but perhaps not 'in flower' as you would expect. I think by July, when you have the Kings Feast your mother has been telling me about.'

'That's good. Give everyone something else to look at. We usually have games for the children but entertaining the adults is sometimes harder.'

'It sounds quite interesting.'

'Can be. Mother might invite you and Mr Chalmers down, if your grandfather can travel. I understand from Mr Wright that he doesn't go out much.'

'Not much, no, but he is passionate about gardens so he might be persuaded to come and have a look. I have talked to him about it at length; indeed, he selected the plants I brought down.'

Roddy and Maryjane strolled back just at this moment and it was agreed that they pack up and head back before the afternoon grew colder. In the evening, his parents had decided, instead of a formal dinner, to have a buffet supper for the tenants and their families and some of their neighbours.

The great hall had been cleared and the fire was well alight, the saloon had been laid out with tables and the buffet, crowned by an enormous cake, was laid in the adjoining room. Everyone agreed Grace had done a splendid job and as Robert came downstairs, he found all the tenants making a corridor for him to pass through, to general applause.

Juliet Chalmers, standing next to Maryjane, looked surprised.

'It's because he's the heir. The future of the estate. They look to the family for their homes and livelihoods. I know my cousin though, this would never go to his head.'

Robert was far too polite to ignore the tenants but after all, Juliet Chalmers was his mother's guest and he made sure she had a plate of food from the buffet and a glass of punch. He danced with each of the tenant's wives and daughters until his mother came over with a glass of lemonade.

'Robert, my dear, I think you should ask Miss Chalmers to dance. She knows no-one here and is our guest.'

'Very well, Mother.' But he did not look too unhappy at the idea.

Simon, coming to claim a dance with his wife, glanced at his son and then back to his wife.

She whispered in his ear, 'He likes her but she is a little harder to read.'

They young couple, dancing sedately together, were also talking.

'Do the tenants get invited here a lot, Mr Amory?'

'Not a lot, no. Couldn't you call me Robert?'

She hesitated before trying it out. 'Robert.'

'May I call you…Juliet?'

She smiled. 'Yes. So this kind of gathering is not usual.'

'It's because of my birthday. Normally they are invited for the Kings Feast, the Yule Log ceremony and on Christmas Eve for punch and mince pies after the carol services.'

'Are all these families your tenants?'

'Not all. They bring their children, you see, some of whom don't work on the estate but when Mother issues an invitation, it is understood that it includes all their families. Makes for a jolly time. But I am pleased we didn't have the usual dinner. A bit stuffy for me if I have to make small talk with the county people I don't see very often.'

'You don't mix with the county?'

'Not much. There's so much to do here and I'm still at Cheltenham. I have two friends from school I keep in touch with, I go to see them and they come here every few months. Trouble with the county is they are stuffed shirts. Thank goodness Dad and Mother aren't like that.'

'How stuffy?' The dance ended, they applauded and carried on into the next dance.

'Look at the Cartwrights, standing next to Mother. The large lady in red.'

Juliet followed his eye and saw a majestic figure standing beside a small thin man.

'Is that her husband?'

'Yes. They would have liked a formal dinner, processing in and toasts, bridge or small talk after. Of course, we had to invite the neighbours but Mother said as it was my birthday, we should do something more suitable for me.'

'Are your friends here?'

'Bunny is. I'll introduce you.'

'Bunny?'

'Edward Charles. At school, we were known as Bobby and Bunny.'

Juliet Chalmers, taken unawares, laughed spontaneously and half the dance floor looked at them. It was a joyous unaffected laugh and several people found themselves smiling as well, though they had no idea why.

Simon, dancing with his wife, saw that the young lady was not quite so aloof as he had first thought. Mrs Cartwright, however, looked put out and Juliet, seeing her face, sobered at once.

'I have upset Mrs Cartwright by being too happy.'

Robert blushed slightly and coughed.

'Fact is, she hopes I will marry her daughter. That's Rose, in yellow, dancing with her younger brother.'

Juliet had a moment of compassion for Rose Cartwright, dressed in an unbecoming colour with frills and flounces everywhere. She was quite plainly dressed in comparison but she also knew that with her height, she could easily look ridiculous.

'You are considered a "catch", I suppose.' There was an edge to her voice that he did not miss. Time for a little honesty.

'I will inherit one day, yes, but Mother and Dad want me to be happy with a girl who loves me for myself.'

The dance ended and he took her back to his mother, but Robert felt he had explained his circumstances well. He couldn't help but know that half the mothers in the county with marriageable daughters looked at him hopefully because at new year, his parents had talked to him frankly.

'The truth is, Robert, now you've turned 18, all anyone will think about is who you might marry.'

His father was realistic but it was Grace who was quick to say, 'We're not saying you should be thinking of marriage yet, but every eligible girl will be trying to impress you.'

'I suppose so. Like Rose Cartwright.'

'Don't blame her, or any of the other girls. Their mothers will be pushing them forward.'

He was silent for a moment before saying slowly, as if it had only just occurred to him, 'And whoever I marry will become mistress of all this.'

Simon looked at his wife lovingly. 'If I have one wish for my son, it's that he will meet someone and feel the same way I felt—and still feel—about his mother.'

Grace smiled as her husband put a hand on his son's shoulder.

'Robert, we want you to enjoy life and not feel obliged to marry yet or even worse, end up trapped into something you don't want.'

'And if you do meet someone you like, don't be afraid to introduce us. We'll try not to scare her too much.'

His father laughed before saying lightly, 'And now, wife, how about some tea?'

Grace took the hint and rang for Mostyn but he came in to say that Celia was on the telephone so she escaped to leave father and son alone.

The next morning saw Grace and Juliet in what Grace hoped would be her herb garden, marking out areas with the help of Batch. They paced and marked, re-read all Mr Chalmers' instructions and went to see how the plants looked. Batch was quite convinced it was wrong to plant them now because the ground was so hard and cold and in the end, they had to agree.

'So we must wait for a while.' Grace was unhappy.

'Perhaps at Easter, Mrs Amory?

'I suppose so. Will you come back and stay to supervise?'

'If Grandfather is happy, yes I will.'

If Robert had hoped to drive their guest to the station, he was disappointed. His mother drove her in the pony and trap.

'Your trunk will be lighter now all the plants have gone.' Grace laughed.

'Yes indeed. I hope you can spare the time to take me to the station.'

'Of course. I have more time to myself than you might think.'

Juliet glanced up at the imposing house front.

'So many rooms. Are they all used?'

'No, not all. The war changed so many things. These days, some of the maids are village girls who go home in the evening. My husband tells me your grandfather's house is quite large. How do you manage?'

'The Larches looks imposing but there are no wings. The butler has been with us forever, of course, cook is his sister and we have two live-in maids. I think Robert—that is, Mr Amory—is right when he says that although it looks very grand, most of it is frontage.'

Grace overlooked the slip with her son's name and confided, 'I can foresee a time when at least one more wing will be demolished. Families will be living in a much simpler way and staff will be harder to find, especially in the country.'

She let this thought take root and before long, the station was in sight.

'I am really grateful for all your help, Miss Chalmers, and I hope we see you again. If your grandfather feels well enough, please come and stay for the Feast.'

'I hope we shall be able to. My grandfather is so very interested in its progress.'

***

Juliet did not come at Easter and it was a nervous Grace, assisted by Batch, who did the planting. It was not as hard as she had thought and by the time she issued an invitation to Mr and Miss Chalmers to stay for a week, the little garden could always have been there.

Grace wrote that a suite of rooms was ready for them in the west wing, very quiet and overlooking the gardens where the Feast would be held. A sitting room was also made ready in case he didn't feel like being social. She was pleased to receive a grateful acceptance and over lunch, read out part of the letter.

'My grandfather is looking forward to seeing the herb garden, Mrs Amory, and at least part of the Feast. He doesn't care too much for noise and crowds but if he can sit somewhere quiet and observe, he will be content. I should tell you he has been looking up some of the old country traditions and wonders if he will see any of them.'

Robert smiled. 'I can just imagine Mr Chalmers in his library looking up medieval dances and Elizabethan masques.'

'I hope he doesn't expect a masque.' Grace was alarmed but Simon looked thoughtful.

'I've just had a great idea.'

'Care to share, Dad?'

'No. Might not work.'

If Grace had been following her husband over the next few days, she would have noticed that he could be found talking to Jenks or Eliza or casually asking Celia if her sons would be at the Feast.

Two days before the festivities, Robert drove to the station to collect their guests. The young lady looked beautiful as always but he was concerned to see the old gentleman looking tired.

'How are you, sir?'

'Tired, young man. But after a rest and a cup of tea, I shall be happy to see your mother.'

Robert, primed by his mother, had put a travelling rug in his car and he tucked 'the old gentleman', as he always mentally called him, neatly in.

'Front seat or back, Juliet?'

'Front please, so Grandfather can stretch out.'

As they drove away, she murmured quietly, 'Thank you for thinking of the rug.'

'Not at all. How are you?'

'Well, thank you, and looking forward to seeing the Feast.'

'If Mr Chalmers is tired, he can sit in his chair and look down on everything, quite undisturbed.'

She smiled. 'He is tired now but I think he will surprise you after a rest.'

Kingscourt glowed softly in the sun and Juliet said spontaneously, 'How welcoming it looks.'

'I'm glad you think so. To me it's just home and I'm always happy to be back.'

Mostyn opened the door as soon as the car drew up and coming down the steps was Dukes, his valet, who had come on an earlier train. Very soon, the old gentleman was settled with his tea and Robert turned to the girl.

'Do you want to stay with your grandfather or come down to the saloon for tea?'

'I'll just tidy myself up before I meet your mother, if you don't mind.'

'Not at all.'

His parents were already in the saloon and as he went to kiss his mother, he said, 'I was beginning to think you had all left the country. There was no-one about.'

'Your mother's idea. She thought he wouldn't want a lot of fuss and people around. How is Mr Chalmers?' his father asked.

'He's looking frail. Much older than the last time we saw him.'

'And Miss Chalmers?'

To his parents, the tone of his voice said 'more beautiful than ever' when in reality, he simply replied, 'Very well, and looking forward to the Feast. She will be down shortly, Mother.'

Juliet proved right and Grace, calling into his rooms to see if he had everything, found the old gentleman much better.

'Dear me, Mrs Amory, how very remiss you must think me. Not to come downstairs to greet my hostess.'

Grace shook his hand. 'Not at all, Mr Chalmers. I merely came to see if you have everything you need.'

'Oh yes, I am quite comfortable. And Juliet tells me I can see everything from my window if I wish.'

'That's why I picked this suite, as it looks straight down onto the lawns. If you want to come downstairs, you are welcome. We have a large library here if you care to see it.'

'Perhaps tomorrow after breakfast.'

Over dinner that evening, Grace outlined her plans for the next day and said to her son calmly, 'Robert, I hope you will put yourself at Mr Chalmers' disposal tomorrow, if he wishes to see the library or be driven anywhere.'

'Certainly, Mother. What about Juliet, I mean, Miss Chalmers?'

'We shall be looking at the herb garden in detail first thing, and in the afternoon checking the final details for the Feast.'

Grace half turned to her guest. 'You see, Miss Chalmers, my niece, Maryjane, normally helps me with the last-minute details but we don't know if they will be attending yet.'

Simon suddenly smelt a very large red herring but his wife carried calmly on.

Robert dutifully escorted their guest into the library after breakfast and did his best to explain, helped by a ledger he had found, what the various sections were. He did not mention his midnight visit to the library, rummaging frantically through his grandfather's large desk and drawers he had never looked in, until he found an old book marked 'Catalogue 1895'. Some dim recollection of his grandfather telling him of an eccentric old cousin who had lived here in the last century and catalogued the library surfaced, and he smiled.

'Now young man, it is very kind of you to spend your day with me, but you can run along now.'

'Are you sure, sir?'

'Yes, I am quite happy here. Is there a bell?'

'I will send Mostyn to you, sir, and come back in an hour.'

On his way to find his mother, Robert asked the butler to keep an eye on their elderly guest. He found his mother and Juliet happily exploring the herb garden.

'Mother, do you want some coffee?'

'Goodness, is that the time? How is Mr Chalmers?'

'Perfectly happy in the library and Mostyn is keeping an eye on him.'

'Then let us all go into the library and have coffee together. I haven't had chance for a good talk with him yet.'

A jolly hour followed before the stable bell rang at noon and Grace jumped up.

'The noon bell. Robert, you have let me forget the time. Mr Chalmers, will you join us for lunch?'

'That will be most pleasant, thank you.'

The 'arrangements' Grace had spoken of so calmly were nothing like as frightening as Juliet had imagined and she even made a small suggestion, which Grace agreed with.

They had gathered for tea when Celia and Hugo arrived with their sons, followed soon after by Roddy and Maryjane. Mr Chalmers was introduced to all the adults but the children seemed to have disappeared. On a sign from Simon, Mostyn opened the door and Eliza, Ed, Fred and Edmund all came in procession, Eliza carrying a cushion. They looked charming in a sort of Elizabethan costume and for a moment, Grace wondered where all their costumes had come from until she remembered the dressing up box.

As they approached Mr Chalmers, the boys bowed and Eliza curtsied.

'Mr Chalmers, sir, honoured guest. We beg your kind indulgence to consider an invitation.'

Grace, Celia and Hugo all glanced at Simon and saw the beginning of a smile. Juliet and Robert glanced at each other, wondering what would happen next.

The cushion was offered and on it sat what looked like an old parchment roll with a seal hanging from it. The old man broke the seal, read the invitation and began to laugh gently before handing it to his granddaughter.

Juliet read it before passing it to Robert, who read it aloud:

An invitation from the Kingscourt players to a performance two days hence in the Great Hall.

'Juliet, my dear, I think I will retire for an hour. I require your assistance, Mr Amory.'

They went off together as everyone began to speak at once.

'It was Dad's idea, but we did it all.' Eliza was laughing.

'Simon, what have you been up to?'

'Nothing, my darling. It was Robert's idea.'

'I must ask him.' Grace was mystified. 'Do we know who the Kingscourt players are?'

'John, Ed and Fred, Eliza and Edmund.'

'But what will they do exactly?'

'For that, you will have to wait "two days hence".'

Juliet, looking around the large family group, all laughing and talking at once, had a moment's envy. Life with her grandfather was so very quiet.

In deference to his age, Mr Chalmers had been offered a tray in his room instead of joining the family for dinner but an hour later, he sent a message to ask if everyone, including all the children, would join him in the great hall for a few minutes.

He came down on Robert's arm and sat in the large chair Simon and Hugo had selected as being the most comfortable. The children came and sat on the floor in front of him as he began to speak.

'When a gentleman receives an invitation, it is only polite to give an answer as soon as possible. Mostyn, where is my bag?'

A velvet pouch was produced; he opened it and a card was taken out, which to Grace seemed somewhat battered.

'Now you will have to imagine the cushion,' Mr Chalmers apologised but Mostyn, obviously entering into the spirit of it all, produced the heavy silver serving tray Grace never used because it was too ornate; the old man placed the card on it with a small bow and Mostyn presented it to Eliza with another bow.

The children all leant over to read it before Eliza passed it to her mother. Grace saw the paper had been aged, even the edges were slightly burnt.

'How did you manage that, sir?'

'Ah well, I had some help.'—with a wink at Robert.

Edmund began to clap and Fred replied, 'We are happy you will be attending, sir. You are our most important guest.'

Grace and Celia spoke together, as they sometimes did, 'Are we invited as well?'

'Of course, you are all invited but as our principal guest, we thought Mr Chalmers should have a proper invitation.' Ed sounded quite surprised they should have to ask.

'Besides,' Eliza intervened, 'we need a big audience; the bigger the better.'

Simon murmured to his wife, 'Perhaps we should invite the tenants as well.'

He meant it as a joke but his daughter, who was sometimes quite literal, instantly said, 'Oh yes, the tenants as well!'

Seeing his wife's look of alarm, Simon shook his head. 'No, you will have Mr and Miss Chalmers and all of us. That's quite enough of an audience.'

'Now that I have delivered my acceptance, I shall retire. Mostyn, your arm if you please.'

'Allow me to see you upstairs, Mr Chalmers.' Robert was already moving but the old gentleman shook his head.

'Thank you, young man, but I require only Mostyn, goodnight everyone.'

He waved to them happily as Juliet said, 'I shall come and see you for dessert, Grandfather.'

***

The day of the Feast dawned bright and clear. Robert was up early and out on the lawn supervising the setting up of the children's games when Juliet went to say good morning to her grandfather. The old gentleman was placidly eating some toast and so she went downstairs to breakfast. Grace was already finishing her coffee and had a list in her hand. 'You must excuse me, Miss Chalmers. I have to see to the buffet.'

Juliet breakfasted alone and wandered outside, to be immediately claimed by Maryjane to help with the children. By the time everyone was gathering on the lawns, Mr Chalmers had decided to come down, helped by Robert. He was installed in the comfortable library chair they had put in the shade and watched happily as the tenants proposed the toast and Simon replied. Juliet, going to see if he wanted something from the buffet, found Eliza next to him with a plate and some lemonade.

'I see you don't need any help, Grandfather.'

'Thank you, my dear, so many are anxious to feed me I fear I must look like a skeleton.' He smiled. 'Mostyn and all the young people are looking after me; off you go and have some fun.'

So Juliet strolled around with Maryjane and Roddy before going to see if Grace needed any help and to eat some buffet with Robert. Her grandfather was soon ready to retire for a rest and when she looked in on him later, he was already asleep.

The tenants stayed until tea time but what Robert called the county seemed as if they never wanted to go home. Juliet saw several people glancing her way, especially if she was talking to Robert, and she began to feel uncomfortable.

She was rescued by Maryjane who strolled over with Roddy and asked to be shown the herb garden. Of course, Juliet did not know they had already seen it but Roddy guessed correctly it was meant to keep her away from curious eyes.

Eventually, even the most hardened guest had to go and Grace and Celia retired to the sitting room for a rest as Robert and Roddy began to move chairs.

'Well, Miss Chalmers, what did you think of the Feast?'

'I enjoyed it; the children had a good time and I know my grandfather did. I saw him talking to some of them.'

'Apparently, Eliza was introducing some of them in case he might be bored.'

'He doesn't get bored easily, only tired. He's asleep at the moment.'

'Robert, I am going to sit down as it's so hot.' Maryjane fanned herself.

'We'll have a drink then, Juliet, let's go and see if there's any lemonade left; my greedy cousins might have drunk it all.' He started to laugh as John came around the corner with a nearly empty jug.

'Robert, is there any more lemonade?'

'No, you've drunk it all.'

Juliet's calm amused voice said, 'Why not ask Mrs Hughes if she has any more?'

'Off you go, John, and if you find some, bring a jug back here.' Roddy sat down next to his wife.

Maryjane had picked up on her favourite cousin's studied casual air when he talked to their guest and she wondered if there was an attraction, it would pay to know the young lady.

'During the war, of course, the Feast was different; usually just tea and a concert.'

'Did you perform, Mrs Allen?'

'Call me Maryjane, my dear; yes, Roddy and I used to duet; we raised money for the war charities, of course. Robert, is anything planned for this evening?'

'We could set up the gramophone and have a little dance.'

'Where? Eliza says the great hall is out of bounds.'

Roddy chipped in, 'We could move a few tables in the saloon; that would make enough space for us.'

'Oh yes, let's. I'll go and find Mother.' Robert jumped up and was off, leaving the other three staring after him.

'I think this must be in your honour, Miss Chalmers.'

'Mrs Amory might not agree,' Juliet sounded worried as she had no evening dress suitable for a dance with her.

But Grace agreed and Simon removed Juliet's unspoken fear by saying easily, 'Well, I'm not changing so everyone will have to take me as I am.'

'I shan't change either. It's only family after all.' Grace agreed.

A few tables and chairs were moved and Hugo set up the gramophone; it was all quite informal, everyone danced with each other and Juliet quite enjoyed it.

With his quick eye, Roddy had noted that Grace had completely ignored the fact that Juliet was a guest and in their room later, he tackled his wife, 'So is Miss Chalmers to be one of the family?'

'Not sure. Robert is clearly smitten and Aunt Grace likes her. He's young though.'

'Not as young as you were when you knew I was the one.' Roddy put an arm around his wife.

The next afternoon brought the performance by the Kingscourt players. Mr Chalmers had lunch in his room and by the time he came downstairs, the great hall was arranged like a small theatre with his large chair placed directly in front of it.

When everyone was assembled and the curtain came up, they all recognised the set from the New Year theatricals. The Elizabethan costumes had been replaced by what was meant to be Lincoln Green and the small play bill announced a performance of Robin Hood and his merry men.

The whole performance was full of sword fights and all agreed that John was a most believable sheriff of Nottingham. Eliza was a winsome Maid Marian and five-year-old Edmund played her brother; there were several characters who made no appearance at all—as explained by the leading lady afterwards, there could be no Friar Tuck or Robin Hood.

'You see, sir, Ed and Fred both thought they should be Robin so in the end, we wrote him out altogether.'

The idea of a performance of Robin Hood and his merry men with no Robin or Tuck made the old gentleman laugh heartily.

'My dear young lady, you should be a politician to arrive at such a diplomatic solution.'

Eliza shook her head. 'But did you enjoy it?'

'Very much. I particularly liked you dancing around the maypole.'

She frowned. 'It wasn't a very large maypole.'

'No my dear, but you must remember that in the theatre, it is illusion you aim for and your illusion was very good.'

The next day their guests were to leave but were at pains to say what an enjoyable time they had and Juliet, belatedly remembering her manners, invited Simon and Grace to the Larches.

'How kind. We should enjoy that, don't you think, Simon?'

'Yes indeed. And Robert will look after everything in our absence.'

If the young lady looked a little downcast, Grace admitted to herself that Simon had made exactly the right reply; best not to assume too much too soon.

***

In the end, it was the three of them who motored to Cambridge one hot August day, Juliet had made it a general invitation and Simon had taken pity on his son.

Grace enjoyed seeing the Larches and watched closely how Juliet ran it. Her private opinion was that the young lady was more than competent to run a large establishment but she didn't voice that thought even to her husband.

'I'm afraid it can be quiet here, Mrs Amory. I hope you won't be bored.'

'I shan't be bored, my dear. It's a treat to have someone else ordering meals and directing the staff.'

While they were at the Larches, Simon took the opportunity to invite William Wright to a lunch but he ended up being invited to the college with Robert.

'I'm sorry, my dear, but the college doesn't allow women in the halls.'

Grace sniffed. 'Oh for goodness sake, it's 1921, not 1821!'

Juliet had an idea. 'Why don't we go into town anyway and look around on our own, Mrs Amory? We can do things on our own.'

They all drove into Cambridge together, parted just before lunch and met up again as arranged at four o'clock; the old gentleman had already retired for the evening and they had a quiet dinner but the next morning after breakfast, their host appeared, wanting to know all about their day.

'Grace and I …' Robert instantly picked up the use of his mother's name but her face remained calm 'looked at some of the stores. It's amazing what is available now. Cambridge shops make Exeter look about a hundred years old. And Juliet found a lovely little place to eat.'

Juliet understanding her grandfather perfectly turned to him and said, 'I'm sure you will want talk to Major Amory about their lunch, so we'll leave you in peace.'

They walked around the grounds and talked over everything they had seen the day before.

'You wouldn't believe how out of date our shops are, Juliet; wait until I tell Celia about the things I've seen.'

'You see her a lot?'

'Yes, we live very close to each other. Maryjane is in London, John is at OTC and Ed and Fred are at school.'

'They were very good at the theatricals.'

'Holy terrors both of them. Hugo decided they must go away to school after they almost blew Kingscourt up!'

'Blew...how on earth?'

'First, they tried to find out how much coal would be needed to overheat the boiler. That took us two days of constantly watching the temperature to get back to normal. Then they tried to make gunpowder in the old nursery wing.'

The joyous laugh could be heard clearly by the three men inside and Mr Chalmers smiled. 'My granddaughter is being well entertained.'

Juliet apologised, 'I'm sorry for laughing. It must have been frightening.'

Grace laughed. 'It is funny looking back on it now. The windows all blew out and the rumble I heard made me think the roof had caved in. I rushed into the hall and began to bang the dinner gong as loudly as I could.' She stood up and acted her words.

'What happened then?'

'I shouted to Mostyn to find Simon and Robert. Then Ed—he's the younger—appeared on the stairs. He was black with soot but said quite calmly, "It's alright, Aunt Grace, we didn't get the gunpowder mixture quite right but we will next time."'

Another laugh made the old gentleman say to Robert, 'I must remember to ask your mother at lunch what was so funny.'

As lunch was being served, he asked Grace what had been amusing his granddaughter so much and heard again the story of what had become known in the family as the gunpowder plot.

'Goodness me, what a pair! I would never have guessed from meeting them.'

'My sister and her husband only want their high spirits toned down a little but so far, school does not seem to be having any effect.'

'I hope I shall see them again.' The old gentleman smiled and Grace had a sudden impulse.

'Come and stay, sir, whenever you like; your room will always be ready.'

A pair of shrewd old eyes glanced from her to his granddaughter, who coloured a little. 'That's very kind. I might just accept.'

They did not see him again and in the evening, it was the four of them for dinner. 'The staff are not used to entertaining, it is out of their routine, but very nice for me. Grandfather doesn't come down until nearly lunch and so I have breakfast alone and dinner too, if he is tired.'

Her three listeners had a momentary pang thinking of this quiet young woman spending so much time alone but Juliet spoke in a matter-of-fact tone.

After dessert, Juliet went upstairs to check on the old man and the three sat a while but she did not return and Grace began to feel anxious.

'I hope he's alright.' Just as she voiced the thought the door opened and Juliet came in.

'I'm sorry I was so long.'

'Is he settled for the night?'

'Yes. Dukes has been with my family for many years and understands grandfather perfectly; however, tonight he wished me to read to him. I believe he had forgotten that we have visitors; when he remembered, he sent me away.'

'What does he like to read?' Robert liked the old gentlemen and was interested.

'We have been working through Dickens; at present, we are on *David Copperfield*.'

Robert stored up this fact and went to collect his mother's coffee cup.

Juliet was instantly apologetic. 'I have been neglecting you; would you like more coffee? Grace? Major Amory? Robert?'

'If you call my wife Grace, you really must call me Simon and no, thank you, I won't; too much coffee at night keeps me awake.'

'Then I will ring for the tray to be taken away; the servants are not used to late hours.'

'Your grandfather is quite elderly.'

'I did ask him once and he said he remembers very well as a young man Prince Albert's funeral but he never said exactly when he was born.' Juliet spoke matter of factly but her two older listeners mentally calculated that the old gentleman must be well into his eighties.

'Well, my dear, these two elderly guests are going to retire. Robert, I shall see you in the morning.'

'Goodnight Mother, Dad.'

Robert kissed his mother and opened the door for her; going upstairs, Simon smiled at his wife. 'Neatly done, my dear.'

'If Robert likes her, they must get to know each other better.'

Her son, having closed the door behind his parents, hesitated before saying, 'I expect you will want me to go as well?'

'Not at all; the staff will have locked up so we can sit a while if you wish. Drink?'

'No thanks. Fact is…well, I'm not too keen on alcohol, never have been.'

'Grandfather has a cellar but it's not used much. Sometimes, I like a small glass of wine but nothing more.'

'Mother says we won't entertain now the way Grandfather King used to before the war; definitely no house parties.'

Juliet smiled. 'I should think Grace would be pleased. Running Kingscourt must be a full-time job.'

'Mother didn't always know how to do it because grandmother died so suddenly; she was just thrown into it.'

'Our neighbours, Sir John and Lady Louisa, had a daughter; she came to help Mother and ended up marrying uncle Billy. She died giving birth to my cousin Marybeth.'

'Very sad.'

'Yes, but if you ever meet my very tiresome cousin, you certainly won't feel sorry for her.'

'Why tiresome?'

'Always has to be the centre of attention, thinks everything revolves around her. When Maryjane married Roddy, she assumed she would be chief bridesmaid.'

'Was she?'

He smiled. 'No. Marybeth and Maryjane don't get on at all. The wedding was at the 1918 Kings Feast and as it was wartime, Maryjane decided she would have my sister Eliza as a flower girl but no other attendant. Roddy's mother had just died and his brother was killed in action during that summer, you see, so it was not a grand wedding.'

'They live in London, I think?'

'Yes; sometimes when he's away for a few days, Maryjane comes to stay. When Aunt Celia was so ill with the influenza and Mother was staying at The Risings to nurse her, Maryjane came to help us out.'

The clock chimed loudly and Robert, conscious he was talking too much, stood up suddenly. 'Goodness, it's eleven. You must be longing to retire. Thank you for a lovely dinner and I will see you in the morning.'

'Robert.' His name was quietly spoken and he paused at the door. 'Would you help me turn out the lights and make the fire safe?'

'Of course.'

Robert carefully attended to the fire and Juliet turned all the lights off until only the lamp near the door was left; seeing her standing in the half gloom, he had a sudden urge to kiss her.

'Juliet…you know, I quite like you…' He paused.

'And I like you, Robert.'

'I should like desperately to kiss you.'

Her face gleamed in the light. 'Then why don't you?'

As first kisses sometimes are, it was all wrong but he tried again and managed a gentle kiss on her lips. Juliet held out her hand and they went upstairs together and as she turned towards her room, he whispered gently, 'Goodnight, dear Juliet.'

'Goodnight Robert.'

He went to his room, sat on the bed and realised he had just had his first kiss with the only girl he could ever love. It was quite a moment for him; his mother had taught him to respect all women and he was not a flirt. He was asleep the moment his head touched the pillow but he woke with a start; it was five in the morning by his travelling clock and his mind was full of one horrible thought.

Suppose—just suppose—she thought he had been forward, thought he always went around kissing girls? What had he done?

He spent the miserable two hours before he could reasonably disturb his parents, pacing up and down his room worrying. He knew his father was always about early and at seven, he couldn't wait any longer; a light tap on his parents' door brought his father.

'Dad, can I talk to you?'

One look at his son's face and Simon knew something was wrong. 'Quiet lad, your mother is still asleep.'

They found the butler already opening up and went into the garden, Simon resolving he would not be the first to speak if it was an affair of the heart—and what else could it be? – He must work it out for himself.

At last Robert sighed. 'Dad, I need your advice.' He paused and swallowed. 'Last night after you and Mother went to bed, Juliet and I sat talking.'

'And?'

'I said I liked her and she said she liked me.'

His father said nothing and Robert, gazing at his feet, went on, 'I said I should like to kiss her and she said why didn't I.'

Simon had a moment's envy of his son, remembering the first time he had kissed Grace. 'And so you kissed her.' He took pity on his struggling son. 'Then why the worried look?'

'We said goodnight, I didn't kiss her again, but I have been awake for hours, worrying. Suppose she thinks I'm…well, thinks I go around kissing girls all the time.'

Simon bit down an impulse to laugh, the young face looked so tragic.

'Robert, you like each other and you kissed her; she did invite you to, remember?'

'That's true. I didn't see it that way.'

There was a long moment's silence before his father spoke again, 'You are young and your life is all before you, but remember, I am always here if you want to talk.'

'Thanks Dad.'

'One more thing; don't try to pretend it didn't happen, that would be insulting to her.'

They were so long talking that Juliet, seeing them out of the dining room window, came to say breakfast was ready.

Simon rose easily and said, 'I will see if my wife is ready; excuse me.'

Juliet smiled. 'Good morning, Robert,' and held out her hand.

He smiled back and took it. 'Good morning, Juliet.'

After breakfast, they were ready to leave and went to take their leave of the old gentleman. Grace and Simon were not detained long but Robert was asked to stay.

'Young man, I want a word with you.'

'Yes sir.'

'Sit down here, facing me.'

Robert took the seat apprehensively.

'You like my granddaughter.' It was not a question and Robert knew honesty was his only hope.

'Yes sir, very much.'

'And she feels the same?'

'I hope so; I believe so.'

'I must ask then—how do you see this mutual liking continuing?'

'I should like permission to write to her, sir, with a view to us becoming better acquainted.'

Robert felt this was a sure way to keep in touch with her.

'You have asked her?'

'No sir, I would like your blessing before I do.'

'Well, well, you are a polite well-brought up young man and I approve of you; go and ask her.'

'Thank you, sir, and I hope to see you again soon.'

He flew off to find her. 'Juliet, I want to ask you something.'

Instantly, her guard was up. 'What?'

'May I write to you?'

She relaxed. 'Certainly; my grandfather will love to hear more about Ed and Fred.'

'No. I mean write to you, we could talk about anything, everything.'

She hesitated and he said boldly, 'I have Mr Chalmers' blessing.'

'You asked him?'

'He said he approves but I should ask you.'

They were standing just inside the hall and his parents were supervising loading the car so Robert seized the opportunity. 'Thank you for a lovely visit and I will write next week.'

He took her hand and held it for a moment; she thought he would kiss her again but it was only a gentle peck on her cheek.

Chapter 11

Robert was happy writing to Juliet every other week, telling her all the news and always asking about her grandfather and what she had been doing; in November, Grace decided to ask them for Christmas.

'Will the old gentleman be fit enough, Mother?' Robert asked hopefully.

'If he is not then Juliet will decline; it would be lovely if he could see a Kingscourt Christmas.'

But the old gentleman replied himself to say he would be delighted and a few days before Christmas, Grace sent Robert to bring them comfortably to Devon when he arrived.

Dukes was already waiting having come by train and Mr Chalmers, after a short rest, went downstairs to meet the family. Robert and Mostyn helped him downstairs and settled him into a chair by the fire.

Presently, he found Ed and Fred had called to see him and insisted on hearing the whole saga of the gunpowder plot.

Juliet seeing him well entertained, took the opportunity to ask about the festivities.

'I understand Christmas has certain rituals?'

Robert replied, 'Yes. On the day before Christmas Eve, we drag the yule log into the hall and it burns—we hope—until Epiphany.'

'How do you choose it?'

'Usually very seriously; all the men go out and when we have chosen one, the tenants drag it up the hall, usually singing as they go. On Christmas Eve, we go to church for the carols, then the tenants and their families all come back here for mince pies and to see the tree lit.'

'I'm not sure Grandfather could do all that.'

'He can do whatever he likes; if he wants to rest, just send his apologies and Mostyn will keep an eye on him.'

'Your mother has been so kind; we have the same rooms we had in the summer so Dukes is close to him. Grandfather has a special present for her, but please don't say anything.'

'I won't. We used to have presents on Christmas morning before church when we were young but now, we have them about tea time. In the evening, we have a buffet to give the servants a night off.'

Grace came over then and he had no further talk with Juliet; he hadn't told her that his mother had decided to recreate the kind of family Christmas they had enjoyed before the war. Tonight, as a special concession to the guest of honour, dinner was moved an hour forward.

The next day, the men went to select the yule log, leaving Mr Chalmers happily in the library with Mostyn keeping an eye on him and Grace took Juliet to The Risings for a long lunch; they arrived back just as the log did and Juliet, wondering aloud if her grandfather wanted to see the ceremony, found him already in a prime position and attended by Robert.

'Juliet, come and sit by me, you too, young man.'

The three sat together, watching as the tenants dragged the log into place and Robert explained how they chose it.

'We are usually guided by Anderson to a specific area. I think he probably chooses the site weeks before and then we wander up and down to pick the log and a tree.'

Just then, Simon came up with the old flambeau that had been used to light the log since Haydn King's time. He lit it ceremoniously and said loud enough for all the tenants to hear, 'Friends, we gather here once again to light the yule log and give thanks for a good year; tonight, I am going to ask a very special guest to light the log for us while I recite our usual words.'

He turned to the old gentleman. 'Will you do us the honour, sir?'

The old man, considerably touched, took Robert's arm and led by Simon, they walked in procession to the huge fireplace. Simon placed the flambeau into his hands as he recited the words and between old and young hands, the log was lit. A cheer went up from the tenants and Juliet felt a sudden urge to cry.

After the tenants had gone, Mr Chalmers decided he would have dinner in his room and as the gong sounded, Juliet came downstairs alone.

Grace, taking her usual pre-dinner sherry, announced that Eliza would be joining them and soon after, feeling very grown up, that young lady came in; she was allowed a glass of fruit cup by her mother and Robert, glancing a question at Juliet, poured two glasses.

At the buffet, Juliet found herself sitting next to Eliza and they chatted amiably enough for an hour and then Eliza was sent off to bed; the small dessert was soon finished and Grace said with a laugh, 'A plain meal tonight for we shall indulge far too much over the next two days.'

Christmas Eve brought a light covering of snow and in mid-afternoon, Maryjane and Roddy came.

'How are you, Robert?' Roddy shook hands.

'Fine. Maryjane looks quite stylish.'

His cousin smiled as she kissed him. 'You like my new hairstyle?'

'It's very modern.'

It was certainly short, Juliet thought, *but it must be very convenient. I wonder if Robert would like my hair cut short?*

Just then, Dukes came to find her. 'Miss Juliet, your grandfather has decided he would like to attend church.'

'Very well. I'll come up.'

The snow was only powdering the ground but Robert drove carefully to church and installed their guest in a pew where he could see everything. The Christmas Eve service was always short: mostly carols and the retelling of the birth and when they arrived back, the long table was piled high with platters of mince pies and bowls of mulled wine. Grace lit the lights on the enormous Christmas tree and the room began to fill with noise.

'Let's take your grandfather up, Juliet, it's getting noisy.'

But the old gentleman wouldn't budge; he was deep in conversation with one of the tenants who farmed near Oakley's Bottom and was quite obviously well entertained.

Christmas morning brought more snow and after breakfast, Grace was summoned to the old gentleman's room; she was gone some time and when Simon finally found her, it was in her little sitting room and she had obviously been crying.

'There you are, wife. I was beginning to think you had run off with Mostyn.' This was a private joke between them but he saw the tell-tale signs and slid an arm around her. 'Hey, what's up?'

'Oh Simon, just look at this.' *This* was a beautiful brooch nestled in an old box, a central turquoise surrounded by seed pearls. 'And look,' she turned it over, 'it's a pendant as well.'

'Where on earth did you get it? It's obviously valuable.' Simon was astonished.

'The old gentleman summoned me to his room. I thought he wanted something but he gave me this; it belonged to his mother and he wanted me to have it.'

'It's a family heirloom; surely Juliet should have it?' Simon frowned.

'He said,' she swallowed, 'he said we have made him so welcome, part of the family. Juliet knew he was going to do it.'

A light tap on the door announced Mostyn. 'Excuse me, madam, Mrs Phillips is on the telephone.'

'Thank you, Mostyn.'

Celia was calling to say they would see them at church and everyone, except Mr Chalmers, went to the usual morning service. He joined them in time for turkey and plum pudding and after that, they all went as usual into the saloon where two trestle tables had been set up, laden with presents.

Robert installed their guest near the fire and waited for his mother to signal that presents could be exchanged. It was mid-afternoon before Grace finally took the first present and handed it to her husband. Robert, standing near the table, took a small parcel and handed it to Mr Chalmers.

'This is for you, sir, with my best wishes.'

The old man adjusted his glasses, untied the paper slowly and opened an old book, beautifully bound; he read the spine. 'My dear Mr Amory, where did you find this?'

'Ah, that's my secret, sir. Are you pleased?'

'Beyond words. Juliet, this is a first edition of *A Christmas Carol*, published in December 1843.'

'Grandfather, it looks brand new; what a thoughtful present.' She glanced at Robert who grinned.

Presents were opened, the tea tray appeared and Grace announced it was time to tidy up.

'Now come along everyone. Robert, can you begin gathering the wrapping paper and Eliza, do you have a list for your thank you letters?'

'Yes Mother.'

'Juliet, my dear, I will retire now,' Mr Chalmers spoke quietly but Grace heard and turned.

'My dear sir, you are welcome to join us tonight for our buffet or would you prefer a tray in your room?'

'You are very kind, Mrs Amory, but a tray will suffice. I'll leave you young people to enjoy the evening.'

Simon and Grace smiled at being called young people as Robert and Juliet helped him out.

When they gathered again later, the saloon was tidy, opened presents still piled up on the table. Juliet reported that her grandfather was having a nap followed by a tray and Simon tackled his son.

'Come on, Robert, spill the beans. A first-edition Dickens?'

His son smiled. 'William Wright. But please,' he appealed to Juliet, 'don't give me away.'

She laughed. 'I won't; it was a thoughtful present and he will cherish it.'

'It seemed entirely appropriate.'

Grace looked out the window and said, 'Oh dear it's snowing again. I hope the hunt won't be called off. Cook has been making an awful lot of punch.'

'Grace, do stop worrying about the weather.'

'It'll be alright, Mother, honestly.'

Robert and Juliet decided to play cards and they sat happily until hunger pangs called them to the buffet.

The Boxing Day Hunt was quite in the pre-war tradition; the start watched from upstairs by their guest; the hounds were just coming back as it began to snow again and Grace invited her guest to stay until New Year. Juliet hesitated but the old gentleman accepted readily.

New Year's Eve was cold but it did not snow again and during the morning, Maryjane and Roddy arrived, followed by Celia and Hugo. Ed, Fred and John had all arrived the day before and there were mysterious comings and goings in the east wing.

Everyone was requested to be in the great hall by three and the players performed Peter Pan, a pantomime, being very seasonal, with Maryjane playing the piano. It was all a success, with Grace asking her usual blessing for the new year and wondering what 1922 would bring.

***

The first three months of the new year were quiet and Grace began making changes to some of her mother's routines. Life would never be the same as pre-war, she explained to Celia, and it saved the staff many duties they would normally have had.

Billy arrived unexpectedly at Easter and told Simon he was going to sell his estate. His brother-in-law, speechless, gazed at him.

'It's alright for you,' Billy said irritably. 'You're here all the time. I'm in the army.'

'But selling…?' Simon found his voice.

'Snyder was a mistake, I know that now. I can't be worrying about Nether Bassett, Marybeth and everything else.'

The bombshell news was given to the family over tea but as Billy had so obviously made up his mind, there was very little anyone could say. The next morning though, Simon had a long talk with his son and Jonathan Anderson.

'Fact is…we could buy the estate; we've plenty of money from the sale of Oakley's Bottom.'

'But Dad—'

Simon held up his hand. 'No, listen. It seems to me…'

They gathered around the estate maps and argued but in the end, Simon had his way and the day before Billy was leaving, the idea was put to him.

'I didn't know you could afford it, Simon.' Billy tossed off a whisky.

'It's not generally known in the neighbourhood, Billy, but we've sold some land at Oakley's Bottom.'

'That worthless piece of land?' 'It's not worthless. There's a rare plant growing there and we've had a handsome offer, which we accepted so we have some cash.'

'Thing is, Uncle Billy, what about the hall? We don't need another house,' Robert spoke quite clearly and Simon was struck again by his son's acute observations.

'Alright then. I might need a house. Or Marybeth might. so not the hall and the gardens. Let's look at the estate maps.'

The maps were pored over, boundaries suggested and in the end, a handshake was all it took. Drinks were produced to celebrate and Billy invited them to London in the summer.

'My lads are trooping the colour this year.'

'That's an honour, should be a fine sight.'

'Come up; bring Grace.'

'I'll try.'

The news that Kingscourt was to acquire most of Nether Bassett was soon generally known and Simon, Robert and the agent spent many hours talking. Every dinner seemed to include some conversation about it and Grace became used to seeing Jonathan Anderson several times a day.

Meeting him one morning in the hall, she said teasingly, 'You should move in, Mr Anderson, save you having to come up every day.'

He smiled, having become used to the more relaxed atmosphere of this family. 'There is a great deal to do just now, Mrs Amory. Tenants to be interviewed and farms inspected.'

'Anything I can do?'

'No thank you.' He paused. 'Actually, there might be something.'

She waited patiently but he would not be drawn out. 'I need to think it over.'

'You know where I am when you're ready.'

She went to her sitting room but before she had even opened her account book, a timid knock announced Jessie, the newest maid. 'Please madam, Mrs Hughes would like a word with you.'

Grace sighed. 'Very well, Jessie. Tell her in fifteen minutes.'

Cook's 'word' took half an hour and Grace had just begun to add up her monthly accounts when the door went again.

'Please madam, Mr Anderson would like to see you.'

Grace closed the book. 'Very well, send him in.'

'I hope I'm not disturbing you, Mrs Amory.'

She put on her smile and denied it. 'No, not at all. How can I help you?'

'As you know, we are taking on new farms and I felt we should make some kind of gesture to mark the occasion; what about a dinner to welcome them?'

She frowned. 'It's very close to the King's Feast.'

'Yes but Mrs Amory, if you could only see how those tenants have been treated, Major Amory has told me that the late Mr King would have been appalled to see a fine small estate ruined.'

'I had no idea it was so bad.'

'We'll be looking at two years' work at least to bring the land up to Kingscourt standards. That is, apart from the work needed to the farm building and so on. Snyder very nearly wrecked the estate.'

Grace was instantly diverted. 'Do we know what happened to him? My husband never mentioned it.'

'Major King let him go, with a reference, I believe.'

'Who is looking after the hall?'

'No-one; the house is shuttered up and the gardens are a ruin.'

'Aunt Louisa's prized roses! Such a shame. But surely...no, never mind, let me think about your idea, Mr Anderson, and I'll let you know.'

Simon had a high regard for his agent, Grace knew and she included him as a matter of course in any festivities to do with the estate and he was frequently invited for tea or dinner if they entertained. Compared to some of his acquaintances, Jonathan Anderson knew he was fortunate.

At dinner that evening, Grace tackled her husband. 'Simon, Mr Anderson has been telling me about the hall shuttered up, and the gardens in ruins.'

'Yes, you would be horrified, my dear, but it is now Billy's responsibility.'

'But surely, he must know someone should be there to look after it. Old Hawkes is well past anything now; suppose the roof falls in, or anything?'

'It is Billy's responsibility, my dear, but if it bothers you so much, I'll write to him and suggest he employ someone.'

Her next suggestion was rather more radical. 'We should do the Feast differently this year.'

'How different?' Though a traditionalist, Simon was open to suggestion.

'Concentrate more on the new tenants and less on inviting the county; we need to integrate the new tenants, show them how we do things and include them. Mr Anderson tells me they suffered much under Snyder.'

'True, they did.'

Robert, when told, grinned. 'The county won't like it.'

'The county will get used to it. It's only this once.'

But Simon would have been surprised at the letter Juliet received from Robert.

'You know, Juliet, I think this is a good idea, concentrating more on the tenants and estate and less on the county; when I take over—and I hope that is many years away—things will be different.'

If the county had a view on not being invited, the only person brave enough to mention it was Mrs Williams.

'What Silas King would have thought of this plan, Major Amory, I shudder to think.'

'He would completely understand, Mrs Williams; the estate must always be our first concern.'

Juliet had come for a three-day visit but Mr Chalmers had politely declined.

'He does get tired so easily these days,' she explained to her hostess.

'Not surprising given his age, still, it's lovely to see you, Juliet.'

It was after dinner before Robert finally saw her alone and took his chance. 'Juliet, I want to ask you something. Come and sit here.'

Unsuspecting, she sat in the chair and was dumbfounded when he dropped onto one knee. 'Juliet, my darling, you know I love you. Have done since the first moment I saw you. Will you marry me?'

For a moment, her heart leapt but she remembered her duties and responsibilities. How could she follow her heart?

Her silence unnerved the young man and his voice was flat as he said, 'I'm sorry. I misunderstood your feelings. Naturally, I wouldn't press any unwanted attentions on you.'

Juliet swallowed the hard lump in her throat and managed to say, 'I could never leave Grandfather.' She fled to her room, leaving Robert kneeling and staring open-mouthed at the door.

The next morning, Roddy and Maryjane arrived and while her husband went to see Simon, Maryjane took the chance to wander quietly around the garden; she had admired the herb garden and was passing the roses when she heard, or thought she heard, muffled sobbing. Turning the corner quietly, she saw Juliet sitting in the little arbour overlooking the rose garden.

Maryjane hesitated a moment before going to sit beside her. The girl did not turn and presently, Maryjane took a cold hand and sat waiting.

Finally, Juliet sniffed and blew her nose; the face she turned to Maryjane was haggard and dark shadows under her eyes spoke of a sleepless night.

'Care to talk about it?'

'No, it's all hopeless, quite hopeless.'

Another pause before Maryjane said calmly, 'Nothing is ever quite hopeless and I sometimes find that to talk aloud whatever is on my mind puts it into perspective.'

The silence was long but she knew better than to break it.

'It's Robert.'

She smiled. 'Then it can't be that bad. I'll tell you something I've never even told Roddy. Robert is my favourite cousin.'

'He has...asked me to marry him.'

'Ah, you don't love him?'

'Yes I do, very much, but...Grandfather! Of course, I can't leave him.'

Maryjane paused before replying carefully, 'My cousin wouldn't want or expect you to leave Mr Chalmers.'

'Noooooo, I suppose not.' Another sniff.

'What would you like to say?'

'Yes, of course.'

'Your grandfather wouldn't wish you to be unhappy and you are both very young. I had a very long written courtship with Roddy, which meant I understood him pretty well before we married.'

Juliet stood up and for a long moment stared into the distance before walking off without a word. That she did accept was obvious when, going into lunch with Roddy, her cousin bounded over and gave her a hug while kissing her heartily on both cheeks.

'Unhand my wife, sir.' Roddy laughed but Robert simply said, 'Maryjane is amazing, Roddy.'

'I know that, but how did you find out?'

A finger to the lips was his only answer and Maryjane had no chance to tell him anything until later that day.

'They must mean to keep it a secret because nothing has been said so we mustn't say anything.'

'Fine by me; she seems a nice girl and Aunt Grace likes her. And I like your cousin because he values my girl so highly.'

She blushed. 'I was only trying to make her see that she shouldn't say no to Robert and they are so very young.'

'Unlike another of your cousins whose problem may not be so easily solved.'

'Will you have to say anything yet?'

'Not yet but soon if nothing changes.'

The Feast was a success and Grace spoke to all the new tenants, promising each of them a visit soon; so busy was she that her son's quiet glow passed unnoticed and when Juliet went back to Cambridge, it was Robert who drove her back.

He went straight to the old gentleman and asked permission to marry Juliet.

Mr Chalmers eyed him carefully. 'You love Juliet.' It was not a question and Robert nodded.

'Yes sir, she's the only girl for me.'

'You are very young to say that. She is the first girl you have fallen in love with.'

'I am perfectly sure there could never be anyone else for me. I would like your blessing, sir, and your approval.'

'If you want to marry my granddaughter, you had best know about her history.'

'It's not necessary, sir. I love her and respect you; what more do I need?'

'To know something she does not and I hope will never find out. I must tell you about my son, Juliet's father.'

Theo Chalmers calmly explained the dreadful event of spring 1900 and Robert listened, open-mouthed.

'Now young man, are you still intent on marrying my granddaughter?'

'Yes sir, what you have told me doesn't change how I feel. Nothing could.'

A withered old hand was held out. 'Then I happily give my consent.'

'Your consent has made me very happy, sir, and Juliet will never hear anything of what you have just told me.'

'There is something else we must speak of—money.'

'I'm not bothered if Juliet is a pauper, sir.'

The old man's shoulders shook. 'Oh no, young man, certainly not a pauper.'

By the time Robert found his fiancée, anxiously waiting to hear how her aged relative had responded to the news, he had dismissed everything from his mind but how happy he was. She put a gentle hand to his cheek. 'I love you, Robert.'

He turned the hand and kissed it. 'And I love you. Now I must tell my parents.'

'I should like to be there when you do the next time I visit.'

'Alright but it will seem a very long time.'

***

Robert found his promise very hard to keep and in the end, he wrote and asked her to bring her grandfather for the August bank holiday. Over dinner on the Saturday evening, he broke the news and his parents, after a moment's surprise, were very happy.

Only his father, as they shook hands, said quietly to him, 'Sure, old man?'

'Very sure, Dad.'

'So Mr Chalmers gave his approval. Very proper to ask him first.'

'I felt awful not telling you, Mother, but there will be so many difficulties.'

Grace swallowed the lump in her throat. 'Let's just get used to the idea of your engagement first.'

Juliet intervened, 'We don't want it announced yet, Grace, we want to wait.'

'Quite right. But if we do nothing else, we must have some champagne.'

Grace happily began to work her way through the tenant visits until the day Celia telephoned to say Roddy and Maryjane were coming to stay for the weekend.

'And they've suggested a family dinner,' Celia reported.

'Good. Come and stay here then. I'll talk to Mrs Hughes about a menu.'

After an excellent dinner, Grace led the way into the saloon, thinking happily that although only a family dinner, her mother would have no fault with the menu; it was quite like the old days. Not quite everything was the same though—the ladies did not withdraw early and after dinner cigarettes were smoked in the saloon. A new innovation had come from London via Maryjane—the cocktail cabinet. At first Grace was convinced they would never use one but Robert persuaded the estate carpenter to make some adjustments to a cupboard he had found in the west wing; it looked better than the old drinks tray and Grace admitted it was an improvement.

Simon opened the cabinet and offered drinks all around. Maryjane shook her head but Roddy took a brandy and drank it quickly. His wife glanced anxiously at him, knowing what was to come; her parents, aunt and uncle and cousin were in happy ignorance.

'I'm glad you came down for the weekend, Maryjane,' her mother smiled. 'It seems ages since we've seen you.'

'About two months, Mother; we were here for the Feast.'

Maryjane began to be anxious that Roddy had missed his chance to begin a difficult conversation but her aunt gave the perfect opening.

'I have had another letter from Mrs Hopkins…you remember her. I'm sure, my dear, her eldest son is married and living in London but I don't think you ever met him. Anyway, she writes about Marybeth.'

Hugo smiled. 'Nothing good, I'm sure, after how she behaved when she came down here.'

Everyone was quiet, remembering last autumn when Marybeth had been the talk of the neighbourhood. Maryjane, glancing at her husband, spoke quietly, 'We wanted to come and see you…because Roddy has something to tell you.'

Every one instantly looked at him.

'Fact is… Well, it's about Marybeth.'

'I'm sure my tiresome cousin can't have done anything to attract your attention, Roddy.'

Senior family members knew that Roddy was 'something' in intelligence but questions were never asked.

'No, not exactly Marybeth; it's more the…company she keeps.'

Hugo and Celia exchanged glances before his father-in-law asked, 'Can you be more specific?'

'She's seeing someone. A young man. It's his father who is of interest to us.'

'Why?'

'He's a wealthy Austrian Jew. Made lots of money during the war selling armaments.'

'Ah! To both sides, I expect,' Simon spoke bitterly, having a low opinion of war profiteers.

Roddy stubbed his cigarette out. 'That's not all though; it's who he is…'

Grace poured herself another cup of coffee before asking the obvious question, 'Can you tell us his name?'

'The lad is called Toby. Marybeth is quite taken with him, thinks they have a common bond as they are close in age and his mother also died in childbirth.' Roddy put off the moment a while longer. 'Thing is, Mother Celia, it's who his father is.' He looked unhappy as he delivered the fatal fact. 'Sir Mark Goldburg.'

For a moment, there was a terrible silence as each remembered the catastrophic events of October 1900, before Simon spoke irritably, 'Oh my lord, is that never to be forgotten?'

'Does Billy know?' Both sisters said in unison.

'We don't think so. He's carrying on as usual.'

Robert said nothing. He hadn't been born or his parents married when his uncle Julian had attempted to run off with Lady Goldburg, but he had been told the story years ago after a school friend told him he had another uncle.

'Will it affect us, Roddy?'

'Given that you don't see Marybeth, probably not. I wanted to tell you—had to clear it with my chief first and tell him why I wanted you to know—because we're not sure how Billy will react when he finds out.'

'I suppose Julian is still in America?' Grace queried.

'Yes, one of the richest men on the east coast.'

'Julian rich? And still married to Alice?'

'Very rich, yes, and they have adopted two children who are extremely spoilt.'

Silence fell again; he spoke calmly, 'Thing is…well, my chief thinks his CO might have to tell Billy. Tricky business.'

'Because Billy is in the army and his daughter is seeing someone whose father is…questionable. This will finish Billy,' Simon voiced his wife's thought.

Celia looked at her daughter for the first time. 'That's why you were so keen to come!'

Maryjane nodded. 'Roddy and I talked about it and thought that you should be prepared. 'Once Billy knows, the old scandal will surface again.'

Hugo suddenly went to the cocktail cabinet and poured brandies all around. As he gave his son-in-law a glass, he said quietly, 'Thanks Roddy, for letting us know. Nothing we can do, of course, but we are prepared when anything happens.'

***

They didn't have long to wait because in mid-October, Billy turned up unannounced. Simon and Robert were out and Grace was turning out the old laundry room when Mostyn came to announce him.

'Major King in the saloon, madam.'

'Thank you, Mostyn. Tell him I'll be there soon and bring some coffee.'

Grace composed herself before facing her brother; they had all agreed that the only choice was to pretend ignorance until told; they couldn't let Billy know Roddy had told them.

Grace hugged him. 'Billy, how good to see you home and so unexpected; are you on leave?'

He looked furious so he knows, she thought.

'Yes, for a fortnight.'

'You will have to stay here. Nether Bassett isn't in a fit state to live in, even for a short time. I'll ask Hugo and Celia to come over tonight. It's ages since we had a family dinner.'

She said all this as Mostyn brought the tray in and quietly retreated.

'Simon about?'

'He and Robert are looking at Oakley's Bottom. I expect them for lunch.'

'I'll see him later. I'm going to ride over to the hall, take a look around.'

When her brother had gone, Grace flew to the telephone to tell her sister and she had just rung off when her husband and eldest son came in.

'Billy's back and he knows.'

'What did he say?'

'Not much. Wants to see you. I have told Celia. Oh yes and he's got a fortnight's leave.'

'That's his CO telling him to clear up the mess before he goes back, if he can go back.'

'Why shouldn't he go back?'

'Think about it, Robert. If Marybeth does marry this chap, Billy could be forced into resigning his commission.'

'This Goldburg lad must be underage and his father might not give him permission to marry; besides, Uncle Billy loves the army.'

'He may not have a choice. Once,' Simon lowered his voice, 'the security services are involved, the normal standards don't apply.'

'Oh for goodness sake, why can't Marybeth be more like her mother?' Grace had voiced this thought so many times over the years.

They had a quiet family dinner but it turned out that the sisters had no time to worry about their brother's troubles. The next morning, the telephone jangled and Grace, answering it herself, heard her sister's tearful voice.

'Grace, Fred's got pneumonia. I must go to the school.'

'Cee, that's awful; what about Ed?'

'I'm sending him to you. Hugo and I are leaving almost at once. He's in some danger.'

She began to cry again and rang off hurriedly.

Grace went to see about a room for Fred. But her thoughts ran on. *He won't want to leave his brother so he'll make a scene. Celia will change her mind and let him stay; still, I'll order the room.*

It was four o'clock and Mostyn was about to serve tea when the telephone rang again.

'Exeter 21.'

'Grace, it's Juliet.'

'Hello my dear, how are you?'

'Grandfather's ill. He's been out of sorts for days but the doctor says he must go into hospital. He's adamant he will stay at home and…' In the silence, an appalled Grace heard her crying. 'I don't know what to do.'

In a moment, her mind was made up.

'Now Juliet, don't upset yourself. I'm coming to Cambridge first thing tomorrow.'

'But you can't just—'

'Yes I can, Robert would never forgive me if I didn't.'

Grace rang off, called for Mostyn and began to run through what she would need. Eliza would have to go to The Risings—no, that was no good and Ed was coming here as well.

She was pacing up and down when her husband and son came in.

'Grace, why is there luggage in the hall?'

'I'm going to Cambridge first thing tomorrow but we are in a mess.'

'Now darling, slow down and tell us calmly.'

'Celia called, Fred's dangerously ill with pneumonia and they are on their way to the school; she's sending Ed to us. Then Juliet called to say Mr Chalmers is ill and they want to send him hospital but he's refusing; poor girl broke down in tears, she's so desperate.'

'Of course, you must go. Robert, you'll drive your mother.'

'Yes Dad, I'll ring up now and see how the old gentleman is.'

Simon, drinking a cup of tea thoughtfully, said to his wife, 'I'll stay here and look after Ed and Eliza.'

But when his son came back, the look on his face was not happy.

'He can't breathe very well, that's why the doctor is insisting on the hospital. Dad, suppose he…you know…'

'I'll come as well.' Simon made up his mind. 'If…anything happens, Juliet will need all our support.'

'But what about Ed and Eliza?' Grace's mind was numb.

'The Risings will need supervision as well; we'd better see if Maryjane can come down and help us.' Simon hurried to the telephone and Robert took his mother's hand.

'Thanks, Mother, for doing this.'

She winked away a tear. 'Nonsense, we can't leave her all alone in such a crisis but it would happen all at once.'

Maryjane said she would be there the next day and so, very early the following morning, they drove to Cambridge in a depressed silence, not sure what they would find; the door was opened by Juliet and she threw herself into Grace's arms and began to cry.

'He won't go. I've tried and tried. And the doctor is adamant.'

Robert patted her hand and said, 'Let me go and talk to him.'

Whatever he said had the right effect because presently, he came down and said the doctor would telephone the hospital. Grace would not leave Juliet and so they went in the ambulance together, leaving the two men to wait.

It was early evening when the telephone rang and Simon just beat Robert to answer.

'Hello. Hello. Ah, Maryjane.' He paused. 'That's good. Thank you for dropping everything, my dear, and we'll keep you informed.'

'Roddy's swung a couple of days' leave as it's a family emergency. He's dropped Maryjane off and now he's going to the school to collect Ed and bring him back.'

Robert, his thoughts absorbed in Juliet, only nodded. The night and the following day seemed very long to both men, the silence broken only by calls from Grace saying that there was no change and one from Maryjane. The butler brought in sandwiches neither of them could eat and for the first time in his life, Robert took to cigarettes.

Maryjane said that Fred was on the danger list and Celia and Hugo were with him. Ed had made a scene until told firmly by his father that either he would stay with the headmaster or go back to Kingscourt. He had reluctantly agreed to leave and Roddy was on his way back with a very sullen brother-in-law.

For several days, the news on both fronts was bad but Fred turned the corner just as Mr Chalmers was declining. Maryjane, running both houses, was the focal point for all the news; she told Simon that Billy was very much annoyed that both his sisters were away.

'He can solve his own problems,' Simon said grimly.

'How's Juliet?'

'Exhausted. Grace has persuaded her to come back for an hour or two's rest and Robert has coaxed her to drink some soup; otherwise, no change.'

'Alright Uncle Simon, I'll call again tomorrow.'

'Bless you for everything, my dear.'

But the next call was from Jonathan Anderson wanting instructions and Simon began to feel guilty about his absence.

'I really should go home, Robert, but I don't like to leave you and your mother.'

'You go, Dad; after all, you'll only be a few hours away if…when anything happens.'

So Simon went off on the train leaving Robert and his mother to hold Juliet's hand. He was there when, as he later phrased it to his wife, all hell broke loose.

It began with the arrival of Marybeth accompanied by what Jenks called a right old dragon named Miss Dawson. No mention was made of Mrs Rodgers and Billy had engaged this new companion, though the neighbourhood thought a more fitting term might have been jailer.

Simon, calling his wife for the daily progress report, said that it seemed Marybeth was to stay at Nether Bassett for the time being. Several local girls were recruited to clean the place and the ladies would lead a retired life.

Grace dismissed it all. 'Time Billy did something as a parent. Now, about Juliet…

***

Robert was summoned to the hospital and said goodbye to Mr Chalmers and the three of them were present when the old gentleman finally breathed his last.

Juliet cried in Robert's arms and Grace went off to call Simon.

'I'll be there tomorrow, darling, on the first train. How's Juliet?'

'Crying. He went so peacefully, just one breath and then nothing and we were all with him.'

'That's something at least. Now try and get some rest, all of you, and I'll be with you soon.'

By the time Simon arrived, the doctor had sedated Juliet and she was asleep. Grace and Robert were trying to eat something but not quite managing it but

Simon brought good news: Fred was pronounced out of danger but still very weak and Maryjane would stay on until Grace returned.

'That will be at least two weeks, because we'll stay for the funeral.'

In the end, they had two funerals because within days of his master's death, Dukes died peacefully in his sleep. Juliet told Robert it was as if everyone was leaving her. His reply was to put an arm around her and say firmly, 'I'm not going anywhere, Juliet Chalmers.'

She put her head on his shoulder and sighed. 'How does one organise a funeral, Robert? I have never had to.'

'That's why Mother and Dad are here, to help you.'

'Thank goodness for your mother; what would I do without her?'

'We are all here to support you.'

'I know; it's what keeps me going.'

Grace had been right to say two weeks because the arrangements were lengthy and as Juliet didn't know where her grandmother was buried, in the end it was a double funeral in the local churchyard; they all agreed it was fitting that Dukes be buried near his master.

Juliet didn't take much persuading to return with them for a rest and soon after they arrived, Celia and Hugo came home with a very weak Fred, who was to convalesce in the bracing air of Brighton.

The following afternoon, Celia, Grace and Maryjane were in the sitting room, discussing everything.

'I am glad you brought Juliet back, Aunt Grace.'

'Couldn't leave the poor girl all alone in that big house; she won't be bothered here but she won't be alone.'

'It's good to be back.' Celia stretched in her chair and sighed. 'I feel about a hundred.'

'When does Fred go?'

'At the end of this week; the convalescent home seems very nice, we have seen photographs.'

'What about Ed?'

'He's going back to school.'

'How did he take it?'

'Badly; wants to go with Fred. But he's too lively just now for his brother. Fred needs peace and quiet and rest.'

They were all silent for a moment, trying to imagine Ed being quiet, and then Maryjane coughed. 'You won't be needing me now, will you, Aunt Grace?'

Grace looked guilty.

'My dear, you have been marvellous through all this and of course, you must go back now.'

Her mother smiled. 'I don't know how we would have managed without you, my dear, but now I want to hear all about Marybeth.'

'Mostyn has seen Miss Dawson and he says she is not the dragon Jenks implied; she is quietly spoken and neatly dressed. I gather he was impressed.'

The news of their arrival home was soon known in the neighbourhood and the next morning as Maryjane was packing, a note arrived from her cousin inviting them to lunch.

'Goodness. Miss Dawson must be a miracle worker, Maryjane. This note was never her idea.'

Maryjane telephoned Roddy saying she would be back on a later train because, as she told her mother, the suspense would have been too much if she had gone back to London just now.

The three ladies presented themselves in time for lunch and were surprised to find the door opened by a maid.

'Come in please, Miss Dawson is in the parlour.'

Grace and Celia, glancing around with sharp eyes, saw a house that looked exactly as it had when Aunt Louisa had been alive.

Miss Dawson proved to be a lady in her late thirties, slim and neatly dressed but not fashionable.

'Ladies, how good of you to accept Marybeth's invitation. She will be pleased to see her family.'

Not necessarily, was the thought in three minds but the social niceties were observed. Marybeth came in quietly and they were all surprised by her appearance; she seemed a different person to the lively girl they had last seen. She was sober and her whole appearance was subdued.

'Aunt Grace, Aunt Celia, Maryjane. How are you all?' She kissed each one in turn but her manner was hesitant.

'We are very well, my dear, how are you?' Celia kissed her.

'Daddy says I am to live here now with Miss Dawson.'

A small nod of her companion's head and Marybeth offered drinks before luncheon.

It was a while later before Grace realised that in every room they entered, prominently displayed was the portrait of Beth King taken when she was married. Celia looked at the happy face of her sister-in-law wearing the King rubies and remembered holding her hand as she died.

The meal was not exactly a success but a conversation of sorts was carried on between the other ladies and Marybeth seemed to be minding her manners. They left early so that Maryjane could get the afternoon train to London, leaving the two sisters to discuss the matter at length.

'Did you see the portrait of Beth in every room?'

'Yes and I wonder what that's all about.'

They didn't have long to wonder because Simon had heard the whole story of the letter, which he lost no time in telling them over the Tuesday evening dinner.

'Billy had a letter from Sir Mark Goldburg.'

'No!' Both sisters spoke at once.

'Yes, and it went something like this… Sir Mark said bluntly that there could be no question of any relationship between his son and the young person; apparently, he didn't even refer to Marybeth by name.'

'How did Billy react?'

'He was livid; the maid who handed it to him thought he was going to have a heart attack.'

'We knew Marybeth was fast though. Old Mrs Hopkins wrote to me about her.'

'I did hear something else.'

'Go on.' Hugo poured another small glass of wine.

'The pictures of Beth in every room.'

'We saw them.'

'Billy ordered them. He told Marybeth she must never forget the sacrifice her mother had made so that she could live and that in dying, Beth had broken his heart forever.'

Grace whistled—a very unladylike habit Ed had taught her. 'That's a bit heavy.'

'Well, perhaps he was too blunt but it is true, and he told Marybeth about Julian and Lady Goldburg and how Beth saw her death notice in the paper and never recovered.'

There was silence, broken at last by Grace, 'That's old history now but we always knew how Billy felt—that giving up the army ruined his life. Beth gave him back his purpose but not for long.'

Simon slid a hand across the table to his wife. 'I was the lucky one; coming here saved me and you gave me purpose and I was lucky enough not to lose you.'

Celia's calm voice cut across the table, 'He should have married again, provided an heir and Marybeth with a stepmother. Grace and I did our best but where this wild streak comes from is beyond me.'

'I expect Mrs Rodgers encouraged her. How did the hall look?'

'Just as it did when Aunt Louisa was alive. Miss Dawson seems a sensible person so perhaps our wild niece will settle down.'

Simon remained unimpressed and spoke with foresight, 'Won't last and if she ever wants to marry, none of the local families will look at her even though she has a sizeable dowry.'

Grace thought no more about this casual remark until a week later when she had another note from Marybeth, saying she would like to call.

'I suppose I must agree but whatever can she want?' she asked her sister.

'I'll come over as if by accident, then you can ask me to stay for tea.'

It soon became apparent, as Miss Dawson began asking discreet questions about the local families. Marybeth said very little and when Juliet, dressed in black, came in, she received only a passing glance of indifference.

'I'm sorry. I didn't know you were entertaining.'

'Come in, my dear, this is a young friend of ours, Miss Chalmers. Her grandfather died recently so she is staying with us; this is my niece, Marybeth King, and her companion, Miss Dawson.'

Despite herself, Juliet found herself looking with interest at Robert's tiresome cousin. She was pretty to be sure, in a porcelain doll way, but there seemed no liveliness in her.

Later, talking to Robert, Juliet said she thought his cousin seemed "flat".

'She's caused a scandal and her father has sent her home in disgrace.' Juliet, not sorry to have her thoughts diverted, soon heard the whole story.

'She will find it very quiet here after London and Paris.'

'Do her good. Teach her that not everything revolves around her. Anyway, that's enough about her. How are you today?'

They began to talk of other things and the visit was soon forgotten. Fred was leaving for Brighton and each of them dropped in to say goodbye. Robert was quite shocked at how much his lively cousin had changed.

Juliet had been with them a month when her grandfather's solicitor wrote to her and she went at once to find Robert. He was out on the estate with his father and she went to Grace's sitting room.

'I have had a letter from Mr Oakes and I don't know what to do.'

'Come and sit here and we'll have some tea. I'm sure we can work it out.'

The letter was full of business matters and asking for instructions. Grace was at a loss and suggested waiting until lunch for a family council and she took the precaution of sending an invitation to Jonathan Anderson.

They waited until Mostyn had finished serving coffee before Juliet asked Simon for his help.

'I can't understand half of it. The bequests I knew about, Grandfather told me long ago but Mr Oakes wants instructions, on the bequest to Dukes in particular.'

The agent coughed as Simon glanced a question at him.

'Perhaps I might see the letter, Miss Chalmers. Lawyers do love to dress language up instead of making it simple.'

'Thank you, I would be obliged.' Juliet handed over the stiff white envelope with relief and waited.

'Hmm. You have enough liquid assets to pay the bequests without touching your capital.'

'What are liquid assets?'

'Cash, Miss Chalmers. Your grandfather, it seems, was in the fortunate position of not only having a sizeable fortune in cash but also other assets, stocks and shares and so on.'

'That I understand, I think, but why does he need instruction from me?'

'In some respect, it is a courtesy because your grandfather has appointed him executer and so he could act on his own but he consults you.'

'And why is he mentioning Dukes?'

'Ah, that is because a beneficiary died before the will could be enacted; we would need to know if he had any family who could inherit his share. Otherwise, the bequest goes back into the estate.'

She frowned. 'I always understood he was alone in the world; how will I know if he had family?'

Jonathan Anderson hesitated a moment as he folded the letter up. 'You could write to Mr Oakes and authorise him to pay those bequests that he can and instruct him to begin enquiries into Dukes' background and report back to you. There are agencies lawyers can use to track people down.'

She smiled. 'You have explained it simply and I thank you for that. Will you help me with the letter?'

'Certainly, if you wish. You will also have to consider how to manage the estate. It seems your grandfather's assets are substantial.'

Juliet sighed and shook her head. 'I must go back to Cambridge and see about a headstone. And what about the Larches?'

Robert glanced at his father who at once took his cue.

'My dear, you will have many decisions to make and you may need advice. If any of us can help, please ask us.'

'The Larches is so big. I don't want to live there.'

'Then don't come back here until we are married.'

Simon, seeing the surprise on his agent's face, smiled. 'We can't announce it yet, Anderson, because of mourning, but Robert and Juliet are engaged.'

'May I wish you every happiness?' He bowed slightly.

'Thank you.'

'May I make a suggestion?'

'Suggest away.'

'Perhaps Miss Chalmers could write now to the lawyer with immediate instructions. Then bring your grandfather's papers here to go through and decide what to do with the house.'

'That's a good idea. I will.'

Juliet began making plans and one bright day in November, she drove back to Cambridge with Robert, loaded the car up with boxes of papers and drove back again.

The Christmas festivities were muted and Juliet, remembering last year's happy events with regret, stayed in her room quite a lot, though she did go to the Christmas Day lunch and on New Year's Eve 1923, she went to the church with the family and prayed for a better year.

Chapter 12

The first post of the New Year brought Juliet a solicitor's letter that was sent her, not to Robert, but to Simon, asking him to look it over.

'What worries you, Juliet?'

'These figures can't be right. That would mean I'm quite rich.'

'And you had no idea?'

'No, Grandfather never told me. And this list…' she waved the attached notes, 'what does "Jewellery: value not known" mean?'

'You could write to Mr Oakes and query that.'

She still looked troubled. 'What will Robert say when he sees this?'

When appealed to, Robert simply said he had always loved her and wasn't marrying her for money, as far as he was concerned she could give it all away. His appalled father, when he finally got his son alone, was blunt.

'Robert, what are you doing suggesting Juliet gives her money away?'

His son shrugged. 'I don't care about the money, Dad, I love *her*.'

'Don't be such a simpleton, lad.' His father's tone was sharp. 'Of course, money matters, not as much as love but it matters. And look at it from her point of view; she has money and you will have land, meaning you are both on an equal footing. How would she feel coming to you with nothing?'

There was a silence before Robert said quietly, 'I never thought of it that way.'

Later, telling Grace, Simon sighed. 'Robert should know by now how this estate runs. We are doing pretty well but anything could happen—a run of bad weather, a bad harvest. A sizeable injection of cash is just what we need and while I love Juliet and approve his choice, it's a happy chance she is rich. I didn't put it to him in those words, of course, but they will both benefit from her circumstances.'

So Robert said no more and Juliet wrote to her solicitor enquiring about the jewellery; at Easter, she decided it was time to return to the Larches but after a week there alone, she admitted it was impossible for her to do it all. An appeal to her future mother-in-law resulted in Celia and Grace descending on Cambridge, soon followed by Maryjane. Roddy was away for a few days, she explained, and another pair of hands was welcome in what Robert called 'an orgy of cleaning out'. Boxes were piling up in all the rooms, furniture was being labelled and Juliet, looking at the library in a depressed silence, decided to enlist William Wright to look at the books.

Over tea the next day, she told them what he had said.

'There are about a thousand books, he thinks, so he's sending two librarians over to look at them. And Mr Oakes has written again about the house.'

'If the college took the books, it would be a tremendous compliment to your grandfather and a weight off your mind. Have you decided about the house?'

Grace was careful not to lead her into any decisions and Maryjane, replacing her cup and saucer on the tray, suggested Juliet might want to keep some family items.

By the time the first auctioneer arrived, she had decided what she would keep and she talked it over with Robert.

'Mother's portrait, of course, though sadly, I can't find one of Father. They died young, did you know?'

Robert knew the unhappy story of Juliet's parents but kept his mouth firmly shut.

'I believe your grandfather did mention it; what else are you keeping?'

'This little workbox, which was grandmother's, although I'm hopeless at sewing. Also, my writing desk and chair, and my own books and everything from my bedroom.'

'Take whatever you want, my darling, there's plenty of room at Kingscourt. I expect Mother will arrange for us to have our own set of rooms after we are married.'

After two weeks of frantic activity, Celia and Maryjane left. Removal vans turned up and the house began to empty. They wandered around the servants' quarters and kitchens, and Grace rattled a door in the butler's passage.

'Where does this lead to?'

Juliet stared aghast. 'It's the wine cellar. I'd forgotten about it.'

'Is it full?'

'Yes, I believe so.'

'You could sell it as part of the estate or bring it back with you.'

All too soon it seemed, Juliet was giving final instructions to Mr Oakes and saying goodbye to the servants who were retiring.

Robert came to collect her and they drove away for the last time. When they arrived in Devon, she found a bedroom sitting already for her, full of her furniture and boxes.

Not normally demonstrative, she found herself hugging Grace and bursting into tears.

***

After some discussion with Robert and Simon, it was decided to keep the wines and Mostyn was summoned to be told. The news that an entire cellar full of rare wines and spirits would soon be arriving threw him into a complete panic and on his next afternoon off, he hurried to the Merridews' cottage to seek advice from his mentor, arriving just in time for tea.

Over Mrs Merridew's substantial fruit cake, the whole subject was reviewed. The old butler, his interest and curiosity fired, agreed to come 'out of retirement' and oversee the shipping and storage of everything. He also referred to 'keeping the wine book' which his puzzled former pupil said he was already keeping.

One fine day Mostyn and Merridew, driven by Robert, went back to Cambridge and watched an expensive firm of specialist wine shippers carefully load dusty crates and boxes into a large van, which made a very slow journey to Devon. Merridew then talked to Mr Chalmers old butler, took possession of The Larches wine book and instructed Mostyn about keeping two wine books running at the same time.

A letter from Mr Oakes regarding the jewellery asked Juliet to visit his offices and inspect it but Simon suggested Robert should go and collect it on her behalf. When he arrived back it was with two large metal boxes and everyone gathered in the library to see what 'jewellery, value not known' consisted of.

Four boxes marked 'Great Exhibition 1851' contained a beautiful set of carved coral and ivory flowers on delicate gold stems. Everyone exclaimed how beautiful it was and Juliet tried on the necklace and earrings. Three more boxes also marked 'Great Exhibition' had ruby, sapphire and emerald brooches and two boxes of what looked like diamond earrings. The other, much smaller, metal box held miniatures of people whose faces meant nothing to Juliet and two sets of silver hair brushes and combs.

'You should perhaps have it valued my dear. Where are you going to keep it?'

Grace, seeing the slightly dazed look on the girl's face murmured 'Perhaps you should put it in the silver safe for now my dear, while you decide.'

Juliet nodded slowly and so everything was repacked and taken to the large room with heavy grill doors handily situated in the below stairs servants in the quarters, next to what had been the under butler's bedroom. Grace and Simon decided to go and have a look at the room themselves, she couldn't ever remember seeing it.

The sight of so much silver was daunting and Simon gazed at huge heavily chased silver platters and enormous engraved trophies.

'Grace, surely your mother never used any of these?'

She frowned. 'Occasionally I think the sideboards in the dining room were dressed up if we were having really important guests father wanted to impress, but not usually.'

'Mostyn, how often do you clean all this stuff?' Simon turned to the butler.

'Every two months sir, but it takes days.'

'Maybe we'll think about disposing of some of it.'

Barely had Juliet's boxes been stored when Simon had a letter from his own solicitor. Beades, Beades & Jacobs of Lincolns Inn had acted for the King family since the eighteenth century. Apparently 'young Mr Beades', now well over 70, had decided to retire and having no son had decided to wind up his practice. He asked Simon to come to London as soon as possible and instruct a new firm to look after the estate affairs.

Simon and Robert went to London and came back feeling depressed. Over tea they explained why to Grace.

'It's not just the estate mother. There are dozens of boxes of papers, really old family stuff to go through.'

'And there are the King rubies and other jewels they hold.'

Grace frowned. 'What on earth are we going to do?'

'No idea. I suppose we shall have to go through it all, which will take forever.'

Robert munched a scone thoughtfully.

'We could ask Mr Wright if he knows anyone at Cambridge who might help.'

***

Grace was well advanced with preparations for the Feast before William Wright 'found someone' in the shape of a retired librarian called Edward Johnson. He came with William Wright and was cautiously interviewed by Simon. Explaining the position they were in to this mild inoffensive looking man Simon began to feel more depressed than ever. He did not see how this quiet little man could help them but Edward Johnson surprised him.

'Have you found another solicitor yet Major Amory?'

'No, and it's a daunting prospect.'

Jonathan Anderson, sitting quietly across the table, lent forward.

'I think Mr Johnson has an idea.'

'Well more a suggestion really. Why do you need a London firm?'

Robert spoke hastily. 'Our affairs have been dealt with at Lincolns Inn since the eighteenth century.'

'Times change though, and perhaps you should consider a more local west country firm. Do you really want to be travelling to London every time you want to consult your solicitor?'

'We'll think about it.' Simon temporized.

The result of this conversation was that Simon and Robert went to Exeter for two exhausting days and came back to say they had appointed Messrs. Phillips, Davis Jones as the family's new solicitors. All the boxes of old King family papers would be delivered to Kingscourt and Edward Johnson agreed to come and stay for three months to put them in order. Grace, told there would be about seventy boxes arriving, cleared her father's old study which Simon never used, and told Edward Johnson that would be his office.

'I'll tell the maids not to disturb any papers you leave around.'

'Very kind of you Mrs Amory, I should like to start as soon as possible.'

Grace smiled. 'Don't work too hard, and feel free to come to the Feast if you wish.'

The boxes of papers arrived along with four boxes of jewellery and the next morning Celia came over and, together with Juliet, they began to look at the family jewels.

'We knew about the rubies, they came down when Billy married. But what on earth is all this?'

Celia gazed at the leather boxes in amazement. From the look on her sister's face it was obvious she had never seen them before either.

'Look Cee, brooches.' Grace was opening them one after another.

'Earrings. Oh look, pearls.'

They stared at open boxes scattered all over the table.

'Why didn't Daddy mention this in his will?'

'He died not long after his will was made so perhaps he forgot. He was more upset, I think, at having to split the estate than he let on.'

'Of course the rubies usually go to the mistress of the house, but I can't imagine ever wearing them.'

Grace looked at the huge stones elaborately set with diamonds and closed the box with a snap. She opened another box and dropped it on the table with a scream.

'What on earth? Celia what is this…hideous thing?'

'This' was a large eye, the centre sapphire surrounded by mother of pearl and the whole framed in diamonds.

'Maybe Hadyn King brought it back from his travels.' Celia mused as she turned it over and saw from the pin that it was a brooch. The ancestor who had re-founded the family fortune had, they all knew, travelled extensively in India and the far east.

Grace shuddered. 'The diamonds are lovely but fancy wearing an eye.'

They stared at the unblinking eye until Grace said slowly 'Let's just leave it for now. Think about it later.'

Juliet, picking up the box to put it away, found a small piece of paper folded inside the lid.

'Grace, there's a note here.'

She opened it carefully and read *The Eye of the Odalisque.*

'What is an odalisque?'

Juliet, whose knowledge came from reading everything in her grandfather's library, said soberly 'They were concubines, mistresses if you like, usually in a sultan's harem.'

Celia put it back into its box and Grace opened the rest of the boxes nervously but nothing more exotic was found and, looking at a small mountain of jewellery boxes, she suddenly said 'Celia, Juliet, you should have some of this.'

'But Grace I don't want anything. Besides I have grandfather's jewels.'

'And I would never wear some of this stuff.'

'Look, there's no point in keeping them in the bank. They are family jewels and it's right they should be shared round, worn. Here's a lovely diamond brooch, not too big. And these pearl earrings.'

'I've never seen any of these before. Mother certainly never wore them.'

Grace smiled. 'Mother always wore her pearls.'

Her sister smiled, remembering the day long after Mary King's death when Silas had called them into his study and given each of them a two-strand pearl necklace.

'Daddy, we couldn't. They were mother's.'

'Nonsense, she would have wanted you to have them. No point in leaving them in the drawer gathering dust.'

Celia wore hers occasionally but Grace somehow couldn't bring herself to even take hers out of the box.

'Father was right, no point having these lying round. I'd like you both to have some, and Maryjane. I'll keep something for Eliza when she's older.'

'What about Marybeth?' Juliet asked.

Celia smiled. 'She would probably say they were too old fashioned for words. I'll write to Billy and see what he thinks.'

'Let's pick something for Maryjane. What about this sapphire star brooch and the matching earrings? And here's a lovely turquoise bracelet. We'll give them to her next time she's here.'

Juliet, after first refusing, fell in love with a small diamond pendant and was persuaded to take it.

The morning passed happily with them trying on everything in the boxes, though by unspoken agreement no-one tried on the rubies or the elaborate brooch. After lunch Celia, loaded up with six jewellery boxes, went home Grace repacked the boxes and had them put in the safe.

***

Edward Johnson, it turned out, had a mind like a filing cabinet and Grace, knocking on the library door the day before the Feast, saw that her father's old table was now stacked with old deeds and documents, all in order. She smiled.

'Mr Johnson, I hope you are coming to the Feast tomorrow.'

'A day off would be very agreeable and the weather looks promising.'

He enjoyed the Feast and found an interesting companion in Juliet. They wandered around watching the children enjoying themselves.

'My grandfather would have enjoyed talking to you Mr Johnson.'

'I understand he died recently. My condolences.'

'Yes, it was last November and I still miss him so much. And trying to go through his papers is a nightmare.'

Though he did not listen to gossip certain comments had already made him aware of this young lady's special place in the family and he had no hesitation in offering to help.

Later, talking innocently to Robert, she mentioned that the librarian had offered his services but her fiancée frowned.

'Surely you don't need any help? You should have said if you were struggling and I'd have helped.'

'You haven't time. Besides Mr Johnson says looking through old documents is not as easy as it looks.'

Juliet carried on eating calmly, unaware how nervous she was making him. So worried was he that next day he sought out the librarian for a chat. He found the older man methodically working through a large box marked 'King 1790'.

'How can I help Mr Amory?' He folded his hands and waited.

Robert cleared his throat. 'The fact is – well, I understand Miss Chalmers has asked you to go through her family papers.'

'Yes, and I am happy to help.'

Robert hesitated before going on. 'I need a favour please.'

The other man waited.

'There are – um – certain events in the family history which her grandfather wished kept secret. He felt they would distress her too much and it was all so long ago. I'm sure you understand.'

'You wish me to consult you before I tell her if I find anything?'

'Only if you find any papers relating to Italy or her parents stay there. Nothing more.'

The older man nodded. 'Very well'

It was late autumn before he was finally able to say to Robert there was nothing relating to Italy anywhere in the Chalmers' family papers. On his way to the estate office Robert heaved a sigh of relief and smiled to think he had ever doubted the old gentleman. Of course there would be no trace of…anything.

The winter drew on quickly and at the Christmas Eve gathering Simon had the happy task of announcing his son's engagement. Amidst great cheering from the family and tenants the happy couple shyly thanked everyone for their good wishes and looked forward happily to 1924.

***

The year did not begin quietly because at the end of January Miss Dawson called early one morning to enquire if anyone had seen Marybeth. Apparently she had disappeared late the evening before and no-one had any idea where she was. After a short talk with Grace she went away visibly upset and later, on the telephone to Celia, both shook their heads over their wild niece.

Robert's birthday was celebrated lavishly and his father proudly announced that the Feast would once again see a family wedding as well. The celebrations were barely over before Billy arrived in search of his missing daughter. He discovered she had impressed one of the maids with her pitiful tale and had been helped to escape. Miss Dawson was positive she had very little money with her and no-one appeared to have seen her. Billy had to return to his regiment leaving Miss Dawson in charge 'just in case', but he dismissed the maid and told Grace he was instructing a private enquiry agent to search for his daughter.

It was Easter when Edward Johnson, still with them on what had turned out to be a much larger task than anyone expected, asked if he could join the family for afternoon tea, which surprised Simon as he had thought it was understood that the librarian was always welcome. He came into the saloon greatly excited and enthusiastically waving an old parchment hung with seals.

'Major Amory, I've found the most amazing document.'

He was too intent on his news to even sit down so Grace had no opportunity to offer him a cup of tea.

'Amazing how?'

'This is a grant of land given to Antony King in 1674 by King Charles II. The land granted was where Kingscourt, originally called The King's Court in his honour, now stands. It seems he visited here in 1681, there are references to provisions for the King's party and retinue. This means your family have been here for two hundred and fifty years.' He paused for dramatic effect.

If he had hoped to stun his audience with this, he was amply rewarded. Simon was shocked into silence, Grace and Juliet stared at him and Robert let out a yell.

'Hurrah! Dad, we have to mark this event. Don't you see – two hundred and fifty years of the estate, our wedding. We can have the biggest Feast ever.'

'But how do we know this?' Grace found her voice.

'Partly luck. It was in another box marked 'Miscellaneous'. There were quite a lot of them.' The librarian smiled. 'I doubt if we'll find anything earlier.'

He paused and Grace offered him a cup of tea before he carried on.

'Also you must decide what you want to do with these family papers. They are very important. I strongly advise a fire proof room.'

Simon frowned. 'We've nothing like that. They'll have to go to Exeter.'

'I have made a catalogue of everything for you to keep here.'

Grace had an idea. 'Simon, if all the papers are going to our solicitors we could send the larger pieces of jewellery as well. Better than having them here.'

'That's settled then, I'll write to Phillips and ask them to store everything for us.'

***

Simon took some persuading to have an extravagant Feast but eventually he was overruled by his wife and son. They began to plan a very grand event, Juliet began to think about her wedding dress and Maryjane and Roddy arrived for a weekend, during which they announced they were expecting a happy event.

For Celia, excited at the idea of being a grandmother, the news came a week after Fred was declared fit enough to come home.

Grace rang for some more tea and the three women settled down to an absorbing talk on baby clothes.

'Of course we shall have to move. Roddy has been doing the rounds of estate agents.'

'What are you looking for?'

'Three bedrooms and a small garden we think. But I shall miss our cosy place.'

'You couldn't bring up a child in a flat Maryjane.'

'I know. And we thought it should happen before I grow too big to move.'

'I'll come and help you of course. Now that Fred is fit I feel quite carefree.'

Grace looked at her sister seriously. Celia never looked any older but soon she would be a grandmother! And she wondered suddenly if she might soon be in the same position.

They took the opportunity of Maryjane's visit to give her the jewellery they had put aside and Celia had the unusual sight of her normally placid daughter crying.

'They are beautiful but honestly mother, when will I wear them?'

'My dear, these are not elaborate. You should have seen some of the pieces we have. Your mother and I have had pieces, I am keeping some for Eliza when she's old enough and Juliet also picked some things. They are family jewels and it's only right they should be shared round.'

Roddy thought them lovely and said how appropriate it was for her to have something, so Maryjane put her objections in her pocket and the next morning, leaving for London, wore the brooch and earrings and felt ridiculously overdressed.

Grace soon had something much bigger to worry about because Eliza at sixteen, told her parents over tea that she had made a decision about her life.

'Mother, Dad, I've decided what I want to do.'

'Darling I'm so pleased.'

Eliza paused for dramatic effect before saying proudly 'I'm going to be an actress.'

If she had hoped for a reaction she certainly succeeded because her mother choked and turned pale.

'An actress!'

Robert, staring at his sister, said grimly 'Over my dead body.'

Juliet stared at her future sister in law incredulously.

Eliza, seeing her mother's white face, panicked.

'Mother, are you alright?'

Simon took his wife's cold hand and said calmly 'Grace, there is no need to worry.'

Eliza smiled winningly at her father and said 'I'm a good actress Dad, everyone says so. I'll be famous, I might even ...'

She got no further. Her father seldom raised his voice but now he said 'Go to your room Eliza. I will speak to you later.'

'But Dad ...'

'Go now.'

She went out quietly and Simon spoke calmly to his wife. 'She will not be an actress my dear.'

'I should hope not. I wouldn't like to see my sister on a stage professionally.' Robert spoke sharply.

The next day, talking it over with Celia, Grace was calmer but still worried.

'I was so surprised I couldn't say anything. An actress!'

'She's had her head turned by the theatricals.' Celia was as ever practical.

'Simon says she won't be one and I trust him.'

Celia laughed softly. 'Oh Gracie, our children. They will keep on surprising us.'

'Well I can do without any more surprises of that kind thank you.'

The next morning Simon, having thought it all over, went to find his daughter and finally caught her sitting astride Dobbin, the rocking horse Silas had bought when Robert was born.

'Well miss, you have upset your mother.'

'I didn't mean to, Dad, but it's what I want to do. You know I'm a good actress because you've seen me on stage.'

Simon sat at the table where nanny used to serve tea and smiled.

'A few family theatricals are not an indication that you could be a good actress my dear. You haven't seen any professional productions.'

Eliza looked unhappy.

'I've never even seen amateur ones.

'How would you like to go to London and see a play?'

She clapped her hands in delight. 'Oh, yes please Dad. When?'

He laughed. 'When I have had time to arrange it Miss Impatience.'

He left a very happy daughter but his wife and son were not enthusiastic.

'Simon, this is a very bad idea. It's only encouraging her.'

'Dad, I have to agree with other. She'll think you want her…to go on stage.'

Simon took his wife's hand and looked her straight in the eye.

'Do you trust me?'

'You know I do.'

'Then leave it all to me. And Robert, not another word to your sister about this.'

Simon arranged a trip to London but in the end it was with his wife and daughter and Celia made up the party. Juliet really didn't want to go and Robert said he would also stay behind.

Maryjane found a hotel near them but Simon disappeared as soon as they arrived, leaving his wife and Celia to talk to Maryjane. Eliza was happily scanning all the newspapers for theatre reviews. When he arrived back in time to dress for dinner he looked pleased but wouldn't say where he had been.

The next day they did some sightseeing, had an early meal and were at the theatre in good time for the performance. Eliza watched everything with great excitement, made happier by her father asking her casually if she might like to go backstage.

'Oh Dad, can I?'

'Yes, you can. Your aunt is going back to the hotel with Maryjane and Roddy but your mother and I are taking you to meet some of the cast.'

While everyone else was finding coats Grace whispered in his ear 'What are you up to Simon Amory?' but he only shook his head.

Eliza was soon deep in conversation with three young actresses and her mother, observing from a little distance and seeing a happy face, hoped her husband wasn't making a big mistake. She glanced across at him, he looked altogether too – casual was the first word she thought of – and not a bit worried. It was time to find out what was going on and she worked her way round the room to him and tapped his arm. He glanced quizzically at her.

'Do you think Eliza is enjoying herself?'

'A little too much. Simon, if you don't tell me what is going on ...'

'Enjoying a family evening at the theatre. But just look at the time! Eliza should be in bed.'

He knew he couldn't dodge the issue for long and later that night, in their hotel room, he waited for his wife to bring the subject up again.

'Now tell me all.'

'I went to the theatre this afternoon and had a chat with the stage manager. Nice chap. Told him all about Eliza and her plans.'

'What did he say?'

'He was sympathetic to our view. Said he wouldn't want his own daughter on stage even though it is respectable. He talked to a few of the girls and told them to paint a picture, not too gloomy but not rosy.'

'How clever of you. Will it work?'

'Don't know yet, but ...' he paused and kissed his wife's cheek before whispering in her ear, 'I'm going to do the same tomorrow.'

She turned and kissed him on the lips. 'You are devious.'

'We have to go along with this because the more we oppose it the more determined she will be. This way she will see rather more of what a professional actress has to endure than taking part in a few amateur theatricals.'

He disappeared again the next morning, Celia and Maryjane were going baby shopping and Eliza wanted to see the Tower so Grace took her daughter and, with a heroic effort, made no mention of theatres or acting.

The first performance they had seen was a light comedy but tonight was Romeo and Juliet at a different theatre and as it progressed Eliza became very quiet. In the interval Roddy invited Simon and Grace for a drink, leaving their daughter with Celia and Maryjane.

'So, will Eliza be put off?' Roddy sipped a brandy.

'I hope so. She is certainly not enjoying tonight's performance.' Grace smiled.

'She's very young to be making decisions about her future but I don't want her on the stage. The girls seem very nice but…it's not the life I want for my daughter.'

'Theatrical lodgings, long hours rehearsing, stage door jonnies. No, I wouldn't either Simon.' Roddy finished his brandy just as the interval bell rang.

In the train going home the next day Grace asked her daughter if she had enjoyed London.

'Yes mother, I did.'

'You've seen comedy and drama, talked to actresses to have some idea of what they do.' Grace glanced across at her husband but the look said 'enough said' and she picked up a magazine at once.

For a day or two no reference was made to acting and then Eliza went to find her mother.

'Mother, can I talk to you?' She put her head round the sitting room door and Grace instantly abandoned her wedding list.

'Of course darling, come and sit here.'

Eliza sat down, sighed, stood up and sat down again.

'You seem distracted. Something on your mind?'

'I've been thinking about the plays we saw in London. Shakespeare's too complicated and there are so many lines to learn.'

'Well of course tragedies are difficult. Perhaps we should have seen one of his comedies, though I don't think there were any on.'

Eliza was pursing her own train of thought. 'And did you know they have to rehearse all day and then perform in the evening? And on Wednesdays and Saturdays there are matinees too. It's really hard work.'

Her mother paused before replying.

'I suppose it would be. To them it's a job and even if they feel unhappy or out of sorts every time they step on stage they have to leave all that behind and entertain an audience.'

Eliza sighed again. 'I don't know what to think mother.'

Grace patted her hand.

'My dear, there's no need to decide anything just now. Enjoy this summer, and the wedding. I think Juliet might want you as a bridesmaid.'

To Simon, in the privacy of their bedroom later that night, Grace confided 'Your plan might just be working.'

'If it does then we'll all be happy.'

***

The sisters had thought Marybeth might try to find Toby Goldburg but a discreet question to Roddy said that father and son were in Vienna.

'I don't see how she could get to Vienna. And Miss Dawson is adamant she had no money.'

'I'm not going to worry about her any more. She's Billy's problem now. I have my son back, and I'll be a grandmother, that's enough for me. And you'll have another daughter.'

A few days later Billy arrived with a very sulky daughter. The private detective told him Marybeth had made it to London and was staying with Mrs Rodgers. Billy, really angry by now, went to London and escorted her back to Devon.

He marched unannounced into his sister's sitting room and said baldly 'Grace, please call Miss Dawson and ask her to come and collect Marybeth.'

'Alright, but why not go to Nether Basset yourself?'

'I only have a day pass so I won't have time. And I want to tell my daughter a few facts.'

He waited while Grace telephoned and Marybeth sat in sulky silence.

'She'll be here presently.' Grace, curiosity getting the better of her, waited.

'Now Marybeth why were you in London?'

'I was staying with Mrs Rodgers.'

'Yes but what then? Were you hoping to go to Vienna?'

'So he knows where the lad is then' was Grace's thought.

Marybeth flushed.

'You're trying to keep us apart because of something that happened years ago.'

Her father sighed and took a letter out of his pocket.

'I was hoping not to do this. I'm going to read you a letter I had from Sir Mark Goldburg last year.'

So Grace heard the famous letter in full and it was not pleasant. The stinging assessment of her niece's character not only made that young lady flush but caused her aunt to turn pink in embarrassment.

The final paragraph was devastating. "When my cherished only son takes a bride she will naturally be modest and ladylike with an impeccable reputation, not someone with a taste for flirtation who has acquired a reputation for notorious behaviour."

'So you see his father's opinion of you. Of course he will never permit a marriage – in his eyes you are wild and fast.'

Grace felt sorry for her niece for the first time.

'Billy, don't be so harsh.'

'Why not? Grace, my daughter has acquired such a reputation that even that man doesn't consider her suitable bridal material.'

'But Daddy he loves me and I love him.'

Billy turned away and it was left to her aunt to say gently 'That may be true Marybeth, but if his father disapproves of you that's an end of it. The young man will not go against his father's wishes.'

'Unlike my own child, who has no hesitation in flouting my wishes.' Billy spoke bitterly but was unprepared for the response.

His daughter turned a furious and resentful face to him. 'You've never acted like a father to me. You only ever remember I'm your daughter when I do something wrong.'

Grace's mouth dropped open and Billy choked. 'What did you say?'

'You never cared about me. You were never with me.'

'That's nonsense. We lived in the same house.'

'But you never read with me like Uncle Hugo did with Maryjane or played games with me like Uncle Simon did with Eliza. I was left to nanny.'

This was so true that Grace nodded despite herself. Quite how the conversation would have gone was a guess but it was a relief when Miss Dawson arrived.

'Miss Dawson, my daughter is to stay at the Hall with you for an indefinite period. She will be strictly supervised at all times and all staff must be instructed to ignore anything she tells them. You will check on her every hour or two and make sure she is occupied.'

'Certainly Major King.'

Billy stood up and began to put his gloves on.

'Marybeth, you will behave properly in future and if there is one more escapade your allowance will be stopped and pocket money will be given you by Miss Dawson who will also choose your clothes. Do I make myself clear?'

Marybeth flushed and bit her lip.

'Do you understand?'

'Yes.'

At that point Grace slipped out to find Simon. She said Celia was right that her brother should have married again and given Marybeth a stepmother and brothers and sisters.

'Well he didn't and we see the result. Now Grace, about the Feast ....' and with that she forgot about everything but her son's wedding.

Grace and Celia, ransacking the attics for yet another wedding, found an evening dress with a bodice of old lace. They packed it carefully in tissue paper to take to London. Juliet had liked the dress worn by the Duchess of York for her wedding the year before and so Celia and Grace took her to London to visit Madame Handley-Seymour. A faithful copy of the dress was of course impossible, if only because the new royal duchess was petite and Juliet was most definitely not, but between them a dress was designed which set off the bride's tall slight figure and red hair. After all, as Madame airily remarked, Juliet wearing white would be a fashion disaster; she just happened to have some beautiful cream silk which would be perfect. They produced the coffee coloured lace and Madame was in raptures, it would be perfect. Now all that was necessary was to choose shoes, a veil, jewellery – she had discovered that Juliet was a considerable heiress. Grace said firmly that of course Juliet would wear family jewels and they would determine what sort of veil later.

Over tea at The Ritz with Maryjane the talk was all wedding clothes.

'Am I wearing family jewels Grace?'

'You have several choices my dear. The King rubies, traditionally the heir's bride wears them.'

Juliet thought of that beautiful face, the folds of lace, the blazing red necklace and shivered. She was not particularly imaginative but somehow that red collar seemed to be choking the life out of Beth King.

'No, perhaps not.'

Celia said smoothly 'We thought that, although the rubies would suit your colouring, they are rather .... flamboyant.'

Grace carried on. 'Or you could look again at the jewellery you inherited. The coral and ivory flowers would look lovely with the neckline of your dress.'

Maryjane, privy to her cousin's intentions, said nothing.

'Yes, I suppose they would.' The bride sounded doubtful and her future mother in law said calmly 'Well you have time to decide.'

Four days of shopping gave Juliet a trousseau with so many boxes Madame agreed to deliver them to Maryjane's for Robert to collect. Juliet looked again at her jewellery and selected the coral and ivory necklace but two days before her wedding Robert presented her with his wedding present – a pearl necklace set with a diamond clasp.

'Robert, it's perfect.'

'Wear it on our day?'

'Of course.'

Grace loaned her a pair of pearl earrings and Celia gave her a beautiful pale blue chemise to wear under her dress, so with the something old, something new, something borrowed and something blue Juliet was ready to marry her Prince Charming.

Kingscourt and The Risings had been full of young people all summer as John, Eliza, Ed and Fred and Edmund invited their friends for tennis parties, picnics, dance evenings and any excuse they could think of for a party. Simon had the croquet lawn re-laid and Hugo was talked into a swimming pool. The weather was fine and somehow it was all fun and laughter. Between all the parties and general merriment Grace and Celia went to London for a week to help Roddy and Maryjane move into the house he had found for them.

'I'm not sure you needed to make it a week mother.' Maryjane commented over tea.

'We didn't, but your aunt was determined to be away and let Juliet run everything.'

Grace nibbled a teacake. 'I just wanted her to see that running the house is not difficult.'

Her sister laughed. 'No doubt you gave Mrs Hughes countless instructions.'

'Maybe.' Grace grinned.

On a beautiful summers day the family gathered for the triple celebration of the Feast, the anniversary and the wedding. The ceremony was to be held first with just family and as the stable bell chimed noon Juliet came slowly into the chapel on Simon's arm and Robert, turning to look at his bride, felt tears well into his eyes. She was so very beautiful! Grace, watching her son become a husband, felt both proud and happy that he had found the right girl. Juliet was everything she could want in a daughter and she knew they would be happy. Beside her Simon reached for her hand and squeezed it.

'She looks beautiful' Grace murmured.

'Not as beautiful as you' her husband replied.

'She's a lovely bride. Robert is so lucky' Maryjane whispered to Roddy.

'Not as lucky as me' Roddy whispered.

'Juliet looks so happy, and absolutely gorgeous' Celia told her husband.

'The most beautiful bride I ever saw was you,' Hugo replied.

***

While Kingscourt was toasting the new bride and groom another family were also ordering champagne on the Atlantic crossing from New York to Southampton in the most luxurious suite the Carinthia could provide.

Julian King Junior, always known as JJ, and his brother Charles were running round the suite opening drawers and banging doors until their mother complained of a headache.

'Where is nanny JJ?'

'Seasick. She says she is quite prostrated.' JJ mimicked his nurse.

'Alice my dear, let's have some champagne. Cure your headache. And boys, do be quiet for your mother's sake.'

The two boys had learned at a young age how to manipulate their parents and Charles now sidled up to his mother and held her hand. He was well built for his age and with a pronounced American accent.

'Gee mom, I'm sorry you feel rotten. We'll be quiet, I promise.'

His brother skipped to the service bell and rang it merrily. The steward, who had taken an instant dislike to the young Kings, entered warily.

'You rang sir.'

He looked at Julian but it was JJ who answered.

'A bottle of champagne and make it snappy.'

His father smiled at how grown up and important his son sounded.

'Very good sir.' There was an edge to the steward's voice he missed, being too used to American ways to think he might be giving offence. but as the door shut behind him Hill mentally worked out how much longer he would have to serve these obnoxious Americans.

'Dad, can we have a drink too?' JJ grinned at his father, who nodded his head.

'But only a small glass JJ.'

'Sure thing Dad.' JJ's face was as angelic as he could make it but he fully intended to have a glass the same size as his father's.

After more than a decade away another King family, extremely rich even by American standards, were returning home …

Ingram Content Group UK Ltd.
Milton Keynes UK
UKHW021928220623
423799UK00003B/25